Narcissus and Goldmund

Hermann Hesse was born in Calw, Germany, in 1877. After a short period at a seminary he moved to Switzerland to work as a bookseller. From 1904 he devoted himself to writing, establishing his reputation with a series of romantic novels. During the First World War he worked for the Red Cross. His later novels – *Siddartha* (1922), *Der Steppenwolf* (1927), *Narziss und Goldmund* (1930) and *Das Glasperlenspiel* (*The Glass Bead Game*, 1943) – poems and critical essays established him as one of the greatest literary figures of the German-speaking world. He won many literary awards including the Nobel Prize for Literature in 1946. Hermann Hesse died in 1962.

HERMANN HESSE

Narcissus and Goldmund

Translated from the German by Leila Vennewitz

PENGUIN BOOKS

Published in association with Peter Owen Publishers

PENGUIN CLASSICS

UK | USA | Canada | Ireland | Australia
India | New Zealand | South Africa

Penguin Books is part of the Penguin Random House group of companies
whose addresses can be found at global.penguinrandomhouse.com

Penguin
Random House
UK

First published in German as *Narziss und Goldmund* by Fischer Verlag 1930
First published in Great Britain by Peter Owen Ltd 1959
This translation first published 1993
First published in Penguin Classics 2017
005

Copyright © Hermann Hesse, 1959
Translation copyright © Leila Vennewitz and Surhkamp Verlag, 1988
This edition published by arrangement with Peter Owen Publishers

The moral right of the translator has been asserted

Set in 11.25/14 pt Dante MT Std
Typeset in India by Thomson Digital Pvt Ltd, Noida, Delhi
Printed in Great Britain by Clays Ltd, Elcograf S.p.A

A CIP catalogue record for this book is available from the British Library

ISBN: 978-0-141-98461-2

www.greenpenguin.co.uk

Narcissus and Goldmund

Chapter One

At the Mariabronn monastery entrance, with its rounded arch resting on double columns, stood a venerable Spanish chestnut tree, a solitary offspring of the south, brought back generations earlier by a pilgrim returning from Rome. Its broad, curving crown spread protectively across the path as it breathed in the wind, and in the spring, when everything around it had turned to green and even the monastery walnut trees were already showing their fresh, russet foliage, the chestnut's leaves were still taking their time. Then, when the nights were shortest, it would thrust up through the clusters of leaves the milky-green shafts of its exotic blossoms with their evocative, pungent scent. In the autumn wind of October, well after fruit and grapes had been harvested, its yellowing crown would shed the prickly crop that did not ripen every year, and the monastery boys would scuffle for the nuts that Subprior Gregor, himself a native of the south, would roast on the hearth in his room. Protective and exotic, the great tree gently waved its crown above the entrance to the monastery, a sensitive guest from a different, warmer climate, mysteriously related to the slender sandstone columns of the doorway and to the carved stonework of the window arches, sills and posts – beloved by southerners, gaped at as an alien by the locals.

Many generations of monastery pupils had passed below this alien tree, their slates tucked under their arms, chattering, laughing, playing, arguing; barefoot or shod, a flower between their lips or a nut between their teeth or a snowball in their hand, according to the season. New pupils kept coming; over the years the faces would change, but the boys tended to resemble each other, fair-skinned and curly haired. Some stayed on, became novices, then monks, had their heads shorn, wore cowl and rope, studied books, taught the boys, grew old, died. Others, their years of study completed, were taken home by their parents, to castles, to merchants' or artisans' houses, went out into the world to carry on their pastimes and trades, came back perhaps once to the monastery for a visit, now grown to manhood, bringing small sons to the monks as pupils, smiled as they gazed up at the chestnut tree, then dispersed again.

In the monastery cells and halls, among the heavy, rounded window arches and massive double columns of red stone, life went on with its teaching, studying, administering and governing. Many forms of art and science were practised here and handed down from one generation to the next – devout and secular, clear and obscure. Books were written and annotated, systems devised, ancient scriptures collected, manuscripts illuminated; the people's faith was nurtured, the people's faith smiled at. Scholarship and piety, naïveté and subtlety, wisdom of the Evangelists and wisdom of the Greeks, white magic and black. Some of all this flourished here; there was room for everything, as much room for isolation and penance as for conviviality and good living. Which of these became dominant depended on the personality of the abbot and on the prevailing trends of the day. At times the monastery was much sought out for its exorcists and demonologists, at others for its excellent music; at times for a saintly father who performed cures and miracles, at others for its fish soups and venison-liver pâtés, each in its own time. And always among the multitude of monks and pupils, the fervent and the lukewarm, the fasters and the fat, among the many who came, lived and died, there had always been the occasional individual, the outstanding one, who was loved by all or feared by all, one who seemed chosen, who continued to be talked about long after his contemporaries had been forgotten.

At this time the Mariabronn monastery also contained two outstanding individuals, an old man and a youth. Among the swarm of brothers filling the dormitories, chapels and study halls there were two whom all knew and respected. There was Abbot Daniel, the old man, and the pupil Narcissus, the youth, who had only recently entered the novitiate. Nevertheless, because of his exceptional gifts Narcissus had already, contrary to all tradition, been assigned to teaching, especially Greek. These two, the abbot and the novice, had a special standing in the monastery. They were watched and aroused curiosity; they were admired and envied as well as secretly derided.

The abbot was loved by almost everyone. Full of goodness, simplicity and humility, he had no enemies. Only the scholars of the monastery tempered their affection with a little condescension, for while Abbot Daniel may have been a saint, a scholar he was not. He possessed the simplicity that is wisdom, but his Latin was modest, his Greek non-existent.

Those few who occasionally smiled at the abbot's simplicity were all the more enchanted by Narcissus, the wonder boy, the handsome youth with such elegant Greek, with the faultless aristocratic bearing, the quiet, penetrating thinker's gaze and the narrow, finely chiselled lips. The scholars loved him for his wonderful Greek. Almost everyone loved him for his nobility and refinement; many fell in love with him. Some resented his extreme quietness and self-control, his courtly manners.

Abbot and novice: each in his own way bore the fate of the chosen; dominating in his own way, suffering in his own way. Each felt more akin to the other, more attracted to him, than to the rest of the monastic community. Yet neither could get close to the other; neither could warm to the other. The abbot treated the youth with the utmost care, the utmost consideration, was concerned for him as for a rare, delicate, perhaps precocious, perhaps endangered, brother. The youth accepted every order, every advice, every word of praise from the abbot with perfect composure, never contradicting, never put out; and if the abbot's assessment of him was correct and his only vice was pride, he was wonderfully skilful at concealing it. There was nothing that could be said against him; he was perfect, superior to everyone. Yet few, apart from the scholars, really became friends with him, and his superiority enveloped him like a chilling cloud.

'Narcissus,' the abbot said one day after hearing his confession, 'I must admit to being guilty of having judged you harshly. I have often considered you proud, and I may have done you an injustice. You are very much alone, my young brother. You are lonely, you have admirers but no friends. I wish I had cause to rebuke you now and again, but I never have reason to do so. I wish you would sometimes misbehave, the way most young people of your age so readily do. You never do. There are times when I am a little anxious about you, Narcissus.'

The youth raised his dark eyes to the old man.

'I greatly desire, gracious Father, not to cause you any anxiety. It may well be that I am proud, gracious Father. I ask you to punish me for that. At times I even wish to punish myself. Send me to a hermitage, Father, or order me to perform lowly duties.'

'For both those things you are too young, dear brother,' said the abbot. 'Moreover, you have a great capacity for

4

languages and thinking, my son. It would be a waste of those gifts from God if I were to assign you to lowly duties. Probably you will become a teacher and a scholar. Do you not wish that yourself?'

'Forgive me, Father, I am really not so sure about my wishes. I shall always take pleasure in scholarly pursuits – how could I do otherwise? But I do not believe that those will be my only sphere. After all, it may not always be a person's wishes that determine his destiny and mission. It may be something else, something predestined.'

The abbot listened gravely, yet there was a smile on his old face as he said: 'From whatever knowledge I have acquired about human beings, it seems we all tend, especially in our youth, to confuse providence with our wishes. But since you believe you have some foreknowledge of your destiny, tell me something about it. For what do you believe yourself destined?'

Narcissus half closed his dark eyes so that they disappeared under his long black lashes. He said nothing.

'Speak, my son,' the abbot prompted him after a long wait.

In a low voice and with downcast eyes, Narcissus began to speak: 'I believe I know, gracious Father, that above all I am destined for the monastic life. I shall, I believe, become a monk, a priest, a subprior and perhaps an abbot. I do not believe this because I wish it. My wish is not to hold office, but offices will be imposed upon me.'

For a long time neither spoke.

'Why do you believe this?' the old man asked hesitatingly. 'What can there be in your character, apart from your erudition, that finds expression in that belief?'

'It is the attribute,' Narcissus said slowly, 'of having a feeling for the nature and destiny of people, not only for my own but for those of others, too. This attribute compels me to serve others by having power over them. Had I not been born to the monastic life I would have to become a judge or a statesman.'

'That may be,' the abbot nodded. 'Have you tested your ability to recognize people and their destinies on any examples?'

'I have.'

'Are you prepared to give me an example?'

'I am.'

'Good. Since I would not like to pry into the secrets of our brothers without their knowledge, perhaps you would care to tell me what you believe you know about me, your abbot Daniel.'

Narcissus raised his lids and looked the abbot in the eye.

'Is that an order, gracious Father?'

'An order.'

'I find it difficult to speak, Father.'

'I, too, find it difficult, my young brother, to compel you to speak. Yet I do so. Speak!'

Narcissus bent his head and continued in a whisper: 'There is not much that I know about you, reverend Father. I know that you are a servant of God who would rather be a goatherd, or ring a little bell in a hermitage and take confessions from the peasants, than rule over a great monastery. I know that you have a special love for the holy Mother of God and pray most often to Her. Sometimes you pray that Greek and other knowledge pursued in this monastery may not confuse or endanger the souls of those in your charge. Sometimes you pray that you may not lose patience with Subprior Gregor. Sometimes you pray for a peaceful end. And your prayers will, I believe, be heard, and you will have a peaceful end.'

There was silence in the abbot's little reception room. At last the old man spoke. 'You are a visionary,' the aged abbot said with a smile. 'Even pious and kindly visions can deceive. Do not rely upon them, even as I do not. Can you see into my heart, Brother Visionary, and know what I am thinking about this matter?'

'I can see, Father, that you are thinking most kindly about it. You are thinking as follows: "This young pupil is in some slight danger. He has visions, he may have meditated overmuch. I could impose a penance on him. It would do him no harm. But I shall also take upon myself the penance I impose upon him." That is what you have just been thinking.'

The abbot rose. With a smile he indicated to the novice that it was time for him to leave. 'Very well,' he said. 'Do not take your visions too seriously, my young brother. God requires many things from us other than having visions. Let us assume that you have flattered an old man by promising him an easy death. Let us assume that for a moment the old man was glad to hear this promise. Now it is enough. You are to pray a rosary, tomorrow after early mass. You are to pray with humility and devotion and not perfunctorily, and I shall do the same. Now go, Narcissus, we have talked enough.'

On another occasion Abbot Daniel had to mediate between the youngest of the teaching monks and Narcissus, who could not agree on a certain point in the curriculum. Narcissus argued passionately for the introduction of certain changes in the teaching methods and was able to justify these convincingly. Father Lorenz, on the other hand, out of a kind of jealousy, refused to consider them, and each new discussion was followed by days of hurt silence and sulking, until Narcissus, convinced that he was right, would bring up the subject again. Finally Father Lorenz said, in a slightly offended tone: 'Very well, Narcissus, let us put an end to this argument. You know that it is for me to decide, not you. You are not my colleague but my assistant, and it is for you to yield to me. However, since the matter seems to be of such great importance to you, and since, although superior to you in authority, I am not your superior in knowledge and talent, I shall not make the decision myself. Instead we shall put it before our Father Abbot and let him decide.'

This they did, and Abbot Daniel listened patiently and benignly to the two scholars' argument about their views on teaching grammar. After they had both presented and backed up their opinions at length, the abbot looked at them with a twinkle, shook his old grey head a little, and said:

'Dear brothers, I am sure neither of you believes that I know as much about these matters as you do. It is laudable of Narcissus that he should have the school so much at heart, and that he should be trying to improve the curriculum. But if his superior is of a different opinion, Narcissus must be silent and obey, for no amount of improvement in the school could be set above any disruption of the order and obedience in this house that would result. I must rebuke Narcissus for not knowing when to yield. And as for you two young scholars, I wish you may never lack for superiors who are more stupid than you! There is no better remedy for pride.'

With this good-natured little joke he dismissed them. But he was careful to keep an eye on them during the next few days to see whether the two young teachers were once again on good terms.

And now it came about that a new face appeared in the monastery which saw so many faces come and go, and that this new face was not among the unnoticed and fast forgotten. It was a youth who, already enrolled in advance by his father, arrived one spring day to become a pupil at the monastery school. They, the youth and his father, tethered their horses to the chestnut tree and were met by the doorkeeper emerging from the entrance.

The boy looked up at the still leafless tree. 'I have never seen a tree like that,' he said. 'What a strange, beautiful tree! I wish I knew what it was called!'

The father, an elderly gentleman with a careworn, somewhat pinched face, ignored the boy's words, but the doorkeeper, who immediately took a liking to the boy, told him the name of the tree. The boy thanked him politely, held out his hand, and said: 'My name is Goldmund, and I am to go to school here.' The man gave him a smile and led the new arrivals through the entrance and up the wide stone staircase. Thus Goldmund entered the monastery with confidence and the feeling of having already met two beings in this place whose friend he could be: the tree and the doorkeeper.

The new arrivals were received first by Father Principal, then in the evening by the abbot himself. On both occasions the father, an imperial official, presented his son Goldmund; and although he was invited to remain in the house for a while as a guest, he made use of his right to hospitality for only one night, stating that he would have to return home the next day. As a gift he offered the monastery one of his two horses, and the gift was accepted. The conversation with the two clerics was polite and cool, but both the abbot and the principal looked upon the respectfully silent Goldmund with favour. They immediately liked the handsome boy with the delicate features. As for the father, they felt no regret at his departure the following day, whereas they were glad to keep the son.

Goldmund was introduced to the teachers and assigned a bed in the pupils' dormitory. Respectfully and with a sad expression he said goodbye to his father as the latter rode away, gazing after him until he disappeared between granary and mill through the narrow arched gate of the outer courtyard. A tear hung from one fair eyelash when the boy turned round, but the doorkeeper was already at hand to welcome him with an affectionate pat on the shoulder.

'Young master,' he consoled him, 'you mustn't be sad. At first most of the boys feel a bit homesick for their father and mother or their brothers and sisters. But you'll soon find out – life's quite good here too, in fact not bad at all.'

'Thank you, Brother Doorkeeper,' the boy replied. 'I have no brothers or sisters, and no mother. I have only my father.'

'Well then, you'll find friends instead, and scholarship and music and new games you've never heard of, all kinds of things, you'll see. And if you need a helping hand at any time, just come to me.'

Goldmund smiled at him. 'Oh, thank you so much! And if you want to do me a favour, please show me sometime where our horse is kept, the one my father left here. I'd like to go and see it and make sure it's being looked after.'

The doorkeeper took him along at once and led him into the stable next to the granary. In the dim light there was a sharp smell of horses, of manure and barley, and in one of the stalls Goldmund found the brown horse that had carried him there. The animal had already recognized him and stretched out its head towards him. Goldmund placed his two hands around its neck, leaned his cheek against the broad forehead with the white patch, stroked the animal fondly and whispered into its ear: 'How are you, Blaze, dear pony, good boy, are you all right? Do you still love me? Have they fed you? Are you homesick too? Dear Blaze, dear little fellow, how glad I am you're staying here too, I'll come and visit you often and make sure you're all right.' From his cuff he pulled a piece of bread he had saved from breakfast and fed it in little pieces to the animal. Then he said goodbye and followed the doorkeeper across the courtyard, which was as wide as the market square of a big town and had linden trees growing here and there on it. At the inner entrance he thanked the doorkeeper, but after shaking hands with him realized he had forgotten the way to his classroom, which he had been shown the previous day. He gave a little laugh, blushed and asked the doorkeeper to show it to him, which he gladly did. In the classroom Goldmund found a dozen boys and youths seated on benches, and Narcissus, the teaching assistant, turned round.

'I am Goldmund,' he said, 'the new pupil.'

Narcissus nodded briefly. Without smiling, he indicated a place on a bench at the back and at once resumed the lesson.

Goldmund sat down. He was amazed to find such a young teacher, scarcely a few years older than himself – amazed and pleased to find this young teacher so handsome, so distinguished-looking, so serious, yet so attractive and charming. The doorkeeper had been kind, the abbot had given him a friendly welcome; over in the stable stood Blaze, a little bit of home, and now here was this amazingly young teacher, with the gravity of a scholar and the nobility of a prince, and with such a disciplined, cool, compelling voice! He listened gratefully, yet without immediately grasping the nature of the subject. He felt at ease. He had landed among good, worthy people, and he was prepared to love them and to seek their friendship. As he lay in bed after waking up that morning, still tired from the long journey, he had felt apprehensive, and in saying goodbye to his father he had been unable to hold back a few tears. But now everything seemed all right: he was content. Gazing long and often at the young teacher, he delighted in the firm, slender figure, the coolly flashing eyes, the firm lips forming clear, crisp syllables, the vibrant, untiring voice.

But when the lesson was over and the pupils scrambled noisily to their feet, Goldmund was startled and somewhat ashamed to realize that he had been asleep for quite a while. Nor was he the only one to notice: the other boys on his bench had noticed too and had passed along the information in whispers. The young teacher was scarcely out of the room before the other boys started tugging and cuffing Goldmund from all sides.

'Had a good sleep?' one of them asked with a grin.

'Fine pupil!' mocked another. 'Sure to become a great luminary of the Church! Nods off in the very first lesson!'

'Take the little brat to bed!' someone suggested, and amid general laughter they seized him by the arms and legs to carry him off.

Furious at being roused in this way, Goldmund hit out in all directions, trying to get free, and was cuffed and finally dropped while one of them still hung on to his foot. He violently kicked him away, hurled himself at the nearest boy who didn't back off, and was immediately involved in a fierce fight. His opponent was a hefty fellow, and the rest of them watched the contest gleefully. When Goldmund did not succumb and landed a few good punches on his hefty adversary, he quickly gained some friends among the others even without knowing the name of a single one of them. But suddenly they all scattered in haste, seconds before Father Martin, the school principal, entered and stood before the sole remaining boy. In some surprise he stared at Goldmund, whose blue eyes looked with embarrassment out of his beet-red, somewhat battered face.

'Well, well, what's the matter with you?' he asked. 'You're Goldmund, aren't you? Did they do you any harm, those young ruffians?'

'Oh no,' said the boy. 'I took care of him!'

'Took care of whom?'

'I don't know. I don't know any of them yet. One of them fought me.'

'I see. Did he start it?'

'I don't know. No, I think I started it myself. They were teasing me, and I got angry.'

'Well, you're off to a fine start, my boy. Now remember this. If you ever get into another fight here in the schoolroom, you'll be punished. And now hurry up and go to supper – off you go!'

Smiling, he watched the contrite Goldmund running off and trying as he ran to comb his ruffled fair hair with his fingers.

Goldmund was himself of the opinion that his first deed in this monastic life had been pretty stupid and naughty. Somewhat remorseful, he went in search of his schoolmates and found them at supper, but he was welcomed with friendly respect. He made honourable peace with his enemy and from then on felt accepted by the group.

Chapter Two

Although before long Goldmund was on friendly terms with everyone, it was some time before he found a friend. There was no one among his schoolmates to whom he felt especially close, let alone attracted. They in turn were surprised to find the plucky pugilist, whom they tended to regard as an amiable ruffian, to be a very peaceable fellow who seemed more intent on achieving fame as a model pupil.

There were two people in the monastery to whom Goldmund felt emotionally drawn, who occupied his thoughts, whom he admired, loved and revered: the abbot Daniel and the teaching assistant Narcissus. He was inclined to regard the abbot as a saint. His simplicity and goodness, his clear, thoughtful gaze; the way he governed and issued orders, humbly as if performing a service; his benevolent, quiet gestures: all this exerted a powerful attraction on him. He wished he could have become the personal servant of this pious man; then he could always have been at his side, in obedience and attendance, could have offered up to him as a perpetual sacrifice all his boyish yearnings for devotion and dedication, could have learned from him how to live a noble, pure and saintly life. For it was Goldmund's intention not only to complete his schooling at the monastery, but if possible to remain entirely and permanently at the monastery and dedicate his life to God. That was his purpose, that was his father's wish and bidding, and that no doubt was God's own will and command. No one seemed to perceive that this fair and smiling boy carried a burden from his past, that he was secretly destined for atonement and sacrifice. Even the abbot failed to see this, although Goldmund's father had dropped a few hints and made it clear that he wished his son to remain indefinitely at the monastery. There seemed to be some secret blemish associated with Goldmund's birth, something unspoken that demanded atonement. But the abbot had not cared very much for the father; he had met his words, in fact his whole somewhat pompous demeanour, with polite aloofness and had attached no particular importance to those hints.

The other person who aroused Goldmund's love had a keener eye and suspected more, but he held back. Narcissus was well aware that a beautiful golden bird had winged its way to him. Isolated as he was in his superiority, Narcissus had quickly sensed their kinship, although seeming to be Goldmund's very opposite in all things. Whereas Narcissus was dark and lean, Goldmund was sunny and rosy-cheeked. Whereas Narcissus was a thinker and an analyst, Goldmund appeared to be a dreamer and a childlike soul. But the contrasts were overarched by one common quality: both were exceptional people; both were set apart from others by conspicuous gifts and signs, and on both of them destiny had conferred a special mandate.

Narcissus passionately empathized with this young soul, whose nature and destiny he had soon recognized. Goldmund ardently admired his personable, erudite teacher. But Goldmund was shy; he knew of no other way to gain Narcissus's favour than by striving to the point of exhaustion to be an attentive, studious pupil. Nor was it shyness alone that restrained him: he also had a feeling that Narcissus was a danger to him. He could not have the good, humble abbot as his ideal and model and at the same time the sophisticated, erudite, astute Narcissus. Yet with all the spiritual strength of his youth he strove to emulate both irreconcilable ideals. This struggle was often painful. During his first months as a pupil, Goldmund sometimes felt so emotionally confused and torn in different directions that he was strongly tempted to run away, or to vent his distress and pent-up rage in the company of his schoolmates. Good-natured though he was, some minor teasing or juvenile prank would often cause such rage to flare up inside him that he could contain himself only with the utmost effort and, deathly pale, eyes closed, would turn silently away. Then he would go off to the stable, to his pony Blaze, to lean his head against its neck, to kiss the animal and weep as he stood beside it. And gradually his suffering increased and became noticeable. His cheeks grew hollow, his eyes lost their lustre, his laughter, loved by all, was seldom heard.

Even he did not know what was happening to him. It was his honest desire and determination to be a good pupil, to be accepted before long into the novitiate, and then become a pious, unassuming brother of the monks. Convinced that all his powers and gifts tended towards that mild, religious goal, he knew no other aspirations and felt strangely sad when forced to acknowledge that this simple, beautiful goal was so hard to attain. At times he was discouraged and puzzled to note some reprehensible tendencies in himself: reluctance and lack of concentration at his studies; day-dreaming or dozing in the classroom; rebelliousness and aversion towards the Latin teacher; irritability and angry impatience with his schoolmates. And most confusing of all was that his love for Narcissus was so greatly at odds with his love for Abbot Daniel. Yet sometimes he believed with profound certainty that Narcissus loved him too, that he sensed his plight and was waiting for him.

In fact, Narcissus's thoughts were far more occupied with him than the boy suspected. He wanted this handsome, bright, lovable boy as his friend; in him he sensed his opposite and complement. He would have liked him at his side, to guide and enlighten him, enhance him and bring about his flowering. But he refrained, for many reasons, and he was aware of almost all of them. Above all he was inhibited by his disgust for those far from rare teachers and monks who fell in love with pupils or novices. All too often he had himself felt with repugnance the lustful eyes of older men resting on him; all too often he had silently warded off their advances and attempted caresses. Now he understood them better: he, too, saw the temptation of becoming attached to this charming Goldmund, of evoking his innocent laughter, of running affectionate fingers through his fair hair. But he would never do that, never. Moreover, as an assistant with the rank of teacher but without a teacher's status and authority, he made a habit of being especially careful and vigilant, of dealing with youths only a few years younger than himself as if he were twenty years older. He consistently refrained from showing preference to any pupil and forced himself to treat with particular fairness and solicitude any pupil who aroused his aversion. His service was a service of the spirit. It was to the spirit that his strict life was dedicated, and only secretly, in his most unguarded moments, did he allow himself to indulge in the pleasure of pride, of knowing better and being cleverer than others. No: however alluring a friendship with Goldmund might be, it was a danger, and he must not permit it to touch the very kernel of his life. The kernel and meaning of his life were service to the spirit, service to the word; the quiet, exemplary, selfless guidance of his pupils – and not only *his* pupils – towards lofty spiritual goals.

Goldmund had already been a pupil at Mariabronn for over a year, and times without number he had played schoolboy games beneath the magnificent chestnut and the linden trees in the courtyard: racing, ball games, robbers, snowball fights. Now it was spring, but Goldmund felt tired and out of sorts.

His head often ached, and in class he had trouble staying awake and alert.

Then one evening he was approached by Adolf, the boy with whom his first encounter had been a fist-fight and with whom he had begun that winter to study Euclid. It was the free hour after supper when playing in the dormitories, chatting in the classrooms and even strolling in the outer courtyard were permitted.

'Goldmund,' Adolf said, drawing him by the arm down the stairs, 'I've something to tell you, something you might enjoy. But of course you're a paragon, and I'm sure you want to be a bishop one day – first give me your word you won't betray our friendship and sneak on me to the teachers.'

Goldmund did not hesitate to give his word. There was a code of monastery honour and a code of schoolboy honour, and at times the two conflicted. He was aware of that. But, as everywhere else, the unwritten laws were stronger than the written ones, and as long as he was a pupil he would never refuse to live up to schoolboy notions of honour.

After drawing him through the doorway and under the trees, Adolf told him in a whisper that there was a group of daring fellows, of whom he was one, who had adopted a traditional custom of recalling from time to time that after all they weren't monks, and they would leave the monastery to spend an evening in the village. It was great fun, an adventure in which a regular fellow wouldn't refuse to take part. They would be back that night.

'But the gate will be closed then!' exclaimed Goldmund.

Yes, of course it would, that was part of the fun! But they knew a secret way of getting in again unnoticed. It wouldn't be the first time.

Goldmund remembered: he had already heard the expression, 'going to the village'. It meant nocturnal excursions by the inmates to participate in all kinds of secret pleasures and adventures, and it was forbidden by monastery law on pain of severe punishment. He was shocked. 'Going to the village' was a sin, was forbidden. But he was fully aware, for this very reason, that it might be part of the 'regular fellows'' code of honour to take a risk, and that there was a certain distinction in being invited to join in the escapade.

His first instinct was to say No, to run back and go to bed. He was so tired and felt so miserable, and he had had a headache all afternoon. But he was a bit ashamed in front of Adolf. And who knows, maybe there was some adventure out there, something exciting and new, something that could make one forget a headache, apathy and general misery. It was a sortie into the world – a secret and forbidden one, true, and hardly a creditable one, but perhaps it would be a liberation, an experience. He stood there hesitating while Adolf egged him on, until suddenly he gave a laugh and said Yes.

Unnoticed he disappeared with Adolf under the linden trees in the big courtyard, dark now, whose outer gate was already locked at this hour. His friend led him into the monastery mill, where the dim light and steady clatter of the wheels made it easy to slip through unheard and unseen. Climbing through a window, by this time in total darkness, they landed on a damp, slippery pile of wooden planks, one of which had to be pulled out and laid across the stream. And now they were outside on the faintly glimmering highway that vanished into the black forest. All this was thrilling and mysterious and appealed greatly to Goldmund.

Another boy, Konrad, was already standing at the entrance to the forest, and after a long wait yet another, Eberhard, came trudging up. The four of them walked through the forest as startled nightbirds fluttered up over their heads; a few stars twinkled between motionless clouds. Konrad chattered and

19

joked, and sometimes the others joined in, but an uneasy, solemn nocturnal sensation hovered over them, and their hearts beat faster.

Beyond the forest, after less than an hour, they reached the village, where everything seemed to be asleep. The low gables gleamed palely, crisscrossed by the dark ribs of beams; not a light was to be seen. Adolf walked ahead. Silently they slipped round a few houses, climbed over a fence, stood in a garden, stepped into the soft earth of beds, stumbled over steps and came to a halt by the wall of a house. Adolf knocked on a shutter, waited, knocked again. There was a sound inside, and presently a light showed, the shutter opened, and one after another they climbed in, into a kitchen with a black chimney-cowl and an earthen floor. On the raised hearth stood a little oil lamp, its feeble flame flickering on a thin wick. A skinny peasant girl was standing there. She offered her hand to the intruders, and behind her, out of the darkness, stepped a second girl, a mere child with long, dark plaits. Adolf had brought along some gifts, half a loaf of white monastery bread and something in a twist of paper – Goldmund assumed it to be a bit of stolen incense or candlewax or something of the kind. The girl with the plaits left the room, groping her way through the door without a light, and after a few minutes returned carrying a grey earthenware pitcher painted with a blue flower. She handed it to Konrad, who drank from it and passed it on. They all had a drink; it was strong cider.

In the light shed by the tiny flame they all settled down, the two girls on wooden stools, the boys round them on the floor. They spoke in whispers and drank from the cider, with Adolf and Konrad doing most of the talking. From time to time one of them would stand up, stroke the skinny one's hair and neck and whisper in her ear. The younger one was never touched. Probably, Goldmund thought, the older one was the maidservant, the pretty, younger one the daughter of the house. But it didn't matter anyway and was no concern of his, for he would never come back here. The secret escape and the walk in the dark through the forest: that he had enjoyed, it had been something new, exciting, mysterious yet not dangerous. Although it was forbidden, the infringement did not weigh on his conscience. But this, this nocturnal visiting of the girls, was more than merely forbidden, he felt. It was a sin. To the others, perhaps, even this was no more than a minor escapade, but not to him. To him, knowing himself destined for asceticism and the monastic life, no dallying with girls was permitted. No, he would never come back here, yet he could feel his heart thumping apprehensively in the dim lamplight of the humble kitchen.

His schoolmates acted like heroes in front of the girls, showing off with Latin phrases which they inserted into the conversation. All three evidently found favour with the maidservant as one after another they approached her with clumsy little caresses, of which the most intimate was a shy kiss. They seemed to know exactly how far they could go. And since the whole conversation had to be carried on in whispers, there was actually something comical about the scene, although Goldmund did not find it so. He stayed hunched up on the floor, staring at the little flame and not uttering a word. Sometimes, with an almost lustful glance, he would catch one of the caresses being exchanged among the others. While continuing to stare straight ahead, he longed to fix his gaze on the younger girl, the one with the plaits, but this was the very thing he would not allow himself to do. Yet whenever his will-power weakened and his eyes strayed to that calm, sweet, girlish face, he found her dark eyes riveted on his own face, staring at him as if spellbound.

Perhaps an hour had passed – never had Goldmund known an hour to be so long – before his schoolmates ran out of phrases and caresses. Silence fell, and as they sat there, somewhat embarrassed, Eberhard began to yawn, at which point the maidservant told them it was time for them to leave. They all got to their feet, and each offered his hand to the maidservant, Goldmund last. Then each offered his hand to the young girl, Goldmund last. Konrad was the first to climb out of the window, followed by Eberhard and Adolf. When half-way out Goldmund felt a hand on his shoulder holding him back. He could not stop, but when he was standing on the ground outside he did reluctantly turn round. The young girl with the plaits was leaning out of the window. 'Goldmund!' she whispered.

He stood still.

'Will you come back?' she asked, her shy voice barely breathing the words.

Goldmund shook his head.

Stretching out both hands she clasped his head; he felt the warmth of her small hands on his temples. She leaned over until her dark eyes were close to his. 'Come back!' she whispered, and her lips touched his in a childish kiss.

He quickly ran after the others through the little garden, stumbled across beds, smelling damp earth and manure, scratching his hand on a rose-bush, and finally climbed over the fence to hurry after the others out of the village and towards the forest. 'Never again!' commanded his will-power. 'Tomorrow!' implored his sobbing heart.

No one encountered the nightbirds; unmolested they found their way back to Mariabronn, across the stream, through the mill, across the linden-tree courtyard, and by devious routes over low roofs and through columned windows into the monastery and finally the dormitory.

Next morning, tall Eberhard was so fast asleep that he had to be punched awake. They were all in time for early mass, morning gruel and class. But Goldmund looked wretched, so much so that Father Martin asked him if he was ill. Adolf shot him a warning glance, and Goldmund said there was nothing the matter. During Greek, however, towards noon, Narcissus kept an eye on him. Although he could also see that Goldmund was not well, he said nothing and observed him closely. At the end of the lesson he summoned him. So as not to attract the attention of the other boys, he sent Goldmund on an errand to the library and soon followed him.

'Goldmund,' he said, 'can I do something to help? I can see you are in trouble. Maybe you are ill. In that case we will put you to bed and send you up a bowl of soup and a glass of wine. You have no head for Greek today.'

He waited a long time for an answer. The pale boy looked at him out of distraught eyes, sank his head, raised it again, twitched his lips, tried to speak, could not. Suddenly he slumped to one side, leaned his head on an oak reading desk between the two cherubs' heads flanking the desk, and burst into such sobs that Narcissus, embarrassed, looked away for a while before touching the weeping boy and lifting him up.

'Now then,' he said, in a kinder tone than Goldmund had ever heard him use. 'Now then, *amice*, cry all you want, you will soon feel better. That's right, sit down, you don't have to talk. I can see you have had enough. I expect you have had to make an effort all morning to sit up straight and not show anything, and you did a good job of that. Now cry all you want, it's the best thing you can do. No? Already finished? Sitting up again? Very well, we'll go over to the sickroom and you can get into bed, and by this evening you will feel much better. Come with me!'

Avoiding the pupils' quarters, he led him to a sickroom, indicated one of the two empty beds and, when Goldmund obediently began to undress, left the room to report him sick to the superintendent. Also, as promised, he ordered a bowl of soup and a glass of invalid wine for him from the kitchen.

These two customary monastery *beneficia* were very popular with most patients.

Goldmund lay in his sickbed, trying to find his way back out of his confusion. An hour earlier he might have been able to unravel what had made him so unspeakably weary that day, to grasp the nature of the mortal exertion of spirit that had made his head feel empty and his eyes smart. It had been the enormous effort – ever renewed, ever unsuccessful – to forget the preceding night; or rather, not the night, not the foolish, delightful escape from the locked-up monastery, not the walk through the forest, or the slippery makeshift bridge over the black millstream or the climbing over fences and through windows and passages, but solely the moment at that dark kitchen window, the breath and the words of the girl, the clasp of her hands, the kiss of her lips.

But now something else had been added, a new terror, a new experience. Narcissus had taken him under his wing, Narcissus loved him, Narcissus had come to his aid – Narcissus, so refined, so distinguished, so clever with his thin, slightly mocking lips. And he, Goldmund, had lost control in his presence, had stood before him disgraced, stammering and finally sobbing! Instead of winning this superior being with the noblest of weapons, with Greek or philosophy, with spiritual heroism and dignified stoicism, he had collapsed in front of him, weakly and shamefully! Never would he forgive himself for that; never would he be able to look Narcissus in the eye without shame.

But the weeping had broken the tension; the solitude in the sickroom, the comfortable bed, were soothing. His despair had been robbed of more than half its strength. After an hour or so, a serving brother entered, bringing a bowl of gruel, a piece of white bread and a small beaker of red wine such as the pupils were otherwise given only on feast days. Goldmund drank the wine, finished half the gruel and put aside the bowl, then began thinking again, but it was no use. He picked up the bowl and had a few more spoonfuls. And when a little later the door was gently opened and Narcissus came in to see how the patient was doing, he found Goldmund asleep, the colour back in his cheeks. Narcissus gazed at him for a long time, with love, with searching curiosity, and also with a degree of envy. He could see that Goldmund was not ill; there would be no need to send up any wine to him the next day. But he knew the spell was broken: they would be friends. This time it was Goldmund who needed him, to whom he could be of service. Another time it might be he himself who was weak and in need of help, of love. And from this boy he would be able to accept these, should it ever come to that.

Chapter Three

It was a strange friendship that now began between Narcissus and Goldmund, approved of by only a few, and at times they seemed to disapprove of it themselves.

At first it was Narcissus, the thinker, who had the greatest difficulty. To him all was spirit, including love; it was not in his nature to surrender unthinkingly to an attraction. In this friendship he was the leading spirit, and for a long time it was he alone who consciously realized the destiny, extent and meaning of this friendship. For a long time he remained solitary in loving, aware that his friend would not be truly his until he had led him to enlightenment. Ardent, playful and reckless, Goldmund abandoned himself to the new life; knowing and responsible, Narcissus accepted the lofty destiny.

For Goldmund it was at first a release and a recovery. At the sight and kiss of a pretty girl, his youthful need for love had just been powerfully aroused and at the same time hopelessly frightened off. In his heart of hearts he felt that all those dreams for his future, everything he believed in, everything to which he believed himself preordained and called, was threatened by that kiss at the window, by the look from those dark eyes. Destined by his father for the monastic life and accepting this fate unreservedly, aiming with youthful fervour towards an ascetic, heroic ideal of piety – at the first fleeting encounter, at the first visceral appeal to his senses, at the first signal from a feminine creature, he had felt without the shadow of a doubt that here was his enemy and demon, that in women lay his danger. And now fate offered him deliverance; now, in his direst need, this friendship came towards him, offering his desire a flower garden, his worship a new altar. Here he was allowed to love, here he was allowed to surrender without sin, to bestow his heart on an admired, older, more astute friend, to sublimate the perilous flames of his senses, to transform them into noble sacrificial fires.

But even in the first spring of this friendship he met with strange inhibitions, with unexpected, mysterious aloofness, with dismaying demands. For it did not occur to him to think of his friend as the reverse and counterpart of himself. To him it seemed that love, sincere devotion, was all that was needed to turn two into one, to wipe out differences and bridge opposites. How severe and assured, how unequivocal and remorseless was this Narcissus! He seemed neither to know nor wish for an innocent devotion in which they could gratefully roam the land of friendship together; neither to know nor tolerate the concept of dreamy, aimless wandering. True, when Goldmund had been sick he had shown concern for him; true, he had loyally helped and advised him in all matters of school and learning, explaining difficult passages in books, opening Goldmund's eyes to the realm of grammar, logic and theology. But he never seemed really to approve of his friend. In fact quite often he seemed, with his faintly superior smile, not to take him seriously. Goldmund felt that there was more to this behaviour than mere schoolmasterly self-importance, that there was something deeper, more significant, behind it, but because he could not define this deeper element his friendship often made him feel sad and at a loss.

In reality Narcissus knew very well what kind of person his friend was. He was not blind to his radiant beauty, to his innate vitality and exuberance. He was far from being a schoolmaster intent on feeding an ardent young soul with Greek, responding to an innocent love with logic. Rather did he love the youth too well, and for him this was a danger, since for Narcissus loving was not a natural condition but a miracle. It was not permitted to him to fall in love, to find satisfaction in the pleasing gaze from those bright eyes, in the proximity of that shining fairness; he must not allow this love to dwell even for a moment on the sensual aspect. For if Goldmund believed himself preordained to the life of a monk and an ascetic and to a lifetime striving for holiness, Narcissus was genuinely destined for such a life. To him, love was permitted only in a single, the most sublime, form. And Narcissus did not believe that Goldmund was destined for the ascetic life. More clearly than anyone else, he knew how to read human beings, and here, loving as he did, he read with intensified clarity. He saw Goldmund's nature which, despite their polarities, he intimately understood, since it was the other, lost half of his own. He saw it as being armoured with a hard shell of illusions, faulty upbringing, paternal exhortations, and he had long since discerned the whole uncomplicated secret of this young life. His task was clear to him: to expose this secret to its bearer, to free him from the shell, to give him back his own true nature. It would be difficult, and the most difficult part was that as a result he might lose his friend.

Almost imperceptibly he approached his goal. Months passed before an initial onslaught, a deeply revealing conversation between the two, became possible, so far were they apart despite their friendship, so wide was the gap to be bridged between them. One who could see and one who was blind: thus they walked side by side. The fact that the blind one knew nothing of his own blindness made things easier only for himself.

The first breakthrough was made by Narcissus when he tried to find out what experience had driven the distraught boy to him in an hour of weakness. The process was less difficult than he had imagined. Goldmund had long felt the need to confess the experience of that night, but there was no one beside the abbot in whom he felt enough confidence, and the abbot was not his father confessor. So when Narcissus, in an hour that seemed favourable to him, reminded his friend of that first beginning of their bond and gently touched upon the secret, Goldmund said without hesitation: 'It's a pity you haven't been ordained yet and can't hear confession. I would gladly have shed the burden of that affair by confessing, and I would have willingly done penance for it. But my father confessor wasn't the one I could tell about it.'

Cautiously, cunningly, Narcissus went on probing; he had found the trail. 'You remember,' he tried, 'that morning you seemed to be ill. You will not have forgotten it, for that was when we became friends. I have often reflected on it. Perhaps you did not notice, but at the time I felt rather helpless.'

'You, helpless?' cried the boy incredulously. 'But I was the helpless one! It was I who stood there swallowing, unable to get a word out and finally bursting into tears like a child! To this day I am still ashamed of that hour. I thought I should never be able to face you again. To think you saw me so wretchedly weak!'

Tentatively Narcissus advanced a little further. 'I can understand,' he said, 'that you felt awkward about it. A sturdy, brave fellow like you, and crying in front of a stranger – what's more, in front of a teacher. That certainly was not like you. Well, at the time I just thought you were ill. Shaken by fever, even an Aristotle may behave strangely. But it turned out you were not ill! You had no fever whatever! And that was what you were ashamed of. No one is ashamed of succumbing to a fever, is he? You were ashamed because you had succumbed to something else, because something had overwhelmed you. Tell me, had something special happened?'

Goldmund hesitated a moment, then slowly said: 'Yes, something special had happened. Let me pretend you are my father confessor. It must be told sometime or other.'

With bent head he recounted the story of that night.

Narcissus commented with a smile: 'Ah yes, "going to the village" is indeed forbidden. But a person can do many a forbidden thing and laugh about it, or he can confess and put it behind him. Why shouldn't you, like almost any schoolboy, occasionally commit a little folly of that kind? Is it really so bad?'

Losing his temper Goldmund angrily burst out: 'You're really talking like a schoolmaster! You know exactly what it's all about! Of course I don't regard it as a great sin to snap one's fingers at the house rules once in a while and take part in a schoolboy lark, although that isn't exactly part of the preparation for the monastic life.'

'Stop!' exclaimed Narcissus sharply. 'Do you not know, my friend, that for many pious monks these very preparations were necessary? Do you not know that one of the shortest routes to the life of a saint can be the life of a rake?'

'Oh, don't talk like that!' retorted Goldmund. 'What I mean is, it wasn't the trivial disobedience that weighed on my conscience. It was something else. It was the girl, it was a feeling I can't describe to you! A feeling that, if I were to yield to that temptation, if I were merely to reach out my hand to touch the girl, I would never be able to turn back, that sin would then swallow me up like a maw of Hell and never spew me out again. A feeling that that would be the end of all beautiful dreams, all virtue, all love of God and what is good.'

Narcissus nodded, very thoughtful. 'The love of God,' he said slowly, searching for the words, 'is not always identical with love of what is good. Ah, if only it were that simple! We know what is good. It is written in the Commandments. But God is not only in the Commandments, my friend. They are only the smallest part of Him. You can be close to the Commandments yet far away from God.'

'Don't you understand me?' Goldmund wailed.

'Certainly I understand you. You see in women, in sex, the quintessence of everything you call "world" and "sin". You believe that either you would not be capable of all the other sins or, if you did commit them, they would not weigh you down. They could be confessed and redeemed. But not that one sin!'

'Yes, that's exactly how I feel.'

'So you see I do understand you. And you are not all that wrong either. The story of Eve and the serpent is indeed no idle fable. And yet you are wrong, dear friend. You would be right if you were Abbot Daniel, or your patron saint Chrysostom, if you were a bishop or a priest or even just an ordinary little monk. But you are not, you see. You are a pupil, and even if it is your wish to remain permanently in the monastery, or if it is your father's wish for you, you still have not taken any vow or been consecrated. If today or tomorrow you should be seduced by a pretty girl and were to succumb to temptation, you would have broken no vow.'

'No written vow!' cried Goldmund, greatly agitated. 'But an unwritten one, the most sacred that I carry within me. Can't you see that what may apply to many others doesn't apply to me? Isn't it true that, although you have not yet been consecrated or taken a vow, you would never allow yourself to touch a woman? Or am I mistaken? Aren't you like that at all? Aren't you at all the person I took you for? Didn't you long ago make in your heart the vow you haven't put into words in the presence of your superiors, and don't you feel for ever committed by it? So aren't you the same as I am?'

'No, Goldmund, I am not the same as you, not the way you think. It is true that I, too, am keeping an unspoken vow – you are right about that. But I am far from being the same as you. I shall tell you something now that you will one day remember. It is this. Our friendship has no other goal and no other meaning whatever than to show how completely different you are from me!'

Shocked, Goldmund stood still; Narcissus had spoken with a look on his face and in a voice that could not be gainsaid. He was silent. But why did Narcissus say such things? Why should Narcissus's unspoken vow be more sacred than his? Didn't Narcissus take him the least bit seriously? Did he see nothing but a child in him? The confusions and sad moments of this strange friendship were beginning all over again.

Narcissus was no longer in doubt as to the nature of Goldmund's secret. It was Eve, the primal mother, who was behind it. But how was it possible that in such a handsome, healthy, radiant youth, awakening sex should encounter such fierce hostility? There must have been a demon at work, a secret enemy that had succeeded in splitting this splendid human being and setting him at odds with his primal urges. Very well, the demon must be found, conjured up and made visible. Then it could be conquered.

Meanwhile Goldmund was being increasingly avoided and deserted by his schoolmates; or rather, they felt deserted and, as it were, betrayed by him. None of them quite approved of his friendship with Narcissus. The spiteful ones discredited it as being unnatural, especially those who had themselves been in love with one of the two youths. But even the others, those who were aware that in this case there was no question of any vice, shook their heads. They all begrudged those two their friendship, for by their bond they had, it seemed, arrogantly distanced themselves as aristocrats from the others, who were not good enough for them. That was not being co-operative, not in the spirit of the monastery, was not Christian.

Many things came to the ears of Abbot Daniel about those two: rumours, accusations, defamations. In more than forty years of monastic life he had observed many friendships between youths. They were part of the monastery scene, a pleasant bonus, sometimes amusing, sometimes dangerous. He stayed in the background, kept his eyes open and did not interfere. A friendship of such intensity and exclusiveness was rare and undoubtedly not without danger, but since he did not for an instant doubt its purity he let the matter take its course. If Narcissus had not occupied an exceptional position between pupils and teachers, the abbot would not have hesitated to impose a few separating ordinances between the two. It was not good for Goldmund to withdraw from his schoolmates and cultivate such a close and exclusive association with someone older, a teacher. But was one justified in disturbing Narcissus – that extraordinary, highly gifted person regarded by all the teachers as their intellectual equal, indeed superior – in his privileged career and removing him from his teaching activities? If Narcissus had not proved his worth as a teacher, if his friendship had led him to be neglectful and partisan, the abbot would have removed him immediately. But there was no evidence against him, nothing but rumours, nothing but jealous suspicion on the part of others. Moreover, he knew of Narcissus's special gifts, of his remarkably penetrating, perhaps somewhat arrogant, insight into human nature. He did not overestimate such gifts, and there were others he would have preferred to see in Narcissus; yet he did not doubt that Narcissus had perceived something exceptional about his pupil Goldmund and knew him far better than he himself or anyone else knew him. Apart from the winning charm of Goldmund's personality, the abbot had noticed nothing beyond a certain premature, perhaps even precocious, zeal with which Goldmund – a mere pupil and guest – already seemed to consider himself part of the monastery, almost one of the brothers. The abbot did not believe he had to fear that Narcissus would favour and further stimulate that touching but immature zeal. He was more afraid for Goldmund that his friend would infect him with a certain spiritual pride and scholarly vanity, but that did not seem much of a danger in regard to this particular pupil; it was a risk one could accept. When he reflected on how much simpler, more peaceful and comfortable it was for a superior to govern average human beings instead of strong, outstanding characters, he had to sigh and smile at the same time.

No, he did not want to let himself be infected by those suspicions, nor did he want to be ungrateful for having been entrusted with two exceptional human beings.

Narcissus gave much thought to his friend. His special talent for perceiving and empathizing with human types and destinies had long since informed him about Goldmund. Everything vital and radiant about this boy spoke so clearly. He bore all the signs of a strong nature richly endowed in his senses and his soul. Signs of an artist, perhaps, in any case of someone with great power to love, whose destiny and happiness consisted in being able to take fire and dedicate himself. So why was this person, born to love, this person with the rich, fine-tuned senses, who could so deeply respond to and love the fragrance of a flower, the morning sun, a horse, the flight of a bird, music: why, oh why, was he obsessed with being a man of the spirit, an ascetic?

Narcissus pondered long over this. He knew that Goldmund's father had favoured this obsession. But could he have caused it? With what magic had he bewitched his son to make him believe in such a destiny, such an obligation? What kind of person could this father be? Although he had very often deliberately brought up the subject of his father and Goldmund had talked a good deal about him, Narcissus could not form a mental image of him. Surely that was rather strange and suspicious? When

Goldmund mentioned a trout he had caught as a boy, when he described a butterfly or imitated a bird-call, told him about a playmate, a dog or a beggar, images were created, one could see something. When he spoke of his father, one saw nothing. No, if this father had really been such an important, powerful, dominant figure in Goldmund's life, the boy would have been able to describe him differently, would have been able to present different images of him. Narcissus did not think highly of this father; he did not care for him; at times he even doubted whether he actually was Goldmund's father. He was an empty idol. But from what source did he draw that power? How had he been able to fill Goldmund's soul with dreams that were so alien to the core of the boy's soul?

Goldmund, too, pondered a great deal. However certain he felt of the warmth of his friend's love, the troublesome feeling kept recurring that Narcissus did not take him seriously enough and always treated him a little bit as a child. And what did it mean, his friend's constant emphasis that he was not the same as Goldmund?

Meanwhile, all this ruminating did not fill Goldmund's days. He was not given to long bouts of rumination. There were other things to be done throughout the long day. He often spent time with Brother Doorkeeper, with whom he was on very good terms. He would often wheedle and wangle an opportunity to ride the pony Blaze for an hour or two, and he was very popular with the few retainers of the monastery, especially the miller. With the miller's help he would often lie in wait for the otter, or they would make pancakes with the fine 'prelates' flour' that Goldmund, with his eyes closed, could distinguish from all the other types of flour merely by the smell. Although he spent a lot of time with Narcissus, there still remained many hours in which he pursued his old habits and pleasures. He usually enjoyed the religious services, too. He loved singing in the boys' choir, loved telling his beads before a favourite altar; he would listen to the beautiful, solemn Latin of the mass, see the gold of the implements and ornaments gleaming through the clouds of incense, the motionless, venerable figures of the saints standing on their pedestals: the Evangelists with their animals, St James with his hat and pilgrim's pouch.

He felt drawn to these statues of stone and wood and liked to think of them as having some mysterious relation to himself, perhaps as immortal, omniscient godfathers, as protectors and mentors of his life. In the same way he loved the columns and capitals of the windows and doors, felt a mysterious and beautiful kinship with them, with the ornamentation of the altars, with those finely chiselled lines and circles, the flowers and proliferating foliage that broke forth from the stone of the columns and interleaved so tellingly and forcefully. It seemed to him a secret of great and touching value: that in addition to nature with all its plants and animals, there was this second, mute, man-made nature, there were these humans, animals and plants carved from stone and wood. Quite often he would spend a free hour copying these figures, animal heads and clusters of leaves, or trying to draw real flowers, horses and human faces.

He was also very fond of liturgical singing, especially of hymns celebrating the Virgin Mary. He loved the firm, austere progression of that singing, its refrains of supplication and glorification. He could prayerfully follow their time-honoured meaning or, ignoring the meaning, merely revel in the solemn measures of the verses, soaking up the sonorous, long-drawn-out notes, the full, resounding vowels, the devout repetitions. In his heart of hearts he was not a lover of erudition, or of grammar and logic, although they, too, had their beauty. His real love was for the liturgical world of image and sound.

From time to time he would briefly interrupt the alienation that had developed between him and his classmates. In the long run he found it a nuisance and a bore to be surrounded by rejection and coldness. Sometimes he would make a surly boy at the next desk laugh, or persuade a taciturn boy in the next bed to chat. For an hour or so he would exert himself, turn on the charm and temporarily win back a few eyes, a few faces, a few hearts. Twice these approaches resulted, very far from his intention, in his being asked again to join in 'going to the village'. He was shocked and quickly drew back. No, he wasn't going to the village any more, and he had succeeded in forgetting the girl with the plaits, in never thinking of her again, or almost never.

Chapter Four

For a long time Goldmund's secret, despite Narcissus's attempted siege, had remained inviolate. For a long time Narcissus had tried, vainly it seemed, to rouse him, to teach him the language in which the secret could be communicated.

Whatever his friend had told him about his background and home had yielded no image. There was a shadowy, amorphous but revered father, and then the legend of a mother who had either vanished or perished many years before, a mother who was now no more than a colourless name. Narcissus, an expert in reading souls, had gradually come to realize that his friend was one of those people who, having lost a part of their lives and being under pressure from some extremity or spell, have found themselves compelled to forget a part of their past. It was clear that mere questioning and advising were useless; he also saw that he had placed too much faith in the power of reason and had said many things in vain.

But not in vain was the love that still bound him to his friend and their habit of spending many hours together. Despite all the profound differences in their natures, each had learned a great deal from the other. Side by side with the language of reason, a language of the soul, of signs, had slowly evolved, just as between two dwellings there can be a road along which carriages can be driven and horses ridden, while beside it many little paths have been worn – paths for children, for lovers, or a barely visible track made by dogs and cats. Gradually Goldmund's inspired imagination had crept on magical paths into his friend's thoughts and their language, while in turn his friend had, without words, gained insight into much of Goldmund's mind and character. Slowly, in the light of love, new bonds matured between soul and soul; the words came only later. Thus quite unexpectedly, on a day when there were no classes, a conversation arose between them in the library – a conversation that brought them to the very core and meaning of their friendship and shed new, far-reaching light.

They had been discussing astrology, which was not pursued in the monastery and was in fact forbidden. Narcissus had said that astrology was an attempt to bring order and system into the many different kinds of people, their past fates and future destinies. At this point Goldmund interjected: 'You're always talking about differences – I have gradually come to see that this is your most striking characteristic. When you speak about the great difference between you and me, for instance, I get the impression that the difference consists of nothing more than your strange obsession with finding differences!'

Narcissus: 'Very true, you have hit the nail on the head! Indeed, to you the differences are not that important, while to me they seem to be the only thing that *is* important. I am by nature a scholar. I was born to pursue scholarship. And scholarship is, to quote you, nothing but that "obsession with finding differences". There could be no better description of its nature. For those of us dedicated to scholarship, all that matters is to determine differences. Scholarship equals the art of differentiation. For instance, finding in each person those marks that distinguish him from all others means recognizing him for what he is.'

Goldmund: 'Good enough. So one man wears peasant shoes and is a peasant, another wears a crown and is a king. I grant you those are differences. But they can be seen by children, without all that scholarship.'

Narcissus: 'But if the peasant and the king are both wearing the same clothes, the child can no longer tell them apart.'

Goldmund: 'Neither can scholarship.'

Narcissus: 'Perhaps it can. It is no cleverer than the child, I will admit that, but it is more patient. It takes note of more than the most obvious distinguishing marks.'

Goldmund: 'Any bright child will do the same. The child will recognize the king by his look or his posture. In a nutshell, you scholars are arrogant. You always see the rest of us as lacking in intelligence. A person can be very intelligent without all that scholarship.'

Narcissus: 'I am glad you are beginning to realize that. Now you will soon also realize that I do not mean intelligence when I speak of the difference between you and me. Don't you see, I am not saying you are more intelligent or less intelligent, better or worse? All I am saying is that you are different.'

Goldmund: 'I see no difficulty in understanding that. But you speak not only of the differences in distinguishing marks. You often speak also of the differences in destiny. Why, for instance, should you have a different destiny from mine? Like me, you are a Christian. Like me, you have decided on a monastic life. Like me, you are a child of our good Lord in Heaven. We both have the same goal – eternal salvation. Our destiny is the same – the return to God.'

Narcissus: 'Very good. In the textbooks of dogmatics, one human being is of course exactly like another, but not in real life. Surely the Redeemer's favourite disciple, on whose breast He rested, and that other disciple, the one who betrayed Him – surely those two could not have had the same destiny?'

Goldmund: 'You are a sophist, Narcissus! If we continue on this path we'll come no closer together!'

Narcissus: 'There is no path that will bring us closer together.'

Goldmund: 'Don't talk like that!'

Narcissus: 'I am serious. It is not our task to come closer together, no more than sun and moon or sea and land come closer together. We two, my dear friend, are sun and moon, we are sea and land. Our goal is not to blend into one another but to know one another, and for each to learn to see and honour in the other what he himself is – the other's counterpart and complement.'

Crestfallen, Goldmund kept his head bent; his expression had grown sad. At last he said: 'Is that why you so often don't take my thoughts seriously?'

Narcissus hesitated a little before replying, then said in a bright, hard voice: 'That is why. You must get used to the fact, my dear Goldmund, that the only thing I take seriously is you yourself. Believe me, I take every nuance in your voice, every one of your gestures, every smile, seriously. But your thoughts – those I take less seriously. What I take seriously in you is what I deem essential and necessary. So why do you want particular attention paid to your thoughts when you have so many other gifts?'

Goldmund gave a bitter smile: 'Just as I said, you've always taken me for a mere child!'

Narcissus stood firm. 'Some of your thoughts I do regard as those of a child. Remember how we were just saying that a bright child had by no means to be less intelligent than a scholar. But when the child wants to discuss scholarly matters, the scholar will not take him seriously.'

At that Goldmund burst out: 'Even when we're not discussing scholarly matters I can see your patronizing smile! For example, you always behave as if all my devoutness, my efforts at progress in learning, my desire to become a monk, were mere childishness!'

Narcissus looked at him gravely: 'I take you seriously when you are Goldmund, but you are not always Goldmund. All I wish for is that you become Goldmund through and through. You are not a scholar, you are not a monk – a scholar or a monk can be fashioned from inferior wood. You believe that you are not learned enough for me, not enough of a logician or not devout enough. Not at all – but you are not enough yourself for me.'

Although Goldmund had withdrawn after this conversation with a sense of shock and even injury, only a few days later he showed a desire to continue it. This time, however, Narcissus was able to give him a picture of the difference in their natures that his friend could more easily accept.

Narcissus had warmed to his subject; he felt that today Goldmund was absorbing his words more openly and willingly, that he had power over Goldmund. Seduced by success into saying more than he had intended, he let himself be carried away by his own words.

'Look,' he said, 'there is only one point in which I am superior to you: I am awake while you are only half awake and sometimes completely asleep. I call a person awake who, with his reason and consciousness, knows himself, knows his innermost, irrational forces, urges and weaknesses, and how to take them into account. The real sense of our meeting is that it may enable you to learn this. In your case, Goldmund, intellect and nature, consciousness and dreamworld, are very far apart. You have forgotten your childhood. It is crying out to you from the depths of your soul. It will make you suffer until you listen to it. But enough of that! In being awake I am, as I said, stronger than you. In this I am superior to you and therefore can be of use to you. In everything else, dear friend, you are superior to me – or rather, you will be as soon as you have found yourself.'

Goldmund had listened in amazement, but at the words 'You have forgotten your childhood' he flinched as if pierced by an arrow. This went unnoticed by Narcissus who, as was often his way while speaking, kept his eyes closed or stared straight ahead, as if that would make it easier for him to find the words. He did not see Goldmund's face twitch and begin to crumple.

'Superior – I to you!' Goldmund stammered, just for something to say. He was as if transfixed.

'Of course,' Narcissus continued. 'Natures of your kind, those with strong and delicate senses, the inspired, the dreamers, poets, lovers, are almost always superior to us men of intellect. Your origin is maternal. Your kind live life to the full, to you is given the power of love and the capacity to experience. We intellectuals, although we often appear to lead and govern you others, do not live life to the full. We live a parched existence. To such as you belong the fullness of life, the juice of the fruits, the garden of love, the beautiful land of art. Your home is the earth, ours is the idea. Your danger is of drowning in the world of the senses, ours of suffocating in a vacuum. You are an artist, I am a thinker. You sleep on your mother's breast, I keep vigil in the desert. On me shines the sun, on you shine the moon and the stars. Your dreams are of girls, mine of the boys in my care . . .'

Goldmund had listened wide-eyed to Narcissus speaking in a kind of oratorical auto-intoxication. Some of his words had smitten him like swords; at the final words he turned pale and closed his eyes, and on Narcissus noticing this and questioning him in alarm the white-faced youth answered in an expiring voice: 'It has happened to me once that I collapsed in your presence and burst into tears – you remember. That mustn't happen again. I would never forgive myself – or you either! Now go away, quickly, and leave me alone – you have said terrible things to me.'

Narcissus was greatly upset. His words had carried him away; he had felt he was more eloquent than usual. Now he saw with dismay that some of what he had said had upset his friend, had somehow cut him to the quick. Reluctant to leave him to himself just then, he hesitated but, at the sight of Goldmund's frown, hurried off in confusion so as to allow his friend the solitude he seemed to need.

This time the tension in Goldmund's soul was not resolved in tears. With a sense of the most profound and despairing injury, as if his friend had suddenly plunged a knife into his breast, he stood there breathing heavily, with a mortally constricted heart, his face waxen, his hands numb. Again it was that old agony, only intensified by a few degrees; that old retching sensation, that feeling of having to look something terrible in the eye, something absolutely intolerable. But this time there were no sobs to help him overcome the agony. Holy Mother of God, what was it? Had something happened? Had he been murdered? Had he killed someone? What terrible things had been said?

His breath came in gasps; as if by poison, he was filled to bursting with the sense of having to rid himself of something lethal deep inside him. With the movements of a swimmer he dashed out of the room, fleeing blindly into the quietest, most unfrequented parts of the monastery, along passages, down stairs and into the open air, finding himself at last in the innermost refuge of the monastery, the cloister. Above the few green beds arched the clear, sunny sky. Through the cool, cellarlike air wafted the scent of roses.

Unwittingly, Narcissus had done in this hour what he had so long yearned to accomplish: he had called by name the demon that possessed his friend, and had challenged it. The secret in Goldmund's heart had been touched by something Narcissus had said, and it had reared its head in a paroxysm of pain. For a long time Narcissus wandered through the monastery looking for his friend, but he could not find him anywhere.

Goldmund stood under one of the heavy, round stone arches leading from the passages into the little cloister garden. From the columns supporting the arch, three stone heads of dogs or wolves looked down on him with bulging eyes. The wound churned horribly inside him, with no escape to light, no escape to reason. Mortal fear was clutching his throat and stomach. Glancing up mechanically, he saw one of the clusters of stone heads above him and immediately felt as if the three wild beasts were glowering and barking deep in his bowels.

I'm about to die, he felt in horror. And right away, trembling with fear: Now I'm losing my mind, now the beasts are devouring me!

His body twitching, he sank to the foot of the column. The pain was too great, it had reached its uttermost limit. Unconsciousness engulfed him. As all expression left his face he sank into longed-for oblivion.

Abbot Daniel's day had been less than pleasant. Two of the older monks had come to him, agitated, shrill, complaining jealously about ancient trivialities, once again in furious conflict. He had listened to them, for much too long, had admonished them, but without success, finally sternly dismissing them after imposing a fairly severe punishment on each yet feeling in his heart that what he had done was useless. Exhausted, he had withdrawn to the chapel of the lower church, prayed, and risen again unrefreshed. Now, attracted by the gently wafting scent of roses, he stepped for a moment into the cloister for a breath of air and found the pupil Goldmund lying unconscious on the flagstones. He regarded him sadly, dismayed by the pallor and lifelessness of that normally handsome young face. Today was not a good day, and now this! He tried to lift up the youth, but the weight was too much for him. With a deep sigh the old man walked away to call two of the younger brothers to carry him upstairs, then told Father Anselm, who was skilled in the art of healing, to see to the boy. At the same time he sent for Narcissus, who was soon found and appeared before him.

'Have you heard?' the abbot asked him.

'About Goldmund? Yes, gracious Father, I have just heard that he is ill or has had an accident, that he had to be carried inside.'

'Yes, I found him lying in the cloister, where he really had no business to be. He did not have an accident – he fainted. I do not like it. I sense that you must have something to do with the matter, or at least know something about it. After all, he is your close friend. That is why I summoned you. Speak.'

Narcissus, self-possessed as always in demeanour and speech, reported briefly on his conversation that day with Goldmund and on its surprisingly violent impact on the boy.

The abbot shook his head, not without displeasure. 'Those are strange conversations,' he said, forcing himself to remain calm. 'What you have just described is a conversation that might be called an intrusion into another soul, a conversation, I would say, such as might be conducted by a spiritual adviser. But you are not Goldmund's spiritual adviser. You are not a spiritual adviser at all. You have not yet been ordained. How can you explain your speaking to a pupil in the manner of an adviser about matters that concern only his spiritual adviser? The consequences, as you see, are deplorable.'

'The consequences,' said Narcissus in a mild voice, but firmly, 'are not yet known to us, gracious Father. I was startled at the violent effect, but I have no doubt that the consequences of our conversation will be beneficial to Goldmund.'

'We shall await the consequences. I am not talking about them now, I am talking about your actions. What prompted you to conduct such conversations with Goldmund?'

'As you know, he is my friend. I have a special affection for him, and I believe I understand him especially well. You call my behaviour towards him that of a spiritual adviser. I have not presumed to claim any spiritual authority whatever. I merely thought I knew him a little better than he knows himself.'

The abbot shrugged. 'I know – that is your speciality. Let us hope that you have caused no harm. Tell me, is Goldmund sick? I mean, is there something the matter with him? Is he in delicate health? Does he sleep badly? Does he eat properly? Is he in any kind of pain?'

'No, until today he has been in good health. In good physical health.'

'But otherwise?'

'In his soul he is indeed sick. You know that he is at an age when struggles with the sexual urge begin.'

'I know. He is seventeen?'

'He is eighteen.'

'Eighteen. Hm. Late enough. But these struggles are quite natural, something everyone has to go through. That is no reason to say he is suffering from a sickness of the soul.'

'No, gracious Father, not for that reason alone. But Goldmund has long been ill in spirit. That is why these struggles are more dangerous for him than for others. He suffers, I believe, from having forgotten a part of his past.'

'Really? What part is that?'

'It is his mother, and everything connected with her. I don't know anything about it either. I only know that that must be the source of his illness. The fact is that Goldmund apparently knows nothing about his mother except that he lost her at an early age, but he gives the impression that he is ashamed of her. Yet she must be the one from whom he has inherited most of his gifts because, from what he has to say about his father, that parent seems hardly the kind of man who would have such a handsome, variously talented and unusual son. I have not gathered any of this from reports. I deduce it from certain indications.'

The abbot, who had at first been inclined to dismiss this speech as being precocious and presumptuous and to whom the whole affair was a nuisance and an added burden, began to reflect. He recalled Goldmund's father, that somewhat stilted, inhibited man; then suddenly, because he was searching his memory for it, he also recalled something the boy's father had told him at the time about Goldmund's mother: that she had disgraced him and left him. He had done his best, he had said, to suppress in his little son any memory of the mother as well as any vices he might have inherited from her. He believed he had succeeded, and the boy was prepared, in order to atone for the mother's misdeeds, to offer his life to God.

Never had the abbot cared so little for Narcissus as today. And yet – how accurately this introspective youth had guessed, how well he seemed to know Goldmund!

After being examined once more about the day's events, Narcissus said: 'The violent turmoil into which Goldmund was thrown today was not intended by me. I reminded him that he does not know himself, that he has forgotten his childhood and his mother. Something I said must have hit him hard and penetrated the darkness I have been fighting so long. He was thunderstruck, and he looked at me as if he no longer knew me or himself. I often told him he was asleep, that he was not truly awake. Now he has been awakened, of that I have no doubt.'

Narcissus was dismissed, without rebuke, but forbidden for the time being to visit the patient.

Meanwhile Father Anselm had had the unconscious boy placed on a bed and was sitting beside him. He did not think it advisable to use forceful means to shock him back into consciousness: the boy looked too ill. The old man with the kind, wrinkled face looked down benignly at the youth. He began by feeling his pulse and listening to his heart. No doubt, he thought, the young fellow has eaten something outrageous, like a bunch of clover or something equally silly, one knows the sort of thing they do. He could not see the boy's tongue. He liked Goldmund but had no use for his friend, that precocious, far-too-young teacher. This was the result. Doubtless Narcissus was partly to blame for this stupid affair. Why did such a fresh, clear-eyed boy, such an appealing child of nature, have to take up with that arrogant scholar of all people, with that conceited grammarian to whom his Greek was more important than any living thing in this world!

When eventually the door opened and the abbot came in, Father Anselm was still sitting there staring at the face of the unconscious boy. What a sweet, young, innocent face, and here one sits, expected to help and probably unable to. Of course the cause could be colic; he would order some mulled wine – rhubarb, perhaps. But the longer he gazed at that drawn, sickly face, the more he tended to suspect another possibility, a more worrisome one. Father Anselm was experienced. In the course of his long life he had seen more than one possessed person, but he hesitated to voice the suspicion even to himself. He would wait and observe. But, he thought grimly, if this poor boy has really been bewitched, one wouldn't have to look far for the guilty party, who must be made to suffer for it.

The abbot came closer, looked at the patient and gently raised one of his eyelids. 'Can he be roused?' he asked.

'I should like to wait a little. His heart is sound. We must not allow anyone to visit him.'

'Is he in any danger?'

'I think not. No injuries, no traces of blows or a fall. He is unconscious. It may have been colic. Intense pain can cause a person to faint. If it were poisoning, he would have a fever. No, he will regain consciousness and survive.'

'Mightn't it have been emotionally induced?'

'I would not deny that. Do we have no information? Did he perhaps suffer a great shock? News of a death? A violent argument, an insult? That would explain everything.'

'We do not know. See to it that no one is allowed to visit him. Please stay with him until he wakes up. If he takes a turn for the worse, call me, even if it should be during the night.'

Before leaving, the old man bent once again over the patient. He was thinking of the boy's father and of the day when this handsome, cheerful tow-head had been presented to him, and how they had all, including himself, liked him immediately. But on one point Narcissus really was correct: there was nothing about this boy to remind one of his father! Oh, so many worries everywhere, how inadequate were all our deeds! Might he not have failed this poor lad in some respect? Had he been assigned to the most suitable father confessor? Was it right for no one in the monastery to be as well informed about this pupil as Narcissus? Could *he* help him, a youth still in his novitiate, who was neither a brother nor ordained and about whose thoughts and views there was something so disagreeably superior, indeed almost hostile? God knew whether Narcissus, too, had not also been wrongly treated over a long period. God knew whether, behind his mask of obedience, he was not hiding something evil, was not a heathen perhaps. And he, the abbot, shared responsibility for everything these two young people would one day become.

When Goldmund came to, it was dark. He felt empty-headed and dizzy. Aware that he was lying in a bed, he did not know where he was, nor did he wonder about it – he didn't care. But where had he been? Where had he come from, from what unknown world of experiences? He had been somewhere, very far away; he had seen something, something extraordinary, something glorious, something terrible too, and unforgettable – and yet he had forgotten it. Where was it? What had emerged before his eyes, so huge, so agonizing, so blissful, only to vanish again?

He listened deep within himself, down to where something had opened up that day, had happened – but what? Fierce, tangled images came spiralling up; he saw dogs' heads, three dogs' heads, and smelled the fragrance of roses. Oh, the agony he had been in! He closed his eyes. Oh, the terrible agony he had been in! He fell asleep again.

Once more he wakened and, just as the evanescent dream-world was slipping away, he saw the image, found it again, and flinched as if in a spasm of voluptuous pain. He saw, he was able to see. He saw *her*. He saw that figure, tall, radiant, with full ripe lips and shining hair. He saw his mother. And he seemed to hear a voice: 'You have forgotten your childhood.' Whose voice was that? He listened, wondered and found. It was Narcissus. Narcissus? In a single instant, with a sudden jolt, it all came back: he remembered, he knew. Oh, Mother, Mother! Mountains of rubble, oceans of oblivion, were gone, had vanished. Out of regal, clear-blue eyes, the lost one, the ineffably beloved one, was looking at him again.

Father Anselm, who had dropped off to sleep in the armchair beside the bed, woke up. Hearing the patient moving and breathing, he carefully rose from the chair.

'Is someone there?' asked Goldmund.

'I am here, do not be alarmed. I will give us some light.'

He lit the hanging lamp, and the light fell upon his kindly, wrinkled face.

'Am I ill?' the youth asked.

'You fainted, my son. Give me your hand, we will take your pulse. How do you feel?'

'I feel well, and I thank you, Father Anselm, you are very kind. There is nothing wrong with me any more, I'm just tired.'

'Of course you are tired. You will soon fall asleep again. But first have some mulled wine. It is all ready. Let us each drink a beakerful, my boy, with a toast to our good fellowship.'

He had thoughtfully been keeping a little pitcher of mulled wine ready in a vessel of hot water.

'So we have both been asleep for quite a while,' laughed the physician. 'A fine sickroom attendant, you will think, who cannot keep awake! Ah well, we are human. Now let us drink a little of this magic potion, my boy. There is nothing nicer than a little secret tippling in the night. To your health, then!'

Goldmund laughed, raised his beaker of wine and took a sip. The hot wine was spiced with cinnamon and cloves and sweetened with sugar. He had never tasted anything like it. It occurred to him that he had been ill once before, and then it had been Narcissus who had looked after him. This time it was Father Anselm who was being kind to him. He liked this very much; it was extremely pleasant and strange to be lying there in the lamplight and sharing a beaker of sweet hot wine with the old man in the middle of the night.

'Have you a stomach-ache?' Father Anselm asked.

'No.'

'You see, I thought you must have had colic, Goldmund. So that is not it. Show me your tongue. Ah well, once again your old Anselm has shown his ignorance. Tomorrow you will stay in bed like a good boy and I shall come and examine you. Finished your wine already? Good, may you feel all the better for it. Let me see whether there is any left. There is just enough for half a beaker for each of us, share and share alike. You know, you gave us quite a shock, Goldmund! Lying there in the cloister like the corpse of a child. Are you sure you haven't a stomach-ache?'

They laughed and shared the rest of the invalid wine. The physician made his little jokes, and Goldmund looked at him, grateful and amused, out of eyes that had regained their bright-ness. Then the old man left to retire to bed.

Goldmund remained awake for some time. Slowly the images welled up again from his innermost self, the words of his friend flared up once more, and the radiant, fair-haired woman, his mother, reappeared in his soul. Like a warm wind her image passed through him, like a cloud of vitality, warmth, intimacy, of tender exhortation. Oh, Mother! How was it possible that he could have forgotten her!

Chapter Five

In the past Goldmund had known a few things about his mother but only from what others had told him. He no longer had any memory of her, and of the little he thought he knew about her he had withheld the greater part from Narcissus. His mother was something one must not speak about, someone to be ashamed of. She had been a dancer, a beautiful, wild creature of cultivated but unworthy and heathen origin. Goldmund's father, according to his account, had rescued her from poverty and shame. Not knowing whether or not she was a heathen, he had had her baptized and instructed in religion. He had married her and made a well-respected woman of her. But after a few years of a tame and orderly life, she had resorted to her old skills and habits, had created scandals and seduced men and stayed away from home for days and weeks. She had acquired the reputation of being a witch, and finally, after her husband had repeatedly brought her home and taken her in again, she had disappeared for ever. For a while her reputation continued to be talked about, an evil reputation flashing like the tail of a comet. Then it had died away.

Her husband slowly recovered from the years of disruption, shock and shame, of the perpetual surprises for which she had been responsible. In place of the wayward wife he now brought up his little son, who greatly resembled his mother in face and figure. The husband had become careworn and given to excessive piety, and he cultivated in Goldmund the belief that he must offer his life to God in order to atone for the sins of his mother.

This was the gist of what Goldmund's father used to say about the wife he had lost, reluctant though he was to discuss the subject. He had also given some hints to the abbot when he delivered Goldmund. And all this was also known to the son, as a terrible legend, although he had learned to push it aside and almost forget it. However, he had totally forgotten and lost the true image of his mother, that other, quite different image which was not composed of the tales told by his father and the servants and of dark, frightening rumours. He had forgotten his own true, personal memory of his mother. And now that image, that star of his earliest years, had risen again.

'It is inexplicable that I should have forgotten that,' he said to his friend. 'Never in all my life have I loved anyone as much as my mother, so unreservedly, so ardently. Never have I so worshipped, so admired anyone – she was sun and moon for me. God knows how it was possible to obscure that shining image in my soul and gradually turn her into the evil, pale, formless witch that she was throughout all these years for my father and for me.'

Narcissus had recently completed his novitiate and been invested. His behaviour towards Goldmund had strangely altered. Goldmund, who had formerly often rejected his friend's hints and admonitions as a tiresome affectation of intellectual and moral superiority, was now, after his great experience, filled with wonder at his friend's wisdom. How much of what Narcissus had said had been fulfilled as prophecy! How profound and uncanny had been his insight, how precisely had Narcissus divined his life's secret, his hidden wound! How cleverly he had healed him!

For healed was what the youth appeared to be. Not only had there been no dire consequences from his fainting spell, but that which had been somewhat flippant, precocious, spurious in Goldmund's nature had, as it were, melted away: that somewhat precocious ideal of monkhood, that conviction of being obligated to serve God in some unique manner. The youth seemed to have grown both older and younger since he had found himself. For all that he had Narcissus to thank.

Narcissus, on the other hand, had for some time been behaving with curious caution towards his friend. He now looked at him with great modesty, no longer in the least superior or didactic, while the youth was full of admiration for him. He saw Goldmund as being nourished from secret sources with powers that were alien to himself. Although able to promote their growth, he had no share in them. He was glad to see his friend liberate himself from his leadership, yet at times he was sad. He felt left behind, discarded and saw the end of this friendship approaching, the friendship that had meant so much to him. He still knew more about Goldmund than Goldmund did himself; for, although Goldmund had rediscovered his soul and was prepared to follow its call, he still had no idea where it would lead him. Narcissus had an inkling and was powerless; his darling's path would lead him into realms in which he would never set foot.

Goldmund's craving for scholarship had markedly decreased. His delight in their friendly arguments was also a thing of the past: it embarrassed him to recall some of their former conversations. Meanwhile there had recently awakened in Narcissus – whether due to the completion of his novitiate or as a result of his experiences with Goldmund – a need for withdrawal, asceticism and spiritual exercises, an inclination towards fasting and lengthy prayers, frequent confession, voluntary penances. Goldmund could understand this inclination, almost share in it. Since his recovery his instincts had become much more acute. Although he still knew nothing whatever about his objectives, he was aware, with great and often alarming clarity, that his destiny was in the making, that a certain respite of innocence and peace was now over and that everything in him was tense and prepared. Often the premonition filled him with joy, keeping him awake half the night as if he were exquisitely in love. His long-lost mother had returned to him. That was a sublime happiness. But where would her siren-call lead? Into uncertainty, entanglement, anguish, perhaps into death. It certainly would not lead into the quiet, gentle security of the monk's cell and a life spent in a religious community. Her call had nothing in common with those paternal injunctions he had for so long confused with his own desires.

It was from such feelings, which were often as vehement, frightening and burning as a violent physical pain, that Goldmund's devoutness drew its nourishment. By repeating long prayers to the holy Mother of God he gave vent to the torrents of emotion drawing him to his own mother. Frequently, however, his prayers would end in another of those strange, glorious dreams he was now so often experiencing: day-dreams, his senses half aroused, dreams of her in which all his senses were involved. Then the maternal world would envelop him with its fragrance, regard him darkly out of enigmatic eyes of love, roar like the ocean, like Paradise, babble sounds of endearment – meaningless sounds, or rather, sounds overflowing with meaning – taste of sweetness and salt, brush thirsting lips and eyes with silky hair. In his mother was not only all loveliness, not only the sweet, blue-eyed look of love,

the beautiful smile of promise, the caress of consolation: somewhere beneath those enchanting veils was also all that was
terrible and dark, all lust, all fear, all sin, all misery, all birth, all
inescapable death.

The youth sank deep into these dreams, into these multiple
weavings of his inspired senses. In those dreams it was not only
the beloved past that magically re-emerged: childhood and
mother love, the radiant, golden morning of life; in them there
also reverberated a menacing, promising, enticing and perilous
future. At times these dreams, in which mother, Madonna and
lover were one, would later appear to him as terrible crimes
and blasphemies, mortal sins beyond all atonement; at other
times he found in them all salvation, all harmony. Full of
secrets, life stared at him, a murky, unfathomable world, an
impenetrable, thorny forest full of fabulous perils – but they
were secrets of his mother, they came from her, they led to her;
they were the small, dark circle, the small, menacing abyss, in
her luminous eye.

Much forgotten childhood surfaced in these mother-
dreams. Out of lost, bottomless depths blossomed many
small flowers of memory: fair to behold, with menace in their
fragrance; memories of childhood feelings, or perhaps of
experiences, perhaps of dreams. Sometimes he would dream
of fish that swam towards him, black and silvery, cool and
smooth: swam into him, through him, like messengers with
good tidings from a more beautiful reality, then vanished,
weaving and shadowy, were gone, having brought not tidings
but new secrets. He often dreamed of fish swimming and birds
flying, and each fish or bird was his creature, was dependent
on him and controllable like his breathing, radiated from him
like a glance or a thought, and re-entered him. And there was
a garden he often dreamed of, a magic garden with fabulous
trees, enormous flowers, deep, dark-blue caverns; from out of

the grass flashed the eyes of unknown beasts, and along the branches slithered smooth, sinuous snakes. From vines and shrubs hung huge, moistly glistening berries which, when picked, swelled in his hand and spilled warm juice like blood, or had eyes they moved, salacious and sly. Leaning against a tree and groping for a branch, he saw and felt between trunk and branch a tangle of thick, curly hair nestling there like the hair in the hollow of an armpit. Once he dreamed of himself or his patron saint, of Goldmund, Chrysostom: he had a mouth of gold, and with that golden mouth uttered words, and the words were swarms of little birds fluttering away in flocks.

Another time he dreamed that he was big and grown-up but was sitting like a child on the ground. In front of him was some mud that he was kneading into figures: a little horse, a bull, a little man, a little woman. He enjoyed the kneading, and he gave the animals and the men absurdly large genitals. In his dream this struck him as very comical. Then he tired of the game, and as he walked on he sensed something alive, something looming, approaching soundlessly from behind. Looking back he saw to his shocked surprise, but not without pleasure, that his little mud figures had grown and come alive: enormous giants, the figures marched wordlessly past him, still growing. Gigantic and silent, on they marched, into the world, as tall as towers.

In this dream-world he lived more than in the real one. The real world – classroom, monastery courtyard, library, dormitory and chapel – were only the surface, only a thin, quivering membrane over the dream-filled, surreal world of images. The slightest thing was enough to pierce a hole in this membrane: something evocative in the sound of a Greek word in the midst of a prosaic lesson, a whiff of herbal fragrance from Father Anselm's botany bag, a glance at a stone tendril sprouting from the top of a column in a window arch. Such small stimuli sufficed to pierce the membrane of reality and to release, behind that peaceful, arid reality, those churning abysses, rivers and galaxies of the world of mental images. A Latin capital letter became the sweet-smelling face of his mother, a long-drawn-out note in the *Ave* became the gateway to Paradise; a Greek letter turned into a galloping horse or a rearing snake, which then silently slithered away among the flowers, to be instantly replaced by the rigid page of the grammar book.

He rarely spoke of all this; only very occasionally did he give Narcissus a hint of this dream-world. 'I believe,' he once said, 'that a flower petal or a little worm on the path conveys much more than all the books of the entire library. With letters and words one can't convey anything. Sometimes I write a Greek letter, a theta or an omega, and as I twist my pen a little bit the letter wriggles and is a fish and in one second evokes all the streams and rivers of the world, all that is cool and wet, Homer's ocean and the water on which St Peter walked; or the letter turns into a bird, lifts up its tail, ruffles its feathers, puffs out its chest, laughs and flies away. Well, Narcissus, I imagine you don't think much of such letters? But I tell you, it was with them that God wrote the world.'

'I think very highly of them,' Narcissus said sadly. 'They are magic letters with which all demons can be conjured. The trouble is that they are unsuitable for the pursuit of learning. The intellect loves what is solid, formed. It wants to be able to rely on its symbols. It loves what is, not what is becoming, what is real and not what is possible. It does not tolerate an omega turning into a snake or a bird. The intellect cannot live *in* nature, only *against* it, only as its antithesis. Do you believe me now, Goldmund, when I say that you will never be a scholar?'

Oh yes, Goldmund had long believed that; he had accepted the fact. 'I'm no longer in the least obsessed with striving after your intellect,' he said, half laughing. 'I feel about intellect and scholarship the way I used to feel about my father: I thought I loved him and was like him, I swore by everything he said. But hardly had my mother returned when I knew for the first time what love is, and beside her image that of my father had suddenly become small and unhappy and almost repellent. And now I'm inclined to regard everything intellectual as paternal, as unmotherly and anti-maternal, and to look down on it a little.'

He spoke jokingly, yet without managing to bring a smile to his friend's sad face. Narcissus looked at him in silence; his gaze was like a caress. Then he said: 'I understand you very well. We need argue no more. You have awakened, and you have now also recognized the difference between you and me, the difference between maternal and paternal origins, between soul and intellect. And now you will also soon recognize that your life in the monastery and your striving for a monastic life have been a mistake, an invention of your father's who wanted in this way to atone for the memory of your mother, or perhaps merely to avenge himself on her. Or do you still believe that it is your destiny to spend your whole life in a monastery?'

Goldmund looked pensively at his friend's hands, those fine, thin white hands, as severe as they were tender. No one could doubt that these were the hands of an ascetic and a scholar. 'I don't know,' he said in that lilting, hesitant voice with its lingering emphasis, the voice he had recently acquired. 'I really don't know. You judge my father somewhat harshly. He has not had an easy time. But perhaps you are right about that too. I have been here more than three years, and he has never come to see me. He is hoping I shall stay here for good. Perhaps that would be best. After all, that's what I always wanted myself.

But today I no longer know what I really want or wish for. Everything was so easy before, as easy as the letters in the primer. Now nothing is easy any more, not even the letters. Everything has acquired many meanings and faces. I don't know what is to become of me. I can't think of such things now.'

'Nor should you,' said Narcissus. 'Time will show where your path leads. It has begun to lead you back to your mother and will bring you even closer to her. But as for your father, I do not judge him too harshly. Would you want to return to him?'

'No, Narcissus, certainly not. Otherwise I would do so as soon as I finish school, or even now. For although I'll never be a scholar, I have actually learned enough Latin, Greek and mathematics. No, I don't want to go back to my father.'

He gazed thoughtfully ahead, and suddenly he cried: 'But how ever do you do it? How do you manage to keep saying or asking me things that shine right into me and reveal me to myself? Now again it was only your question as to whether I would want to return to my father that suddenly showed me that I don't. How do you do it? You seem to know everything. You have told me many things about you and me which, at the moment of hearing them, I did not fully understand and which later have become so important to me! It was you who called my origin a maternal one, and it was you who discovered that I was under a spell and had forgotten my childhood! How do you manage to know so much about human beings? Can't I learn that too?'

Narcissus shook his head with a smile. 'No, my friend, you cannot. There are people who can learn a great deal, but you are not one of them. You will never be a learner. And why should you? You have no need for that. You have other gifts. You have more gifts than I have. You are richer than I am, and you are also weaker, and your path will be more splendid and more difficult than mine. There were times when you did not want to understand me, when you struggled like a colt. It was not always easy, and often I even had to hurt you. I had to waken you, for you were asleep. When I reminded you of your mother, that hurt too at first, very much. You were found lying like a corpse in the cloister. It had to be. No, don't stroke my hair! No, please don't! I can't bear it!'

'And so I can learn nothing? I'll always be stupid and a child?'

'There will be others from whom you will learn. Whatever you could learn from me in your childishness – that's all over and done with.'

'Oh no!' Goldmund cried. 'We couldn't have become friends for that! What kind of a friendship would it be that has so quickly reached its goal and can simply come to an end! Are you tired of me? Have you turned against me?'

Narcissus paced up and down, his eyes on the ground, then stopped in front of his friend. 'Enough of that,' he said gently. 'You know very well that I have not.'

His eyes lingered doubtfully on his friend; then he resumed his pacing back and forth, stopped again and looked at Goldmund, his gaze steady, his face stern and gaunt. In a low but steady voice he said: 'Listen to me, Goldmund! Our friendship has been a good one. It had a goal and it has reached it. It has awakened you. I hope it is not over. I hope it will renew itself many times and lead to new goals. At the moment there is no goal. Yours is uncertain – I can neither lead nor accompany you there. Ask your mother, ask her image, listen to her! My goal, on the other hand, is not an uncertain one – it is here, in the monastery. It challenges me every hour. I am permitted to be your friend but not to be in love. I am a monk, I have taken the vow. Before being ordained I shall ask to be excused from my teaching duties and withdraw for many weeks of fasting and religious exercises. During that time I shall have no secular conversation, not even with you.'

Goldmund understood. Sadly he said: 'So you will be doing now what I would have done if I had entered the Order for ever. And when you have completed your exercises, when you have sufficiently fasted and prayed and kept vigil – what will you aim for then?'

'You know the answer to that,' said Narcissus.

'Do I? In a few years you will be a head teacher, perhaps even the principal. You will improve the curriculum, enlarge the library. Perhaps you will write books yourself. You won't? Very well, so you won't. But what will your goal be?'

Narcissus gave a faint smile. 'My goal? Perhaps I shall die as a school principal, or as an abbot or a bishop. It doesn't matter. My goal is this: always to place myself where I can best serve, where my nature, qualities and gifts find the best soil, the widest scope. There is no other goal.'

Goldmund: 'No other goal for a monk?'

Narcissus: 'Oh yes, there are plenty of goals. It can be a lifelong goal for a monk to learn Hebrew, to gloss Aristotle or beautify the monastery church, or to become a hermit and meditate, or do a hundred other things. Those are not my goals. I wish neither to increase the wealth of the monastery nor to reform the Order or the Church. Within my own capacities I wish to serve the spirit, as I understand it, nothing else. Isn't that a goal?'

Goldmund pondered long over his reply. 'You are right,' he said. 'Have I been a great hindrance on your path towards your goal?'

'A hindrance? Oh, Goldmund, no one has helped me more than you. You have presented me with some difficulties, but I do not mind difficulties. I have learned from them, and some of them I have overcome.'

Goldmund interrupted him by saying, somewhat facetiously: 'Wonderful, the way you've overcome them! But tell me then: by helping me, by guiding and liberating me and healing my soul – did you really serve the spirit? You probably deprived the monastery of an earnest, hard-working novice. You may have raised an enemy of the spirit, an enemy that will do and believe and strive for the very opposite of what you believe to be good!'

'Why not?' said Narcissus very seriously. 'My friend, after all this time how little you know me! In you I have probably ruined a future monk and instead cleared a path in you for a more than ordinary destiny. Even if tomorrow you were to burn our fine monastery to the ground, or proclaim some crazy heresy to the world, I would not for an instant regret having helped you on to that path.'

He affectionately placed both hands on his friend's shoulders. 'Look, dear Goldmund, part of my goal is this: whether I become a teacher or an abbot, a father confessor or anything else, I would never want to find myself encountering a strong, valuable and exceptional human being and not be able to understand him, to uncover his nature and help him on his way. And I tell you, whatever may become of you and me, whatever may happen to us, the moment you call me and feel in serious need of me, I shall never turn my back on you. Never.'

Those sounded like words of parting, and in truth it was a foretaste of parting. As Goldmund stood before his friend, gazing at that determined face, those eyes fixed on goals, he had an unmistakable sense that they were now no longer brothers and comrades and equals, that their ways had already parted. This person standing before him was no dreamer, nor was he waiting for any summons by Fate. He was a monk, he was committed, was part of a solid system and a firm duty, a servant and soldier of the Order, the Church and the spirit. But he, Goldmund – this had become clear to him today – did not belong here. He had no home; an unknown world awaited him. This was what had once happened to his mother too. Abandoning hearth and home, husband and child, community and social order, duty and honour, she had gone forth into the uncertain world where she must have long since perished. She had had no goal, just as he also had none. To have goals was something given to others, not to him. How well Narcissus had seen all this so long ago, and how right he had been!

Very soon after that day it was as if Narcissus had disappeared, had suddenly become invisible. A different teacher took his classes; his reading desk in the library remained vacant. He was still there, not totally invisible; he could sometimes be seen walking through the cloister, or heard murmuring in one of the chapels as he knelt on the stone floor. It was known that he had begun the great religious exercise, that he was fasting and rising three times a night to perform his devotions. Although still there, he had passed into another world. He could be seen, rarely at that, but was inaccessible; it was impossible to share anything with him or to speak to him. Goldmund knew: Narcissus would reappear. Once again he would occupy his desk, his chair in the refectory, he would speak; but of what had been, nothing would return; Narcissus would not belong to him again. As he thought about this it also became clear to him that it had been Narcissus alone through whom monastery and monkhood, grammar and logic, study and intellect had become important and precious to him. Narcissus's example had enticed him; to become like him had been his ideal. True, there was also the abbot, whom he revered and loved and in whom he had seen a lofty example. But the others, the teachers, schoolmates, dormitory, refectory, school, religious exercises and services, the entire monastery – without Narcissus, all that had ceased to concern him. What was he still doing here? He was waiting; he was standing under the roof of the monastery like an irresolute traveller who stops under some roof or tree during a shower, merely to wait, merely as a guest, merely from fear of the inhospitality of what might lie ahead.

During this time Goldmund's life had been reduced to postponement and leave-taking. He sought out all the places that had become precious or meaningful to him. To his surprise and dismay he noted how few people and faces there were that he would find it hard to part from. There was Narcissus and old Abbot Daniel, as well as dear, good Father Anselm and perhaps also the friendly doorkeeper and the cheerful miller, but even they had already become almost unreal. More difficult than to take leave of them would be to part from the great stone Madonna in the chapel and the apostles of the portal. He stood for a long time in front of them, also in front of the exquisite carving of the choir stalls, the fountain in the cloister, the column with the three dogs' heads, and leaned against the linden trees and the chestnut tree in the courtyard. All this would one day be a memory, a little picture-book in his heart. Even now, when he was still in the midst of it all, it began to slip away from him, to dwindle in reality, to transform itself eerily into something that had once been. With Father Anselm, who was fond of his company, he went looking for herbs; at the mill he watched the men at work, from time to time joining them in a glass of wine and some fish from the oven. But everything was already remote, part memory. Just as in the dim church and penitential cell his friend Narcissus, although alive and pacing the floor, had for him become a shadow, so all his surroundings were now shorn of reality, exhaling the breath of autumn and impermanence.

Nothing was real and alive now but the life within him, the anxious beating of his heart, the pangs of longing, the joys and fears of his dreams. It was to them that he belonged and surrendered. In the midst of reading or studying, in the midst of his schoolmates, he could lapse into himself and forget everything, surrendering to the inner currents and voices that were sweeping him away into deep wells full of dark melody, into multicoloured chasms of fabulous experiences where the sounds were all like the voice of his mother, where a thousand eyes were all the eyes of his mother.

Chapter Six

One day Father Anselm summoned Goldmund to his apothecary, his delightful, wonderfully fragrant herb chamber. Here Goldmund was well versed. The monk showed him a dried plant, neatly preserved between sheets of paper, and asked him whether he could identify it and describe exactly what it looked like when growing outdoors. Yes, Goldmund could; the plant was called St John's wort. He was told to describe all its distinguishing marks minutely. The old monk was satisfied. He instructed his young friend to gather a good bunch of those plants that afternoon and told him where he was most likely to find them.

'In return you will be allowed the afternoon off from school, my boy. You won't object to that, and you won't miss anything, for the understanding of nature is also a science, just as much as your silly grammar.'

Goldmund thanked him for the most welcome assignment of spending a few hours gathering flowers instead of sitting in the classroom. To round out the pleasure he asked the head stableman if he might take Blaze, and soon after the midday meal he went to fetch the horse from the stable. Blaze greeted him enthusiastically, and Goldmund mounted and trotted off happily into the warm, sunny day. For an hour or so he just rode along enjoying the air, the fragrance of the fields and, above all, the riding itself. Then he remembered his assignment and made for one of the places the monk had described. After tethering the horse under a shady maple tree, chatting with it and feeding it some bread, he went off in search of the plants.

A few of the fields were lying fallow, overgrown by various weeds. Skimpy little poppies with their last faded blooms and numerous ripe seed-pods showed here and there among withered tendrils of sweet peas, bright-blue chicory in flower and yellowing knot-grass. A few rough piles of stones between two fields were the home of lizards, and here Goldmund came upon the first clumps of yellow-flowering St John's wort. He began to pick, and after gathering a fair-sized handful he sat down on the stones to rest. It was hot, and he looked longingly towards the dark shade of a forest in the distance, but then decided he did not want to go so far away from the plants or from his horse, which was still in sight. He continued to sit on the warm stones, keeping perfectly still so as to watch the lizards re-emerge from their hiding-places. He sniffed at the St John's wort and held the small leaves up to the light in order to examine the hundreds of tiny pinpricks in them.

How amazing, he thought: into each of these thousands of small leaves a tiny firmament has been pricked, as delicate as embroidery. How amazing, how incomprehensible it all was: the lizards, the plants, even these stones – everything. Father Anselm, who was so fond of him, could now no longer gather his St John's wort himself. He had trouble with his legs; on some days he could not move about, and his medical skills offered no cure. Perhaps one day soon he would die, and the herbs in their chamber would go on spreading their fragrance, but the old monk would no longer be there. On the other hand, he might go on living for a long time, maybe ten or twenty years, and would still have the same sparse white hair and the same funny little crow's-feet round his eyes. But as for Goldmund himself, what would he be like in twenty years' time? Oh, it was all incomprehensible and really quite sad, though also beautiful. One knew nothing. One lived and walked about on the earth or rode through the forests, and so many things looked at one with such challenge and promise, rousing such longing: an evening star, a bluebell, a lake green with reeds, the eye of a human being or of a cow, and at times it seemed as if the very next moment something never seen but long yearned for must happen, as if a veil must drop from everything. But then it passed, and nothing happened, and the riddle was not solved, nor was the secret spell lifted, and finally one became old and looked as shrewd as Father Anselm or as wise as Abbot Daniel, and perhaps one still knew nothing, would still be waiting and listening.

He picked up an empty snail's shell; it clicked faintly between the stones and was warm from the sun. Deeply absorbed he studied the whorls of the shell, the spiral grooves, the delicate tapering to a tiny knob, the empty orifice with its mother-of-pearl sheen. He closed his eyes in order to feel the shapes with his fingertips only, an old, playful habit of his. Turning the snail over, his slack fingers slid caressingly, lightly, over its shape, and he rejoiced at the miracle of the shaping, at the magic of the purely physical. This, he thought dreamily, was one of the drawbacks of school and scholarship: it seemed to be an intellectual tendency to see and represent everything as if it were flat and two-dimensional. Somehow this seemed to indicate a deficiency and a defect in the entire intellectual approach, but he could not hold on to the thought, the snail slipped from his fingers, he felt tired and drowsy. With his head bent over his herbs, whose fragrance was increasing as they wilted, he fell asleep in the sun. The lizards ran across his shoes, the plants wilted on his knees, and Blaze waited under the maple tree and grew impatient.

From the distant forest someone was approaching, a young woman, her face brown from the sun. She was wearing a faded blue skirt and a red scarf tied round her black hair. The woman came closer, carrying a bundle and holding a small, fiery-red wild pink between her lips. She saw the youth sitting there and looked at him a long time from a distance, curious and suspicious. Seeing that he was asleep, she carefully approached on her brown, bare feet, stopped beside him and stood looking at him. Her suspicion vanished: the handsome, sleeping youth did not appear to be dangerous – she liked the look of him. What was he doing here in these fallow fields? He had picked some flowers, she saw with a smile; they had already wilted.

Goldmund opened his eyes, returning from dream-forests. His head lay on something soft, on a woman's lap. The warm, brown eyes of a stranger were looking into his sleepy, surprised eyes. He was not alarmed, there was no danger; the warm, brown stars shone kindly down at him. The woman smiled at his astonished look, the smile was friendly, and slowly he too began to smile. Her mouth descended on to his smiling lips; they greeted one another with a gentle kiss, and Goldmund was immediately reminded of that evening in the village and of the little girl with the plaits. But the kiss was not yet over. The woman's mouth lingered on his, toyed with it, teasing and enticing him, and finally seized his lips fiercely and hungrily, stirring his blood to the innermost depths, and in a long, wordless game the brown-skinned woman, guiding him gently, gave herself to the boy, helped him search and find until he burned with desire, then quenched the fire. The sweet, brief bliss of love arched over him, flared up in golden flames, subsided and died away. His eyes closed, he lay on the woman's breast. Not a word had been spoken. The woman kept still, gently stroking his hair and letting him slowly recover.

At last he opened his eyes. 'Who are you?' he said. 'Who *are* you?'

'I am Lisa,' she replied.

'Lisa,' he repeated, savouring the name. 'Lisa, you're so kind.'

Bringing her mouth close to his ear she whispered: 'Tell me, was that the first time? Haven't you ever loved anyone before me?'

He shook his head. Then suddenly he sat up and looked round, across the field and up to the sky. 'Oh!' he cried. 'The sun is already quite low. I must get back.'

'Back to where?'

'To the monastery, to Father Anselm.'

'To Mariabronn? Is that where you're from? Don't you want to stay with me a little longer?'

'I'd like to.'

'Then stay!'

'No, it would not be right. Besides, I have to pick some more of these herbs.'

'Do you mean you're from the monastery?'

'Yes, I'm a pupil. But I'm not staying there any longer. Can I come to you, Lisa? Where do you live – where's your home?'

'I don't live anywhere, my darling. But won't you tell me your name? So it's Goldmund, is it? Give me another kiss, my sweet Goldmund, then you can leave.'

'You don't live anywhere? Then where do you sleep?'

'If you like, with you in the forest, or in the hay. Will you come tonight?'

'Oh yes! Where to? Where shall I find you?'

'Can you hoot like an owl?'

'I've never tried.'

'Try now.'

He did. She laughed and was satisfied.

'Then come tonight from the monastery and hoot like a tawny owl, I'll be nearby. Do you like me, my little Goldmund, my little one?'

'Oh, I like you very much, Lisa! I'll come. God be with you – now I must go.'

His horse steaming, Goldmund arrived back at the monastery at dusk and was glad to find Father Anselm very busy. One of the brothers had been disporting himself barefoot in the stream and had stepped on a shard of broken glass.

Anxious to find Narcissus immediately, he asked one of the serving brothers in the refectory. No, they said, Narcissus would not be coming for supper; he was fasting that day and would probably be asleep now, since these nights he was keeping vigil. Goldmund hurried off. For the duration of the long exercises his friend had moved to one of the penitential cells in the inner monastery. Without pausing to reflect he ran to the cell. He listened at the door but could hear nothing. Very softly, he entered. The fact that it was strictly forbidden was now irrelevant.

Narcissus was lying on the narrow pallet. In the dim light he resembled a corpse as he lay there rigidly on his back, his face pale and haggard, his hands crossed over his breast. But his eyes were open, and he was not asleep. Silently he looked at Goldmund, without reproach yet without moving, and obviously so caught up in a kind of trance, so removed to a different time and world, that he had difficulty recognizing his friend and understanding his words.

'Narcissus! Forgive me, forgive me, dear friend, for disturbing you. It is not out of wilfulness. I know you are not really allowed to speak to me at this time, but please do – I beg you!'

Narcissus pulled himself together, blinking several times as if trying to wake up. 'Is it essential?' he asked in a faraway voice.

'Yes, it is. I have come to say goodbye.'

'Then it is essential. I would not want you to have come in vain. Come, sit here beside me. We have a quarter of an hour before the first vigil begins.'

He had raised himself and sat, a gaunt figure, on the bare board. Goldmund sat down beside him.

'Please forgive me!' he said, feeling guilty. The cell, the bare pallet, Narcissus's drawn face marked by lack of sleep and over-exertion, the unfocused expression in his eyes: everything pointed clearly to how great an intrusion this was.

'There is nothing to forgive. Don't worry about me – there's nothing wrong with me. You have come to say goodbye, you say? So you are leaving?'

'I'm leaving this very day. Oh, I can't tell you about it! Suddenly everything has come to a head.'

'Has your father come, or a message from him?'

'No, nothing. Life itself has come to me. I am leaving, without my father, without permission. I am bringing shame upon you, Narcissus, I am running away.'

Narcissus looked down at his long white fingers protruding, thin and spectral, from the wide sleeves of his habit. There was a trace of a smile in his voice though not in his stern, exhausted face, as he said: 'We have very little time, dear friend. Tell me only what is essential, and make it clear and brief. Or do I have to tell you what has happened to you?'

'Tell me,' Goldmund asked.

'You are in love, little boy, you have met a woman.'

'How can you possibly know that too!'

'You make it easy for me. Your condition, *amice*, bears all the marks of that type of intoxication known as being in love. But now tell me yourself, please.'

Shyly Goldmund placed his hand on his friend's shoulder. 'You've already said it. But this time you didn't get it right,

Narcissus. This is quite different. I was out in the fields and fell asleep in the heat, and when I woke up my head was lying on the knees of a beautiful woman, and I immediately felt my mother had come to take me away with her. Not that I thought this woman was my mother. She had dark-brown eyes and black hair, and my mother had fair hair, like mine, and looked quite different. Yet it was she, it was her call, it was a message from her. As if emerging from the dreams of my own heart, a beautiful woman, a stranger, had appeared, who held my head in her lap and smiled at me like a flower and was good to me. At her very first kiss I could feel something melt in me and hurt in some wonderful way. All the longing I had ever known, all the dreams, all the sweet dread, all the mystery that had been sleeping in me, was roused. Everything was transformed, enchanted. Everything had acquired meaning. She taught me what a woman is and the secret she holds. Within half an hour she made me many years older. I know many things now. And I also knew, quite suddenly, that I could no longer remain in this house, not a single day longer. I shall leave at nightfall.'

Narcissus listened and nodded. 'It has come suddenly,' he said, 'but it is more or less what I expected. I shall think of you very often. I shall miss you, *amice*. Is there anything I can do for you?'

'If it's at all possible, say a word to our abbot so that he won't condemn me utterly. Apart from you, he is the only person in this house whose opinion I care about. He and you.'

'I know. Have you any other request?'

'Yes, one. When you think of me later, say a prayer for me! And . . . thank you.'

'For what, Goldmund?'

'For your friendship, for your patience, for everything. Also for listening to me today, seeing how difficult it is for you. Also for not trying to stop me.'

'Why should I want to stop you? You know how I feel about it. But where will you go, Goldmund? Have you some place in mind? Are you going to that woman?'

'I am going with her. I have nowhere in mind. She is a stranger, homeless it seems, perhaps a gypsy.'

'I see. But tell me, my friend, are you aware that your path with her may be very short? You should not rely too much on her, I believe. She may have relatives, perhaps a husband. Who knows how you will be received there?'

Goldmund leaned against his friend. 'I know that,' he said, 'though I hadn't thought of it till now. I've already told you, I have no destination. Even that woman, who was so good to me, is not my destination. I am going to her, but I am not going because of her. I am going because I must, because I hear the call.'

He fell silent and sighed, and they sat leaning against each other, sad yet content in the awareness of their indestructible friendship.

Then Goldmund continued: 'You mustn't think I am totally blind and naïve. No. I am going gladly, because I feel that it has to be, and because I have had such a marvellous experience today. But I don't imagine that I'll run into nothing but happiness and pleasure. I imagine the way will be hard. Yet it will also be rewarding, I hope. It is wonderful to belong to a woman, to give oneself to her! Don't laugh if what I'm saying sounds stupid. But look, to love a woman, to give oneself to her, to envelop her totally and to feel enveloped by her – that's not the same thing as what you call being in love and tend to mock. It is not to be mocked. For me it is the path to life and the path to the meaning of life. Oh, Narcissus, I must leave you! I love you, Narcissus, and I am grateful to you for sacrificing some sleep for my sake today. I find it hard to leave you. You won't forget me, will you?'

'Don't make it even harder for both of us! I shall never forget you. You will return – I beg you to, I expect you to. If one day you should find yourself in trouble, come to me or call me. Farewell, Goldmund, God be with you!'

Narcissus had risen to his feet. Goldmund embraced him. Knowing his friend's aversion to caresses, he did not kiss him. He merely stroked his hands.

Night fell. Narcissus closed the cell door behind him and went across to the church, his sandals flapping on the flagstones. With loving eyes Goldmund followed the gaunt figure until it vanished at the end of the passage like a shadow, swallowed up by the darkness of the church door, drawn in and claimed by religious exercises, duties, virtues. How amazing, how infinitely strange and confused it all was! How strange and frightening this, too, had been: to come to his friend with his overflowing heart, with the ecstasy of his newly blossomed love, in the very hour in which this friend, deep in meditation, wasted by fasting and vigils, was nailing his youth, his heart and his senses to the Cross, sacrificing them, and submitting himself to the severest school of obedience so that he might serve only the spirit and become entirely a *minister verbi divini*! There he had lain, exhausted and drained, with his pale face and wasted hands, resembling a corpse, yet he had immediately responded so clearly and kindly to his friend, and had not only lent an ear but sacrificed his meagre rest-time between two penances to the young lover still redolent of a woman! It was strange, and wondrously beautiful, that there could also be this kind of love, one that was selfless, completely spiritualized. How different from that love today in the sun-drenched field, that intoxicated, heedless play of the senses! Yet both were love. And now Narcissus was gone from him after showing once again in this final hour with such clarity how utterly different and dissimilar they were. Narcissus was now on his weary knees before the altar, prepared and purified for a night of prayer and meditation during which no more than two hours' rest and sleep were permitted, while he, Goldmund, was running off to find his Lisa somewhere under the trees and to repeat those sweet carnal games with her! Narcissus would have had some memorable comments to make about that! Well, Goldmund was not Narcissus. It was not his duty to fathom these beautiful, terrifying riddles and confusions and make important pronouncements about them. His sole duty was to continue on his own uncertain, foolish paths. His sole duty was to love and surrender to his friend at prayer in the dark church no less than to the beautiful, warm young woman waiting for him.

Though his heart was quickened by a hundred conflicting emotions as he slipped away below the linden trees and sought the way out through the mill, he could not help smiling at the sudden remembrance of that evening when he and Konrad had left the monastery by that same devious route to 'go to the village'. How excited and secretly nervous he had been as he started out on the forbidden little jaunt! And today he was leaving for ever, following paths that were far more strictly forbidden, far more dangerous, yet he was not afraid, and he had no thought for doorkeeper, abbot or teacher.

This time there were no planks lying beside the stream. He had to cross without a bridge, so he took off his gown, threw it on to the other bank and walked naked through the deep, strong current up to his chest in the cold water.

As he dressed on the other side, his thoughts were again with Narcissus. With great and humiliating clarity he now realized that at this moment he was doing precisely what Narcissus had foreseen and towards which he had guided him. All too clearly he saw again that clever, mocking Narcissus who had heard him say so many foolish things, the Narcissus who had once, in a fateful hour, painfully opened Goldmund's eyes. Something Narcissus had said at the time now vividly returned to him: 'You sleep on your mother's breast, I keep vigil in the desert . . . Your dreams are of girls, mine of the boys in my care.'

For a moment his heart contracted icily as he stood there, terribly alone, in the night. Behind him was the monastery, an illusory home only but a loved and long-familiar one.

Yet at the same time he was conscious of something else: that Narcissus was now no longer his admonishing and more knowledgeable guide and awakener. Today he felt that he had set foot in a country where he had to find the paths on his own, where no Narcissus could continue to guide him. He was glad to have become aware of this; he had felt depressed and humiliated when looking back on his time of dependence. Now his eyes were opened, and he was no longer a child and a schoolboy. It was good to know that. Yet how hard it was to say goodbye! To know that *he* was over there kneeling in the church, and to be unable to give him anything, to help him, to mean anything to him! And now for a long time, perhaps for ever, to be separated from him, to know nothing about him, no longer to hear his voice, no longer to see his noble eye!

He tore himself away and followed the stony path. A hundred paces from the monastery walls he stopped, took a deep breath and uttered, as best he could, the cry of an owl. A similar owl's cry replied, downstream, in the distance.

Like animals, we cry out for each other, he thought, recalling the hour of lovemaking that afternoon. Now for the first time it struck him that it was only at the very end, when the caresses were over, that any words had been exchanged between himself and Lisa, and then only a few trivial ones.

What long conversations he had had with Narcissus! But now, it seemed, he had entered a world where one did not speak, where one lured the other with owl's cries, where words were irrelevant. He didn't mind this; today his desire was no longer for words or thoughts but only for Lisa, only for that blind, wordless, sensual burrowing, for that sighing and dissolving.

Lisa was there, already approaching from the forest. He reached out his hands to touch her, tenderly cupping her head, feeling her hair, her throat and neck, her slender waist and firm hips. With one arm round her, he walked on with her, not speaking, not asking: Where are we going? Sure-footed she walked into the dark forest. He had difficulty keeping up with her; like a fox or a marten she seemed able to see in the dark without stumbling or colliding. He let himself be led into the night, into the forest, into the blind, mysterious country without words, without thoughts. He no longer thought: not even of the monastery he had left behind, not even of Narcissus.

Silently they walked on through the dark forest, sometimes on soft, cushiony moss, sometimes on ribs of exposed roots. At times the starlit sky above them was visible through tall, sparse treetops; at others the darkness was complete. Bushes struck him in the face; brambles caught at his gown. She seemed familiar with the forest and seldom stopped or hesitated as she found her way through it. After a long while they reached some widely spaced pine trees: the pale night sky opened out, the forest came to an end, a sloping meadow spread before them and there was a sweet smell of hay. They waded through a silently flowing brook. Out here in the open it was even quieter than in the forest – no more rustling bushes, no more startled nocturnal creatures, no more creaking of dry wood.

Lisa stopped beside a big haystack. 'We'll stay here,' she said.

They sat down in the hay, first to catch their breath and enjoy a rest, both being a little weary. They stretched their limbs, listened to the silence, felt their foreheads drying and their faces gradually cooling off. Pleasantly tired, Goldmund idly pulled up his knees and stretched them again; in long breaths he drew in the night and the smell of hay, giving no thought either to the past or to the future. Slowly he let himself succumb to the enchantment of his beloved's warmth and fragrance; his hands stroked her as hers stroked him, and he was filled with joy as her blood began to stir and she moved her body closer and closer to him. No, neither words nor thoughts were needed here. He could clearly sense all that was important and beautiful, youthful strength and the simple, healthy beauty of the female body, its arousal and desire. He also clearly sensed that this time she wished to be loved differently from before, that this time she did not wish to seduce and guide him but was waiting for his initiative and his lust. Silently he let the currents flow through him; blissfully he felt the growing ardour that had been kindled in them both, turning their modest resting-place into the breathing, glowing core of the whole silent night.

While bending over Lisa's face and beginning to kiss her lips in the dark, he suddenly saw her eyes and forehead shimmer in a soft light. In amazement he watched as the light swiftly increased. Then he understood and turned round: the moon was rising above the edge of the spreading black forest. As he watched the soft, white light flow magically over her brow and cheeks and across her round pale throat, he whispered rapturously: 'How beautiful you are!'

She smiled as if at a gift. Drawing her towards him, he gently pulled her dress away from her throat, helped her free herself from it and pulled it down until her bare breasts and shoulders were shimmering in the cool moonlight. With eyes and lips he voluptuously followed the delicate shadows, gazing and kissing. She lay motionless, as if spellbound, her eyes lowered, her face solemn, as if at that moment her beauty were for the first time being discovered and revealed also to herself.

Chapter Seven

While the air over the fields grew cool and hour by hour the moon rose higher, the lovers lay in their softly illumined resting-place, lost in their love-play, dropping off to sleep together, then, on waking, turning afresh towards each other to mingle their limbs in renewed desire before falling asleep again. After the final embrace they lay exhausted. Lisa had pressed her body deep into the hay, and her breathing was laboured; Goldmund lay on his back, motionless, staring up at the pale, moonlit sky. In both of them a great sadness welled up, from which they fled into sleep. They slept deeply and desperately, slept avidly as if for the last time, as if they were condemned to eternal wakefulness and would in these hours have to drink in all the sleep of the world in advance.

As he woke up, Goldmund saw Lisa busy with her black hair. He watched her for a while, absent-minded and only half awake. 'Awake already?' he said at last.

She swung round, as if in alarm. 'I have to go now,' she said, somewhat subdued and embarrassed. 'I didn't want to wake you.'

'Well, now I'm awake. Do we really have to move on already? We're homeless, aren't we?'

'I am, yes,' said Lisa. 'You belong in the monastery.'

'No, I don't, not any more – I'm like you now, I'm all alone and have no destination. I'll go with you, of course.'

She looked away.

'Goldmund, you can't come with me. I have to go to my husband now. He'll beat me for staying out all night. I'll tell him I lost my way, but of course he won't believe me.'

Then Goldmund remembered that this is what Narcissus had predicted. So this is how it would be now.

He stood up and held out his hand. 'I was mistaken,' he said. 'I had thought we would stay together. But did you really want to let me go on sleeping and run off without saying goodbye?'

'Oh, I thought you would be angry and might beat me. For my husband to beat me – well, that's the way it is, that's all right. But I didn't want to get a beating from you too.'

He held on to her hand.

'Lisa,' he said, 'I shan't beat you, not today or ever. Won't you come with me rather than go back to your husband, if he beats you?'

She pulled hard to free her hand. 'No, no, no!' she cried in a tearful voice. And since it was clear that her heart was drawing away from him, and that she would rather have a beating from that other man than kind words from him, he let go her hand. She began to cry but at the same time started running away, holding her hands to her streaming eyes as she ran. He said no more and watched her go, feeling sorry for her as she hurried over the mown meadows, summoned and drawn by some power, an unknown power that caused him to reflect. He felt sorry for her, and also a little bit for himself. He was out of luck, it seemed, so he sat there alone and rather foolish – abandoned, left behind. He was still tired and craving sleep; never had he been so exhausted. There was time later on to be unhappy. He fell asleep immediately, waking only when he became conscious of the heat of the noonday sun.

Feeling rested, he quickly got up, ran to the brook, washed and drank. Many memories came to him now, many images from the night's lovemaking, as fragrant as exotic flowers, many exquisite, tender sensations. All these filled his mind as he strode briskly off; he felt, tasted, smelled and touched everything again and again. How many dreams had that brown-skinned woman, that stranger, fulfilled, how many buds had she caused to open, how much curiosity and longing had she satisfied and how much new longing aroused!

And before him lay meadow and heath, arid fallow fields and dark forest. Beyond them might be farmhouses and mills, a village, a town. For the first time the world lay open to him, open and waiting, ready to accept him, to bring him pleasure or cause him pain. He was no longer a schoolboy who sees the world through a window; his wandering was no longer a stroll that must inevitably end in a return. This great world had now become reality; he was a part of it. In it lay his fate, its sky was his, its weather his. He was but small in this great world, small as he ran like a rabbit, a beetle, through its blue and green infinity. Here no bell rang to get him out of bed, to summon him to church, to class, to dinner.

How hungry he was! Half a loaf of barley bread, a bowl of milk or gruel – what magical memories those were! His stomach had woken up like a wolf. Passing a field of wheat where the ears were half ripe, he peeled some with his fingers and teeth, chewed voraciously on the slippery little grains and picked more and more ears, stuffing them into his pockets. Then he found hazel-nuts, still quite green, and bit eagerly into the brittle shells. Of these he also took a supply.

Now the forest began again, fir trees interspersed with oak and ash, and here there were bilberries in vast quantities. He stopped to rest and eat and cool off. In among the coarse forest grass were bluebells; sunny brown butterflies fluttered up and disappeared in random, zigzag flight. In just such a forest Ste Geneviève had lived; he had always loved her story. How he would have liked to come upon her! Or there might be a hermitage in the forest, with a bearded old monk in a cave or a bark hut. Or maybe there were charcoal-burners living in this forest; gladly would he have saluted them. There might even be robbers, but probably they would have done him no harm. It would be good to come upon some human beings, no matter what kind. But he was well aware that he might continue walking in the forest for a long time – today, tomorrow and for many a day beyond – without meeting a soul. That, too, he must accept if such was his fate. One must not think too much; one must let everything happen as it will.

He heard a woodpecker tapping and tried for a long time to creep up on it. At last he succeeded and could observe it for a while as it clung, solitary, to a treetrunk, hammering away and jerking its industrious head back and forth. A pity one couldn't talk to animals! He would have liked to call out to the woodpecker, make some friendly remark and maybe learn something about its life in the trees, about its work and its joys. If only one could transform oneself!

He recalled how in his free hours he had sometimes taken his slate-pencil and drawn outlines on his slate; flowers, leaves, trees, animals, human heads. He used to spend a long time at this game, and occasionally, like a little Heavenly Father, he would invent creatures of his own will. In the calyx of a flower he would draw eyes and a mouth; a cluster of leaves sprouting from a branch he would shape into figures, to a treetop add a head. At this game he had spent many a blissful, enchanted hour; he had been able to perform magic, had drawn lines and seen them, to his own surprise, turn into a leaf, a fish's mouth, a fox's tail, a human eyebrow. We should all be as capable of transformation, he thought, as the playful lines on his slate had been!

Goldmund wished he could turn into a woodpecker, maybe for a day, maybe for a month; he would live in the treetops, would run high up on the smooth trunks, using his strong beak to peck at the bark as he braced himself against it with his tail feathers, would speak woodpecker language and pick tasty morsels out of the bark. Sweet and robust was the sound of the woodpecker's hammering on the resonant wood.

Goldmund encountered many animals on his way through the forest. At his approach, rabbits would suddenly dart out of the undergrowth, stare at him, turn and race away, ears laid back, white scuts flashing. In a little glade he found a long snake that did not run away: it was not a live snake, only its empty skin. He picked it up and examined it; a beautiful grey and brown pattern covered its back, and the sun shone through it. It was cobweb-thin. He saw blackbirds with yellow beaks, staring at him nervously out of their round black eyes before flying off low over the ground. Robins and finches abounded. At one spot in the forest there was a depression, a pool full of thick green water. Long-legged spiders ran frantically about on it as if obsessed, absorbed in some obscure game, and a few dragonflies with dark-blue wings flew above it. And once, towards evening, he saw something, or rather, he merely saw foliage being violently shaken, heard branches snapping and damp earth splashing, and caught a glimpse of some large animal running and trampling thunderously through the bushes – a stag, maybe, or a wild boar, he didn't know. He stood there a long time, recovering from the shock. Profoundly stirred, he listened to the plunging animal, listened with a pounding heart until long after the sound had died away.

Unable to find his way out of the forest, he was forced to spend the night in it. While looking for a place to sleep and preparing a bed of moss, he tried to imagine what it would be like if he never did find his way out of the forest and had to stay in it for ever. And he concluded that this would be a great misfortune. He could, if necessary, live on berries and sleep on moss, and he would doubtless manage to build himself a hut, perhaps even to make a fire. But to be alone for ever and ever and dwell among the silent, sleeping treetrunks and to live among creatures that ran away from one and with which one couldn't converse – that would be unbearably sad. Never to see another human being, never to wish anyone good-morning or good-night; not to be able to look into faces and eyes, never again look at girls and women, feel a kiss, play that lovely, secret game of lips and limbs – oh, that would be unthinkable! If that were to be his fate, he thought, he would try to become an animal, a bear or a stag, even if it meant renouncing eternal salvation. To be a bear and love a she-bear, that wouldn't be so bad. At least it would be much better than keeping his reason and language and living on with all that, solitary and sad and unloved.

On his mossy bed, before falling asleep, he listened with uneasy curiosity to the incomprehensible, mysterious night-sounds of the forest. They were now his companions; he had to live with them, become used to them, adapt to them and get along with them. He was one with fox and deer, with fir and spruce; he must live with them, share air and sun with them, await the dawn with them, share their hunger and be their guest.

Then he slept and dreamed of animals and humans, was a bear and devoured Lisa even as he caressed her. In the middle of the night he awoke in sudden terror, not knowing why. He felt an immense fear in his heart and puzzled over this for some time; then remembered that the previous night and this present one he had lain down to sleep without saying his prayers. He got up, knelt beside his couch and recited his evening prayers twice, for both nights. Soon he was asleep again.

Next morning he looked round the forest in surprise: he had forgotten where he was. His fear of the forest began to subside. With new joy he gave himself up to life in the forest, but always moving on and taking his direction from the sun. At one point he came upon a section of the forest that was completely flat, with little undergrowth, and the trees were all very old, straight, thick-stemmed white firs. After he had walked for a while among these columns, they began to remind him of the pillars of the great monastery church, that very church into whose black doorway he had recently seen his friend Narcissus disappear – when was that? Was it really only two days ago?

Two days and two nights passed before he emerged from the forest. He was cheered by the signs of human proximity: tilled land, strips of field planted with rye and oats; meadows through which a narrow footpath, visible here and there, had been trodden. Goldmund picked some rye and chewed it. The cultivated land smiled at him; after the long forest wilderness, everything seemed human and companionable – the footpath, the oats, the withered, blanched cornflowers. Soon he would come upon people. In less than an hour he passed a field with a wayside cross, and he knelt and prayed at its foot. Rounding a projecting hill, he suddenly found himself standing in front of a shady linden tree and heard with delight the melody of a spring, its water flowing out of a wooden pipe into a long wooden trough. He drank some of the cold, delicious water and saw to his joy a few thatched roofs showing beyond elderberry-bushes whose berries were already dark. What touched him more deeply than all these homely signs was the lowing of a cow: the sound was so comforting, so warm and friendly, a greeting and a welcome.

Cautiously he approached the hut from which the lowing had come. In the dust outside the door sat a little boy with reddish hair and bright blue eyes. He had an earthenware pot of water beside him, and with the dust and water he was making a paste with which his bare legs were already coated. Happy and solemn, he squeezed the wet mud in his hands, watching it ooze out between his fingers, then made it into little balls, using even his chin to knead and shape them.

'Good-morning to you!' cried Goldmund in a cheerful, friendly voice. But the child, on looking up and seeing a stranger, gaped, contorted his plump face and started to howl before scuttling on all fours into the hut. Goldmund followed and found himself in the kitchen, which was so dimly lit that, coming in from the bright noonday glare, he could at first see nothing. To be on the safe side he called out a pious greeting. There was no response, but over the screams of the frightened child a thin, ancient voice gradually became audible as it spoke consolingly to the boy. At last a little old woman stood up in the darkness and came closer, holding one hand in front of her eyes and peering up at the visitor.

'God be with you, Mother,' Goldmund said, 'and may all the dear saints bless your good face! For three days I have seen no human face.'

The little old woman looked at him dully out of far-sighted eyes. 'What do you want?' she asked uncertainly.

Goldmund took her hand and stroked it gently. 'To bid you good-day, Granny, and rest a little and help you light a fire. And I wouldn't say No to a piece of bread if you would like to give me some, but there's no hurry.'

Seeing a bench attached to the wall, he sat down on it while the old woman cut off a slice of bread for the child, who was now staring across at the stranger, intent and curious but still prepared to burst into tears at any moment and run away. The old woman cut another slice from the loaf and brought it to Goldmund.

'Thank you,' he said. 'May God reward you.'

'Is your stomach empty?' asked the woman.

'Not really, it is full of bilberries.'

'Well, then, eat! Where have you come from?'

'From Mariabronn, from the monastery.'

'Are you a priest?'

'No. A student. Travelling.'

She looked at him, half mocking, half foolish, and shook her head a little on her gaunt, wrinkled neck. She left him to eat some of the bread while she took the child outside again into the sunshine. Then she came back, curious, and asked: 'Have you anything new to tell?'

'Not much. Do you know Father Anselm?'

'No. What about him?'

'He is sick.'

'Sick? Is he going to die?'

'Don't know. It's his legs. He has trouble walking.'

'Is he going to die?'

'I don't know. Perhaps.'

'Well, let him die. I have to make the soup. Help me cut some kindling.'

She gave him a chunk of fir wood, well dried on the hearth, and a knife. After cutting as much kindling as she wanted he watched her push the pieces into the ash, stoop over them and blow hard until they caught fire. Then, following some obscure system of her own, she proceeded to add layers of fir and beech wood. When the fire blazed up on the open hearth, she moved the big black cauldron, which hung from the chimney on a sooty chain, into the flames.

At her orders, Goldmund fetched water from the spring and skimmed the cream off the bowl of milk. He sat in the smoky dimness, watching the play of the flames and the old woman's bony, wrinkled face appearing and disappearing above them in the red glow. Next door, behind the plank wall, he could hear the cow rootling and bumping its head in the manger.

All this pleased him very much. The linden tree, the spring, the flickering fire under the cauldron, the cow snorting and munching and its muffled thuds against the wall, the semidark room with its table and bench, the little old woman pottering about: it was all fine and good, smelled of food and peace, of people and warmth, of home. There were also two goats, and from the old woman he learned that there was a pigsty at the back, and the woman was the farmer's grandmother, the great-grandmother of the little boy, who was called Kuno. He would come inside from time to time, and although he didn't say a word and looked a bit scared, at least he wasn't crying any more.

When the farmer came home with his wife, they were very surprised to find a stranger in the house. The farmer was about to speak out angrily and, full of suspicion, drew the youth by the arm to the door to inspect his face in daylight. Then he laughed, clapped him approvingly on the shoulder and invited him to share their meal. They all sat down, and each of them dipped bread into the common bowl of milk until most of the milk was gone. The farmer drank up the rest.

Goldmund asked if he might stay until the next day and sleep under their roof. No, the man replied, there was not room enough for that, but outside there was plenty of hay lying around everywhere and he'd have no trouble finding a place to sleep.

The farmer's wife had the little boy beside her. She did not share in the conversation, but during the meal her curious eyes took possession of the young stranger. His curly hair and his gaze had impressed her right away; then she took in with satisfaction his handsome white neck, his smooth hands with their easy, pleasing gestures. What a distinguished-looking stranger this was, and so young! But what attracted and enamoured her most was the stranger's voice, that subtly melodious, warm, gently seductive young male voice that sounded like a caress. She could have gone on listening to that voice for hours.

After the meal the farmer busied himself in the stable. Goldmund had gone outside to wash his hands at the spring and was now sitting on its low rim, cooling off and listening to the water. He sat there irresolutely: there was nothing to keep him here, yet he was sorry to have to move on again. Just then the farmer's wife came out, carrying a bucket. She placed it under the stream of water and while it filled up said in a low voice: 'Listen – if you're still nearby this evening I'll bring you something to eat. Over there, beyond the long barley field, there's some hay that won't be brought in till tomorrow. Will you still be here?'

He looked into her freckled face, watched her strong arms shift the bucket; her large bright eyes looked at him warmly. He smiled at her and nodded; she left at once with the full bucket and disappeared in the dark doorway. Full of gratitude, he sat there very content, listening to the running water. A little later he went inside, looked for the farmer, shook hands with him and the grandmother and thanked them. There was a smell of open fire, soot and milk in the hut. Only a few minutes ago it had been shelter and home; already it had become remote. With a final salutation, he left.

Beyond the huts he came upon a chapel and close to it a copse, a group of fine, sturdy old oak trees with short grass under them, where he stayed in the shade, strolling back and forth among the massive trunks. Strange, he thought, this thing about women and love; they really did require no words. The woman had needed no more than a word or two to indicate the site of their rendezvous; everything else she had expressed without words. With what, then? With her eyes, yes, and with a certain intonation in her slightly husky voice, and with something else still, a scent, perhaps, a delicate, soft emanation of the skin by which women and men could immediately perceive that they desired one another. It was remarkable, like a subtle, secret language, and how quickly he had learned that language! He was looking forward to the evening, full of curiosity as to how this tall, fair-haired woman might be, how she would look and sound, what limbs, movements and kisses she would have – quite different, no doubt, from Lisa's.

Where might she be now, Lisa, with her smooth black hair, her brown skin, her brief sighs? Had her husband beaten her? Did she still think of him? Had she already found a new lover, just as today he had found a new woman? How quickly it all went by, how much happiness was to be found along the way, how lovely and hot it was and how strangely impermanent! It was a sin, it was adultery; until a short while ago he would have let himself be killed rather than commit this sin. And now this was already the second woman he was waiting for, and his conscience was quiet and calm. Or rather, perhaps it wasn't all that calm; but it was not the adultery and the lust that sometimes troubled and burdened his conscience. It was something else; he could not name it. It was the feeling of a guilt one had not incurred but a guilt with which one had come into the world. Perhaps this was what theologians called original sin? Quite possibly. Yes, life itself carried in itself something like guilt – why else would so pure and knowing a man as Narcissus submit himself to penitential exercises like a condemned person? Or why would he, Goldmund, have to feel this guilt somewhere deep inside himself? After all, wasn't he happy? Wasn't he young and healthy, wasn't he as free as a bird in the air? Didn't women love him? Wasn't it wonderful to feel that as a lover he could give the woman the same deep sensual pleasure he experienced himself? Why, then, wasn't he totally and utterly happy? Why would his young happiness, like Narcissus's virtue and wisdom, sometimes be shot through by these strange pangs, this shadowy fear, this lament for the transient nature of things? Why did he spend so much time brooding and thinking, although he knew he was no thinker?

Well, in spite of all this, it was beautiful to be alive. He picked a little mauve flower from the grass, held it close to his eyes and looked into its slender cup: veins ran inside it, and minute organisms lived in it. As in a woman's womb or a thinker's brain, life pulsed and lust quivered there. Why, oh why, are we so hopelessly ignorant? Why couldn't we talk to this flower? But then not even two human beings could really talk to each other; for that, a lucky chance was required, a special friendship and readiness. No, it was a blessing that love needed no words; otherwise it would be full of misunderstanding and folly. How the light in Lisa's half-closed eyes had been extinguished in the throes of her ecstasy, with only a white slit showing between the fluttering lids – that could never be expressed by ten thousand erudite or poetic words! Nothing, nothing whatever, could be expressed or imagined in any way; yet within us was that constant urge to speak, that eternal need to think!

He studied the leaves of the little plant, arranged so neatly, so ingeniously, round the stalk. Virgil's poems were beautiful and he loved them; but they contained many a verse that was not half as clear and ingenious, not half as beautiful and meaningful, as the spiral symmetry of these tiny leaves ascending the stalk. What a delight, what bliss, how noble and meaningful it would be if a human being were able to create a single such flower! But no one could; no hero and no emperor, no pope and no saint.

When the sun was low on the horizon he went off in search of the place described by the farmer's wife. There he waited. It was wonderful to wait and know that a woman was on her way bringing sheer love.

She came carrying a linen cloth in which she had wrapped a big piece of bread and a slice of bacon. After undoing it she spread it out in front of him.

'For you,' she said. 'Eat!'

'Later,' he said, 'I'm not hungry for bread, I'm hungry for you. Show me what good things you have brought for me!'

She had brought many good things for him: strong, thirsty lips; strong, sparkling teeth; strong arms red from the sun, though below her neck and farther down she was white and delicate. She knew few words, but her throat throbbed with a lovely, seductive sound; and when she felt his hands upon her, such tender, sensitive hands as she had never felt before, a shiver ran over her skin, and from her throat came a sound like the purring of a cat. She knew few love-games, fewer than Lisa, but she was wonderfully strong; she pressed against her lover as if wanting to break his neck. Her love was childlike and voracious, simple yet, in all its strength, chaste. Goldmund was very happy with her.

Then she left, with a sigh: it was hard to tear herself away, but she must not stay.

Goldmund remained behind alone, happy and also sad. Much later he remembered the bread and bacon and ate his solitary meal. It was already dark.

Chapter Eight

Goldmund had been on the move for quite a while, rarely spending two nights in the same place, desired and made happy by women everywhere, tanned by the sun, grown thinner from his wanderings and meagre fare. Many women had parted from him in the early hours, some with tears, and more than once he had thought: Why does none of them stay with me? Why, if they love me and will commit adultery for the sake of one night's lovemaking – why do they all immediately return to their husbands, from whom most of them can expect a beating? Not one of them had urged him to stay; not a single one had ever asked him to take her along, had been prepared out of love to share with him the joys and hardships of life on the road. True, he had not invited any of them to do this, or even hinted as much. In his heart of hearts he acknowledged that his freedom was dear to him, and he could not remember any woman for whom he had felt a desire that did not desert him in the arms of the next one. Yet he found it strange and a little sad that love seemed everywhere to be so fleeting, the women's as well as his own: that it was as quickly sated as it was kindled. Was that right? Was it always and everywhere like that? Or had it something to do with him – was he perhaps so constituted that women, although they desired him and admired his looks, wanted no further association with him beyond the brief, wordless tumble in the hay or on the moss? Was it because he was a wanderer, and people with homes had a horror of the life of the homeless? Or had it to do solely with him, as a person, that women desired him and pressed him to their breasts like a pretty doll, but then all went back to their husbands even if they had to face a beating? He didn't know.

He never tired of learning from women. Although he was more attracted by girls, by the very young, the ignorant ones who had no husbands yet – with these he could fall passionately in love – most of those cherished, shy, sheltered girls were out of reach. But he also enjoyed learning from women. Each one left something with him – a gesture, a way of kissing, a special kind of love-play, a special way of surrendering or resisting. Goldmund went along with everything, as insatiable and flexible as a child and open to every kind of seduction: it was this that made him so seductive. His beauty alone would not have sufficed to draw women so easily to him. It was this childlike quality, this receptiveness, this inquisitive innocence of desire, this absolute readiness to do whatever a woman might want of him. With each woman he was, unwittingly, exactly what she wished and longed for him to be: tender and patient with one, swift and aggressive with another, sometimes as childlike as a newly initiated boy, sometimes sophisticated and knowing. He was prepared for playfulness or struggle, for sighs or laughter, for modesty or shamelessness. He did nothing to a woman that she did not desire, nothing that she did not lure out of him. This was what every sensually discriminating woman quickly perceived in him. This was what endeared him to her.

And he learned. In a short time he learned many of the ways and arts of love and absorbed the experiences of many lovers, learning also to see, feel, touch and smell women in all their diversity. He developed a sensitive ear for every kind of voice and learned from the very sound of a woman's voice to guess infallibly the nature and extent of her capacity for love. With recurring delight he observed the infinitely varied ways a head could be set on a neck, a forehead be separated from the hairline, a kneecap move. In the dark, with closed eyes, he learned with gently inquiring fingers how to distinguish one type of feminine hair from another, one type of skin or complexion from another.

It was not long before he began to wonder whether this might be the meaning of his wanderings: to be driven from one woman to the next so that he might learn and practise, ever more subtly, in ever greater variety and depth, the skills of knowing and distinguishing. Perhaps this was his destiny: to attain perfect knowledge of the thousand kinds and thousand varieties of women and love, just as some musicians can play not only one instrument but three, four, many. But of what use this was, to what it would lead, he did not know; he merely felt that he was on his way. Although in Latin and logic he might be competent yet not especially or surprisingly gifted, he did have a rare gift for love, for dalliance with women. Here he learned effortlessly, here he forgot nothing, here experiences accumulated and fell into place on their own.

Once, after spending a year or two on the road, Goldmund arrived at the manor of a wealthy knight who had two beautiful young daughters. It was early autumn; soon the nights would grow chilly. In the previous autumn and winter he had had a taste of that, and it was with some anxiety that he thought of the months ahead; winter was hard on the wayfarer. He asked for food and a night's lodging. He was courteously taken in, and when his host heard that the stranger was educated and knew Greek, he had him brought from the servants' table to his own, where he treated him almost as an equal. The two daughters kept their eyes lowered; the elder one was eighteen, the younger barely sixteen: Lydia and Julie.

The next day Goldmund intended to move on. There was no hope of winning one of these beautiful fair-haired young ladies, and there were no other women around for whose sake he might have wanted to stay. After the morning meal, however, the knight took him aside and led him to a chamber he had furnished for special purposes. The old man spoke modestly to the youth of his own love of learning and books. He showed him a small chest filled with manuscripts he had collected, a writing-desk he had had made for himself and a supply of the finest paper and parchment. In his youth this pious knight, as Goldmund later gradually found out, had attended schools but then devoted himself entirely to a life of war and worldly pleasures until, in the course of a serious illness, a divine exhortation had prompted him to set out on a pilgrimage and to repent his sinful youth. He had travelled as far as Rome and even Constantinople. Finding on his return that his father had died and the house was empty, he had settled there, married, lost his wife, brought up his daughters and now, with the onset of old age, had sat down to compose a detailed account of his pilgrimage. He had managed to write several chapters, but – as he confessed to the young man – his Latin was sadly inadequate and held him up everywhere. He offered Goldmund new clothes and free accommodation if he would correct what had already been written, make a fair copy of it and help him with the remainder.

It was autumn, and Goldmund knew what that meant for a wayfarer. The new outfit was also desirable. But above all the young man liked the prospect of a lengthy stay under the same roof as the two beautiful sisters. He accepted on the spot. Within a few days the housekeeper was instructed to unlock the closet where the bolts of cloth were kept. Some fine brown cloth was available from which garments and a cap for Goldmund were to be made. The knight had been thinking of black and some sort of scholarly gown, but his guest would have none of that and was able to talk him out of it. A charming suit of clothes was produced, half page, half huntsman, which was very becoming.

Things went well with the Latin too. Together they reviewed what had already been written, and Goldmund not only corrected the many inaccuracies and omissions but here and there transformed the knight's short, awkward sentences into elegant Latin periods, with solid constructions and a precise *consecutio temporum*. The knight enjoyed this greatly and was not sparing with praise. They spent at least two hours every day engaged in this work.

At the castle – a large, partly fortified estate – Goldmund found many diversions. He took part in the hunt, learned from Hinrich the gamekeeper to shoot with a crossbow, made friends with the dogs and could ride as much as he liked. Rarely seen alone, he would be talking to either a dog or a horse, or to Hinrich, to Lea the housekeeper (a fat old woman with a masculine voice and much inclined to jokes and laughter), or to the boy in charge of the dogs, or to a shepherd. It would have been easy to carry on an affair with the miller's wife, a near neighbour, but he held back, feigning inexperience.

He was charmed by the knight's two daughters. The younger was the more beautiful, but so prudish that she hardly spoke a word to Goldmund. He behaved towards both with the utmost consideration and courtesy, but both sensed his proximity to be an unremitting courtship. The young one was completely unapproachable, shyness making her appear sulky. The elder one, Lydia, adopted a special manner towards him, treating him – half respectfully, half mockingly – as some kind of a prodigy of a scholar, plying him with questions, including many about life in the monastery, but always displaying a mocking and ladylike superiority towards him. He went along with everything, treating Lydia as a lady, Julie as a little nun; and when he succeeded by his conversation in keeping the girls longer than usual at table after supper, or when Lydia occasionally addressed him in the courtyard or the garden and permitted herself a little banter, he was satisfied and felt he had made progress.

That autumn the foliage clung for a long time to the tall ash trees in the courtyard, and asters and roses continued to bloom in the garden. One day visitors arrived on horseback, a neighbouring landowner with his wife and a groom, the mild weather having tempted them to make an unusually long excursion. Now they were there and asked to stay the night. They were received very courteously, and Goldmund's bed was immediately moved from the guest-room into the study. The guest-room was prepared for the visitors, a few chickens were killed, and someone was sent to the mill for some fish. Goldmund enjoyed sharing in the festive excitement and was at once aware that the knight's lady had her eyes on him. And hardly had he noticed, in her voice and something in her look, that he pleased and aroused her, when he also became aware, with even greater intensity, that Lydia was changing, becoming silent and reserved and starting to watch him and the lady. During the festive evening meal, the lady's foot began to toy with Goldmund's under the table, and he was delighted not only by this game but even more so by the scowling, silent intensity with which Lydia observed it from blazing eyes that missed nothing. Finally he deliberately dropped a knife on the floor, bent down for it under the table to caress the lady's foot and leg, and saw Lydia grow pale and bite her lip. As Goldmund continued to tell anecdotes about the monastery, he felt that the visitor was listening intently, not so much to the stories as to his seductive voice. The others also listened to him, his patron benevolently, the guest with an impassive expression, though he too was touched by the youth's fiery ardour. Never had Lydia heard him speak like that; he blossomed, desire hung quivering in the air, his eyes flashed; happiness sang and love pleaded in his voice. The three women felt it, each differently: young Julie with violent resistance and rejection, the knight's lady with radiant satisfaction, Lydia with a painful surge of the heart, a blend of intense longing, slight resistance and extreme jealousy, which narrowed her face and made her eyes burn. Goldmund was conscious of all these waves flooding back to him like covert responses to his wooing. Like birds, those love-thoughts fluttered round him, surrendering, resisting, fighting one another.

After the meal Julie withdrew. Night had long since fallen and, carrying her candle in its earthenware holder, she left the hall, as calm as a little nun. The others stayed up for another hour; and while the two men discussed the harvest, the Emperor and the bishop, Lydia listened ardently as a casual conversation about nothing was spun between Goldmund and the lady – a conversation, however, in whose loose threads a close, sweet network of glances exchanged, of emphasis and little gestures, was created, all overloaded with meaning, overheated with fervour. The girl absorbed the atmosphere lasciviously but also with revulsion; and when she saw or felt Goldmund's knee touching the stranger's under the table, she felt as if he were touching her and flinched. Later, she lay awake half the night, listening with beating heart, convinced that the two would come together. In her imagination she completed that which was denied them: saw them entwined, heard their kisses. At the same time she was trembling with agitation, as she both feared and wished that the betrayed husband would surprise the lovers and thrust his knife into the heart of that horrible Goldmund.

The following morning the sky was overcast, and a damp wind blew. The guest, refusing all invitations to prolong his stay, insisted on a speedy departure. Lydia was present when the guests mounted their horses. She shook hands and spoke words of farewell, but she was oblivious to everything, all her senses being concentrated in the look with which she watched the knight's lady placing her foot in Goldmund's proffered hands as she mounted, and his broad right hand firmly gripping the shoe and for a moment holding the woman's foot in his strong clasp.

The visitors had ridden away, and Goldmund had to go to the study and work. After half an hour he heard Lydia's voice issuing orders below and a horse being led up. His employer stepped to the window and looked down, smiling and shaking his head; then the eyes of the two men followed Lydia as she rode out of the courtyard. That day they made less progress in their Latin composition. Goldmund was absent-minded, and his employer kindly dismissed him earlier than usual.

Goldmund managed to get himself and his horse out of the courtyard unseen. Facing the cool, damp wind, he rode into the autumnal landscape, trotting faster and faster and feeling his horse growing warm under him as his own blood caught fire. With a sense of release he rode across stubble and fallow fields, across moor and bog patches covered with horsetail and reeds, through the grey day, through little alder hollows, through a dank fir forest, and once again across dun, empty moorland.

He discovered Lydia's figure on a high ridge. Sharply outlined against the pale-grey sky, she sat erect on her slowly trotting horse. He raced towards her. As soon as she saw that she was being pursued, she spurred on her horse and took flight. At times she would disappear, then reappear with flying hair. He chased her as if hunting down a prey, his heart exultant. With affectionate little cries he urged on his horse, and as he flew along he gleefully counted off the landmarks of the countryside – the low-lying fields, the alder thickets, the stand of maples, the muddy banks of the ponds, while constantly casting his eye ahead again at his quarry, the beautiful fugitive. He knew he would catch up with her before long.

When she knew he was near her, Lydia abandoned her flight and slowed her horse to a walk. She did not turn towards her pursuer. Proudly, seemingly indifferent, she rode along as if nothing had happened, as if she were alone. He brought his horse level with hers, and the two horses walked peacefully side by side, but animal and rider were heated by the chase.

'Lydia!' he called out softly.

She made no reply.

'Lydia!'

She remained silent.

'How lovely it was, Lydia, to see you from a distance as you rode with your hair streaming behind you like golden lightning! How lovely that was! Oh, how wonderful that you fled from me! Only then did I see that you do love me a little. I hadn't known – even last night I was in doubt. Only now, when you tried to escape from me, did I suddenly understand. My beautiful, my beloved, you must be tired, let us dismount!'

He sprang down from his horse, at the same moment seizing her reins to prevent her galloping off again. With a snow-white face she looked down at him, and when he lifted her off her horse she burst into tears. Gently he led her a few steps, then made her sit down on the dry grass and knelt beside her. She sat there struggling with her sobs, struggling bravely and overcoming them.

'Oh, how can you be so wicked!' she began when able to speak. She could hardly get the words out.

'Am I so wicked?'

'You are a seducer of women, Goldmund. Let me forget what you said to me just now – those were shameless words, it is not seemly for you to speak to me like that. How can you believe that I love you? Let us forget that! But how am I to forget what I was obliged to see last evening?'

'Last evening? What did you see?'

'Oh, don't pretend, don't lie to me! It was horrible, shameless the way you showed off to that woman before my very eyes! Have you no shame? You even stroked her leg under the table, under our table! In front of me, before my very eyes! And now the moment she's gone you come after me! Really, you don't know the meaning of shame!'

Goldmund had already regretted the words he had spoken before lifting her off the horse. How stupid he had been! In love, words were not necessary; he should not have spoken.

He said no more. Kneeling beside her as she looked at him, so beautiful and so unhappy, he was affected by her suffering and felt there had been something to be deplored. But despite all she said, he still saw love in her eyes, and even the suffering on her trembling lips was love. He believed her eyes more than her words.

But Lydia was expecting an answer. When none came, she narrowed her lips even more, turned her tear-stained face to him and repeated: 'Have you really no shame?'

'Forgive me,' he said humbly. 'We are speaking about things that should not be spoken of. It is all my fault, forgive me! You ask whether I have no shame. Yes, I have! But then I love you, and love knows nothing of shame. Don't be angry!'

She seemed scarcely to hear him but sat there with that bitter mouth and looking out into the distance, as if she were quite alone. Never before had he been in such a situation. It all came from speaking.

He gently laid his face on her knee, and at once the feel of it comforted him. Yet he was somewhat at a loss, and sad, and she too still seemed sad as she sat there motionless, silently gazing out into the distance. So much embarrassment, so much sadness! But the knee accepted his nestling cheek kindly and did not reject it. His eyes remained closed as his face lay on her knee, slowly absorbing its noble, graceful shape. It pleased and touched him to think how, in its elegant, youthful form, this knee corresponded to the long, shapely, gentle arches of her fingernails. Gratefully he nestled against the knee, making cheek and mouth speak to it.

Now he felt her hand, shy and light as a bird, being laid on his hair. Dear hand, he thought, as he felt it, gentle as a child's, stroking his hair. He had often studied and admired her hand, knew it almost as well as his own; the long, slender fingers with those long, shapely, rosy arches of her fingernails. Now the long, delicate fingers were conversing shyly with his curls. Their language was childlike and timid, but it was love. Gratefully he nestled his head in her hand, feeling her palm with his neck and cheeks.

Then she said: 'It is time, we must leave.'

He raised his head and looked at her tenderly as he gently kissed her slender fingers.

'Please, get up,' she said, 'we must go home.'

He obeyed at once. They got to their feet, mounted their horses and rode off.

Goldmund's heart rejoiced. How beautiful Lydia was, pure and delicate as a child! He had not even kissed her, yet he felt she had bestowed a precious and fulfilling gift on him. They rode fast, but on reaching the gates of the courtyard she suddenly said in alarm: 'We should not have arrived together – how foolish we are!' And at the very last moment, as they were dismounting and a groom was already running up, she whispered urgently in his ear: 'Tell me if you were with that woman last night!' He shook his head emphatically and set about unsaddling his horse.

That afternoon, while her father was out, she appeared in the study. 'Is it true?' she burst out passionately, and he knew at once what she meant.

'Then why did you toy with her like that, so disgustingly, and make her fall in love with you?'

'It was meant for you,' he said. 'Believe me, I would a thousand times rather have stroked your foot than hers. But not once did your foot come to me under the table to ask whether I loved you.'

'Do you really love me, Goldmund?'

'Oh, I do!'

'But what can come of it?'

'I don't know, Lydia. And I don't care. It makes me happy to love you – what may come of it is something I don't think about. I am happy when I see you riding, and when I hear your voice, and when your fingers stroke my hair. I shall be happy when I am allowed to kiss you.'

'A man may kiss only his betrothed, Goldmund. Have you never thought of that?'

'No, never. Why should I? You know as well as I do that you can never be my betrothed.'

'You are right. And because you cannot become my husband and stay with me for ever, it is very improper of you to speak to me of love. Did you believe you could seduce me?'

'I believed nothing and thought nothing, Lydia. And anyway, I think much less than you imagine. My only wish is that you should one day want to kiss me. We talk too much. Lovers don't do that. I believe you don't love me.'

'This morning you said the opposite.'

'And you did the opposite!'

'I did? What do you mean?'

'At first you galloped away from me when you saw me coming. That made me believe you love me. Then you had to cry, and I believed it was because you love me. Then my head was lying on your knee, and you stroked me, and I believed that was love. But now you're doing nothing to show me love.'

'I am not like the woman whose foot you stroked yesterday. You seem to be accustomed to such women.'

'No, thank God, you are much more beautiful and refined than she.'

'That's not what I mean.'

'Oh, but it's true. Do you know how beautiful you are?'

'I have a mirror.'

'Have you ever looked at your forehead in it, Lydia? And then your shoulders, and then your fingernails, and then your knees? And have you seen how all that has a harmonious resemblance, how it all has the same shape, a firm, slim, elongated shape? Have you seen that?'

'The things you say! I have never actually noticed it, but now that you say so I do know what you mean. Listen, you *are* a seducer – now you're trying to make me vain!'

'What a pity I can't do anything right for you. But why should I be interested in making you vain? You are beautiful, and I should like to show you that I am grateful for that. You force me to tell you so in words – I could say it a thousand times better with words. With words I can give you nothing! With words I can learn nothing from you and you nothing from me.'

'What am I supposed to learn from you?'

'I from you, Lydia, and you from me. But you're not interested. You want to love only the man whose bride you will be. He will laugh when he finds out that you have learned nothing, not even how to kiss.'

'I see. So you would like to give me lessons in kissing, would you, Mr Schoolmaster?'

He smiled at her. Although he did not like what she said, he could sense that, behind her vehement but unconvincing irony, her maidenly innocence was being seized by sensuality and nervously resisting it.

He did not reply. Smiling at her, he held her uncertain gaze captive with his eyes, and while she surrendered to the spell, not without resistance, he slowly brought his face close to hers until their lips touched. He lightly brushed her lips, which responded with a little childlike kiss and parted with a pang of surprise when he did not release them. In his gentle wooing he followed her retreating mouth until it hesitantly approached again, then, without force, taught the spellbound girl the taking and giving of kisses until, exhausted, she pressed her face against his shoulder. He let it rest, breathed in the scent of her abundant blonde hair, murmured tender, soothing sounds into her ear, and recalled how he, a naïve pupil, had once been initiated into the secret by Lisa the gypsy. How black her hair had been, how brown her skin; how scorching the sun, and how fragrant the wilting St John's wort! And how far in the past that already lay, across what distances did it all seem to flash. How quickly everything wilted that had scarcely had time to bloom!

Slowly Lydia straightened up, her face transformed, and looked at him solemnly out of big, loving eyes. 'Let me go, Goldmund,' she said. 'I've spent so much time with you. Oh Goldmund, oh my dear one!'

Each day they found their clandestine hour, and Goldmund let himself be guided entirely by Lydia. He was touched, made wonderfully happy, by this maidenly love. Sometimes for a whole hour she wanted nothing more than to hold his hands in hers and look into his eyes, and she would leave with a childish kiss. At other times she would kiss him passionately and insatiably but would not let him touch her. Once, blushing deeply and overcoming her reluctance in her desire to give him special pleasure, she let him look at one of her breasts, taking the little white fruit shyly out of her dress. When, on his knees, he had kissed it, she carefully covered it again, still blushing to the roots of her hair. They talked, too, but in a new way, no longer as they had the first day. They invented names for one another, and she loved to tell him about her childhood, her dreams and games. She also spoke about their love being wrong, since he could not marry her. Of this she spoke sadly and resign-edly, and she adorned her love with the secret of this sadness as with a black veil.

For the first time Goldmund felt himself not merely desired but loved by a woman.

One day Lydia said: 'You are so handsome and look so serene. But deep in your eyes there is no serenity, there is only sadness, as if your eyes knew that there is no such thing as happiness, and that what we find beautiful and lovable does not stay with us for long. You have the most beautiful eyes in the world, and the saddest. I believe that is because you are homeless. You came to me out of the forests, and one day you will go away again and sleep on moss, a wayfarer. But then, where is *my* home? When you leave I shall still have a father and a sister, have a room and a window where I can sit and think of you, but I shall no longer have a home.'

He let her speak; sometimes he would smile, sometimes feel distressed. Instead of consoling her with words, he would merely stroke her gently as he held her head against his chest and softly hum meaningless magic tunes the way a nurse hums to comfort a crying child.

Once Lydia said: 'I wish I knew, Goldmund, what's going to become of you – I think about it often. You won't have an ordinary life, or an easy one. Oh, how I hope that life turns out well for you! Sometimes I think you should be a poet, one who has visions and dreams and can express them beauti-fully. Oh, you will roam the whole world, and all the women will love you, yet you will remain alone. It would be best for you to go back to the monastery, to the friend you have told me so much about! I shall pray for you that you may not some day lie alone in the forest.'

That is how she could speak, deeply serious, with a faraway look in her eyes. But then again she could ride laughing with him across the autumnal countryside, or ask him nonsense riddles and pelt him with dead leaves and shiny acorns.

One night Goldmund was lying in bed in his room, waiting for sleep. His heart was heavy, in a sweet and painful way; it beat heavily in his breast, filled to bursting with love, with sadness and perplexity. He could hear the November wind rattling the roof. It had already become a habit with him to lie awake quite a while before sleep came. Under his breath he sang a hymn to the Virgin Mary, as he usually did at night:

> Tota pulchra es, Maria,
> et macula originalis non est in te.
> Tu laetitia Israel,
> tu advocata peccatorum!

With its gentle music the hymn sank into his soul, but at the same time the wind was singing outside, singing of restlessness and wayfaring, of forest and autumn and the life of the homeless. He thought of Lydia, he thought of Narcissus and his mother; his troubled heart was full and heavy.

Suddenly he gave a start and stared in disbelief: the door had opened, and in the darkness a figure in a long white gown entered. Without a sound, walking with bare feet on the stone floor, Lydia came in, softly closed the door and sat down on his bed.

'Lydia,' he whispered, 'my little doe, my white flower! Lydia, what are you doing?'

'I have come to you,' she said, 'just for a moment. I wanted to see my Goldmund lying in his bed, my Goldheart.'

She lay down beside him. They lay still, with pounding hearts. She let him kiss her, let his adoring hands play along her limbs: no more was permitted. After a short while she gently pushed his hands away, kissed his eyes, got up without a sound and disappeared. The door creaked. In the rafters the wind clattered and banged. Everything seemed to be under a spell, full of mystery and foreboding, full of promise and menace. Goldmund did not know what to think, what to do. After a restless sleep he awoke to find his pillow wet with tears.

A few days later she came again, the sweet white ghost, and as before, lay beside him for a quarter of an hour. Held in his arms, she whispered in his ear; she had much to say and to lament. Lovingly he listened while she lay on his left arm and he stroked her knee with his right hand.

'Dearest Goldmund,' she said in a muffled voice close to his cheek, 'it is so sad that I must never belong to you. It won't last much longer, our little happiness, our little secret. Julie is already suspicious, and soon she will force me to tell her. Or Father will notice. If he were to find me in bed with you, my golden bird, things would go badly for your Lydia. Her eyes red with weeping, she would stand looking up at the trees and see her lover dangling up there, swaying in the wind. Oh my darling, you had better run away, right now, rather than that Father should have you bound and hanged. I once saw a man who had been hanged, a thief. I couldn't bear to see you hanging like that, I'd rather you ran away and forgot me – just so you don't have to die, Goldie, just so the birds don't peck at your blue eyes! But no, my darling, you mustn't go away – oh, what shall I do if you leave me here all alone!'

'But don't you want to come with me, Lydia? We'll run away together, the world is big!'

'That would be wonderful,' she moaned. 'Oh, how wonderful to roam the whole world with you! But I can't. I can't sleep in the forest and be homeless and have straw in my hair – I can't do that! And I can't bring such disgrace on Father. No, don't tell me – I'm not pretending. I can't! No more than I could eat from a dirty plate or sleep in a leper's bed. Oh, everything that seems good and beautiful is forbidden to us – we were both born to suffer. Goldie, my poor boy, it seems I shall have to see you hanged after all. As for me, I'll be locked up and then sent to a convent. Dearest, you must forsake me and go back to sleeping with the gypsies and peasant women. Oh go, go, before they catch you and tie you up! We shall never be happy, never!'

He softly stroked her knee and, as he very gently touched her pudenda, asked: 'Little flower, we could be so very happy! Won't you let me?'

Firmly, but without displeasure, she pushed his hand aside and moved slightly away from him.

'No,' she said, 'no, I won't. That's forbidden. Little gypsy that you are, you probably don't understand that. It's true, I'm doing wrong, I'm a bad girl, I'm bringing disgrace on the whole house. But somewhere deep in my soul I still have my pride – no one is allowed in there. You must grant me that, otherwise I can never come to your room again.'

Never would he have disregarded a refusal, a wish or a hint on her part: in fact he was surprised at how much power she had over him. But he suffered. His senses remained unsatisfied, and his heart often rebelled against his dependence. Sometimes he made an effort to shed it. Sometimes he paid court to young Julie with exquisite politeness, and of course it was also essential to maintain good relations with this important person and if possible to deceive her. He felt strangely ambivalent towards this Julie who often behaved so childishly yet often seemed so omniscient. There was no doubt that she was more beautiful than Lydia; she was an outstanding beauty, and this, together with her somewhat precocious innocence, was a great attraction for Goldmund. He was often strongly enamoured of Julie. And it was precisely this fascination exerted on his senses by the sister that made him recognize, often with surprise, the difference between desire and love. At first, he had looked at both sisters with the same eyes, had found both desirable but Julie more beautiful and worthier of seduction. He had courted both equally and always kept his eye on both. And now Lydia had gained this power over him! Now he loved her so much that his love made him even renounce total possession of her. Her soul had become familiar and dear to him; in its childlike nature, tenderness and inclination towards melancholy it seemed to resemble his own. He was often amazed and delighted to find how greatly this soul matched her body: she might do something, say something, express a wish or an opinion, and her words and the attitude of her soul were fashioned in exactly the same mould as the shape of her eyes and the form of her fingers!

These moments, when he believed he could perceive the basic forms and laws shaping her very being, both soul and body, had often prompted in Goldmund the wish to capture and copy something of this shape, and on a few well-hidden sheets of paper he had attempted to sketch from memory the outline of her head, the line of her eyebrows, her hand, her knee.

The situation with Julie had become a little difficult. Obviously sensing the wave of love on which her elder sister was being carried along, her senses turned, full of curiosity and desire, towards that paradise, although her stubborn mind refused to admit it. She displayed an exaggerated aloofness and antipathy towards Goldmund, yet in unguarded moments she could watch him with admiration and lascivious curiosity. With Lydia she was often very affectionate, sometimes even coming into her bed, where with hidden lust she would breathe in the atmosphere of love and sex, touching boldly on the forbidden, longed-for secret. Then again she would indicate in an almost offensive manner that she knew about Lydia's secret misconduct and despised it. Charmingly, disturbingly, the beautiful moody child flickered between the two lovers, feeding in thirsty dreams on their secretiveness, sometimes pretending to be naïve, sometimes hinting at her dangerous connivance. In a very short time she had turned from a child into a power. Lydia had to suffer more from this than Goldmund, who seldom saw the younger sister except at meals. Nor could it escape Lydia's notice that Goldmund was not insensitive to Julie's attractions; sometimes she saw his approving, appreciative gaze resting on her. She could say nothing; everything was so difficult, so fraught with danger. Above all, Julie must not be annoyed or offended: every day, every hour, the secret of their love might be discovered and an end, perhaps a terrible one, put to their fear-filled happiness.

At times Goldmund wondered why he had not cleared off long ago. It was hard to live as he was living now: loved, but without hope of either legitimate and lasting happiness or the easy fulfilments to which his desires had so far been accustomed, with urges that were perpetually aroused, hungry but never satisfied, while he was in constant danger. Why did he stay and endure all this, all these entanglements and confused emotions? Weren't they experiences, emotions and crises of conscience for established, legitimate people, for those living in heated rooms? Didn't he have the right of the homeless and the undemanding to withdraw from these delicate and complex situations and to laugh at them? Yes, he had that right, and he was a fool to look for something like home here and to pay for it with so much pain, so many predicaments. And yet he did and he suffered for it, suffered gladly, and was secretly happy doing so. It was stupid and difficult, it was complicated and exhausting, to love in such a manner, but it was wonderful: wonderful, that darkly beautiful sadness of this love, its folly and hopelessness; they were beautiful, those meditative, sleepless nights. All this was as lovely and precious as the mark of sadness on Lydia's lips, as the dreamy, resigned sound of her voice when she spoke of her love and her fear. In only a few weeks, those lines of suffering on Lydia's young face had appeared and come to stay, and it was these lines that he found so gratifying and important to copy with his pen. He felt that in these few weeks he had also changed and grown much older, not cleverer but more experienced, not happier but much more mature and spiritually enriched. He was no longer a boy.

In her gentle, dreamy voice Lydia said to him: 'You mustn't be sad, not on my account. I want only to make you smile and see you happy. Forgive me, I've made you sad, I've infected you with my fear and my melancholy. I have such strange dreams at night: I am walking along in a desert that is vaster and darker than I can describe, I walk on and on searching for you, but you aren't there, and I know I've lost you, and I shall always, always, have to walk like that, all alone. Then when I wake up I think: Oh, how wonderful, how glorious, that he is still there and I shall see him, maybe for weeks, maybe for a few days, never mind, he is still there!'

One morning Goldmund awoke soon after dawn and lay in bed for a while, thinking. Images from a dream still floated about him, but randomly. He had been dreaming of his mother and of Narcissus and could still distinctly see both figures. When he had shaken off those wisps of his dream he became aware of an unusual light, a strange brightness entering through the little window opening. He jumped up and ran to the window, where he saw that the sill, the stable roof, the courtyard entrance and the whole countryside beyond reflected a bluish-white shimmer: the first snow of winter had fallen. The contrast between the restlessness of his heart and the silent, submissive winter world saddened him. How quietly, with what touching devotion, did field and forest, hill and moor surrender to wind, rain, drought and snow; with what beauty and patient suffering did maple and ash bear their winter burden! Couldn't one become like them, couldn't one learn something from them? Deep in thought he went out into the courtyard, waded through the snow, felt it with his hands, walked across to the garden and looked over the snow-topped fence at the stems of the rose-bushes weighed down by the snow.

Over their breakfast gruel they all discussed the first snow. They had all, even the girls, already been outside. The snow came late that year; Christmas was not far off. The knight told them about southern lands where snow was unknown. But what made that first winter day unforgettable for Goldmund did not occur until long after nightfall.

That day the two sisters had had a quarrel of which Goldmund knew nothing. At night, when all was quiet and dark in the house, Lydia came to him in her usual way. In silence she lay down beside him with her head on his chest so she could hear his heart beating and find solace in his closeness. She was despondent and anxious, fearing betrayal by Julie, yet reluctant to worry her lover by speaking of it. So she lay silently against his heart, hearing him whisper an occasional endearment and feeling his hand in her hair.

But suddenly – she had not been lying there very long – she received a terrible shock, which made her sit up with wide-open eyes. And for Goldmund the shock was no less when he saw the door open and a figure enter which in his alarm he did not immediately recognize. Only when the apparition stood close by the bed and bent over it did he see with quaking heart that it was Julie. She slipped out of the cloak she had thrown over her nightgown and let it fall to the floor. With an agonized cry, as if she had been pierced with a knife, Lydia sank back and clung to Goldmund.

In a mixture of mockery and gloating triumph, yet in an uncertain voice, Julie said: 'I don't like lying all by myself in our room. Either you let me join you and the three of us will lie together, or I'll go and wake Father.'

'By all means, get in!' said Goldmund, throwing back the cover. 'Your feet must be freezing.' She got in, though he had difficulty making room for her in the narrow bed, for Lydia had buried her face in the pillow and would not budge. At last all three lay together, Goldmund with a girl on each side, and for a moment he could not suppress the thought of how, not so long ago, this situation would have answered all his desires. Oddly disquieted yet secretly thrilled, he felt Julie's hip against his side.

'I had to see,' she went on, 'what it's like to lie in your bed, which my sister is so fond of visiting.'

In order to quieten her, Goldmund gently rubbed his cheek against her hair, while his hand lightly stroked her hips and knees, the way one fondles a cat; silent and curious she surrendered to his exploring hand and, enraptured by the magic, offered no resistance. While weaving this spell, however, he also attended to Lydia, murmuring soft, familiar sounds of love into her ear and gradually prevailing upon her at least to raise her face and turn it towards him. Silently he kissed her mouth and eyes, while his hand on the other side kept the sister enthralled and the awkwardness and weirdness of the whole situation were borne in on him almost beyond endurance. It was his left hand that taught him; while it was becoming acquainted with Julie's lovely, quietly expectant limbs, he felt for the first time not only the beauty and profound hopelessness of his love for Lydia but also its absurdity. Now, while his lips were with Lydia and his hand was with Julie, he felt that he should have either forced Lydia to yield or continued on his way. To love her and yet renounce her had been foolish and wrong.

'Dear heart,' he whispered in Lydia's ear, 'we are suffering to no purpose. How happy we three could be now! Let us follow the call of our blood!'

As she withdrew from him with a shudder, his desire fled to the sister, to whom his hand was giving so much pleasure that she responded with a long, trembling, voluptuous sigh.

When Lydia heard that sigh, jealousy constricted her heart, as if poison had been dripped into it. She suddenly sat up, flung the cover off the bed and jumped to her feet crying: 'Julie, let's go!'

Julie flinched; that thoughtless outburst, which could betray them all, was enough to show her the danger, and without a word she sat up. But Goldmund, in all his urges insulted and betrayed, quickly threw his arms round her, kissed both her breasts, and whispered ardently in her ear: 'Tomorrow, Julie, tomorrow!'

Lydia was standing barefoot in her nightgown, her toes on the stone floor curled against the cold. She picked up Julie's cloak and hung it round her sister's shoulders in a suffering, humble gesture which, even in the darkness, did not escape Julie and both touched and reconciled her. Quietly the sisters flitted from the room. Beset by conflicting emotions, Goldmund listened to their retreating footsteps and breathed a sigh of relief when deathly silence settled back over the house.

Thus the three young people were transported from a strange and unnatural grouping to a state of lonely reflection, for after reaching their room the two sisters, instead of having a heart-to-heart talk, also lay awake, solitary, unspeaking and defiant, each in her own bed. A spirit of unhappiness and contradiction, a demon of senselessness, isolation and spiritual confusion seemed to have taken possession of the house. Goldmund did not fall asleep until after midnight, Julie not until nearly daybreak. Lydia lay wakeful and tormented until the pale day came up over the snow. She rose at once, dressed, knelt and prayed for a long time before her little wooden Saviour, and as soon as she heard her father's footsteps on the stairs she went and asked if she might speak to him. Without attempting to distinguish between her anxiety for Julie's maidenly virtue and her own jealousy, she had made up her mind to put an end to the affair. Goldmund and Julie were both still asleep when the knight was already aware of everything Lydia had deemed appropriate to tell him. She had said nothing about Julie's participation in the adventure.

When Goldmund appeared in the study at the usual hour, he saw that the knight, who normally attended to his writing efforts in slippers and loose felt jacket, was wearing boots and doublet, his sword at his side, and Goldmund knew instantly what that signified.

'Put on your cap,' said the knight. 'I must take a walk with you.'

Goldmund took his cap from the nail and followed his employer down the stairs, across the courtyard and out through the gateway. Their soles crunched on the ice-crusted snow; the sky was still pink with the dawn. The knight walked ahead in silence; the youth followed, looking back several times at the house, at the window of his room, at the steep, snow-covered roof until it sank out of sight and nothing more was to be seen. Never again would he see that roof and that window, never again the study and his room, never again the two sisters. He had long been used to the thought of a sudden parting, yet a spasm of pain clutched at his heart. It was a bitter wrench to leave.

For an hour they continued walking, the knight ahead, neither of them speaking. Goldmund began to wonder what was in store for him. The knight was armed; perhaps he would kill him. But he did not think so. The danger was slight; he need only run away, and the old man would be left standing there helpless with his sword. No, his life was not in danger. But to walk like this in silence behind the outraged, dignified old man, to be led wordlessly away like this, was becoming more and more of an ordeal with every step. At last the knight halted.

'Now,' he said, his voice cracking, 'you will go on alone, always in this direction, and resume the life of a wayfarer to which you were accustomed. If you should ever again show yourself in the vicinity of my house, you will be shot down. I do not wish to take revenge on you. I should have known better than to allow so young a man to come near my daughters. But should you dare to return, you will forfeit your life. Go now, and may God forgive you!'

As the knight stood there in the wan light of the snowy morning, his bearded face looked drained. Like a spectre he remained rooted to the spot until Goldmund had disappeared over the next ridge. The clouds had lost their pink reflection, the sun did not appear, and snow began to fall slowly in thin, hesitant flakes.

Chapter Nine

From many a ride on horseback Goldmund was familiar with the area. He knew that beyond the frozen marsh there was a barn belonging to the knight, also a farm where he was known. At one or other of these he would be able to rest and spend the night. All else must wait until tomorrow. Gradually he regained the sense of freedom and discovery that for a while he had put aside. On this icy, hostile winter's day, the unknown world did not taste sweet. It smelled strongly of hardship, hunger and need, yet its breadth, its vastness and pitilessness sounded soothing and almost comforting to his indulged and confused heart.

He walked until he was worn out. No more riding for me, he thought. O wide world! It was snowing, but lightly. In the distance, wooded ridges merged with grey clouds. The silence was infinite, reaching to the end of the world. What was Lydia, that poor, anxious heart, doing, he wondered? He felt bitterly sorry for her and thought of her tenderly as he rested in the midst of the empty marsh under a single bare ash tree. Finally the cold drove him away; stiff-legged, he got up and gradually managed to walk more briskly. Already the meagre daylight seemed to be fading. During his long march across barren fields his mind became empty of thought. Now was not the time for thinking or indulging in emotions, no matter how tender, no matter how beautiful. Now the essential thing was to keep warm and reach shelter for the night in time to survive this cold, inhospitable world like a marten or a fox and try not to perish out here in the open. Nothing else mattered.

He looked round in surprise when he thought he heard a distant hoofbeat. Was it possible he was being pursued? He grasped the little hunting-knife in his pocket and loosened the wooden sheath. Now he could make out a rider and recognize from far off a horse from the knight's stable heading straight for him. It would have been useless to flee, so he stood still and waited, not exactly afraid but tense and curious as his pulse quickened. For an instant the thought flashed through his mind: If I managed to kill this horseman, how well off I would be! I would have a horse, and the world would be mine! But when he recognized the rider, young Hans the groom, with his pale-blue eyes and good-natured, embarrassed, boyish face, he had to laugh. To kill this nice young fellow would have required a heart of stone! He greeted Hans warmly, and affectionately greeted the horse Hannibal, which recognized him at once as he patted its warm, damp neck.

'Where are you heading for, Hans?' he asked.

'For you!' laughed the young fellow with shining teeth. 'You've already covered quite a distance! Well, I mustn't linger, I'm supposed just to bring you greetings and hand you this.'

'Greetings from whom?'

'From Miss Lydia. I must say you've dished up a nice mess for us, Master Goldmund – I'm glad I could get away for a bit. Although my master mustn't find out that I've been off carrying messages – he'd really have it in for me! So here you are!'

He held out a little parcel, and Goldmund took it from him.

'Tell me, Hans, d'you happen to have a piece of bread on you? If so, give it to me.'

'Bread? I suppose I could find a crust.' He fished in his pockets, brought out a piece of black bread, and was about to ride off.

'How is your young mistress?' Goldmund asked. 'Didn't she give you any message? A note, maybe?'

'No, nothing. I only saw her for a moment. Stormy weather in the house, you know. The master is walking around like King Saul. Well, I'm supposed to give you this stuff, that's all. I have to get back.'

'Yes, but just a moment! Listen, Hans – do you think you could let me have your hunting-knife? I only have a small one. If there should be any wolves around, say, I'd be better off with something useful in my hand.'

But Hans wouldn't hear of it. He'd be sorry if anything happened to Master Goldmund, but his hunting-knife – no, he'd never part with that, not for money, not for a swap, oh no, even if Ste Geneviève herself were to ask him for it. That was that, and now he must hurry, and he wished him well, and he was sorry.

They shook hands, and the lad rode away. With a strange pang Goldmund watched him disappear. Then he opened the parcel, glad of the good calf-leather strap with which it was fastened. Inside he found a knitted doublet of thick grey wool, evidently Lydia's handiwork intended for him; also, well wrapped up in the woollen garment, something hard which turned out to be a chunk of ham, and cut into the ham was a little slit containing a shiny gold ducat. There was no written message. Holding Lydia's gifts he stood there in the snow, indecisively, then took off his jacket and slipped on the woollen garment, which provided a pleasant warmth. He quickly dressed again, hid the gold coin in his safest pocket, fastened the strap round his waist and continued across country. It was time to reach shelter. By now he was very tired, but he did not feel like going to the farm, although it would have been warmer there and probably some milk would have been obtainable. He was not in the mood for talking and answering questions, so he spent the night in the barn and, despite frost and a sharp wind, continued on his way early next morning. The cold drove him to long marches, and when he slept he often dreamed of the knight and his sword and the two sisters. For many days, loneliness and melancholy weighed on his heart.

One evening he found shelter in a village, where the poor peasants had no bread but only barley soup. New experiences were awaiting him there. The farmer's wife, whose guest he was, gave birth to a child during the night. Goldmund was present, having been hauled out of the straw to help, although as it turned out all he had to do was hold the flare while the midwife was busy about the woman. For the first time he witnessed a birth; his astonished eyes fastened avidly on the face of the woman in labour, and suddenly he was richer by a new experience. At least it seemed to him that what he was observing in the woman's face was truly remarkable; for in the light of the pine torch, while he stared with his intense curiosity into the face of the woman in her labour pains, he was struck by something unexpected: the lines in the face of the screaming woman differed little from those he had seen at the moment of supreme passion in the faces of other women. Granted the facial expression of great pain was more extreme and more distorting than that of great ecstasy, yet basically the one was no different from the other; there were the same grimaces, the same spasms, the same climax and subsiding. He was amazed, although uncomprehendingly, by this revelation that pain and ecstasy could resemble one another like siblings.

An additional experience awaited him in this village. Because of the neighbour's wife, of whom he had caught sight the morning following the birth and who had responded at once to the question in his lovelorn eyes, he spent a second night in the village, making the woman very happy, for after a long interval and all the inflammatory and ultimately disappointing love affairs of the past weeks, this was the first time his sexual urge could be satisfied again. And this postponement led to yet another experience. It was due to her that on the second day in that very hamlet he met a brother-wayfarer, a tall, devil-may-care fellow by the name of Viktor, in appearance part-priest and part-highwayman, who hailed him with scraps of Latin and declared himself to be a travelling student, although in years he was well beyond the student stage.

This man with the pointed beard greeted Goldmund with a certain cordiality and a vagabond humour with which he immediately won over the youth. When asked where he had been a student and where he was heading, the odd fellow declared:

'Upon my soul, I have attended more than enough seats of learning! I have been in Cologne and Paris, and rarely has anything more profound been said about the metaphysics of liver sausage than in my dissertation at Leyden. Since then, *amice*, I, poor wretch that I am, have been travelling throughout the German Empire, my precious self suffering agonies of hunger and thirst. They call me the Peasants' Ogre, and my profession is to instruct young women in Latin and to conjure the smoked sausage from the chimney into my belly. My goal is the bed of the burgomaster's wife, and I fear that, unless I am first devoured by the crows, I shall not be spared the need to devote myself to the tiresome occupation of archbishop. It is better, my young friend, to live from hand to mouth than vice versa and, after all, no roast hare has ever felt more comfortable than in my poor stomach. The King of Bohemia is my brother, and the Father of us all feeds him as well as me, but He leaves me to do the best part myself, and the day before yesterday, hard-hearted as fathers are, He wanted to misuse me to save the life of a half-starved wolf. Had I not slain the beast, sir, you would never have had the honour of making my pleasant acquaintance. *In saecula saeculorum, Amen.*'

Although Goldmund, not yet familiar with the gallows humour and tall stories of this species, was a little afraid of the lanky, uncouth fellow and the disagreeable laughter with which he accompanied his own jokes, there was something about the hard-boiled vagabond that appealed to him, and he was easily persuaded that they should continue their journey together; for whether or not the story about slaying the wolf was a fabrication, together they would in any case be stronger and have less to fear. However, before moving on, Brother Viktor wanted to talk Latin, as he called it, with the peasants and found one to take him in. But his behaviour was not such as Goldmund had deemed proper in all his wanderings when given hospitality: Viktor went from cottage to cottage, chatting with each farm-wife, stuck his nose in every stable and every kitchen and seemed unwilling to leave the hamlet until he had exacted tribute from every house. He regaled the peasants with tales of war in southern lands; at the hearthside he sang the ballad of the battle of Pavia; to the old folks he recommended cures for rheumatism and loss of teeth. He seemed to know everything and to have been everywhere, and he stuffed his shirt above his belt with as much donated bread, nuts and dried pears as it would hold.

In amazement, Goldmund watched him tirelessly pursuing his campaign, sometimes scaring the locals, sometimes winning them over by flattery. He observed him putting on airs and soaking up admiration, at times spouting scraps of

Latin and feigning scholarship, at others cutting a figure with his colourful, impudent thieves' cant and, in the midst of all his story-telling and bogus learned speech, registering with sharp, watchful eyes every face, every drawer being opened, every bowl and every loaf. Goldmund realized that this was a crafty sort, a vagrant who had seen and experienced much, had known severe hunger and cold and who, in the grim struggle for a marginal, precarious life, had become wily and brazen. So that was what became of those who spent long years on the road. Would he in time become like that too?

The next day they moved on, and for the first time Goldmund had a taste of companionship on the road. During the three days they travelled together, Goldmund picked up a thing or two from Viktor. The by now instinctive habit of relating everything to the three primary needs of the homeless – protecting life and limb, finding shelter for the night and acquiring food – had taught the inveterate tramp many things. To recognize the proximity of human habitation from the most inconspicuous signs, even in winter, even at night, or to examine minutely every nook and cranny in forest and field for its suitability as a place to rest or sleep, or upon entering a room to sense instantly the level of affluence or poverty in which the owner lived as well as the degree of his benevolence, or of his curiosity or fear: these were skills of which Viktor had become a master, and he passed on much useful information to his young companion. When Goldmund once countered that he did not like to approach people in such a calculating manner and maintained that, although he was not acquainted with all these skills, his courteous request for hospitality had rarely been refused, Viktor laughed and said good-naturedly:

'Well, of course, young Goldmund, you may succeed with that, you're so young and handsome and innocent-looking – that will always open doors for you. The women fancy you, and the men think: Oh well, he's harmless enough, he won't hurt anyone. But look, young feller, a man gets older, and the child's face grows a beard and acquires wrinkles, and the breeches get holes, and before he knows it he is an ugly and unwelcome guest, and now, instead of youth and innocence, only hunger stares from his eyes. When that happens, he has to have grown tough and learned something of the world, otherwise he'll soon be lying on the dungheap with dogs pissing on him. But I have a feeling that you won't be on the road like this for long anyway. Your hands are too delicate, your curls too handsome. Soon you'll be sneaking off to where life is easier, into a nice warm conjugal bed or a nice fat monastery, or a well-heated study. Besides, you're wearing such fine clothes you could be taken for a young nobleman!'

With a laugh he passed his hand over Goldmund's clothing, and Goldmund could feel the hand searching out and groping at all the pockets and seams, so he pulled away, thinking of his ducat. He told Viktor about having stayed in the knight's household and how he had earned his fine clothes by Latin scribblings. But Viktor wanted to know why he had left such a cosy nest in mid-winter weather, and Goldmund, unused to lying, told him a little about the knight's two daughters. This set off the first quarrel between the companions. Viktor declared Goldmund to be an unmitigated ass for simply running away and abandoning the manor house and the maidens to their fate. That would have to be rectified, he said, and he would see to it. They would go to the manor, where of course Goldmund must keep out of sight, but Goldmund was to leave everything to him. Goldmund must write a note to Lydia, saying such and such, and with that Viktor would go to the manor and, by the wounds of our Saviour, would not return from it without bringing money and suchlike with him. And so on. Goldmund would not agree and finally lost his temper; he refused to listen to another word on the matter or to reveal the knight's name or the way to the manor.

On seeing him so angry, Viktor laughed again and adopted his good-natured front. 'Now, now,' he said, 'calm down! All I'm saying is, you're letting a good catch slip away from us, my boy, and that's not really very nice and friendly of you. But you won't do it, you're a noble gentleman. You will return on horseback to your manor and marry the young lady! My, my, how full your head is of noble foolishness! Well, I don't care – let's move on till our toes drop off from frostbite!'

Goldmund remained moody and silent until the evening. However, since they had not come upon any habitation or other human traces that day, he was glad to have Viktor look for a place to spend the night, build a sheltering wall between two treetrunks at the edge of the forest, and spread a pile of fir branches for them to lie on. They ate bread and cheese from Viktor's full pockets. Goldmund, ashamed of his anger and doing his best to be helpful, offered his companion his woollen doublet for the night, and they agreed to take turns keeping watch for wild animals.

Goldmund took the first watch, while Viktor stretched out on the fir branches. For a long time Goldmund stood quietly leaning against a tree so as not to keep his companion from falling asleep. Then, feeling cold he began walking up and down, each time increasing the distance covered. He saw the tops of the fir trees pointing into the pale sky, felt solemn and a bit apprehensive in the deep silence of the winter night, was aware of his warm, living heart beating solitarily in the cold, unresponding night and, returning quietly, listened to the breathing of his sleeping companion. More strongly than ever he was pierced by a sense of homelessness, of having failed to build house or monastery walls between himself and the great fear, a sense of walking alone through the incomprehensible, hostile world, alone among the cold, mocking stars, among the lurking animals, among the patient, steadfast trees.

No, he thought, he would never become like Viktor, even if he were to spend the rest of his life wandering the face of the earth. He would never be able to learn that way of fending off dread, those furtive, thieving survival skills, nor that loud, brazen clowning, that voluble gallows humour of the braggart. Maybe the clever, cocksure fellow was right, maybe Goldmund would never be his equal, never become wholly a vagabond, and would one day crawl back behind walls. Yet he would always remain homeless and purposeless; he would never feel truly protected and secure. The world would always surround him, mysteriously beautiful, mysteriously sinister, and he would always be compelled to listen to the silence in whose midst his heart beat so fearfully and so ephemerally. Only a few stars were to be seen. There was no wind, but high in the sky there seemed to be movement among the clouds.

After a long time Viktor woke up – Goldmund had not wanted to waken him – and called out. 'Come on,' he said, 'you'd better get some sleep now or you'll be good for nothing tomorrow.'

Goldmund obediently lay down on the branches and closed his eyes. Tired though he was, he did not fall asleep. His thoughts kept him awake and, apart from these, a feeling he would not admit to himself, a feeling of nervousness and suspicion on account of his companion. It now seemed inexplicable that he should have told this coarse, boisterous person, this jokester and brazen beggar, about Lydia! He was angry at him and at himself and thought uneasily about the best way to split up with him.

However, he must have dozed off because he was startled and surprised to feel Viktor's hands on him, carefully exploring his clothing. In one pocket was his knife, in the other the ducat; Viktor was bound to steal both if he found them. He pretended to be asleep, drowsily turning from side to side and moving his arms, and Viktor withdrew. Goldmund was furious with him and decided to leave him next day.

But when, after an hour or so, Viktor bent over him again and resumed his exploration, Goldmund was filled with cold rage. Without moving, he opened his eyes and said contemptuously: 'Go away – I have nothing on me worth stealing!'

In a terrified reaction the thief made a grab for Goldmund's neck and pressed his hands round it. When Goldmund struggled to defend himself, the thief tightened his grip and at the same time knelt on Goldmund's chest. When Goldmund could no longer breathe, he writhed and jerked about and, when he could not free himself, mortal fear suddenly transfixed and inspired him: he managed to get his hand into his pocket and, while the thief continued to strangle him, brought out his short hunting-knife and thrust it blindly several times into the man kneeling on him. After a moment, Viktor's grip loosened, there was air to breathe and, panting and gasping, Goldmund drank in the taste of his restored life. When he tried to raise himself, his tall companion, groaning horribly, collapsed in a limp, soft heap on top of him, and his blood ran over Goldmund's face. At last Goldmund could get to his feet. By the night's grey light he saw the long, collapsed figure; his outstretched hand met blood everywhere. He raised the man's head, and it fell back as heavy and limp as a sack. Blood continued to gush from his chest and neck, and life flowed from his mouth in spasmodic, diminishing sighs.

Now I have killed a man, Goldmund thought, and kept on thinking it as he knelt over the dying man and watched the pallor spread over his face. 'Dear Mother of God, now I have killed,' he heard himself say.

Suddenly he could no longer bear to remain. He picked up his knife and wiped it on the woollen doublet the other man was wearing, the one Lydia's hands had knitted for her beloved. Putting the knife into its wooden sheath and back into his pocket, he jumped up and ran off as fast as he could.

The death of the jolly vagabond weighed heavily on his soul. When morning came, he shuddered as he took handfuls of snow to wash off all the blood he had spilled, and he spent another day and night wandering about, scared and aimless. It was the demands of his body that finally roused him and put an end to his fear-racked remorse.

Lost in the desolate, snow-bound countryside, with no shelter, no path, no food and almost no sleep, he was in desperate straits. Hunger was growling in his stomach like a wild beast. Several times he lay down exhausted wherever he happened to be, closed his eyes and resigned himself, wishing only to fall asleep and die in the snow. But again and again his instinct brought him to his feet; desperately, avidly, he would run for his life, and in his extremity he was revived and intoxicated by the irrational power and passion of the refusal to die, the immense force of the naked urge to live. With hands blue with cold he picked the small, withered berries from a snow-covered juniper-bush and chewed the brittle, bitter fruit mixed with fir needles. It tasted harsh and acrid, and he gulped down handfuls of snow to quench his thirst. Breathing into his numbed hands, he sat on a hillock for a brief respite. Avidly he scanned the countryside in all directions: nothing but moor and forest, no trace of human life. A few crows circled overhead, and he looked up at them balefully. No, they were never going to make a meal of him as long as an ounce of strength remained in his legs or a spark of warmth in his blood!

Getting to his feet he resumed his inexorable race with death. He ran and ran. In the fever of exhaustion and ultimate exertion, strange thoughts took possession of him, and he carried on demented conversations, sometimes inaudibly, sometimes aloud. He addressed Viktor, the man he had stabbed, his words rough and mocking: 'Well, my smart brother, how do you feel? Is the moon shining through your guts, fellow, are the foxes tearing at your ears? You say you killed a wolf? Did you bite its throat or tear out its tail, eh? You wanted to steal my ducat, you old scrounger! But young Goldmund surprised you, didn't he – didn't he, old man? He tickled your ribs! And all the time your pockets were full of bread and sausage and cheese, you bastard, you greedy pig!' Choking out and barking such taunts as he ran, he swore at the dead man, gloated over him, jeered at him for letting himself be killed, the clot, the stupid braggart!

But then his thoughts and words ceased to concern poor, lanky Viktor. Now he saw Julie before him, pretty little Julie, just as she had left him that night. He cried out countless endearments to her; with rambling, shameless words of love he tried to seduce her, to persuade her to come to him, to drop her shift, to ascend with him to Heaven, for one hour before he died, for one brief moment before his miserable end. Imploringly, temptingly, he addressed her high little breasts, her legs, the fuzzy fair hair under her arms.

And again, while trotting on stiff, stumbling legs through the withered, snow-covered heath, he began to whisper, reeling with wretchedness, triumphant with a burning thirst for life; and now it was Narcissus to whom he spoke, whom he told of his new ideas, clever thoughts and jests.

'Are you scared, Narcissus?' he asked him. 'Are you horror-struck – have you discovered something? Yes, O revered one, the world is full of death, full of death squatting on every fence, standing behind every tree, and it is useless for you to build walls and dormitories and chapels and churches. Death looks through the window and laughs, Death knows each one of you so thoroughly! In the middle of the night you hear him laughing outside your windows and calling your names. Go ahead and sing your psalms, go and light your candles at the altar, recite your Vespers and Matins, and collect herbs in the laboratory and books in the library! Are you fasting, my friend? Depriving yourself of sleep? He's ready to help you, is friend Death. He will deprive you of everything, right down to your bones. Hurry, beloved friend, run fast, the Grim Reaper is abroad in the fields. Run and see that you keep your bones together, they want to scatter, they won't stay with us. Oh, our poor bones, our poor gullet and stomach, our pathetic little brain inside our skull! Everything wants to get away, everything wants to go to the Devil. The crows, those black-robed priests, are waiting in the tree.'

By now Goldmund was utterly lost, with no idea of where he was running, where he was, what he was saying, whether he was lying down or standing up. He stumbled over bushes and collided with trees, his hands plunging into snow and thorns as he fell. But the urge in him was strong, for ever pulling him on, for ever driving him farther and farther as he fled blindly on. His final and total collapse occurred in the same hamlet where a few days earlier he had met the travelling scholar, where during the night he had held the pine flare over the woman giving birth. As he lay there, the villagers came running up and stood round him chattering, but he was past hearing anything. The woman whose favours he had enjoyed recognized him and was shocked by his appearance. Taking pity on him, and ignoring her husband's protests, she dragged the half-dead man into the stable.

It did not take long for Goldmund to get back on his feet and be able to resume his wanderings. Sleep, the warmth of the stable, and the goat's milk the woman gave him to drink, helped him to recover his senses and his strength, except that his most recent experiences had shifted into the past, as if a long time had elapsed. Tramping the roads with Viktor, the cold, anxious winter night under those fir trees, the terrible struggle on the bed of branches, the shocking manner of his companion's death, the days and nights of cold and hunger when he had lost his way: all that had become the past, and he had almost forgotten it. But it was not forgotten: he had merely weathered it; it was over. Something remained, something inexpressible, something terrible but also valuable, something submerged yet never to be forgotten, an experience, a taste on the tongue, a ring around the heart. In scarcely two years he must have explored the joys and pains of the homeless life to their very depths: the solitude, the freedom, listening to forest and wildlife, the roving, faithless love affairs, the direst extremity. He had spent days as a guest of the summer fields and meadows, days and weeks in the forest, days in the snow, days in mortal fear and mortal danger; and, of all this, the strongest and strangest element had been resisting death, knowing himself to be puny and wretched and threatened yet, in the ultimate desperate fight against death, to feel life's wonderful, terrible force and tenacity within himself. That still reverberated, that remained engraved on his heart, like the gestures and facial expressions of ecstasy that so greatly resembled those of the woman giving birth and the man near death. The way that woman had screamed, her whole face contorted; the way his companion had collapsed as his blood streamed silently away! And he himself – the way during those days of starvation he had felt death lurking all around him; the pain of that hunger, and the cold – how cold he had felt! And how he had fought, how he had punched Death in the nose – with what mortal fear and what grim passion he had defended himself! Beyond that, it seemed to him, there was not much left to be experienced. He might have been able to discuss this with Narcissus, but with no one else.

On first regaining full consciousness as he lay on his straw pallet in the stable, Goldmund felt in vain for the ducat in his pocket. Could he have lost it as he staggered along, half unconscious, that last terrible day of hunger? He mulled this over for a long time. He had grown fond of the ducat and didn't like the idea of losing it. Although money meant little to him and he hardly knew its value, this gold coin had become important to him for two reasons. It was the only gift from Lydia remaining to him now that the woollen doublet had been left with Viktor in the forest, drenched with Viktor's blood. And then it had been the gold coin whose theft he refused to tolerate; for its sake he had defended himself against Viktor, and for its sake he had killed him in his extremity. If the ducat was now lost, the entire experience of that horrible night would in a sense have lost all meaning and value. After much thought he took the farmer's wife into his confidence.

'Christine,' he whispered to her, 'I had a gold piece in my pocket, and now it's not there any more.'

'So you've noticed, have you?' she replied with an oddly affectionate yet knowing little smile which so charmed him that, in spite of his weakness, he put his arms round her.

'What a strange lad you are,' she said tenderly. 'So clever and so refined and yet so stupid! Does one run round with a loose ducat in an open pocket? Oh you childish, adorable little fool! I found your gold piece as soon as I laid you down in the straw.'

'You did? And where is it now?'

'Look for it!' She laughed and actually let him look for quite a while before showing him the place in his jacket into which she had firmly sewn it. She added a quantity of good motherly advice which he promptly forgot, but he never forgot her act of kindness and that sly, good-natured laughter in her peasant face. He did his best to show her his gratitude, and when he was fit to resume his wanderings and wanted to leave she held him back: there would soon be a change of the moon, she said, which was bound to mean milder weather. And so it turned out. As he moved on, the snow lay grey and sickly, and the air was heavy with moisture. He could hear the south wind moaning in the air above.

Chapter Ten

Once again the ice was drifting down the rivers; once again there was a scent of violets under rotting leaves; once again Goldmund travelled through the seasons, with insatiable eyes drinking in the changing colours of forests, hills and clouds, roaming from farm to farm, from village to village, from woman to woman, spending many a chilly evening crouched, depressed and heartsick, beneath a window showing a red glow from a lamp that radiated – unattainable! – all there was of happiness, home and peace on earth. Everything recurred, again and again, everything he thought he knew so well by now. Everything recurred yet each time was different: tramping over field and moor or stony roads, sleeping in summertime in the forest, strolling in villages behind the rows of young girls returning home, hand in hand, from tossing hay or picking hops; the first shivers of autumn, the cruel early frosts – everything recurred, once, twice, endlessly, as the chequered ribbon unrolled before his eyes.

Much rain and much snow had fallen on Goldmund when one day he climbed up through a beech wood where the trees, though bare, already showed green buds. From the ridge he saw spread beneath him a new landscape that gladdened his eyes and released a flood of anticipation, desire and hope in his heart. For days he had known he was not far from this area and was expecting it; now it took him by surprise at this hour of noon, and the impact of his first visual impression confirmed and reinforced his expectations. Between grey treetrunks and gently swaying branches he looked down into a green and brown valley in the middle of which shimmered the glassy blue of a wide river. Now, he knew, there would for a long time be no more roaming through lonely, trackless moor and forest where a farm or a poor hamlet was seldom to be found. Down there flowed the river, and beside the river ran one of the most beautiful and renowned highways of the Empire. Down there lay a rich and prosperous land; rafts and boats were moving along, and the road led to picturesque villages, castles, monasteries and rich cities. Anyone was free to travel this road for many days and weeks without having to worry that it might suddenly, like the miserable little farm-tracks, peter out somewhere in a forest or swamp. Something new lay ahead, and he looked forward to it.

The evening of that same day he found himself in a charming village situated between the river and the red, vine-covered slopes along the great highway. The attractive timberwork of the gabled houses was painted red, there were arched gateways and steep cobbled lanes, and from a smithy a fiery glow and the ringing tones of an anvil issued on to the street. The new arrival investigated all the lanes and hidden corners, breathed in the smell of barrels and wine at cellar doors, and the watery, fishy odour along the banks of the river. He inspected church and churchyard and did not forget to look for a suitable barn to slip into for the night. But first he wanted to try his luck at the parsonage by asking for some food. He found a stout, red-haired priest there who plied him with questions and to whom, with a few suppressions and a few fabrications, he related the story of his life. Thereupon he was kindly received and had to spend the evening over good food and wine in long conversations with his host.

The next day he resumed his journey along the road that followed the river. He saw rafts and barges, and he passed carts, some of which took him along for a stretch. The spring days, packed with images, passed quickly. Villages and small towns gave him shelter, women smiled behind garden fences or knelt on the brown earth planting seedlings, and in the evenings girls sang in the village lanes.

At a mill he met a young girl whom he found so attractive that he spent two days in the area prowling around her. She laughed and chatted happily with him, and he almost wished he were a mill-hand and could stay there indefinitely. He sat with the fishermen and helped the drivers feed and curry their horses, in return for which he was given bread and meat and allowed to ride with them. After being alone so long, he delighted in this companionable world of people on the move, in the laughter among these loquacious, cheerful folk after his months of brooding, in his daily fill of ample food after long privation. He gladly abandoned himself to this happy wave as it bore him along, and the closer he approached the cathedral town, the more crowded and lively the highway became.

In one village, at dusk, he went for a stroll along the river bank under trees already in leaf. Calm and powerful, the river flowed along, the current sweeping and sighing under the roots of trees, and the moon came rising over the hill, casting lights on to the river and shadows under the trees. He came upon a girl sitting there weeping: she had had a quarrel with her lover, and now he was gone, leaving her all alone. Goldmund sat down beside her and listened to her lament. He stroked her hand, told her about the forest and about the deer, comforted her a little, made her laugh a little, and she did not resist his kiss. But at that moment her sweetheart came back to look for her: he had calmed down and was sorry about the quarrel. On finding Goldmund seated beside her, he hurled himself upon him, pummelling him with both fists. Goldmund had trouble fending him off but finally got the better of him. Cursing as he went, the fellow ran back into the village. The girl had long since fled.

Goldmund, not sure that he had seen the last of his opponent, abandoned his shelter and walked on half the night in the moonlight, through a silent, silvery world, very content and glad of his strong legs, until the dew washed the white dust from his shoes and, suddenly feeling tired, he lay down under the nearest tree and fell asleep. The day was well advanced when he was wakened by a tickle on his face. Still half asleep, he flapped at it awkwardly with his hand and fell asleep again, but was soon wakened once more by the same sensation. A peasant girl was standing there looking at him and tickling him with the tip of a willow branch. He scrambled to his feet, they nodded and smiled at each other, and she led him to a shed where, she said, he would find it more comfortable to sleep. For a while they slept there together; then she ran off and returned with a little pail of milk still warm from the cow. He gave her a blue hair ribbon he had found in a lane and tucked in his pocket, and they kissed once again before he went on his way. Her name was Franziska, and he was sorry to leave her.

That evening he found shelter in a monastery and in the morning attended mass. In his heart a thousand memories were churning, and he was seized with nostalgia at the smell of the cool, stone air under the vaulted ceilings, at the sound of flapping sandals in the flagstoned passages. When mass was over and silence had descended on the monastery church, Goldmund remained on his knees, strangely moved. He had had many dreams that night, and he felt a desire somehow to shed his past, somehow to change his life. Why this should be, he did not know: perhaps it was merely the memory of Mariabronn and his pious youth that so moved him. He felt impelled to confess and purify himself. There were so many little sins, so many little vices, to acknowledge, but weighing on him more heavily than anything else was the death of Viktor, who had died by his hand. He found a priest to whom he confessed various misdeeds but mainly the knife thrusts into poor Viktor's throat and back. What a long time it had been since he had last confessed! The number and gravity of his sins seemed considerable to him; he would have been prepared to do a hefty penance for them. But his confessor seemed familiar with the life of wayfarers. He was not shocked but listened quietly, rebuking and admonishing Goldmund earnestly and kindly, without thought of condemnation.

Much relieved, Goldmund got to his feet, prayed at the altar as instructed by his confessor and was about to leave the church when a sunbeam shone through one of the windows. Following its direction he saw in a side-chapel a statue that appealed to him so greatly that he turned to it with eyes of love and studied it with reverence and deep emotion. It was a wooden statue of the Madonna standing with gently bowed head; and the way her blue cloak fell from her slender shoulders, the way she stretched out her delicate, girlish hand, the look in her eyes above the suffering mouth, and the curve of her lovely brow – all this was more alive, more tender and soulful, than anything he remembered ever having seen before. His eyes could not get their fill of that mouth, or of that exquisite movement of the neck. He seemed to be looking at something he had seen many times in dreams and fantasies, something for which he had yearned many times. As often as he turned to go, he was always drawn back again.

When finally he turned to leave, he found his confessor standing behind him.

'You find her beautiful?' the priest asked with a smile.

'Inexpressibly beautiful,' Goldmund replied.

'Many people have said that,' the priest went on. 'And others again say she is not a fitting Madonna, that she is much too modern and worldly and that everything is exaggerated and spurious. One hears many arguments about it. So you like her – I am glad to hear that. She has been in our church for only a year: a patron of our house donated her. She was carved by Master Niklaus.'

'Master Niklaus? Who is he? Where is he? Do you know him? Please tell me about him! He must be a glorious, inspired person to be able to create something like this!'

'I don't know much about him. He is a wood-carver in our cathedral town, a day's journey from here, and enjoys a great reputation as an artist. Generally speaking, artists are not saints, and doubtless he is not one either, but he is certainly a gifted and high-minded person. I have seen him a few times . . .'

'Oh, you have seen him! What does he look like?'

'My son, you appear to be quite bewitched by him. Well, go and see him and take him greetings from Father Bonifazius.'

Goldmund thanked him effusively. With a smile the priest left him, but Goldmund remained standing for a long time before the mysterious figure whose breast seemed to rise and fall and whose face contained so much pain and so much sweetness that it took his breath away.

A changed man, he left the church, his footsteps taking him through a completely altered world. From the moment he stood before that sweet, sacred wooden statue, Goldmund possessed something he had never possessed before, something he had often smiled at or envied in others: a goal! He had a goal, and perhaps he would attain it, and perhaps his whole haphazard life would acquire a higher meaning and value. The new feeling suffused him with joy and fear and lent wings to his steps. This fine, lively highway on which he was travelling was no longer what it had been yesterday, a festive playground and comfortable sojourn. Now it was merely a highway, the road to the city, the road to the master. Impatiently he pressed on. Arriving well before dusk, he saw resplendent towers beyond the walls, coats of arms and shields chiselled and painted above the gateway arch, walked through it with quickened pulse and paying scant attention to the noise and the cheerful throngs in the narrow streets and lanes, to the knights on horseback, the carriages and coaches. Neither knights nor carriages, neither town nor bishop meant anything to him. When he asked the very first person under the arch where Master Niklaus lived, he was bitterly disappointed that the man had never heard of him.

He came to a square surrounded by handsome buildings, many of them decorated with paintings or carvings. Over one entrance stood the tall, flamboyant figure of a soldier of fortune painted in vivid colours. He was not as impressive as the statue in the monastery church, but the way he stood there flexing his calf muscles and thrusting his bearded chin out into the world made Goldmund think this statue might have been carved by the same master. He entered the house, knocked at doors, climbed stairs and finally came upon a gentleman wearing a fur-trimmed velvet coat whom he asked where he might find Master Niklaus. What did he want of him? came the curt rejoinder. Goldmund restrained himself with difficulty and merely declared that he had a message for the master. The gentleman named the lane where the master lived, and by the time Goldmund, after much questioning, had found his way there, darkness had fallen. Apprehensive yet happy, he stood outside the master's house looking up at the windows and was tempted to go in then and there. However, mindful that the hour was late and that he was hot and dusty from the day's journey, he forced himself to wait. But he stood outside the house for a long time. A window lit up, and just as he turned to leave he saw a figure move to the window, a very beautiful young girl with soft lamplight shining through her hair.

The following morning, when the town was once again awake and noisy, Goldmund washed his face and hands in the monastery where he had been a guest for the night, then shook the dust from his clothes and shoes. He found his way back to the lane and knocked at the front door. A servant appeared and at first refused to take him to her master, but he managed to mollify the old woman, and she conducted him into a large room. There in his workshop, wearing an apron, stood the master, a tall, bearded man some forty or fifty years old, Goldmund thought. He looked at the stranger out of piercing blue eyes and brusquely asked what he wanted. Goldmund delivered the greetings from Father Bonifazius.

'Is that all?'

'Master,' said Goldmund, hardly able to breathe. 'I have seen your Blessed Virgin in the monastery there. Ah, don't look at me so sternly – it is sheer love and veneration that have led me to you. I am not easily frightened. I have lived for a long time as a wayfarer and have tasted forest, snow and hunger, and there is no living soul of whom I might be afraid. But I am afraid of you. I have one single, great desire that fills my heart to bursting.'

'And what is that desire?'

'I should like to become your apprentice and learn from you.'

'You are not the only one with that desire, young man. But I do not care for apprentices, and I already have two assistants. Where do you come from, and who are your parents?'

'I have no parents, and I come from nowhere. I was a pupil in a monastery where I learned Latin and Greek. Then I ran away, and for years I have been on the move, until this day.'

'And why do you think you should become a wood-carver? Have you ever tried anything like that? Have you any drawings?'

'I have done many drawings, but I no longer have them. As for why I should like to learn this art, I can tell you that. I have done a lot of thinking, I have seen many faces and figures and I have thought about them, and some of those thoughts continue to haunt me and leave me no peace. I have noticed how in a human figure a certain shape, a certain line, keeps recurring, that a forehead corresponds to a knee, a shoulder to a hip, and how in essence all that is identical with the nature and soul of the person who happens to have a knee like that, a shoulder and forehead like that. And I have also noticed – I saw it one night when I had to help a woman in labour – that the greatest pain and the most intense ecstasy produce a very similar facial expression.'

The master gave the stranger a penetrating look. 'Do you know what you are saying?'

'Yes, Master, it is so. That was the very thing which to my utmost delight and consternation I found expressed in your Blessed Virgin, and that is why I have come. How much suffering there is in that lovely, sweet face, and how all that suffering has been transformed into a smile of pure bliss! When I saw that, I was as if transfixed by fire. All those thoughts and dreams throughout the years seemed confirmed, suddenly they were no longer useless, and I knew at once what I had to do and where I had to go. Dear Master Niklaus, I beg you from the bottom of my heart to let me be your pupil!'

Without relaxing his expression, Niklaus had listened attentively. 'Young man,' he said, 'you can speak remarkably well on the subject of art. Moreover, I am amazed that at your age you can find so much to say about ecstasy and pain. I would deem it a pleasure to spend an evening discussing this topic with you over a beaker of wine. But listen: to have a pleasant, intelligent conversation together is not the same thing as spending several years living and working together. This is a workshop, a place for working, not for chatting, and what counts here is not the ideas a person has and is able to express, but solely what a person is capable of producing with his hands. You seem to be serious about it, so I shall not simply send you away. Let us see what you can do. Have you ever modelled anything out of clay or wax?'

Goldmund immediately recalled the dream he had long ago, in which he had kneaded little mud figures that stood up and grew into giants. But he did not mention this, merely stating that he had never attempted such work.

'Good. So you will draw something. Over there is a table, and paper and charcoal. Sit down and draw. You can stay until noon or even until the end of the day. Perhaps then I shall be able to see what you are good for. So, that's enough talk. I shall return to my work. You go to yours.'

Goldmund sat down at the drawing-table in the chair indicated by Niklaus. He was in no hurry to start. For the time being he sat as still and expectant as any nervous pupil, staring across with curiosity and affection at the master, who stood with his back half-turned to him as he resumed work on a small clay figure. Goldmund looked closely at this man in whose greying head and tough but inspired workman's hands dwelled such magical forces. Niklaus did not look as Goldmund had imagined him: he seemed older, more modest, more down-to-earth, much less exuberant and endearing and far from happy. Now that the relentless scrutiny of the master was focused on his own work, Goldmund was free to take in every detail of his appearance. This man, he thought, might also have been a scholar, a quiet, rigorous researcher dedicated to an undertaking that many of his predecessors had begun and that one day he would have to pass on to his successors: a demanding, never-ending task combining the work and dedication of many generations. That, at least, was what the observer read from the master's face: much patience, much acquired knowledge and deliberation, much modesty and acceptance of the dubious value of all human endeavour, were written there, but also a belief in his commitment. The language of his hands, however, was different; between them and his face there was a contradiction. Those hands worked the clay they were modelling with firm but highly sensitive fingers. They handled the clay as a lover's hands would treat the beloved – ardently, full of tender emotion and desire but without distinguishing between taking and giving, voluptuously and devoutly, with the sure and masterful touch that came from profound, age-old experience. Goldmund watched those inspired hands with delight and admiration. He would have liked to draw the master had it not been for that contradiction between face and hands, which inhibited him.

After about an hour of observing the sculptor quietly working away, Goldmund, full of searching thoughts about the secret of this man, began to feel a different mental image forming inside him, the image of the man he knew better than anyone else, the man he had loved and deeply admired, and this image was seamless, without contradiction, although it, too, had many different facets and recalled many struggles. It was the image of his friend Narcissus. In it, unity and wholeness became ever more condensed and the innate laws governing that beloved person ever more apparent: the fine head shaped by the spirit, the firm, disciplined mouth and the somewhat sad eyes ennobled by service to the spirit; the gaunt shoulders, the long neck and the delicate hands animated by the struggle for spirituality. Never since leaving the monastery had he seen his friend so clearly, possessed his image so entirely.

As if in a dream, almost subconsciously yet full of eagerness and a sense of inevitability, Goldmund began to draw with careful strokes, his fingers moving reverently round the figure dwelling in his heart, forgetting the master, himself and the place where he was. He did not notice the light gradually moving round the room, did not notice the master occasionally glancing across at him. As if engaged in a sacrificial deed, he completed his task, the task his heart had set him: to raise the image of his friend, and to preserve it as it lived this day in his soul. In the back of his mind he perceived what he was doing as the paying of a debt, an act of gratitude.

Niklaus walked over to the drawing-table, saying: 'It is twelve o'clock, I am going for dinner – you can come along with me. Let me see – you've drawn something?'

Stepping behind Goldmund he looked down at the big sheet of paper, then pushed him aside and carefully picked up the sheet in his skilled hands. Goldmund had awakened from his dream and now looked with nervous expectation at the master, who stood holding the drawing in both hands and carefully scrutinizing it with his sharp, pale-blue eyes.

'Who is this person?' asked Niklaus after a while.

'My friend, a young monk and scholar.'

'Good. Go and wash your hands. You'll find a fountain out there in the courtyard. Then we'll go for dinner. My assistants aren't here, they're working out of town.'

Goldmund obediently went in search of the courtyard and the fountain and washed his hands. He would have given much to know the master's thoughts. On his return he found the workshop empty, but he could hear Niklaus moving about in the next room. The master reappeared, having washed his hands and exchanged his apron for a handsome cloth coat in which he looked imposing and dignified. He led the way up a staircase whose walnut newel posts were topped by carved cherubs' heads, then across a landing with many statues, old and new, and into a pleasant room with hardwood floor, walls and ceiling. A table, already laid, stood in the corner by the window.

A young girl came hurrying in, and Goldmund recognized her as the beauty he had noticed the evening before.

'Lisbeth,' said the master, 'you must lay another place – I have brought a guest. This is – why, I really don't even know his name yet!'

Goldmund told him.

'Goldmund, then. Can we eat now?'

'In a moment, Father.'

She brought a plate, hurried out, and soon came back with the serving-woman, who placed the food on the table: pork, lentils and white bread. During the meal the father discussed this and that with his daughter, while Goldmund sat silent, eating sparingly and feeling insecure and depressed. He found the daughter very attractive, a handsome, womanly figure almost as tall as her father, but she sat, demure and quite unapproachable, as if behind glass, directing neither a word nor a glance at the stranger.

When the meal was over the master said: 'I am going to rest for half an hour. You go down to the workshop, or take a stroll outside, and we'll discuss the matter later.'

With a nod, Goldmund left the room. An hour or more had passed since the master had seen his drawing, and not a word had he said about it. Now he was supposed to wait another half-hour! Well, it couldn't be helped: he waited. Not wanting to see his drawing again, he avoided the workshop and went into the courtyard, where he sat down on the edge of the watering-trough and watched the steady trickle of spring water flowing from the pipe into the deep stone basin, causing miniature waves as it fell and carrying down with it a little air that kept struggling up again in tiny bubbles. In the dark mirror of the water he saw his own reflection and thought how this Goldmund looking at him from the water had long since ceased to be the Goldmund of the monastery or Lydia's

153

Goldmund, and even the Goldmund of the forests belonged to the past. He thought how he and every human being was carried along through constant change to final dissolution, whereas the image as created by the artist remained for ever fixed and immutable.

Perhaps, he thought, the root of all art, and perhaps also of all intellectual activity, is the fear of death. We fear it, we shudder at the ephemeral nature of all things, we grieve to see the constant cycle of fading flowers and falling leaves and are aware in our own hearts of the certainty that we too are ephemeral and will soon fade away. So when as artists we create images, and as thinkers we search for laws and formulate ideas, we do so in order to salvage something from the great Dance of Death, to create something that will outlast our lifetime. The woman after whom the master fashioned his beautiful Madonna may have already faded or died, and soon he too will be dead: others will live in his house, others will eat at his table. But his work will remain. In the quiet monastery church it will continue to shine for another hundred years and much longer; it will always remain beautiful, always smile with that same mouth which is as full of life as it is of sadness.

Hearing the master coming downstairs, Goldmund hurried into the workshop. Master Niklaus paced up and down, looking repeatedly at Goldmund's drawing. Finally he stopped by the window and said in his dry, deliberate manner: 'It is customary with us here for an apprentice to learn for at least four years and for his father to pay the master an appropriate fee.'

Here he paused, and Goldmund thought the master was afraid of not receiving a fee from him. Quick as a flash he drew his knife from his pocket, slit open the seam round the hidden ducat, and pulled out the coin. Niklaus watched him in amazement and began to laugh when Goldmund offered him the gold piece.

'Ah, so that's what you have in mind?' he said, laughing. 'No, young man, keep your gold piece. Now, listen to me. I told you about our guild's normal practice in taking on apprentices. But I am no more an ordinary master than you are an ordinary apprentice, for the latter usually begins his apprenticeship at the age of thirteen or fourteen, or at most fifteen, and he must spend half his apprenticeship performing menial tasks and being at everybody's beck and call. But you are already fully mature, and at your age you could have long been a journeyman or even a master. An apprentice with a beard has yet to be seen in our guild. I have already told you that I do not wish to keep an apprentice in my house. Besides, you don't look in the least like someone who lets himself be ordered about or sent on errands.'

Goldmund's impatience had reached its peak. Each of the master's measured words stretched him on the rack and seemed to him intolerably boring and pedantic. Passionately he burst out: 'Why are you telling me all this when you have no intention of accepting me as an apprentice?'

The master continued imperturbably in the same manner: 'I have spent an hour thinking over your request. Now you must have the patience to listen to me. I have seen your drawing. It is not flawless, but it is beautiful. Were it not so, I would have made you a present of half a guilder, sent you on your way and forgotten you. I shall say no more about the drawing. I would like to help you to become an artist. Perhaps you are meant for that, and it is too late for you to become an apprentice. However, someone who has not been an apprentice and served his full apprenticeship cannot become either a journeyman or a master in our guild. Let that be clear. But I want you to make an attempt. If you find it possible to spend some time here in the town, you may come to me and learn a few things. This will be without obligation or contract. You may leave at any time.

But you can break a few wood-carving knives and ruin a few blocks of wood in my workshop, and if it turns out that you are not a wood-carver you will just have to turn to something else. Would you be satisfied with that?'

Goldmund had felt humbled and moved as he listened.

'I thank you most sincerely,' he exclaimed. 'I have no home, and I shall know how to survive in this town as I did out in the forests. I can understand that you do not wish to assume the care and responsibility for me that you would for an apprentice. I consider myself extremely fortunate to be allowed to learn from you. I thank you with all my heart for wanting to do this for me.'

Chapter Eleven

New impressions now surrounded Goldmund, and a new life began for him. Just as this land and this town had taken him in with all their lively, bountiful charm, so this new life took him in joyfully and with many promises. Although the underlying sadness and knowledge remained untouched, on the surface life intrigued him in all its many colours. Now began the happiest, most carefree period of Goldmund's life. Outwardly he came face to face with the rich cathedral town and all its art, its women, and a hundred pleasant pastimes and impressions; from within, his awakening artistic nature enriched him with new emotions and experiences. With the help of Master Niklaus he found lodging in the house of a gilder at the fish-market, and from both master and gilder he learned the art of handling wood and plaster, paint, varnish and gold leaf.

Goldmund was not one of those unfortunate artists who, while doubtless possessing great gifts, never find the right means to express them. There are many such to whom it is given to perceive, deeply and intensely, the beauty of this world and to carry lofty, noble images in their souls, yet who cannot find a way to bring forth such images and to display and communicate them for the delight of others. Goldmund did not suffer from this deficiency. He found it easy and a pleasure to use his hands and to learn the skills of the craft, just as he found it easy, while spending his spare time with a few companions, to learn how to play the lute and on Sundays how to dance on the village greens. All this he learned without effort. He did, to be sure, have to apply himself seriously to wood-carving, and inevitably he ran into difficulties and disappointments, ruined a few good pieces of wood, and on several occasions gave himself a nasty cut in his fingers. But he quickly got over the early stages and acquired skill. Nevertheless, the master was often very dissatisfied with him. He would say, for instance: 'It is a good thing you are not my apprentice or my journeyman, Goldmund. It is a good thing we know that you have come from the highways and the forests and that one day you will return to them. Anyone unaware that you are neither a townsman nor an artisan but a homeless idler might be tempted to demand a number of things of you that every master demands of his employees. You are quite a good worker when you happen to be in the mood, but last week you stayed away for two days. And yesterday, when you were supposed to be polishing the two angels in the outside workshop, you slept half the day.'

He was justified in his reproaches, and Goldmund listened in silence without protest. He was well aware that he was not a reliable, diligent person. As long as a job claimed his interest, confronted him with difficult problems or allowed him to take pride and pleasure in his dexterity, he was an enthusiastic worker. He disliked heavy manual work, and those tasks that were not difficult but required time and diligence – and in his trade there were many of these that needed to be done with painstaking attention – he often found quite intolerable. Sometimes he wondered about this himself. Had those few vagabond years been enough to make him lazy and unreliable? Was it his mother's heritage that was spreading and gaining the upper hand in him? Or what else was wrong? He could well remember his first years at the monastery when he had been such a diligent and successful student. How at that time had he been capable of all the patience he now lacked? How had he managed to devote himself so tirelessly to Latin syntax, and to learn all those Greek aorists that in his heart of hearts really meant little to him?

He spent some time thinking about this. It had been love that in those days had fortified and inspired him; his devotion to study had been nothing more than an intense wooing of Narcissus, whose love could be won only by gaining his respect and appreciation. In those days he had been able, for the sake of an appreciative glance from the beloved teacher, to exert himself for hours and days on end. Then the longed-for goal was achieved: Narcissus had become his friend and, oddly enough, it had been the scholarly Narcissus who had pointed out his unsuitability for the life of a scholar and had evoked in him the image of his lost mother. Instead of scholarship, monastic life and virtue, innate and powerful primal urges had become his masters: sex, the love of women, a craving for independence, for the life of a vagabond. But now he had seen the master's statue of the Madonna and had discovered the artist in himself; he had entered upon a new path and had settled down again. Where did he stand now? In which direction would his path lead him? What were the obstacles?

At first he was at a loss. Only this much was clear to him: although he greatly admired Master Niklaus, he certainly did not love him as he had once loved Narcissus. In fact he sometimes took pleasure in disappointing and annoying him. This had to do, it seemed to him, with the conflicting aspects of the master's character. The statues from Niklaus's hand, at least the best of them, were revered models for Goldmund, but the master himself was not a model for him.

Side by side with the artist who had carved that Blessed Virgin with the agonized and most beautiful mouth, side by side with the man of vision and of knowledge, whose hands were capable of transforming profound experiences and intuitions into visible shape, there dwelled in Master Niklaus another person: a somewhat severe and nervous paterfamilias and guildmaster, a widower who, with his daughter and an ugly serving-woman, led a quiet, unassuming life in his quiet house, a man who violently resisted Goldmund's strongest urges, a man who had settled into a quiet, moderate, orderly and decent life.

Although Goldmund revered his master, and although he would never have permitted himself to question others about him or to criticize him in the presence of others, after a year he knew every detail of all there was to be known about Niklaus. This master meant a lot to him; he loved him as much as he hated him, he was obsessed with him, and so, with love and mistrust, with ever-vigilant curiosity, the pupil delved into the hidden places of the man's nature and his life. He noted that Niklaus had neither apprentice nor journeyman living in his house, although there was room enough. He noted that he very seldom went out and just as seldom invited guests. He observed how touchingly and jealously he loved his beautiful daughter and tried to hide her from all the world. He also knew that, behind the widower's strict and premature abstinence, there were still lively impulses, that when a commission in another town occasionally required him to travel he could for those few days be astonishingly transformed and rejuvenated. And once, too, he had noticed that, in a small town some distance away where they were setting up a carved pulpit, Niklaus had secretly paid a visit to a prostitute one evening and for days afterwards had been restless and bad-tempered.

As time passed there was, apart from Goldmund's curiosity, something else that kept him in the master's house and preoccupied him. It was Lisbeth, the lovely daughter, to whom he was attracted. He rarely caught sight of her; she never set foot in the workshop, and he could not fathom whether her primness and reserve had merely been imposed upon her by her father or also corresponded to her own nature. It could not be overlooked that the master never again invited him for a meal and that he sought to prevent Goldmund from encountering her. Lisbeth was a most precious and sheltered maiden, he realized that, and there was no hope here for love without marriage. Any man wanting to marry her would have to come from a good family and be a member of one of the top guilds, and also, if possible, have money and own a house.

Lisbeth's beauty, so different from that of the gypsies and peasant women, had held Goldmund's eyes that very first day. There was something in her that was unknown to him, something uncommon that strongly appealed to him yet made him suspicious, even annoyed him: a great calm and innocence, a discipline and purity that nevertheless were not childlike. Hidden behind that docility and rectitude was an aloofness, an arrogance, so that her innocence, instead of touching and disarming him (he could never have seduced a child), provoked and challenged him. Almost as soon as her appearance had become somewhat familiar to him as a mental image, he felt the desire to carve a statue of her, not as she now was but with aroused and suffering features, not a young maiden but a Mary Magdalene. Often his desire was one day to see that lovely, calm, impassive face, whether in ecstasy or pain, contorted, laid open and yielding up its secret.

There was also another face that dwelled in his soul but that he did not quite possess, a face he yearned to capture and reproduce as an artist but that kept withdrawing and concealing itself from him: the face of his mother. Some time ago this face had begun to change from the one that, after those conversations with Narcissus, had surfaced from the hidden depths of his memory. During the days on the road, the nights of lovemaking, the times of nostalgia, the times of mortal danger and imminent death, his mother's face had slowly transformed and enriched itself, become more profound and more varied. No longer was it the face of his own mother: from those features and colours a more impersonal maternal image had gradually evolved, the image of an Eve, of a mother of all mankind. Just as Master Niklaus had portrayed in some of his Madonnas the image of the suffering Mother of God with a perfection and expressive power that to Goldmund seemed unsurpassable, so Goldmund hoped, some day when he was more mature and confident of his skill, to fashion the image of the secular Eve-mother that was enshrined in his heart as its most ancient and precious sacred object. But this vision, at one time merely a remembered image of his own mother and his love for her, was in constant process of change and growth. The features of Lisa the gypsy, of Lydia the knight's daughter and of many other women had found their way into that original image; and not only the faces of all the women he had loved but also each of his strong emotions, each of his experiences had helped shape it and imparted certain features. This figure, should he ever succeed in giving it visible form, was not intended to portray one particular woman but rather life itself as primal mother. He often thought he could see it, and sometimes it appeared to him in a dream. But all he could have said about that Eve's face was that he intended it to express the lust for life in its intimate relationship to pain and death.

During that year Goldmund learned a great deal. In draw-ing he had quickly acquired great sureness, and in addition to wood-carving Niklaus would sometimes allow him to try mod-elling in clay. His first successful piece was a clay figure, some eighteen inches high, the sweet, seductive statuette of young Julie, Lydia's sister. The master praised the piece but would not consent to having it cast in metal, finding it too unchaste and worldly for him to feel like giving it his seal of approval. Then came work on the statue of Narcissus. Goldmund carved it in wood as St John the disciple, since Niklaus intended, if it turned out well, to include it in a Crucifixion group for which he had been commissioned and on which his two assistants had for some time been working exclusively, with the finishing touches to be left to the master.

Goldmund worked with profound love at this Narcissus figure. It was here that he regained his artistry and his soul whenever he had gone off the rails, which occurred often enough: caught up in love affairs, village dances, drinking bouts with friends, rolling dice and frequent brawls, he would for a day or more stay away from the workshop or appear listless and distracted at his work. On his St John, however, whose cherished, pensive image was emerging with increasing purity from the wood, he worked only in hours of eagerness, dedication and humility. During those hours he was neither happy nor sad, thought neither of lust for life nor of life's fleeting nature. His heart would again be filled with that pure, reverent and shining emotion with which he had once, glad of his friend's guidance, surrendered to him. It was not Goldmund who was creating a sculpture of his own will; it was the other, it was Narcissus, availing himself of the sculptor's hands in order to shed the impermanence and mutability of life and to present the pure image of his innermost being.

That, Goldmund sometimes felt with a shiver, was how genuine works of art came about. That accounted for the master's unforgettable Madonna, which he had since revisited again on many a Sunday. That accounted, in a mysterious and sacred way, for the best of those old statues that the master kept upstairs on the landing. That was how that other image would some day be created, the unique one, even more mysterious and awe-inspiring: the figure of the mother of all mankind. Oh, if human hands would produce only such works of art, such sacred, essential images unsoiled by vanity or ulterior motives! But, as he had long known, that was not how it was. Artists could create other images, charming objects fashioned with masterly skill, the delight of art lovers, the adornment of churches and council chambers – beautiful things, yes, but not sacred, genuine images of the soul. He knew many such works, not only by Niklaus but by other masters, which, despite all their charm of inventiveness and precision of craftsmanship, were really mere trifles. To his shame and regret he knew in his own heart, had felt in his own hands, that an artist can produce such pretty things out of delight in his own ability, out of ambition, out of playfulness.

The first time he realized this he felt desperately sad. To fashion adorable cherubs or other baubles, no matter how adorable, it was not worth being an artist. For others perhaps, for artisans, for quiet, contented bourgeois souls, it might be worth it, but not for him. For him, art and artistry were worthless if they did not burn like the sun and have the force of storms, if they brought only comfort, only pleasant feelings, only minor happiness. He was searching for something else. To gild a Madonna's lacy crown with some shiny gold leaf was no job for him, be it ever so well paid. Why did Master Niklaus accept all those commissions? Why did he employ two assistants? Why did he spend hours, measuring-rod in hand, listening to all those councillors and provosts when they commissioned a doorway or a pulpit from him? He did it for two reasons, two contemptible reasons: because he was intent on being a famous artist swamped with commissions, and because he wanted to amass money – not for major enterprises or luxuries, but for his daughter, now long since a rich girl. Money for her dowry, and for lace collars, brocade gowns and a walnut marriage bed with costly quilts and linens! As if that beautiful girl could not experience love just as well in any hayloft!

During the hours when he was preoccupied with such thoughts, Goldmund felt his mother's blood stirring deep within him – pride, and the contempt of the homeless for those who were settled and had possessions. At times both the craft and the master were as repugnant to him as fibrous string beans, and he was often on the point of running away.

The master himself had many times been sufficiently annoyed to regret having engaged this difficult and unreliable fellow who often so sorely tried his patience. Whatever he learned about Goldmund's way of life, about his indifference to money and possessions, his extravagance, his many love affairs, his frequent brawls, did nothing to make him more lenient: the man he had taken in was a gypsy, an inexplicable character. Nor had the eyes this vagabond turned on his daughter Lisbeth escaped his notice. If, in spite of all this, he mustered more patience than came easily to him, this was not from a sense of duty or nervousness but because of the St John, the statue he watched being created. With a feeling of love and spiritual affinity, which he would not quite admit to himself, the master watched as this gypsy from the forests now fashioned, slowly and erratically but tenaciously and unerringly, his wooden statue from that touching, beautiful yet inexpert drawing for whose sake Niklaus had allowed him to stay on. Some day, despite all moods and interruptions, the statue – the master had no doubt of this – would be completed, and then it would be a work such as none of his journeymen would ever be capable of producing and such as even great masters rarely manage to achieve. As much as there was for the master to disapprove in his pupil, as often as he chided him, as often as he was furious with him, when it came to the St John he held his tongue.

The last of the boyish charm and childlike naïveté that so many had found attractive in Goldmund had gradually vanished during these years. He had grown into a stalwart, handsome man, much desired by women, not popular with men. His disposition, his mental make-up, had also greatly changed since Narcissus had roused him from the innocent sleep of his monastery years and since the world and his wanderings had moulded him. The charming, gentle, popular, devout and ever-obliging monastery pupil had long since turned into a quite different person. Narcissus had awakened him, women had given him knowledge, his wanderings had stripped him of his bloom. He had no friends; his heart belonged to women, who could conquer him with ease. A melting look was enough. He found it hard to resist a woman and responded to the slightest encouragement. And although he was highly sensitive to beauty and mostly preferred very young girls in the freshness of their springtime, he also pitied and yielded to women who were no longer young and of little beauty. At village dances he sometimes found himself stuck with some despondent spinster whom no one desired but who won him by arousing his pity, and not only pity but also his ever-vigilant curiosity. From the moment he began to concentrate on a woman, whether for weeks or merely hours, for him she was beautiful and he gave himself totally. Moreover, experience taught him that every woman was beautiful and able to give happiness, that the mousy woman whom men ignored was capable of fantastic ardour and surrender, the woman past her prime of more than sad, sweet, maternal tenderness; that every woman had her secret and her magic, the uncovering of which brought bliss. In this all women were the same. Any lack of youth or beauty was compensated for by some special quality. Yet not every woman managed to keep him equally long under her spell. He was not a whit more loving or grateful towards the youngest and loveliest than towards the unprepossessing: he never loved by halves. But there were women who enthralled him more than ever after three or ten nights of lovemaking, and others in whom he lost interest after the first time and whom he quickly forgot.

Love and lust seemed the only things that could truly give warmth and value to life. Ambition was unknown to him; bishop or beggar were the same to him. Acquisitions and possessions had no appeal. He despised them, would never have made the least sacrifice for them, and casually squandered the money that he sometimes earned in abundance. The love of women, sexual games – these had priority for him, and the core of his frequent bouts of melancholy and jaded spirits grew from his knowledge of the fleeting nature of lust. The swift, delicious surge of ecstasy, its brief, rapturous blaze, its rapid extinction – this seemed to him to comprise the core of all experience; this became for him the image of all bliss and all suffering. He could yield to that melancholy, to that dread of impermanence, as utterly as he could to love, and this melancholy also was love, it also was lust. Just as the ecstasy of love is aware, at the moment of the highest, most sublime peak, of having to subside and die away with the next breath, so the deepest loneliness and yielding to melancholy were aware of suddenly being swallowed up by desire, by a new yielding to the sunlit side of life. Death and lust were one. The mother of life could be called love or lust; she could also be called tomb and decay. The mother was Eve: she was the well-spring of happiness and the well-spring of death, giving birth eternally, killing eternally. In her, love and cruelty were one, and the longer he carried her image within him, the more it became for him a parable and sacred allegory.

He knew, not with words or consciousness but with the more profound knowledge of his blood, that his path led him to the maternal, to lust and death. The paternal side of life, the mind, the will, was not where he lived. Narcissus was at home there, and now for the first time Goldmund grasped the full meaning of his friend's words and recognized in him the counterpart to himself. It was this counterpart that he shaped and made visible in his statue of St John. He could long for Narcissus to the point of tears; he could have wonderful dreams about him, but he could never reach him, become like him.

With some mysterious sense Goldmund also divined the secret of his artistic nature, of his profound love of art, his sometimes rampant hatred of it. Not intellectually but emotionally, he sensed by way of many parables that art was a uniting of the paternal and maternal world, of mind and blood; it could begin at the most sensual level and lead to the most abstract realms, or it might have its origin in a pure world of ideas and end in the bloodiest of flesh. All those works of art that were truly sublime, not merely the work of skilful charlatans but imbued with the eternal mystery – such as that Blessed Virgin of the master's – all those indisputable works of art had that dangerous, smiling dual face, that male/female element, that juxtaposition of animal instinct and pure spirituality. But it would be the Eve-mother who would one day most clearly display that dual face if he should ever succeed in creating her.

Art and being an artist enabled Goldmund to reconcile the deepest contradictions in his nature, or at least they presented a glorious, ever new parable of the duality of that nature. But art was not an outright gift; it was not to be had without cost, and the cost was considerable. It demanded sacrifice. For more than three years Goldmund had sacrificed to art that which was all-important to him, apart from the ecstasy of love: freedom. To be free, to roam wherever he pleased, to live the random life of the wayfarer, to stand on his own feet and be independent: all this he had renounced. Let others find him moody, intractable and arrogant whenever in his fury he neglected workshop and work: for him that life was a slavery which exasperated him beyond endurance. It was not the master whom he had to obey, or the future, or pressing need: it was art itself. Art, that goddess who seemed so spiritual, required so many banalities! It required a roof over one's head, and tools, wood, clay, paint, gold; it demanded work and patience. For its sake he had sacrificed the unfettered freedom of the forests, the intoxication of wide open spaces, the voluptuous sting of danger, the pride of poverty, and he had had to make that sacrifice over and over again, with much gnashing of teeth.

Some of what he had sacrificed he did regain, taking a small revenge on the slavish orderliness of his present settled life by indulging in amorous adventures and scuffles with rivals. All the pent-up, untamed side of his nature, all his suppressed energy, was vented through this outlet, and he became a notorious and much-feared ruffian. To be suddenly attacked in a dark alley on his way to a girl or coming home from a dance, to receive a few blows with a cudgel, to swing round like lightning and switch from defence to attack, to press the panting enemy to his panting chest, to punch him in the jaw, drag him by the hair or get a good stranglehold round his throat – all this he relished, and for a while it cured his black moods. And the women liked it too.

This amply filled his days, and it was all worth while as long as the work on his St John continued. This took a long time, and he completed the final delicate modelling of face and hands in solemn, patient concentration, in a little shed behind the journeymen's workshop. Then came the morning when the statue was finished, the hour when Goldmund fetched a broom, carefully swept the floor of the shed clean, and tenderly brushed the last specks of dust from the hair of his St John. Then he stood for a long time in front of the disciple, an hour or more, filled with the solemn feeling of a rare great experience that might be repeated once more in his life but also might remain unique. A man on the day of his wedding or of receiving the accolade of knighthood, a woman after giving birth to her first child, may experience a similar emotion, a lofty consecration, a profound gravity, and at the same time a secret dread of the moment when that sublime and unique occasion would have become part of the past, integrated and swallowed up in the normal course of daily life.

Now he saw his friend Narcissus, the mentor of his youthful years, standing there with face raised and listening, in the robe and role of the Beloved Disciple, with an expression of calm piety that showed something of a budding smile. Pain and death were not unknown to that spiritual face in all its devout beauty, to that poised, slender figure, to those long, fine, uplifted hands, although all were filled with youth and inner music. But unknown to them were despair, disorder and rebellion. Whether the soul behind those noble features was joyful or sad, it was in pure harmony; it suffered no discord.

Goldmund stood there contemplating what he had wrought. This began as a meditation before the monument to his early youth and friendship, but it ended with an onslaught of apprehension and gloomy thoughts. So this was his work, and the beautiful disciple would remain, his exquisite blossoming would never come to an end. But he who had created it must now take leave of his creation; tomorrow it would cease to be his, cease to await his hands, to grow and blossom under them, to offer him refuge, solace and a meaning to life. He was left empty. And it would be best, it seemed to him, to take his leave today, not only of this St John but of the master, the town and art. There was nothing more for him to do here; there were no images in his soul to which he could have given shape. That longed-for image of images, the figure of the mother of all mankind, was still, and would long remain, beyond his reach. Was he now supposed to go back to polishing cherubs and carving ornaments?

He tore himself away and went across to the master's workshop. After entering quietly he remained standing by the door until Niklaus noticed him and called out: 'What is it, Goldmund?'

'My statue is finished. Perhaps before you go to dinner you would come and have a look at it.'

'Of course – at once.'

They walked across together and left the door open so as to have more light. Niklaus had not seen the statue for quite some time, having left Goldmund undisturbed at his work. Now as he studied the finished work with silent attentiveness his reserved expression brightened, and Goldmund saw his stern blue eyes light up with pleasure.

'It is good,' said the master. 'It is very good. With this you have qualified as a journeyman, Goldmund. Your apprenticeship is over. I shall show your statue to the guild members and ask that on the strength of it they grant you a master's patent. You have earned it.'

Goldmund cared little about the guild, but he knew how much approval lay behind Niklaus's words, and he was happy.

While once again walking slowly round the statue of St John, the master said with a sigh: 'This figure is filled with piety and clarity. It is solemn, but full of joy and peace. One would think it was carved by someone in whose heart there is much light and happiness.'

Goldmund smiled. 'You know that in this figure it is not myself whom I have portrayed but my dearest friend. It is he, not I, who has brought clarity and peace to the image. Actually it wasn't I who made that figure – he placed it in my soul.'

'That may well be,' said Niklaus. 'It is a mystery how such an image is created. I am not exactly humble, but I must say that I have carved many works that are far inferior to yours, not in terms of art and painstaking care but in terms of truth. Well, I am sure you know yourself that one cannot repeat such a work. It is a mystery.'

'Yes,' said Goldmund. 'When the figure was finished and I looked at it, I thought to myself: You will never be able to do anything like that again. And that is why, Master, I believe I shall soon be going back to my travels.'

Surprised and annoyed, Niklaus looked at him with eyes that had become stern again.

'We shall discuss that later. Now is the very time when you should start working. This is certainly not the moment to run away. But now you can take the rest of the day off, and you will be my guest at noon.'

At noon Goldmund appeared in his Sunday best, washed and with his hair combed. This time he knew how much it meant and what a rare favour it was to be invited by the master. Yet, as he climbed the stairs to the landing crowded with statues, he was far from being as filled with awe and anxious joy as that other time when with a beating heart he had entered these quiet, pleasant rooms.

Lisbeth was also dressed for the occasion and wore a jewelled necklace. At table, in addition to the carp and wine, there was a surprise: the master presented him with a little leather pouch containing two gold coins, Goldmund's wages for the completed statue.

This time he did not sit silently by while father and daughter chatted. They both addressed remarks to him, and beakers were clinked. Goldmund's eyes were busy as he seized the opportunity of minutely studying the beautiful girl with the refined and somewhat haughty face, and his eyes did not hide how attractive he found her. She treated him courteously, but he was disappointed that she neither blushed nor showed any warmth. Again he longed to force that lovely, impassive face to speak and to yield up its secret.

When the meal was over, he thanked them, lingered briefly by the carvings on the landing, and spent the afternoon, unable to make up his mind, strolling idly about the town. He had been greatly honoured by the master, beyond all expectations. Why did this not make him happy? Why did all this honour smack so little of celebration?

Following an impulse, he hired a horse and rode out to the monastery where he had first seen the master's work and heard his name. That had been only a few years back yet seemed unimaginably remote. In the monastery church he studied the Blessed Virgin, and again the statue charmed and overwhelmed him. It was more beautiful than his St John, its equal in spirituality and mystery, and artistically superior to it in free, ethereal weightlessness. He now saw details in the work that only the artist sees: delicate movements in the gown, boldness in the shaping of the long hands and fingers, sensitive utilization of chance patterns in the structure of the wood. Although these fine details were nothing in comparison with the whole, with the simplicity and deep feeling of the vision, they were there and were very beautiful, and to even an inspired artist they were possible only if he knew his craft from the ground up. To be able to create such a work he must not only harbour images in his soul: he must have eyes and hands that have undergone untold training and practice. So perhaps it was worth while after all to place one's entire life in the service of art at the expense of freedom, at the expense of great experiences, merely in order one day to produce something of such beauty, something that was not only envisioned and conceived in love but, down to the last detail, the product of unerring masterly skill? This was a big question.

Goldmund returned to town late that night on his weary horse. He found a tavern still open where he had some bread and wine. Then he climbed the stairs to his room at the fish-market, at odds with himself, full of questions, full of doubts.

Chapter Twelve

The following day Goldmund could not bring himself to go to the workshop. As on so many other listless days, he wandered aimlessly about the town. He watched housewives and servants going to market, then spent some time by the fountain at the fish-market watching the fishmongers and their coarse womenfolk as they hawked their wares, snatching the cool, silvery fish from their tubs and holding them out for inspection, while the fish, with agonized, gaping jaws and frightened, staring gold eyes, quietly resigned themselves to death, or fiercely and desperately fought it off. As on many another occasion, he was seized by pity for these creatures and by a sorrowful resentment of human beings: why were they so insensitive and brutal, so incredibly stupid and dense? Why were they all so blind, the fishermen and the fishwives as well as the haggling customers? Why didn't they see those gaping jaws, those panic-stricken eyes and thrashing tails, that horrible, futile, desperate struggle, that unbearable transformation of mysterious, wondrously beautiful creatures as the last little quiver rippled across the dying skin and they lay there lifeless and flat, pitiful morsels of food for the tables of jovial gluttons? They saw nothing, these people, they knew nothing and noticed nothing: Nothing spoke to them! It was all one to them whether a lovely, pathetic creature perished before their eyes, or a master-carver made thrillingly visible in a saint's face all the hope, nobility, suffering and gripping fear known to human existence – they saw nothing, nothing touched them! They were all in high spirits or busy, full of importance, always in a hurry, shouting, laughing and belching at each other, raucous, cracking jokes, squabbling over two pfennigs, and they were all smug, untroubled and highly satisfied with themselves and the world. Pigs, that's what they were, only much worse, much fouler, than pigs! Oh well, many a time he had himself been in their midst, had had a good time among their kind, chased the girls and downed a plateful of baked fish with much laughter and no revulsion. But again and again – often quite suddenly as if by magic – joy and tranquillity had deserted him. Again and again that smug illusion had dropped away from him, that complacency, self-importance and spiritual indolence, and he had been snatched away into solitude and brooding, to wander aimlessly, to contemplate suffering, death and the dubiousness of all human activity, to stare into the abyss.

Sometimes, though, a sudden joyousness had sprung from that wallowing in the contemplation of the futile and the terrible – a passionate falling in love, an impulse to sing a lovely tune or make a drawing; or, as he smelled a flower or played with a cat, his childlike acceptance of life would return to him. This time, too, it would return, tomorrow or the next day, and once again the world would be good and splendid – until, of course, that other came back; the melancholy, the brooding, the hopeless, anguished love for the dying fish, the fading flowers, the horror at the dull, brutish existence, the gawking and wilful blindness of human beings. At such times he could not help thinking, with tormenting curiosity and profound anguish, of Viktor the travelling student, of how he had plunged his knife between the man's ribs and left him lying, drenched in blood, on the fir branches. And he would wonder and brood over what had actually become of that Viktor, whether animals had completely devoured him, whether anything was left of him. Yes, he supposed the bones might have remained, and maybe a few handfuls of hair. And the bones – what happened to them? How long might it take – decades or just years – for them, too, to crumble away and turn to dust?

Today, while watching the fish with pity and the market crowds with disgust, his heart full of anxious melancholy and bitter hostility towards the world and himself, he was reminded of Viktor. Perhaps he had been found and buried? And if that were so, had all the flesh already fallen from his bones? Had it all rotted, been eaten by worms? Was there still hair on his skull, were there still eyebrows above his eye-sockets? And of Viktor's life, so filled with adventures and stories and the fantastic range of his droll jokes and japes – what remained of all that? Apart from the few random memories that his murderer retained of him, did anything survive of that human existence which, when all was said, could hardly have been called a humdrum one? Was there still a Viktor in the dreams of the women he had once loved?

Ah well, it was all gone now, had all dwindled to nothing. And that was what happened to everyone and everything: a swift blossoming and a swift withering away, and in the end a blanket of snow. Of all that had blossomed in himself when he came to this town a few years ago, filled with a yearning for art, with a deep reverence for Master Niklaus, what of all that was still alive? Nothing, no more than of poor Viktor, that lanky old scrounger. If someone had told him at the time that a day would come when Niklaus would acknowledge him as his equal and claim a master's patent for him from the guild, he would have believed he was holding all the happiness in the world in his hands. And now it was nothing more than a withered flower, dried up and joyless.

As he was thinking this, Goldmund suddenly had a vision. It was but a moment, a sudden flash: he saw the face of the primal mother, bending over the abyss of life and wearing a faraway smile, beautiful and horrifying; saw it smiling at births and deaths, at flowers and rustling autumn leaves, smiling at art, smiling at putrefaction.

Everything was the same to her, to the primal mother; over everything hung, like the moon, her unearthly smile. She cared as much for the brooding Goldmund as for the carp dying on the cobbles of the fish-market, as much for the cold, proud maiden Lisbeth as for the scattered bones of the Viktor who had once been so eager to steal his ducat.

The lightning flash was already gone; the mysterious maternal face had vanished. But deep within Goldmund's soul its wan light continued to flicker, and a wave of life, of pain, of strangling desire churned through his heart. No, no, he had no use for the good cheer and complacency of those others, of the fish customers, the townsfolk, the bustling crowds. The Devil take them! Ah, that suddenly illumined, pale face, the full, ripe mouth across whose heavy lips had quivered, like wind and moonlight, the ineffable smile of death!

Goldmund went to the master's house. It was almost noon, and he waited until he could hear Niklaus inside leaving his work and washing his hands. Then he went in.

'Allow me to say a few words, Master, while you are washing your hands and putting your coat on. I am thirsting for a mouthful of truth, and I should like to tell you something that perhaps I can say at this moment and then never again. I am at a point where I have to speak to someone, and you are the only one who may be able to understand. I am not speaking to the man who has a famous workshop and receives all these prestigious commissions from towns and monasteries and has two assistants and a grand house. I am speaking to the master who made the Madonna in that monastery, the most beautiful sculpture I know. This is the man I have loved and revered – to become his equal seemed to me the highest goal on earth.

'I have now completed a statue, St John, and could not make him as perfect as your Madonna. But that is the way he is. There is no other statue for me to make, no other that requires me and compels me to make it. Or rather, there is one, a distant, sacred image that one day I shall have to create, but I am not yet ready for that. To be able to make it, I still have much more to learn and experience. Perhaps I shall be ready in three or four years, or ten or even more, or maybe never. But until that time, Master, I don't want just to pursue a craft and varnish figures and carve pulpits and lead an artisan's workshop life and earn wages and become like all the other artisans. No, that's not what I want. I want to live and roam freely, feel summer and winter, look at the world and savour its beauty and its horror. I want to suffer hunger and thirst and to forget and rid myself of everything I have experienced and learned with you. It's true that one day I should like to produce something as beautiful and deeply moving as your Madonna, but to become like you and live the way you do – that's not what I want.'

The master had washed and dried his hands and now turned round to look at Goldmund. His expression was stern but not angry.

'You have spoken,' he said, 'and I have listened. Let that be enough for now. I do not expect to see you at work, although there is much to be done. I do not regard you as an assistant. You need freedom. There are a few things I should like to discuss with you, my dear Goldmund, not now but in a few days. Meanwhile you may pass the time as you please. Look, I am much older than you and have learned a few things. I think differently from you, but I can understand you and what you mean. In a few days I shall send for you, and we shall discuss your future. I have all kinds of plans. Until then, be patient! I am well aware of what it is like to have completed a piece of work that was of great personal significance. I know that empty feeling. It will pass, believe me.'

With a sense of frustration, Goldmund hurried away. The master meant well, but what could he do for him?

Goldmund knew a spot by the river where the water was shallow and flowed over a layer of rubbish and refuse that had been thrown there by the local fisherfolk. He made for this spot, sat down on the embankment and looked into the water. He loved water; all water attracted him. And if one gazed down from here through the fast-flowing, crystalline water to the dark, indistinct river bed, one could see here and there something with an enticing, muted gold sheen flashing and sparkling – unidentifiable objects, maybe a piece of an old plate or a discarded, bent sickle, or a pale, smooth stone or glazed tile, or it might be a mudfish, a plump burbot or a redeye turning over on the bottom and briefly catching a ray of light on its scales and pale pelvic fins – it was never possible to make out exactly what it was, but it was always exquisitely beautiful and enticing, that brief, muted glint of sunken gold treasure in the wet, black depths.

All true secrets, all true images of the soul, it seemed to him, were like these little watery secrets: they had no outline, no shape; veiled and ambiguous, they permitted only a vague perception as of some distant, enchanting possibility. Just as in the twilight of the green river depths something inexpressibly gold or silver might flash for a few seconds, a mere nothing yet full of the most delectable promises, so a vague human profile, glimpsed from behind, could occasionally betoken something overwhelmingly beautiful or unutterably sad; or, when a lantern hanging under a wagon at night threw huge revolving shadows of wheelspokes on to walls, so that shadow-play could, for the duration of a minute, be as replete with scenes, events and stories as the whole of Virgil. It was from the same unreal, magical material that nocturnal dreams were woven; a mere nothing that comprised all the images in the world, a water in whose crystal dwelled the shapes of all humans, animals, angels and demons as constant possibilities for the waking world.

Again he became absorbed in his game as he stared absently into the flowing river, seeing shapeless reflections trembling on the bottom, imagining royal crowns and women's gleaming shoulders. Long ago in Mariabronn, he remembered, he had seen similar dream-shapes and magical transformations in Latin and Greek letters. Hadn't he talked to Narcissus about this at the time? When was that, how many centuries ago? Oh, Narcissus! To see him, to talk to him for an hour, hold his hand, hear his calm, intelligent voice, he would gladly have given his two gold ducats.

Why were these things so beautiful, this subaqueous golden lustre, these shadows and intimations, all these unreal, magical phenomena – why were they so unutterably beautiful, why did they fill one with such happiness, since they were the exact opposite of the beauty an artist could create? For if the beauty of these ineffable objects had no form and consisted purely of mystery, with works of art it was precisely the other way round: they were nothing *but* form; they spoke with complete clarity. Nothing could be more uncompromisingly clear and definite than the line of a head or mouth drawn on paper or carved in wood. He could have drawn an exact copy of the lower lip or the eyelids of Niklaus's Madonna: there was nothing vague about them, nothing illusory or evanescent.

Goldmund pondered deeply over this. He could not understand how it was possible for something completely definite and formed to have an effect on the soul very similar to that of something completely intangible and formless. But one thing did become clear to him during this mental exercise: why so many excellent, well-made art objects failed absolutely to appeal to him – in fact, despite their having a certain beauty, he was bored by them, almost hated them. Workshops, churches and palaces were filled with such unfortunate objects; he had worked on some of them himself. The reason they were so bitterly disappointing was that they aroused a desire for the highest yet did not fulfil it because they lacked the main ingredient: mystery. This was what dreams and supreme works of art had in common: mystery.

Goldmund went on thinking: There is one mystery I love. I am getting close to it, it has more than once appeared to me in a flash, and as an artist I should like, if I am equal to the task one day, to give it form and voice. It is the figure of the great giver of life, the primal mother, and her mystery lies not, as in other figures, in any particular detail, in her being plump or thin, coarse or delicate, in possessing strength or charm, but in the greatest, otherwise irreconcilable opposites having made peace in this figure and existing together within it: birth and death, goodness and cruelty, life and annihilation. If I had concocted this figure, if it were merely a whimsical notion or the ambitious wish of an artist, it would be no loss. I would recognize its flaws and forget them. But the primal mother is not a notion – I did not imagine her, I have seen her! She lives in me, keeps appearing to me. The first time I had an inkling of her was one winter's night in a village when I had to hold a light over the bed of a peasant woman in labour: that was when the image began to live in me. Often it is distant and vague, for a long time, but suddenly it will flare up again, as it did today. The image of my own mother, once so dear to me, has transformed itself completely into this new image; the old dwells in the new like the stone in a cherry.

He was now keenly aware of his present situation, of his uneasiness before coming to a decision. No less than when parting from Narcissus and the monastery so long ago, he was now on a crucial path: the path to his mother. Perhaps one day a concrete image, a work of his hands and visible to all, would evolve from that mother. Perhaps that was the goal, perhaps that was where the meaning of his life lay hidden. Perhaps; he did not know. One thing he did know: to follow his mother, to be on his way to her, to be drawn and called by her, that was good, that was life. Perhaps he would never be able to give form to her image; perhaps she would always remain dream, idea, enticement, the golden glint of a sacred mystery. Well, in any case, he was bound to follow her, to put his destiny in her hands; she was his star.

And now the moment of decision was almost upon him, everything had become clear. Art was a splendid thing, but it was not a goddess or a goal – not for him. It was not art that he had to follow but only his mother's call. What good would it do to make his fingers even more skilful? Master Niklaus was an example of where that led to. It led to fame and reputation, to money and a stable life, to a wilting and withering of those spiritual sensibilities which alone can find access to the mystery. It led to the production of costly, pretty toys, to sundry rich altars and pulpits, to St Sebastians and curly-haired cherubs at four thalers apiece. The gold in the eye of a carp, the delicate silvery bloom along the edge of a butterfly's wing, were infinitely more beautiful, more alive, more precious than a whole roomful of such art objects.

A boy came strolling along the road beside the river, singing as he walked. Sometimes his singing stopped as he bit into a hunk of white bread he had in his hand. Goldmund saw him and asked for a bit of his bread. With two fingers he dug out a soft piece and rolled it into little pellets. Leaning over the embankment wall he threw the bread pellets, slowly, one after another, into the water, saw the white pellets sinking down in the dark water, and saw each one surrounded by a swarm of thrusting heads of fish until it disappeared into gaping jaws. Pellet after pellet sank and disappeared as he watched with deep satisfaction.

After that he felt hungry and sought out one of his sweethearts, a servant-girl in a butcher's house whom he called 'mistress of sausages and ham'. With his usual whistle he summoned her to the kitchen window. He would condescend, he indicated, to accept something to eat which he could stuff into his pocket and consume across the river, sitting on one of the vine-covered slopes where the rich, red soil shone through the succulent vine leaves and where in spring the little blue hyacinths bloomed and smelled so delicately of peaches and apricots.

But today seemed to be a day of decisions and insights. When Kathrine's solid, coarse face appeared at the window and she smiled at him, when he was already holding out his hand to give the usual signal, he was suddenly reminded of other occasions when he had stood and waited here like this. And with stultifying clarity he simultaneously foresaw what would happen in the next few minutes: how she would recognize his signal and vanish, how she would shortly reappear at the back door with some sausage or ham in her hand, how he would accept it while stroking her a little and holding her close, as she expected – and suddenly it seemed to him infinitely stupid and distasteful to set in motion yet again that entire mechanical sequence of a stale routine and to play his part in it, to accept the sausage, to feel her large, firm breasts thrusting against him and to press them gently, as a token of gratitude, so to speak. Suddenly he seemed to see in her coarse, good-natured face a hint of humdrum habit, in her pleasant smile something seen too often, something mechanical and lacking in mystery, something degrading to himself.

He did not complete his usual gesture; the smile froze on his face. Did he still love her, did he still seriously desire her? No, he had been here far too often; far too often had he seen that invariable smile and, his heart not in it, smiled back. That which yesterday he could have done without a thought, today suddenly was no longer possible. The girl was still standing at the window looking out when he swung round and vanished from the alley, determined never to show himself there again. Let someone else stroke those breasts! Let someone else eat those good sausages! Anyway, just think of all the food that was consumed and wasted day after day in this overfed, merry-making town! How lazy, how spoiled, how finicky were these fat burghers for whose benefit so many pigs and calves were slaughtered and so many pitiful, beautiful fish pulled out of the river every day! And as for him – how spoiled and corrupt he was, how disgustingly similar to these fat burghers he had become! When he used to tramp across snowy fields, a dried plum or an old crust of bread had tasted more delicious than an entire guild banquet here amid all this affluence. Oh freedom, oh open road, oh moonlit heath, cautiously studied animal tracks in the dewy grass of early morning! Here in the town, among settled folk, everything was so easy and cost so little, even love.

He had had enough, suddenly; he spat on it. This life here had lost its meaning, was a bone without marrow. It had been pleasant and had had meaning as long as the master had been his model and Lisbeth a princess. It had been bearable as long as he had been working on his St John. Now it was over, the fragrance was gone, the flower had wilted. In a great wave the sense of impermanence engulfed him, the feeling that could often so torment and intoxicate him. How quickly everything withered, how quickly all desire was spent, with nothing remaining but bones and dust. No, one thing remained: the eternal mother, ancient and eternally young, with her sad, cruel smile of love. Again he saw her for a moment or two: a giant figure, with stars in her hair, dreamily sitting on the edge of the world, her fingers absently plucking flower after flower, life after life, and slowly letting them drop into the void.

During these days, while Goldmund saw a finished piece of his life fading behind him, while he roamed the familiar places in a sad frenzy of farewells, Master Niklaus was taking the utmost pains to provide for Goldmund's future and to get this restless young man to settle down for good. He persuaded the guild to grant him a master's patent and was considering a plan to bind him permanently to himself, not as an inferior but as a colleague, to discuss and carry out all major commissions with him and to make him a partner in the proceeds. This might be risky, also on account of Lisbeth, for of course the young man would then soon become his son-in-law. But a figure like the St John could never have been made by even the best of all the assistants Niklaus had ever had in his pay, and he himself was getting old and was no longer as full of ideas and creative energy. He did not want to see his famous workshop sink to the status of an ordinary artisan's business. It would be difficult with this Goldmund, but he had to take the risk.

Such were the worried master's calculations. He would have the rear workshop extended and enlarged for Goldmund and let him have the room in the attic. He would also make him a gift of fine new clothing for his acceptance into the guild. Cautiously he also asked for Lisbeth's opinion; since that dinner she had been expecting something of the kind. And it so happened that Lisbeth was not opposed. If the young man could be persuaded to settle down and was entitled to call himself a master, he was quite acceptable to her. So there were no obstacles here either. And if Master Niklaus and his craft had still not quite managed to tame this gypsy, Lisbeth would be sure to succeed.

So everything was set in motion and the bait for the bird hung nicely behind the noose. And one day Goldmund, of whom nothing had been seen since, was sent for and once again invited to dinner. Once again Goldmund turned up, clothes brushed and hair combed, and sat in the rather too formal room and once again clinked beakers with the master and the master's daughter, until she left the room and Niklaus came out with his great plan and offer.

'You have understood me,' he added to his surprising disclosures, 'and I need not tell you that I doubt whether a young man who has not even completed the prescribed apprenticeship has ever risen so quickly to the rank of master, with a place found for him in a warm nest. Your fortune is made, Goldmund.'

Surprised and ill at ease, Goldmund looked at his master and pushed aside the still half-full beaker of wine. Actually he had expected Niklaus to chide him for the wasted days and then suggest that he stay on as an assistant. Now there was this situation. It saddened and embarrassed him to have to sit facing this man. For the moment he did not quite know what to say.

The master, his expression already showing some tension and disappointment at his generous offer not being immediately accepted with joy and humility, rose and said: 'Well, my suggestion comes as a surprise to you. Perhaps you would like to give it some thought. I do feel a little hurt. I had thought I would be giving you great pleasure. But never mind – take time to think it over.'

'Master,' said Goldmund, struggling for the words, 'don't be angry with me! I thank you with all my heart for your concern for my welfare, and I thank you even more for the patience with which you have treated me as your pupil. I shall never forget my indebtedness to you. But I do not need time to think it over. I have already made my decision.'

'What decision?'

'I had made up my mind before accepting your invitation today and before I had any inkling of your generous offers. I am not staying on here. I am going to resume my travels.'

Niklaus, who had turned pale, scowled at him.

'Master,' Goldmund implored, 'believe me when I say I do not want to hurt you! I have told you of my decision. It cannot be changed. I must get away, I must travel, I must have my freedom. Let me once again thank you most sincerely, and let us part in friendship.'

Close to tears, he held out his hand. Niklaus ignored it; white in the face he began pacing faster and faster up and down the room, his footsteps resounding with fury. Never before had Goldmund seen him like that.

Then suddenly the master stopped, controlled himself with a tremendous effort and, without looking at Goldmund, said between clenched teeth: 'Very well then, go! But go at once, so I do not need to see you again, so I do not do or say anything that I may one day regret! Go!'

Once again Goldmund held out his hand. The master seemed about to spit on it, so Goldmund, by now also very pale, turned, quietly left the room, put on his cap, crept down the stairs while letting his hand run over the carved newel posts, entered the little workshop in the courtyard, stood briefly for one last time in front of his St John, and left the house, his heart filled with a sorrow deeper than he had once felt on leaving the knight's castle and poor Lydia.

At least it was all over quickly! At least no unnecessary words had been spoken! That was his only consoling thought as he crossed the threshold, when lane and town suddenly confronted him with that altered, alien face which familiar objects acquire when our hearts have said farewell to them. He glanced back at the front door – now the door to a house for ever closed to him.

Back in his small room Goldmund began to prepare for his departure. Not that there was much to prepare; the only thing to be done was to say goodbye. On the wall was a picture he had painted himself, a gentle Madonna, and there were a few oddments belonging to him: a Sunday hat, a pair of dancing shoes, a roll of drawings, a small lute, a number of clay figures he had made, and a few gifts from sweethearts – a posy of artificial flowers, a ruby-red drinking glass, an old, dried-up gingerbread heart and similar oddments. Each had its significance and history, each had won his affection, but all this had now become tiresome rubbish, since he could take none of it with him. At least he was able to exchange the ruby glass for a good strong hunting-knife belonging to his landlord. He sharpened the knife on the whetstone in the courtyard, crumbled the gingerbread and fed it to the neighbours' chickens, presented the Madonna painting to the landlord's wife and received a useful gift in exchange: an old leather satchel and ample provisions for his journey. He packed the satchel with the few shirts he owned and some small drawings rolled round a piece of broomstick, together with the provisions. The rest of the stuff had to stay behind.

There were several women in the town from whom it would have been seemly to take his leave; he had slept with one of them only the night before without telling her of his plans. Yes, there were quite a few tag-ends that might bother a wayfarer. One mustn't worry about that. He said goodbye to no one but the landlord and his wife, and this he did in the evening so as to be able to get away first thing in the morning.

Nevertheless, next morning someone was already up and, just as he was about to slip quietly out of the house, offered him a bowl of bread and milk in the kitchen. It was the daughter of the house, a child of fifteen, a quiet, ailing creature with beautiful eyes but a defective hip that made her limp. Her name was Marie and, though pale and wan from lack of sleep, she had dressed carefully and combed her hair. As she served him hot milk and bread in the kitchen she seemed very sad that he was leaving. He thanked her and, in his pity for her, kissed her goodbye on her narrow lips. Devoutly, with eyes closed, she received his kiss.

Chapter Thirteen

In the early stages of his new journeyings, in the first rapture of freedom regained, Goldmund had first to relearn the homeless, timeless life of a wayfarer. Obedient to no man, dependent only on weather and season, with no goal, no roof overhead, possessing nothing and open to all manner of chance, the homeless lead lives that are childlike and courageous, meagre and tenacious. They are the sons of Adam, of the outcast from Paradise, and the brothers of the animals, the innocents. From the hand of Heaven they accept, hour by hour, whatever is given them: sun, rain, fog, snow, warmth and cold, comfort and suffering. For them there is no time, no history, no striving, nor that strange idol of growth and progress in which house-owners so desperately believe. A wayfarer can be tender or rough, skilful or clumsy, courageous or timid, but always he is at heart a child, always living Earth's first day, before the beginning of all history, his life always governed by a few simple urges and needs. He can be clever or stupid. He can have a deep-seated knowledge of the fragility and impermanence of all life, of how pitifully and tremulously all living things carry their scrap of warm blood through the icy spaces of the universe, or he can be like a child and greedily follow the dictates of his poor stomach: but always he is the opponent and mortal enemy of the sedentary property-owner, who hates, despises and fears him because he does not wish to be reminded of that – of the ephemeral nature of all existence, of the continuous withering of all life, of the inexorable, icy death that fills the universe around us.

The childlike quality of the wayfarer's life, Goldmund's maternal origin, his turning his back on law and intellect, his vulnerability and his hidden, ever-present proximity to death had long since permeated and shaped his soul. The fact that, in spite of this, intellect and willpower were still alive in him, that in spite of all he was an artist, enriched and complicated his life, since every life needs division and contradiction to become rich and radiant. What would reason and sobriety be without the knowledge of intoxication? What would sensual desire be if Death were not looking over its shoulder? And what would love be without the eternal mortal antagonism of the sexes?

Summer and autumn were left behind. Goldmund managed to scrape through the bare winter months and continued on his way, intoxicated by the sweet-smelling spring. How the seasons hurried by! How quickly the high summer sun set day after day! Year followed upon year, and it seemed as if Goldmund had forgotten that there was more on earth than hunger and love and this silent, uncanny haste of the passing seasons. He seemed to have become entirely submerged in the maternal, instinctive, primal world. But in all his dreams, and whenever he stopped to rest and look out pensively over blossoming or withering valleys, he was all eyes, all artist, tormented by the desire to conjure with the power of the mind that exquisite, meaningless drift of life and reshape it into meaning.

One day, having invariably travelled alone since that bloody incident with Viktor, he happened upon another wayfarer who imperceptibly latched on to him and whom for quite a while he could not shake off. However, he was not a type like Viktor: he was on a pilgrimage to Rome, a young man in monk's garb and pilgrim's hat whose name was Robert and who came from

Lake Constance. This son of an artisan, and for a time a pupil with the monks of St Gallus, had even as a boy set his heart on making a pilgrimage to Rome and, continuing to nurse this pet project, had grasped the first opportunity of carrying it out. It came with the death of his father, in whose workshop he had been a carpenter. The funeral was hardly over when Robert declared to his mother and sister that nothing could hold him back from immediately embarking on a pilgrimage to Rome in order to satisfy his urge and to atone for his own and his father's sins. In vain did the women complain, in vain did they heap reproaches on him: he remained stubborn, and, instead of providing for the two women, he set out on his journey without the blessing of his mother and with the wrathful abuse of his sister. He was motivated chiefly by wanderlust combined with a kind of superficial piety – an inclination to linger near ecclesiastical sites and religious ceremonies, a delight in church services, baptism, burial, mass, incense and candle flames. He knew a little Latin, but it was not erudition for which his childlike soul strove: it was contemplation and quiet day-dreaming in the shadows of vaulted church ceilings. In his early youth he had served with passionate dedication as an altar boy. Goldmund did not take him very seriously, but he liked him well enough; in a way he felt a kinship with him in his passion for travelling to foreign parts.

So Robert had happily set off and actually reached Rome, claiming along the way the hospitality of countless monasteries and priests' homes. He had viewed the mountains and the south, and in Rome he had felt very happy among all those churches and religious events; he had heard hundreds of masses and prayed at the most famous and sacred places, had partaken of the sacraments and inhaled more incense than was necessary for his minor youthful sins and the sins of his father. After staying away for more than a year, he finally returned to his paternal cottage, where he was not received as the Prodigal Son, the sister having meanwhile taken charge of domestic duties and rights. She had employed and married a hard-working journeyman-carpenter and now ruled both home and workshop so completely that after a brief stay the homecomer realized he was superfluous: no one urged him to remain when he soon spoke again of leaving and travelling. He did not resent this but accepted some of his mother's meagre savings, dressed up again in his pilgrim's outfit and set out on a new pilgrimage with no goal, clear across the Empire, a semi-clerical wayfarer. Consecrated rosaries as well as copper souvenir medals from well-known places of pilgrimage dangled and tinkled on his garments.

It was thus that he met Goldmund. They travelled for a day together and exchanged wayfarers' reminiscences; then Robert disappeared in the next small town, appeared again here and there, and finally remained entirely with him, a congenial and obliging travelling companion. Much attracted to Goldmund, he ingratiated himself with small services. He admired his knowledge, his audacity, his intellect, and he loved his health, strength and sincerity. They became used to one another, Goldmund also being easy to get along with. There was just one thing Goldmund could not tolerate: when overcome by one of his fits of melancholy or brooding, he would remain obstinately silent, looking past his companion as if he were not there, and at such times neither chatter nor questioning nor comforting was tolerated, and he must be left alone and allowed to remain silent. Robert was quick to learn this. Since he had noticed that Goldmund knew many Latin verses and songs by heart, had listened to him expound on the stone statues on a cathedral doorway, and seen him use a piece of red chalk to sketch life-size figures in bold strokes on the blank wall against which they were resting, he regarded his companion as a darling of the gods and almost a magician. That he was also a darling of the women and able to win quite a few of them with a look and a smile, was something else that Robert noticed. It pleased him less, but he could not help admiring it.

One day their journey was interrupted in an unexpected manner. As they approached a village they were confronted by a group of peasants armed with cudgels, poles and flails. The leader shouted at them from a distance to turn back immediately and go to the Devil and never show their faces again, otherwise they would be beaten to death. While Goldmund stood there demanding to know what was going on, he was struck on the chest by a stone. On looking round for Robert, he saw he had taken to his heels. The peasants advanced threateningly, and Goldmund had no choice but to follow his fleeing companion, but more slowly. The trembling Robert was waiting for him beside a crucifix well away from the village.

'You ran like a true hero!' Goldmund said, laughing. 'What's got into the thick heads of those filthy wretches? Is there a war on? Stationing armed guards outside their miserable village and not allowing anyone in! I wonder what's behind it all!'

Neither of them had any idea. It was not until the following morning, when they came upon a lonely farmhouse, that they made certain discoveries and began to solve the mystery. This farm consisted of cottage, stable and barn and stood in a little property of tall green grass and many fruit trees. It seemed strangely silent, as if asleep: no human voice, no footsteps, no children's cries, no scythe-sharpening – not a sound to be heard. A cow stood lowing in the grass, and it was obviously time for it to be milked. They approached the hut and knocked on the door, but there was no answer. They walked over to the stable, which was open and empty, then to the barn, on whose thatched roof pale-green moss glinted in the sun, and found no one there either. They returned to the cottage, baffled and frustrated by the desolation of this homestead, and pounded once again on the door. Again there was no answer. Goldmund tried the door and was surprised to find it unlocked. Pushing it open, he entered the dark room.

'Hello!' he shouted, and 'Anyone at home?' But the silence remained unbroken. Robert had stayed outside. Curious, Goldmund advanced into the room. There was a foul smell in the hut, a strange, repulsive smell. The hearth was heaped with ashes. He blew into them; a few sparks from charred logs were still glowing at the bottom. Then in the dim light he saw someone sitting beyond the hearth, someone in a chair, asleep, apparently an old woman. He called out but with no effect; the place seemed to be under a spell. He gave the woman a friendly tap on the shoulder, but she did not move, and then he saw that she was sitting enveloped in a cobweb, some of its threads being attached to her hair and knees. She's dead, he thought, with a slight shudder, and to convince himself he went to work on the fire, poking and blowing until there was a flame and he could set fire to a long wood-shaving, which he used to illumine the face of the seated woman. He saw under grey hair the bluish-white face of a corpse; one eye was open and shone vacant and leaden. The woman had died here, sitting in the chair. Well, she was past helping now.

Holding the burning wood-shaving, Goldmund continued to explore, and in the same room he found another corpse lying across the threshold to a back room, a boy of about eight or nine, wearing only a shirt, his face swollen and distorted. He was lying face down over the threshold, both hands clenched into small, desperate fists. This is the second one, Goldmund thought. As if in a bad dream he walked on, into the back room, where the shutters were open and daylight streamed in. He carefully extinguished his torch and stamped out the sparks on the floor.

In the back room were three beds. One was empty, with straw protruding from under the coarse grey sheet. In the second was another body, that of a bearded man lying rigidly on his back, chin and beard upthrust from the backward-tilted head. This must be the farmer. His sunken features shimmered wanly in the unfamiliar colours of death; one arm hung down to the floor, where an earthenware jug lay on its side, empty. The spilled water had not yet been entirely soaked up by the floor; it had run towards a little dip that still contained a small puddle. But in the third bed, completely buried and wrapped up in a sheet and blanket, lay a heavy-set woman, her face pressed into the bed, her coarse, straw-coloured hair catching the bright light. Beside her and wrapped up with her, as if entangled and suffocated in the twisted sheet, lay an adolescent girl, also with straw-coloured hair, her dead face showing greyish-blue patches.

Goldmund's eyes went from one body to the other. In the girl's face, although it was already much distorted, there were still signs of a helpless dread of death. In the hair and nape of the mother, who had wound herself so deeply and frenziedly into the bedclothes, there seemed to be rage, fear and a frantic desire to escape. Above all, the unruly hair had refused to capitulate to death. The farmer's face showed defiance and pain grimly borne. He had, it seemed, suffered a hard death but met it manfully. His bearded chin jutted stiffly into the air like that of a warrior felled on the battlefield. That silent, defiant, grimly outstretched body was beautiful. Clearly it had been no inferior or cowardly person who had accepted death in this manner. By contrast, the little body of the boy lying in the doorway was very moving. His face told nothing, but his posture across the threshold, together with those childish clenched fists, conveyed much: uncomprehending suffering, a helpless struggle against excruciating pain. Beside his head was an opening for the cat sawn in the door.

Goldmund observed it all minutely. No doubt about it, everything here looked pretty gruesome, and the smell of corpses was revolting. Yet for Goldmund it all had a profound fascination, was all filled with grandeur and destiny, so true, so genuine. Something about it captured his love and penetrated his soul.

Meanwhile Robert, impatient and anxious, began calling outside. Goldmund liked Robert, but at this moment he thought how very petty and insignificant was a living person, with his fear and curiosity and all his childishness, in comparison with the dead. He did not answer Robert but, with that strange mixture of deep compassion and cool observation such as artists possess, gave himself up entirely to the scene presented by the dead. He looked carefully at the figures on the beds, the floor and the chair: the heads, the hands, the attitudes in which they had stiffened. How silent it was in this spellbound cottage! How strange and dreadful it smelled! How eerie and sad this little human home was, where the remains of a fire still glowed on the hearth: inhabited by corpses, filled and permeated by death! Soon the flesh would fall from the cheeks of these silent forms, and rats would devour their fingers. The process that other people accomplished invisibly and discreetly in the coffin and the grave – the last and most pathetic of all, disintegration and decay – these five were accomplishing here at home, in their rooms, in daylight, with the door unlocked: unconcerned, unashamed, unprotected. Goldmund had seen quite a few dead people, but never before had he come upon such a display of the inexorable work of death. He drank it all in deeply.

When Robert's shouting at the front door finally began to bother him, he went outside. His companion looked at him anxiously. 'What's the matter?' he asked in a low, scared voice. 'Isn't there anyone in the house? Oh, the expression on your face! Say something!'

Goldmund looked him coolly up and down.

'Go inside and see for yourself. It's a queer kind of farm-house. Afterwards we'll milk that fine cow over there. Go on!'

Hesitantly Robert entered the cottage. As he moved towards the hearth he caught sight of the old woman sitting there and, on realizing she was dead, let out a scream. Back he came in a hurry, his eyes bulging.

'For God's sake! There's a dead woman sitting by the hearth! What does it mean? Why is nobody with her? Why don't they bury her? Oh God, what a stench there is!'

Goldmund smiled. 'You're quite a hero, Robert, but you came back much too quickly. Granted, an old woman sitting there dead like that in a chair is a strange sight, but if you go on a few steps you'll see even stranger things. There are five of them, Robert – three in bed and a dead youngster lying right in the doorway. They are all dead. The entire family is lying there dead, there's not a living soul in the house. That's why no one has milked the cow.'

Robert stared at him in horror, then suddenly cried out in a choked voice: 'Oh, now I understand about the peasants who wouldn't let us into their village yesterday! Oh my God, I see it all now. It's the plague! Upon my poor soul, it's the plague, Goldmund! And you were in there for such a long time, you may even have touched the bodies! Get away from me, don't come any closer, I'm sure you've been poisoned! I'm sorry, Goldmund, but I must go – I can't stay with you.'

He was about to run off but found himself impeded by his pilgrim's gown. Goldmund looked at him sternly in silent reproach and held on to him relentlessly as he pushed and struggled to get free.

'My dear young fellow,' Goldmund said, his tone gently mocking, 'you are smarter than one would think. You are prob-ably right. Well, we'll find that out at the next farm or village.

Probably there is plague in this area. We shall see whether we get through it unscathed. But as for running away, young Robert, I can't let you do that. Look, I am a merciful man, my heart is much too soft, and when I think that you might have become infected in there and I let you run away, and you would lie down somewhere out in the open to die, all alone, with no one to close your eyes and no one to dig you a grave and throw a little earth on you – no, my friend, the horror of it is too much to contemplate. So listen, and pay attention to what I say, for I shan't say it twice. We two share the same danger, it can strike either of us. So we'll stay together, and together we'll either perish or escape this cursed plague. If you become ill and die, I'll bury you, I promise you that. And if I'm the one who has to die, then do whatever you like – bury me or clear out, I don't care. But before that, my friend, there's to be no sneaking off, remember that! We shall soon need each other. And now shut up, I don't want to hear another word, and go and look for a bucket somewhere in the stable so we can at long last milk that cow.'

Thus it came to pass, and from that moment on it was Goldmund who gave the orders and Robert who obeyed, and both fared well under this arrangement. Robert made no further attempt to escape, merely saying placatingly: 'For a moment I was afraid of you. I didn't like the look of you after you had been in that house of the dead. I thought you had caught the plague. But even if it's not the plague, your face has changed. Was it as bad as that, what you saw in there?'

'It wasn't bad,' Goldmund said slowly. 'All I saw in there was what's in store for you and me and everyone else even if we don't catch the plague.'

Continuing on their way, they soon saw signs everywhere of the Black Death that had taken hold of the country. Some villages allowed no strangers to enter; in others they could walk round everywhere quite freely. Many farms had been abandoned; many unburied dead lay rotting outdoors or in the houses. In the stables, unmilked or starving cows were lowing, or the cattle were running loose in the open. They milked and fed a few cows and goats, slaughtered and roasted a few piglets and kids at the entrance to the forest, and drank wine and cider from many an abandoned cellar. In the midst of plenty they led the good life, but their enjoyment of it was overshadowed. Robert lived in perpetual fear of the plague, and the sight of the corpses nauseated him. Often he was quite distraught with fear: he kept thinking he had been infected and would hold his head and hands for long periods in the smoke of their camp fire (this was supposed to have a curative effect). Even in his sleep he would feel himself all over to find out if swellings had started on his legs or arms or in his armpits.

Goldmund, who did not share his fear or his revulsion, often scolded him, often scoffed at him. Intent and gloomy, he would walk through the land of death, grimly fascinated by the sight of so much dying, his soul filled with the great autumn of life, his heart heavy with the song of the Reaper's scythe. Sometimes the image of the eternal mother would appear again, a huge, pale face with Medusa eyes and a sombre smile laden with suffering and death.

One day they came to a small, heavily fortified town with a covered passage at housetop level on the wall encircling the town, but there was no guard on the wall or in the open gateway. Robert refused to enter the town and begged his companion not to do so. They heard a bell tolling and a priest emerged from the gate, carrying a cross and followed by three carts, two drawn by horses and one by a pair of oxen. The carts were filled to the top with corpses. A few men wearing strange cloaks, their faces hidden deep inside the hoods, walked alongside, urging the animals on.

Robert turned pale and vanished, while Goldmund followed the death-carts at a short distance. After a few hundred paces they stopped, but there was no graveyard. Instead, a pit had been dug in the empty heath, barely three feet deep but the length and breadth of a great hall. Goldmund stood watching as the men dragged the bodies from the carts with poles and boat-hooks and shoved them in piles into the big pit. The priest murmured a few words, waved his cross over the pit, and left, while the men lit great fires on all sides of the shallow grave and silently walked back to the town, having made no attempt to cover the pit with earth. He looked down: there must have been fifty or more bodies in there, thrown on top of each other, many of them naked. Here and there an arm or a leg stuck stiffly into the air as if in protest and a shirt flapped feebly in the wind.

Back at the gate, Robert begged, almost on his knees, that they move on as fast as possible. He had good reason for his entreaty: in Goldmund's absent look he saw that all-too-familiar absorption and obsession, that concentration on horror, that terrible curiosity. He failed to hold back his friend. Goldmund proceeded alone into the town.

He walked through the unguarded gate and, hearing his footsteps echoing from the cobbles, vividly recalled the many little towns and gates he had walked through like this, and he remembered how he had taken in the sounds of children shouting, boys playing, women squabbling, blacksmiths hammering on resounding anvils, carts rattling, and many other noises, subtle or crude sounds, a medley woven, as if into a net, that had proclaimed the diversity of human labour, joy, accomplishment and conviviality. Now here in this hollow gateway and empty lane, there was no sound, no laughter, no shouting; everything had frozen into the silence of death in which the musical chatter of a flowing fountain sounded almost disturbingly loud. Through a small open window a baker could be seen surrounded by his loaves and rolls. Goldmund pointed to a roll, and the baker carefully passed it out to him on a long shovel, then waited for Goldmund to put money on the shovel. He closed his window angrily but made no further protest when the stranger bit into the roll and walked on without paying. On the window-ledges of a charming house stood a row of earthenware pots in which flowers had once bloomed; now withered leaves hung down over the sides. From another house came the sound of children sobbing and wailing. But in the next alley Goldmund saw a pretty girl beside an upper window, combing her hair, and he watched her until, feeling his eyes on her, she looked down. She blushed as their eyes met, and when he smiled at her a slow, tentative smile spread over her blushing cheeks.

'Almost done?' he called up. With a smile on her fair young face she leaned out of the window.

'Not sick yet?' he asked, and she shook her head. 'Then come with me and leave this town of the dead. We'll go off to the forest and have a good life.'

Her eyes looked a question.

'Don't waste time thinking – I'm serious!' Goldmund called out. 'Do you live with your parents, or do you work for some other people? I see – other people. Then come, dear child. Let the old people die, we're young and healthy and want to enjoy life for a while yet. Come on, my little brunette, I'm serious!'

She looked at him searchingly, hesitantly, surprised. He strolled slowly on, along one deserted lane and then another, then slowly back. The girl was still leaning out of the window and seemed glad he had returned. She waved at him, and he slowly walked on. She soon followed, catching up with him even before he reached the gate. She was carrying a little bundle and wore a red kerchief over her hair.

'What's your name?' he asked her.

'Lena. I'm coming with you. Oh, it's so dreadful here in town – everyone's dying! Let's go away, far away!'

Near the gate he found Robert squatting morosely on the ground. As Goldmund approached he jumped up and stared when he caught sight of the girl. This time he did not submit immediately but wrung his hands and made a great scene. For someone to bring along a female out of that damned pest-hole and then expect him to tolerate her company – that was worse than mad, that was tempting Providence, and he refused, he wouldn't stay with him any longer, his patience was at an end.

Goldmund let him curse and rant until he calmed down. 'Well,' he said, 'you've carried on long enough. Now you'll come with us and be glad to have such charming company. Her name is Lena, and she's going to stay with me. But now I'm going to do you a favour, Robert – listen. For a while we're going to lead a quiet, healthy life and avoid the plague. We'll look for a nice place with an empty hut, or we'll build one ourselves, and Lena and I will be master and lady of the house, and you will be our friend and live with us. Let's find somewhere pleasant to live for a while. Do you approve?'

Oh yes, Robert thoroughly approved. As long as he wasn't required to shake hands with Lena or touch her clothes . . .

'No,' said Goldmund, 'you won't be. In fact, you will be strictly forbidden to touch Lena with as much as a finger. Don't even think of it!'

The three of them set out briskly, in silence at first; then gradually the girl began to speak, saying how glad she was to see sky and trees and meadows again, it had been so ghastly back there with the plague in the town, really indescribable. And she began to talk and rid her spirit of the tragic, terrible scenes she had had to witness. Many tales she told, horrifying ones; the little town must have been pure hell. Of the two physicians, one had died and the other would visit only the rich, and in many houses the dead lay rotting because nobody took them away. In other houses, the men who were paid to remove the bodies had gone on rampages of looting and whoring; often they had even dragged sick but still living people from their beds together with the dead, thrown them on their burial-carts and tossed them into the pits with the corpses. She had all kinds of terrible things to relate. Neither of them interrupted her. Robert listened in fascinated terror; Goldmund remained silent and calm, letting the horror spend itself and making no comment. What was there to say, after all?

At last Lena wearied, the torrent dried up and she ran out of words. Goldmund, slowing his pace, now started to sing, very softly, a song with many verses, and with each verse his voice gathered strength. Lena began to smile, and Robert listened in joyous surprise – never before had he heard Goldmund sing. He could do anything, this Goldmund! There he was, walking along and singing, this strange person! His voice was pure and musical, but he kept it low. At the second song, Lena hummed along softly and soon joined in with full voice. Evening was coming on; in the distance, beyond the heath, there were dark forests and, beyond those, low blue hills that seemed to grow more blue from within. Now cheerful, now solemn, their singing kept time with their footsteps.

'You're in such good spirits today,' said Robert.

'Yes, I am, of course I'm in good spirits today now that I've found such a pretty sweetheart. Oh Lena, what a good thing those gravediggers left you behind for me! Tomorrow we'll find ourselves a little home where we can be comfortable and glad that our flesh is still on our bones. Lena, have you ever been in a forest, in autumn, and seen those fat edible mushrooms the snails like so much?'

'Oh yes,' she laughed, 'I've seen them many times!'

'Your hair is the same brown as those mushrooms, Lena. And it smells so nice too. Shall we have another song? Or maybe you're hungry? There are still some good things in my satchel.'

The next day they found what they were looking for. In a little grove of birch trees stood a log hut, built perhaps by woodcutters or hunters. It was empty, the door could be broken open, and even Robert agreed that it was a good hut and a healthy area. On the way they had come upon some wandering goats with no goatherd, and they had taken along a fine nanny-goat.

'Well, Robert,' said Goldmund, 'although you're not a carpenter you did once work as a cabinet-maker. This is where we're going to live, and you must build a partition in our castle to give us two rooms – one for Lena and me, and one for you and the goat. We've nothing much left to eat, so today we'll have to make do with goat's milk, however much there is. So you must build the partition, and we two will prepare places for us all to sleep. Then tomorrow I'll go out and forage.'

Immediately they all got down to work. Goldmund and Lena went off to find ferns and moss for bedding, and Robert sharpened his knife on a stone to cut saplings for the partition but, being unable to finish the job in one day, slept outdoors that night. In Lena, Goldmund found a sweet playmate, shy and inexperienced but full of love. He gently held her to his chest, and after she had fallen asleep, tired and satisfied, he stayed awake a long time listening to her heart beating. He smelled her brown hair and nestled close to her as he thought of that great shallow pit in which the muffled devils had tossed all those cartloads of corpses. How beautiful was life, how beautiful and fleeting was happiness, how beautiful and swiftly withering was youth!

The partition in the hut turned out very nicely, with all three of them eventually working on it. Robert was keen to show what he could do and spoke enthusiastically of all the things he wanted to build if only he had a work-bench and tools and a try square and nails. Since all he had was his knife and his hands, he had to be content with cutting a dozen birch saplings and using them to build a rough, sturdy fence on the floor of the hut. The gaps, he decreed, had to be filled with interlaced branches of broom. This took time, but the result was very pleasing, and they all cheerfully joined in the work.

From time to time Lena had to go out and look for berries and attend to the goat, while Goldmund made little sorties into the area in search of food, exploring the surroundings and bringing back whatever he could find. Far and wide, no other people were to be found, a fact of which Robert in particular highly approved, as this kept them safe from infection or hostility, although it did mean that the area offered very little in the way of nourishment. There was a deserted farmhouse nearby, this time with no corpses inside, so that Goldmund suggested they choose that for their shelter instead of their log hut. But Robert, with a shudder, refused; he did not like Goldmund entering the empty house, and every object Goldmund brought back from there had to be smoked and washed before Robert would touch it. What Goldmund found did not amount to much: two stools, a milk pail, a few items of earthenware crockery and an axe, and one day he caught two stray chickens outside.

Lena was in love and happy, and all three of them enjoyed building their little home and making it a bit more pleasant every day. There being no bread, they adopted another goat, and they also discovered a small field of turnips. Day followed upon day, the interlacing of the partition was complete, their bedding was improved and a hearth built. A stream was not far off, and the water was clear and sweet. They often sang as they worked.

One day, as they were drinking their milk together and expressing delight in their domestic life, Lena suddenly said in a dreamy voice: 'But what's going to happen when winter comes?'

No one replied. Robert laughed; Goldmund stared straight ahead with an odd look in his eyes. Gradually it dawned on Lena that no one was thinking about the winter, no one was seriously considering staying in one place for so long, and that their home was not home, that she was among vagrants. She hung her head.

Then Goldmund said, in a playful, encouraging way as if to a child: 'You are a farmer's daughter, Lena, and farmers look far ahead. Don't worry, you'll find your way home again when this plague is over – it's not going to last for ever, you know. Then you'll go to your parents or whoever else you have, or you'll go back into the town and earn your keep as a maid. But now it's still summer, and all around us people are dying, while here it's pleasant and we're well off. So we'll stay here for just as long as it suits us.'

'And after that?' Lena burst out. 'After that, it's all over? And you'll go away? And what about me?'

Goldmund reached for her plait and gave it a gentle tug. 'Silly child,' he said, 'have you already forgotten the gravediggers, and the abandoned houses, and the great pit outside the gate with all those fires burning? You should be glad you're not lying in that pit with the rain falling on your shift. Just remember you've escaped – that there is still precious life in your limbs and that you can still laugh and sing.'

She was still not satisfied.

'But I don't want to leave here, and I don't want to let you go – no, I don't! How can one be happy when one knows that everything will soon be over!'

Again Goldmund responded, kindly enough but with a hint of threat in his voice: 'That's something, little one, that all the sages and saints have long been racking their brains over. There is no such thing as lasting happiness. But if what we have now isn't good enough for you and no longer pleases you, then I'll set fire to the hut this very hour, and we can each go our own way. Let's hear no more of this, Lena – enough has been said.'

That was how it was left, and she submitted, but a shadow had fallen over her happiness.

Chapter Fourteen

Even before summer had turned to autumn, life in the hut came to an end, but not in the way they had expected. A day came when Goldmund had been roaming the area for some time with a slingshot in the hope of getting a partridge or some other game, their food supply having run rather low. Lena was not far off, picking berries. Now and then he would pass close to her and glimpse her head and brown neck and the top of her cotton shift above the bushes or hear her singing. Once he helped himself to a few of her berries, then continued his search without seeing her again for a while. He thought about her, with some tenderness but also some annoyance; she had again spoken of autumn and the future, that she believed she was pregnant and that she wouldn't let him leave. It won't be long now, he thought. Soon I'll have had enough, I'll go off on my own and leave Robert behind too. I'll see that I get back to the big town, to Master Niklaus, before winter sets in, then spend the winter there, and next spring I'll buy some stout new shoes and go off again and somehow make my way to our monastery in Mariabronn and see Narcissus again. It must be a good ten years since I last saw him. I must see him, even if only for a day or two.

An unfamiliar sound roused him from his thoughts, and suddenly he was aware that with all his day-dreaming he had already moved far away. He strained to listen: that cry of fear was repeated. Believing he recognized Lena's voice, he followed it, although he somewhat resented her calling him. Soon he was close enough. Yes, it was Lena's voice, and she was screaming his name as if in desperate trouble. He ran faster, still a bit annoyed but, because of her repeated screams, pity and alarm were now uppermost in him. When at last he could see her she was sitting or kneeling in the heather, her shift torn to shreds, and as she screamed she was struggling with a man who was trying to rape her. Goldmund approached in great leaps, and all his annoyance, restlessness and despondency were discharged in a paroxysm of rage directed at the unknown assailant, whom he came upon just as he was trying to force Lena down on the ground. Her bare breasts were bleeding, and the stranger held her fast in his lecherous grip. Goldmund hurled himself upon him and tightened his furious hands round the man's throat, which felt gaunt and sinewy and was covered with a thick beard. Relishing his task, Goldmund increased his pressure until the man let go of the girl and hung inertly in Goldmund's hands. Still throttling him, he dragged the limp, half-unconscious man a short distance away to some bare grey rocks rising in ribs out of the ground. Here he lifted his victim, heavy though the man was, two or three times and smashed his head on to the jagged rock, breaking his neck. He then tossed the body away, but his fury was not yet assuaged; he would have liked to go on abusing it.

Lena looked on, her face aglow. Her breast was bleeding, and she was still trembling all over and gasping for air, but she quickly pulled herself together and watched with voluptuous admiration as her strong lover dragged the molester away, throttled him, broke his neck and flung the body from him. Like a snake that has been beaten to death, the body of the stranger lay twisted and limp, the grey face with its tousled beard and scanty hair tilted pathetically at a grotesque angle. With a cry of joy Lena got to her feet and threw her arms round Goldmund; then, still suffering from shock, she suddenly turned pale and sank, nauseated and exhausted, into the shrubs. However, before long she was able to go back to the hut with Goldmund, where he washed her badly scratched breasts, one of which showed toothmarks where the villain had bitten her.

When Robert heard about the incident he became very agitated and asked feverishly for details of the struggle.

'Broke his neck, you say? Marvellous! Goldmund, you're a man to be feared!'

But Goldmund did not want to talk about it any more; he had cooled down, and in leaving the dead man he had been reminded of poor Viktor, and that this was now the second person to have died by his hand. To get rid of Robert he said: 'And now you can do something too. Go over there and see to removing the body. If it's too difficult to dig a hole you'll have to carry it into the reeds or else cover it well with stones and earth.' But this suggestion was rejected: Robert refused to have anything to do with corpses – after all, one never knew whether they mightn't be contaminated by the plague.

Lena had lain down in the hut. The bite-wound in her breast was painful, but she soon felt better, got up, rekindled the fire and heated the evening milk. Although in very good spirits she was sent to bed early. Such was her admiration for Goldmund that she obeyed like a lamb. Goldmund was taciturn and gloomy, and Robert, being familiar with that mood, left him to himself. Later when Goldmund went to his pallet he bent down over Lena and listened. She was asleep. He was restless, thought of Viktor, felt uneasy and longed to get away, sensing that their game of domesticity had come to an end. There was one thing, however, that made him particularly thoughtful: he had caught the expression in Lena's eyes as she looked at him when he shook that fellow's body and tossed it away. A strange expression that had been. He knew he would never forget it. In those wide-open, horrified, enraptured eyes there had been a gloating pride, a deep and passionate sharing in the lust for revenge and killing such as he had never seen and never expected to see in a woman's face. Were it not for that look, he thought, he might one day, over the years, have forgotten Lena's face. That look had rendered her peasant face majestic, beautiful and terrible. It was months since his eyes had witnessed anything that sparked the desire: What a drawing that would make! At the sight of that look he had once again, with a kind of shock, felt the flash of that desire.

Unable to sleep, he finally got up and stepped outside. It was cool; a slight wind played in the birches. He paced back and forth in the dark, then sat down on a rock and sank into deep thought and melancholy. He felt sorry for Viktor, and he felt sorry for the man he had killed that day; he felt sorry for the lost innocence and childhood of his soul. Was it for this he had left the monastery, deserted Narcissus, offended Master Niklaus and renounced the beautiful Lisbeth – merely to camp out on a heath, lie in wait for stray cattle and kill that poor fellow among the rocks? Did all this have any meaning? Was it worth the experience? His heart contracted with a sense of futility and self-contempt. He sank back on the rock and lay staring up into the pale clouds of the night sky. As he stared he gradually lost track of his thoughts, not knowing whether he was looking at the clouds in the sky or into the murky world of his innermost self. All of a sudden, at the very moment he was falling asleep on the rock, a face appeared to him like sheet lightning among the drifting clouds, the great Eve-face, heavy-lidded and inscrutable. But suddenly its eyes opened wide, huge eyes full of sensuality and murderous lust. Goldmund slept until moistened by the dew.

The following day Lena was ill, so they told her not to get up. There was much to be done: that morning Robert had come across two sheep in the copse, but they had immediately fled from him. He fetched Goldmund, and they spent most of the day hunting the animals, eventually catching one of them. By the time they returned with the sheep towards evening they were worn out. Lena was feeling very ill. When Goldmund examined her he found plague swellings. He did not reveal this, but Robert, on hearing that Lena was still sick, became suspicious and did not stay in the hut. He would look for a place to sleep outside, he said, and he'd take along the goat, too, since it might also become infected.

'Then go to the Devil! I never want to see you again!' Goldmund shouted at him furiously as he grabbed the goat and took it behind the partition. Without a word Robert disappeared, minus the goat. He was sick with fear – fear of the plague, fear of Goldmund, fear of loneliness and the night. He lay down close to the hut.

'I'll stay with you,' Goldmund told Lena, 'don't worry. You'll get better again.'

She shook her head. 'Be careful, dearest, that you don't catch the sickness too. You mustn't come so close to me any more. Don't try to comfort me. I must die, and I would rather die than one day have to see your bed empty and know that you have left me. I have thought of that each morning and been afraid. No, I would rather die.'

Next morning her condition was very much worse. From time to time during the night Goldmund had given her a sip of water, snatching an hour or two of sleep when he could. Now as it grew light he could not fail to recognize the nearness of death in her face, the flesh already shrivelled and wasted. He stepped outside for a breath of air and a look at the sky. A few bent, red pine trunks at the forest's edge were already catching the sun; the air tasted fresh and sweet, and the distant hills were still hidden by early-morning clouds. He walked on a little way, stretching his weary limbs, and took a deep breath. How beautiful the world was on this sad morning! His wanderings were about to begin again. It was time to say goodbye.

Robert called out to him from the forest: Was she any better? If it wasn't the plague, he'd stay, and he hoped Goldmund wasn't angry with him. Meanwhile he'd been minding the sheep.

'Go to Hell with your sheep!' Goldmund shouted back. 'Lena is dying, and I've caught it too!'

The last part was a lie, spoken to get rid of him. Robert was a good-natured fellow, but Goldmund had had enough of him: he was too cowardly, too small, to have around in these fateful, turbulent times. Robert disappeared and did not return. The sun rose in splendour.

On returning to Lena he found her asleep. He fell asleep again too, and in his dream saw his old pony Blaze and the beautiful chestnut tree at the monastery. He felt as if he were looking back across immeasurable distance and desolation at a lost and lovely homeland, and when he awoke tears were running down his bearded cheeks. He heard Lena's weak voice. Thinking she was calling him, he raised himself on his elbow, but she was not speaking to anyone, she was merely mumbling words to herself, words of endearment, words of abuse, laughing a little, then sighing heavily and swallowing, until she gradually fell silent again. Goldmund got up and leaned over her already distorted face. With grim curiosity his eye followed the lines that were being so pathetically twisted and contorted under the scorching breath of death. Dear Lena, his heart called out, dear, good child, do you want to leave me too, have you already had enough of me?

His impulse was to run away. To roam, to walk, to step out briskly, to breathe the air, become tired, see new scenes – that would have done him good, perhaps alleviated his deep depression. But he could not do that; he simply could not leave the child here to die alone. He scarcely dared go outside briefly every few hours for some fresh air. Since Lena could now no longer swallow any milk, he drank his fill of it; there was nothing else to eat. He also let the goat out a few times so it could browse, drink and move around. Then he would stand once more by Lena's bed, murmuring words of tenderness, looking fixedly into her face, sorrowfully but intently watching her die. She was conscious; sometimes she slept, and when she woke up she would only partially open her eyes, the lids being weary and slack. Round her eyes and nose the young girl aged with every passing hour; above the fresh young neck there was now the rapidly withering face of a grandmother. She rarely uttered a word, would say 'Goldmund' or 'dearest', and try to moisten her swollen bluish lips with her tongue, and he would give her a few drops of water.

That night she died. She died without complaint: after a brief little shudder her breathing stopped and a quiver passed over her skin. The sight of it gave a jolt to his heart, and he remembered the dying fish he had so often seen and pitied at the fish-market. They had expired in just the same way, with a brief shudder and a pitiful little quiver that passed over their skin, taking the shine and life with it. For a while he stayed on his knees beside Lena, then went outside and sat down in the heather. Remembering the goat, he went in again and brought out the animal; after briefly sniffing around, it lay down on the ground. Goldmund lay down beside it, rested his head on its flank and slept until daybreak.

Then, for the last time, he went into the hut and behind the partition for a final look at that poor dead face. He could not bear to leave the dead girl lying there so he went out and collected armfuls of dry wood and dead leaves. After tossing these into the hut he struck a flame with his flint – the only thing he had brought out of the hut – and set fire to them. Instantly the partition of dried broom blazed up. Standing outside, his face roasted by the fire, he watched until the whole roof was in flames and the first roof beams collapsed. The goat skipped about, bleating in fear. It would have made sense to kill the animal, roast it and eat some of it to gain strength for his journey. But he could not do that: he chased the goat on to the heath and left, the smoke from the fire following him all the way into the forest. Never had he set out on a journey in such a mood of despondency.

And yet that which awaited him was even worse than he had imagined. Starting at the first farms and villages it continued and grew worse the farther he went. The whole area, the whole wide country, was under a cloud of death, under a veil of horror, fear and spiritual eclipse; and the worst part was not the deserted houses, the decomposing bodies of watchdogs that had starved to death at the end of their chains, or the unburied dead, the begging children, the mass graves outside the towns. The worst was the living who, under the burden of horror and mortal fear, seemed to have lost their eyes and their souls. Everywhere he went the wayfarer witnessed and heard of strange and gruesome things. Parents had abandoned their children, and husbands their wives, when these became ill. The men paid to remove the corpses held sway like hangmen, looting the empty houses of the dead, arbitrarily leaving the bodies unburied or dragging the dying from their beds and on to the death-carts before they had breathed their last. Frightened refugees, ragged and unkempt, wandered aimlessly about, singly, avoiding all human contact, haunted by the fear of death. Others gathered together in a whipped-up, hysterical mania for life, carousing and indulging in orgies of dancing and copulation at which Death played the fiddle. Others – demoralized, grieving or cursing – squatted wild-eyed outside graveyards or their empty houses. And worst of all: each one sought a scapegoat for the unbearable misery; each one claimed to know the villains who were responsible for the plague and were its evil originators. Devilish persons, it was said, gloatingly helped to spread death by removing the plague poison from corpses and smearing it on walls and door handles and by using it to contaminate wells and cattle. Those suspected of such atrocities were doomed unless warned and able to escape: they were punished with death by either the judiciary or the mob. Furthermore, the rich blamed the poor and vice versa, or the Jews were said to be responsible, or the foreigners or the physicians. In one town Goldmund watched in suppressed rage as an entire Jewish sector burned, house after house, while the howling mob stood round and the screaming victims were driven back by force of arms into the flames. In the madness of fear and frustration, innocent people everywhere were being beaten to death, burned to death or tortured. Goldmund looked on with fury and revulsion. The world seemed destroyed and poisoned; there seemed to be no more joy, no more innocence, no more love on earth. Often he would join some frenzied celebrants of the lust to live – Death's fiddle was to be heard everywhere and he soon learned to recognize its sound – or he would participate in those desperate feasts, perhaps play the lute or join in the dancing by the light of pitch flares throughout the feverish night.

He was without fear. In the past he had tasted mortal fear, that winter's night under the fir trees when Viktor's fingers had tightened round his throat; also in the snow and hunger of many a hard day's wayfaring. That had been a death one could fight and resist, and he had resisted, with trembling hands and feet, with an empty stomach and exhausted limbs – had resisted, had conquered and had escaped. But there was no fighting this pestilential death; one had to let it rage, to become resigned to it, and Goldmund had long since become resigned to it. He had no fear: he seemed to have lost interest in life since leaving Lena behind in the burning hut, since wandering day after day through the death-ridden land. But an enormous curiosity drove him and kept him alert; tirelessly he observed the Reaper, listened to the song of the transience of life. Nowhere did he turn away; everywhere he was gripped by the same silent passion to be present and to walk his way through Hell with open eyes. He ate mouldy bread in abandoned houses, joined in the singing and drinking at the frenzied feasts, plucked the short-lived flower of love, looked into the staring, intoxicated eyes of women, into the staring, sodden eyes of drunks, into the dulled eyes of the dying, made love to desperate, feverish women; for a bowl of soup helped carry out the dead, for a few coins helped throw earth on naked corpses. The world had become dark and savage, Death howled its song, and Goldmund listened with open ears, with burning passion.

His goal was the town of Master Niklaus, to which he was drawn by the voice of his heart. The way was long, and it was full of death, of withering and dying. Sadly he walked on and on, intoxicated by Death's song, caught up in the screaming agony of the world, grieving yet passionate, with wide-eyed senses.

In a monastery he saw a newly painted mural, which he studied for a long time. The Dance of Death had been painted on a wall: the pale skeleton of dancing Death was leading the people out of their lives – the king, the bishop, the abbot, the count, the knight, the physician, the peasant, the mercenary – taking them all along with him to a tune played by skeletal musicians on hollow bones. Goldmund's avid eyes drank in the painting. Here an unknown fellow-artist had drawn the lesson from what he had seen of the Black Death, and was shouting into the ears of men the grim sermon of the certainty of dying.

It was good, this mural, it was a good sermon; this unknown fellow-artist had seen and portrayed the whole thing quite well. A gruesome rattling of bones emanated from his frightening painting. Yet it was not what he, Goldmund, had himself seen and experienced. This mural portrayed the harsh inevitability of dying. But Goldmund would have liked a different picture; in him, Death's wild song sounded quite different – not skeletal and harsh but sweet and seductive, beckoning homewards, maternal. Wherever Death reached its hand into life, the sound was not merely strident and martial but also deep and caressing, autumnal and replete, and in the proximity of death the tiny lamp of life shone with a brighter, more ardent light. For others, Death might be a warrior, a judge or an executioner, a stern father: for him, Death was also a mother and lover, its call a call of love, its touch a shiver of love.

After studying the Dance of Death mural and setting off again, Goldmund felt with even greater force the urge to see the master and to create a work of art. But along the way there were many new scenes and experiences to delay him. With quivering nostrils he breathed in the air of death; wherever he went, compassion or curiosity claimed an hour or a day from him. For three days he took along a whimpering little peasant boy, carrying him for hours on his back, a half-starved urchin of five or six who put him to a lot of trouble. He found it difficult to get rid of him but eventually a charcoal-burner's wife took the boy off his hands. Her husband had died, and she wanted some living creature about the place again. For days a stray dog kept him company, eating out of his hand, warming him when he slept, but one morning the dog was gone. He felt sorry: he had become used to talking to the dog, addressing lengthy ruminations to the animal about the wickedness of men and the existence of God, about art, about the breasts and hips of a knight's young daughter by the name of Julie whom he had once known in his youth. For of course on his journey through death Goldmund had become a little mad; everyone in the plague area was a little mad, some completely so. Maybe the young Jewess Rebekka was also a little mad, that beautiful black-haired girl with the burning eyes with whom he tarried for two days.

He found her outside a small town, crouching beside a heap of charred rubble and sobbing as she beat her face and tore at her black hair. He was moved to pity by her hair, it was so beautiful, and catching her frantic hands he held them tight as he tried to soothe her, noticing as he did so that her face and figure were also of great beauty. She was bewailing the death of her father who, with fourteen other Jews, had been burned to ashes by order of the authorities. After managing to escape she had now returned in despair, overcome with remorse at not having let herself be burned with them. He patiently held on to her trembling hands as he tried to calm her and, murmuring words of sympathy and protection, offered to help her. She asked him to help bury her father, and from the hot ashes they collected all the bones, carried them across the fields to a secluded spot and covered them with earth.

Meanwhile night was approaching, and Goldmund looked for a place to sleep. In a copse of oak trees he prepared a bed for the girl, promised to keep watch, and listened to her crying and sobbing until she finally fell asleep. Then he slept for a while too and in the morning began his courtship. He told her she couldn't remain alone like that; she would be recognized as a Jewess and killed, or villainous vagrants would rape her, and there were wolves and gypsies in the forest. However, he would take her with him and protect her from wolf and man, for he felt sorry for her and liked her well, since he had eyes in his head and knew what beauty was, and never would he permit those sweet, clever eyelids and those graceful shoulders to be devoured by beasts or perish at the stake. She scowled as she listened to him, then jumped up and ran away, and he had to chase and catch her before he could continue.

'Rebekka,' he said, 'can't you see that I wish you no harm? You're troubled, you're thinking of your father, at the moment you don't want to hear anything about love. But tomorrow or the next day or the day after I'll ask you again, and until then I'll protect you and bring you food and I shan't touch you. Be sad as long as you need to be. With me you can be sad or happy – I want you always to do only what gives you pleasure.'

But his words were so much chaff in the wind. She didn't want to do anything, she said angrily, that would give pleasure; she wanted to do only what would give pain. Never again would she think of such a thing as pleasure, and the sooner the wolf devoured her the better it would be for her. And now would he please leave? Nothing could help her – they had already talked too much.

'Listen,' he said, 'don't you see that death is all around us, that in every house and every town people are dying, that there is misery and despair everywhere? Even the rage of those stupid people who burned your father to death is nothing but anguish and despair, simply the result of unbearable suffering. Look, soon death will come for us too, and our bodies will decay somewhere under the sky, and moles will play dice with our bones. Until then, let us live and be kind to each other. Oh Rebekka, it would be such a waste of your white neck and your little foot! Dear, beautiful girl, come with me – all I want is to see you and look after you!'

He went on and on pleading until it suddenly became clear even to him that it was useless to woo her with words and reasons. He fell silent and looked at her sorrowfully. Her proud, regal face was rigid with rejection.

'That's how you are,' she said at last, in a voice of hatred and contempt, 'that's how you Christians are! First you help a daughter bury her father, whom your people have murdered and whose little fingernail is worth more than you, and hardly has that been done when the girl is supposed to fall into your arms and go to bed with you! That's how you are! At first I thought you might be a good person. But how could you be good? Oh, you're all pigs!'

While she was speaking, Goldmund saw in her eyes, behind the hatred, a glowing core that touched and shamed him and struck deep into his heart. In her eyes he saw death; not *having* to die but wanting to die, being allowed to die: in homage to the Earth-mother and submission to her call.

'Rebekka,' he said softly, 'you may be right. I am not a good person, though I wanted only the best for you. Forgive me. Now at last I really understand you.'

Doffing his cap, he bowed deeply as to a princess and with a heavy heart walked away; there was no way he could save her. For a long time he remained depressed and shunned all conversation. As little as they resembled one another, this proud, pathetic Jewish child somehow reminded him of Lydia, the knight's daughter. To love such women entailed suffering. But for a while it seemed to him that he had never loved any other than these two: poor, timid Lydia, and the shy, bitter Jewess.

For many a day his thoughts dwelled on this raven-haired, passionate girl, and many a night he dreamed of the slender burning beauty of her body, which seemed made for joy and fulfilment but was already fated to die. Oh, that those lips and breasts should fall prey to 'pigs' and decay somewhere in the open! Was there no power, no magic, to save those precious blossoms? Yes, there was: it would be for them to live on in his soul, for him to give them form and permanence. In fear and rapture he was aware of how his soul brimmed with images, how this long journey through the land of death had crammed the pages of his mind with images. Oh, how his soul was filled to bursting with these images, how he longed to reflect on them in peace, to let them flow by and be turned by him into permanent form! He pressed on, his ardour ever increasing, still with open eyes and inquisitive senses but filled with a fierce desire for paper and charcoal, for clay and wood, for workshop and work.

Summer was over. Many expressed confidence that, with the arrival of autumn or at least the onset of winter, the pestilence would come to an end. It was an autumn without cheer. Goldmund passed through areas where there was no one left to pick the fruit. In some places it fell from the trees and rotted in the grass; in others, roving hordes from the towns came to raid and plunder the orchards.

Gradually Goldmund approached his destination, and during this last stage he was often beset by the fear that he might still catch the plague and die in some barn or other. Now he no longer wanted to die – not before tasting the joy of standing once again in a workshop and devoting himself to artistic creation. For the first time in his life he found the world too wide and the German Empire too big. No pretty little town could entice him to linger; no pretty peasant girl could hold him for longer than a night.

One day he came past a church whose main doorway was framed by deep niches containing ancient stone figures standing on small decorative columns: figures of angels, apostles and martyrs such as he had often seen before. At his own monastery, Mariabronn, there had also been a number of statues of this kind. In the old days, as a youth, he had felt pleasure in looking at them but no emotion, finding them beautiful and dignified but a little too solemn, too stiff and patriarchal. Later on, when at the end of his first long journey he had been so enthralled by that sweet, sad Madonna of Master Niklaus's, he had found those solemn, old-world statues too heavy, too rigid and unapproachable. He had regarded them with a certain condescension, whereas in his master's new style he had seen a much more vital, intimate and spiritual art. Today as he returned from the world, his head full of images, his soul marked with the traces and scars of violent adventures and experiences and yearning for an opportunity to reflect and create, these ancient, austere sculptures suddenly touched his heart with overwhelming power. He stood reverently before the venerable creations in which the essence of a distant era lived on, and the fears and raptures of long-vanished generations, frozen in stone, still defied impermanence after so many centuries. In his unruly heart there arose with a shudder a humble sense of awe as well as horror at his wasted, burned-out life. He did what he had not done for an immensely long time: went in search of a confessional so that he might make confession and receive a penance. But although there were confessionals in the church, in none of them was there a priest. They had died, were in hospital, had fled or were afraid of infection. The church was empty, and Goldmund's footsteps echoed hollowly from the vaulted stone ceiling.

He knelt down beside one of the empty confessionals, closed his eyes and whispered through the grille: 'Dear Lord, see what has become of me. I am returning from the world and have become a bad, useless person. I have squandered my young years like a profligate, and there is little left. I have killed, I have stolen, I have whored. I have been idle and have taken away the bread of others. Dear Lord, why hast Thou created us like this, why dost Thou lead us along such paths? Are we not Thy children? Did not Thy Son die for us? Are there not saints and angels to guide us? Or are these all charming stories invented for children and laughed at by the priests themselves? I have lost faith in Thee, O Lord. Thou hast created an evil world, and Thou dost not look after it well. I have seen houses and streets filled with the dead; I have seen how the rich barricaded themselves in their houses or fled, and how the poor left their brothers unburied, each casting suspicion on the other, and how they slaughtered the Jews like cattle. I have seen so many innocent people suffer and perish, and so many wicked ones wallowing in luxury. Hast Thou then quite forgotten and deserted us? Canst Thou no longer tolerate Thy creation? Dost Thou want us all to perish?'

With a sigh he walked out of the church and saw the silent stone statues, angels and saints, standing gaunt and tall in the stiff folds of their robes: motionless, out of reach, superhuman yet created by human hand and the human spirit. Austere and unheeding, there they stood in their narrow spaces, deaf to all requests or questions, yet infinitely consoling, a triumphant victory over death and despair, upright in their dignity and beauty and outliving one expiring human generation after another. Oh, that the poor, beautiful Jewess Rebekka might be there too, and poor Lena who was burned to ashes with the hut, and lovely Lydia, and Master Niklaus! But one day they would stand there and survive, he would place them there; and their images, which today meant love and torment, fear and passion, to him, would stand without name or history before future generations – mute, motionless symbols of human life.

Chapter Fifteen

At last Goldmund reached his longed-for destination, and he entered the town through the same gate through which, so many years before, he had passed for the first time in search of his master. A few items of news from the cathedral town had reached him on his way. He knew that the plague had been there too, perhaps was still there. He had been told of disturbances and popular uprisings, and that an imperial governor had come to restore order, proclaim emergency laws and protect the possessions and lives of the citizens. The bishop had left the town immediately after the outbreak of the plague and was now residing in one of his palaces far off in the country. The wayfarer had not been much concerned with all this news, as long as the town still stood, and the workshop where he wanted to work! All the rest meant little to him. By the time he arrived, the plague had died out; the return of the bishop was expected, and people were looking forward to the departure of the governor and the resumption of normal peaceful life.

At the sight of the town, Goldmund experienced a surge of nostalgia in his heart, and he assumed an unwonted expression of severity in order to control himself. It was all still there! The gateways, the charming fountains, the massive old tower of the cathedral and the slender new spire of St Mary's, the clear sound of the bells of St Lawrence, the great colourful market-place. How satisfying that all this had waited for him! Hadn't he once along the way dreamed of arriving and finding everything unfamiliar and altered, partly destroyed and in ruins, partly unrecognizable because of new buildings and other disturbing signs of change? He was close to tears as he walked through the streets, recognizing one building after another. When all was said and done, weren't the burghers to be envied, in their nice, safe houses, their peaceable settled lives, soothed and fortified by the sense of having roots, of being at ease in home and workshop, among wife and child, servants and neighbours?

It was late afternoon, and on the sunny side of the lane the houses, the signboards hanging outside taverns and guilds, the carved doors and the flowerpots shone in the warm rays. There was nothing to remind one that this town, too, had been ruled by rampant death and the wild hysteria of the people. The river, clear and cool, pale green and pale blue, flowed under the echoing arches of the bridge. Goldmund sat down on the embankment. Below in the green crystal, the dark, shadowy fish still glided, or hung motionless with their heads against the current; from the twilit depths that faint gold shimmer still flashed here and there, so richly promising, so conducive to daydreams. All this also existed in other waters, and other bridges and towns also presented a pretty sight, yet it seemed to him that for a very long time he had not seen or felt anything like it.

Two butcher-boys were laughing as they drove a calf past him, exchanging looks and banter with a servant-girl who was taking down washing from an arbour above them. How swiftly everything passed! Not long ago the plague fires were still burning and the dreaded corpse-removers holding sway here, and now life was going on again, people were laughing and joking, and he himself was no different, overjoyed and grateful to be back, with even a soft spot for the townspeople, as if there had never been any misery or death, any Lena or Jewish princess.

With a smile he stood up and walked on. Only when he approached Master Niklaus's lane and retraced the route to work that he had taken every day for years did he begin to feel uneasy. He quickened his pace: he must speak to the master this very day and get an answer, it couldn't be put off any longer – it seemed quite out of the question to wait another day. Was it conceivable that the master was still angry with him? That was so long ago: it couldn't possibly still have any significance and, if it did, he would overcome it. So long as the master was still there, and the workshop, all was well. As if he might miss something at the last minute, he hurried towards the familiar house, grasped the door handle, and was shocked to find the door locked. Could that be a bad omen? In the old days he had never known this door to be kept locked in broad daylight. The knocker resounded as he let it fall back. He waited. All of a sudden he felt very much afraid.

The door was opened by the same old serving-woman who had admitted him the first time he came to the house. She had not grown any uglier, but she was older and even more ungracious, and she did not recognize Goldmund. Anxiously he asked after the master. She gave him a vacant, suspicious look.

'Master? There's no master here. Go away, you – no one's allowed in here.'

She tried to push him back out of the doorway, but he took her by the arm and shouted at her: 'Tell me, Margrit, for God's sake! I'm Goldmund – don't you know me? I must see Master Niklaus!'

In those dim, unfocused eyes there was no glimmer of welcome.

'There's no Master Niklaus here any more,' she said in a surly voice. 'He's dead. Be off with you now. I can't stand here and waste my time talking.'

While everything in him was collapsing, Goldmund pushed the old crone aside, and with her at his heels hurried along the dark passage towards the workshop. It was closed. Pursued by the outraged old woman, he ran up the stairs, and in the dim light on the familiar landing he saw the sculptures that Niklaus had collected. Raising his voice he shouted for Mistress Lisbeth.

The door to the chamber opened, and Lisbeth appeared. When he recognized her, although only after a second look, her appearance gave him a pang. If everything in this house, starting with his shock at finding the front door locked, had seemed to be under some eerie, nightmarish spell, the sight of Lisbeth now really sent a shiver down his spine. The beautiful, proud Lisbeth had turned into a shy, stooped spinster with a sallow, sickly face, wearing a plain black dress, uncertain and nervous in gaze and posture.

'Forgive me,' he said, 'Margrit didn't want to let me in. Don't you know me? I'm Goldmund! Please tell me, is it true your father is dead?'

From her expression he could see that she recognized him now, and he could also see that her memory of him was not favourable.

'I see – you're Goldmund?' she said, and in her voice he recognized something of her former haughty manner. 'You have come here in vain. My father is dead.'

'And the workshop?' he burst out.

'The workshop? It's closed. If you are looking for work you will have to go elsewhere.'

He tried to pull himself together.

'Mistress Lisbeth,' he said with a smile, 'I am not looking for work, I merely wanted to pay my respects to the master and to you. I am truly saddened by what I hear! I can see that you have been through a difficult time. If a grateful pupil of your father's can be of any service whatever to you, please say so – it would give me great pleasure. Ah, Mistress Lisbeth, it breaks my heart to find – to find you in such sad trouble.'

She stepped back into the doorway. 'Thank you,' she said after a pause. 'There is nothing you can do for him now, or for me. Margrit will see you out.'

Her voice sounded harsh, half angry, half frightened. He felt that, if she had had the courage, she would have thrown him out in disgrace.

In no time he was downstairs; in no time the old woman had slammed the front door behind him and shot the bolts home. He could still hear the hard impact of the two bolts; it sounded like a coffin-lid being slammed shut.

Slowly he returned to the embankment and resumed his old place above the river. The sun had gone down, cold air rose from the water, and cold too was the stone he was sitting on. The street along the river was silent now; the current swished past the bridge pier, and in the dark depths there were no flashing golden gleams. Oh, he thought, if only I were to fall over the wall now and disappear in the river! Once again the world was full of death. An hour passed, and dusk had turned to night. At last he was able to weep. He sat there and wept, the warm drops falling on his hands and knees. He wept for his dead master, he wept for Lisbeth's lost beauty, he wept for Lena, for Robert, for the young Jewess, for his withered, wasted youth.

After a while he made his way to a wine tavern where at one time he used to carouse with his friends. The landlord's wife recognized him. When he asked her for a piece of bread she gave it to him, kindly adding a beaker of wine, but he was unable to swallow either bread or wine. He slept through the night on a bench in the tavern, and the woman woke him in the morning. He thanked her and went on his way, eating the bread as he walked along.

At the fish-market he saw the house where he had once had a room. Beside the fountain a few fishwives were offering their living wares, and he peered into the tubs at the lovely shimmering creatures. How often he had seen all this before, and how often felt sorry for the fish and been furious with the fishwives and their customers. Long ago, he recalled, he had also spent a morning wandering about here like this, admiring and pitying the fish and feeling very sad. Much time had passed since then, and much water had flowed under the bridge. He had felt very sad, he clearly remembered that, but what it was that he had felt so sad about he could no longer remember. That's how it was: even sadness passed, even pain and despair passed, just as joy did. They passed, faded, lost their depth and their value, and eventually there came a time when one could no longer remember what had been so painful. Even pain wilted and withered. Would even his present pain wither one day and become worthless, his despair over the master's death and the fact that he had died still bearing a grudge against him, and that there was no workshop open to him so he could taste the joy of creation and unload the burden of images from his soul? Yes, without a doubt even this pain, even this bitter suffering, would grow old and weary; even those he would forget. Nothing lasted, not even suffering.

While gazing at the fish, lost in these thoughts, he heard a voice softly speak his name. 'Goldmund!' it called diffidently, and on glancing in that direction he saw it had come from a young girl, rather frail-looking but with beautiful dark eyes. He did not know her.

'Goldmund! It is you, isn't it?' said the diffident voice. 'How long have you been back here? Don't you remember me? I'm Marie!'

But he could not place her. She had to tell him that she was the daughter of his former landlord, and that long ago, early on the morning of his departure, she had heated some milk for him in the kitchen. She blushed as she told him.

Yes, it was Marie, that ailing child with the bad hip who had looked after him so sweetly and shyly that morning. Now it all came back to him: that chilly dawn she had waited for him and been so sad that he was leaving; she had heated some milk for him and he had given her a kiss, which she had received as meekly and solemnly as if it were a sacrament. He had never thought of her since. At the time she was still a child. Now she had grown up and had very beautiful eyes, but she still limped and looked far from robust. He took her hand in his. It pleased him that after all there was someone in this town who remembered him and was fond of him.

Marie took him home with her, and he offered little resistance. Her parents, in whose home his painting still hung on the wall and his ruby-red glass still stood on the mantelshelf, insisted that he share their midday meal, and they invited him to stay for a few days. It was a pleasure, they said, to see him again. It was here that he learned what had happened in his master's house. Niklaus had not died of the plague; it was the lovely Lisbeth who had caught it. She almost died, and her father, having nursed her beyond the limits of his own strength, died before she had fully recovered. She was saved, but her beauty was gone.

'The workshop is empty,' said his host, 'and for a capable wood-carver there would be a nice home and plenty of money. Think it over, Goldmund! She wouldn't say no – she has no choice now.'

He was also told some other things about the time of the plague – that the mob had first set fire to a hospital and later stormed and looted a few houses of the rich. For a while there had ceased to be any order or safety in the town, the bishop having fled. Then the Emperor, who happened to be in the vicinity, had sent a governor, Count Heinrich. Well, he was a forceful gentleman, and with his few horsemen and soldiers he had restored order in the town. But now it was probably time for his rule to end; the bishop was expected back. The townspeople had had to put up with a lot from the count, and they had also had enough of his doxy, Agnes – she was a proper hellcat. Oh well, they'd be leaving soon, the town council was fed up with having their good bishop replaced by this courtier-soldier who was a favourite of the Emperor's and forever receiving ambassadors and delegations like a prince.

And now the guest was asked about his own experiences. 'Ah,' he said, 'better not talk about that. I have been up and down the whole country, and everywhere the plague was raging and the dead were lying around, and everywhere the people were mad and evil with fear. I survived, and perhaps some day I'll forget all that. Now I am back, and my master is dead! Let me stay here and rest a few days, then I'll be on my way.'

He did not stay in order to rest. He stayed because he was disappointed and vacillating, because memories of happier times endeared the town to him and because poor Marie's love gratified him. He could not return it: he could give her nothing but kindness and pity, though her silent, humble adoration did warm his heart. More than all this, however, what bound him to this place was the burning urge to be an artist again, even without a workshop, even with only makeshift tools.

For a few days Goldmund did nothing but draw. Marie had obtained paper and pen for him, and he sat in his room drawing, hour after hour, filling the big sheets with figures – some hurriedly scrawled, others drawn with loving care, letting the bursting picture-book of his mind flow on to the paper. Many times he drew Lena's face, the way it had smiled, full of satisfaction, love and blood-lust, after that vagrant's death; and Lena's face as it had been during her last night, already beginning to melt into formlessness, beginning its return to earth. He drew a little peasant boy whom he had once seen lying dead with clenched fists across a threshold in his parents' house. He drew a cart filled with corpses and drawn by three straining nags, accompanied by hooded men with long poles, their eyes squinting menacingly through the slits in their black plague-masks. Over and over again he drew Rebekka, the slender, black-eyed young Jewess, her narrow, proud lips, her face full of pain and indignation, her graceful young figure that seemed created for love, her arrogant, bitter mouth. He drew himself, as a wayfarer, as a lover, in flight from the Reaper's scythe, dancing at the plague orgies of those with a mania for life. Totally absorbed, he sat over the white paper, sketching the determined, haughty face of Mistress Lisbeth as he had once known her, the ugly visage of old Margrit, the beloved, feared face of Master Niklaus. Occasionally he also sketched, in thin, intuitive lines, a great female figure, the Earth-mother, seated with her hands in her lap, on her face a hint of a smile beneath the brooding eyes. He felt an extraordinary relief at this outpouring, this sensation in the hand as it drew, this mastering of the faces. Within a few days he had covered every sheet of paper. From the last one he cut off a piece and, with a few strokes, drew Marie's face with its beautiful eyes, its resigned mouth. This he gave her as a present.

Through his drawing he had released from his soul the heavy burden of pressure and congestion. As long as he was drawing he forgot where he was; his world consisted only of the table, the white paper and at night the candle. Now he woke up, recalled his most recent experiences, saw himself inescapably faced with new journeyings, and began to roam the town with strangely divided emotions, partly of reunion, partly of farewell.

On one of these walks he encountered a woman, the sight of whom gave a new focus to all his confused emotions. It was a woman on horseback, tall, fair-haired, with probing, somewhat aloof blue eyes, firm, taut limbs and a face alive with the desire for pleasure and power, full of self-confidence and sensual curiosity. Mounted on her chestnut horse she appeared somewhat imperious and haughty, accustomed to giving orders yet not reserved or distant, for under those cool blue eyes were sensitive nostrils open to all the scents of the world, and the wide, soft-lipped mouth seemed supremely capable of both giving and taking. The moment Goldmund saw her he became fully alert and filled with the desire to match himself against this proud woman. To conquer this woman seemed to him a noble goal, and to lose his life on his way to her would have seemed not the worst kind of death. Instantly he sensed that this blonde lioness was his equal, rich in sensuality and soul, open to every assault, as tempestuous as she was tender, versed in all the passions by reason of her ancient, inherited blood.

She rode past. His eyes followed her, glimpsing between blonde curls and a blue velvet collar her firm neck, strong and proud in its delicate, flawless skin. He thought her the most beautiful woman he had ever seen. He wanted to clasp that neck in his hand and wrest the cool blue secret from her eyes. It was not difficult to find out who she was, and he soon learned that she lived in the palace and was called Agnes, the governor's mistress. This did not surprise him: she might have been the Empress herself. He stopped beside a fountain and looked for his reflection in the basin. The image corresponded well with that of the blonde woman, except for its being rather unkempt. Then and there he sought out a barber he knew and persuaded him to cut his hair and beard and comb them into place.

The pursuit lasted two days. When Agnes emerged from the palace, the blond stranger was already standing at the gate looking admiringly into her eyes. When Agnes rode round the bastion, the stranger stepped out from the alders. When Agnes visited the goldsmith, she encountered the stranger as she left the workshop and, her nostrils quivering, flashed him a glance from her imperious eyes. The next morning, finding him already in place as she rode out from the palace, she smiled a challenge at him. He also saw the count, the governor, a bold, imposing figure who was to be taken seriously, but his hair was already tinged with grey, and his face was careworn. Goldmund was sure he was more than a match for him.

These two days made him happy; he was radiant with recaptured youth. It was wonderful to present himself to this woman and offer her a challenge; wonderful to lose his freedom to that beauty; wonderful and deeply exhilarating to stake his life on this single throw of the dice.

On the morning of the third day Agnes emerged from the palace gate accompanied by a groom. Her eyes, combative and restless, immediately looked for her pursuer. Ah yes, he was there. After sending the groom away on an errand, she rode slowly on, alone, through the lower town-gate and across the bridge. Only once did she look back: the stranger was following her. Beside the path to the pilgrimage church of St Vitus, at this time a very lonely spot, she waited for him. She had to wait half an hour; the stranger, not wanting to arrive out of breath, was walking slowly. Fresh and smiling, he approached with a sprig of red rosehip in his mouth. She had dismounted and tethered her horse and was now leaning against the ivy-covered buttress as she watched her pursuer coming towards her. He stopped, eye to eye with her, and doffed his cap.

'Why are you following me?' she asked. 'What do you want from me?'

'Oh,' he replied, 'I would much rather give you something than accept something from you. I would like to offer you myself as a gift, fair lady, to do with me whatever you wish.'

'Very well, I shall see what can be done with you. But if you were thinking of picking a little flower out here with impunity, you were mistaken. I can only love men who will, in case of need, risk their lives.'

'I am at your command.'

Slowly she took from her neck a fine gold chain and handed it to him.

'What is your name?'

'Goldmund.'

'Very well – Goldmund. I will taste how golden you are. Listen carefully. You will take this necklace to the palace at dusk and say you found it. You will not let it out of your hands – I want it returned to me by you in person. You will come just as you are – never mind if they take you for a beggar. If one of the servants should speak roughly to you, you will remain calm. You should know that there are only two people in the palace whom I can trust – Max the groom and my maid Berta. You must seek out one of those two and have yourself led to me. Towards everyone else in the palace, including the count, behave with caution – they are enemies. You have been warned. It might cost you your life.'

She held out her hand. He took it with a smile, kissed it gently and rubbed his cheek lightly against it. Then he tucked away the necklace and left, walking downhill towards the river and the town. The vines were already bare, and one yellow leaf after another was falling from the trees. Smiling, Goldmund shook his head as, looking down on the town, he found it friendly and lovable. Only a few days ago he had been so sad, saddened even by the swift passing of misery and suffering. And now they had indeed passed, fallen away like the golden leaves from the branches. Never, it seemed to him, had love shone so brightly at him as from this woman, whose tall figure and fair-haired, laughing vitality reminded him of the image of his mother as he had carried it in his heart when a boy at Mariabronn. Even two days ago he would not have believed that the world could once again laugh so joyously in his face, that he would once again feel the tide of life, joy, youth flow so fully and urgently through his blood. How lucky that he was still alive, that during all those horror-filled months Death had spared him!

That evening he turned up at the palace. The courtyard presented a lively scene: horses were being unsaddled, messengers were hurrying to and fro, and a small group of priests and church dignitaries were being ushered by servants through the inner gate and up the staircase. Goldmund was about to follow them but was held back by the doorkeeper. He produced the gold chain, saying he had been instructed not to hand it to anyone but the lady herself or her personal maid. A servant was sent with him, and he was left to cool his heels in the corridors. At last a pretty, light-footed woman passed him and whispered 'Are you Goldmund?', then signalled to him to follow her. She disappeared silently through a door, reappeared after a while and beckoned him inside.

He entered a small room redolent of fur and sweet perfume. Gowns and cloaks hung in profusion along the walls, women's hats were perched atop wooden stands, and an open chest contained a variety of footwear. Here he stood and waited for perhaps half an hour, sniffing at the scented garments, stroking the furs and smiling in curiosity at all the pretty things hanging there.

At last the inner door opened and, instead of the maid, Agnes herself entered, wearing a pale-blue dress trimmed at the neck with white fur. Slowly she advanced towards him, one step at a time, with a serious expression in her cool blue eyes.

'You have had to wait,' she said in a low voice. 'I think we are safe now. A delegation of clerics is with the count. He will be dining with them and no doubt will have long negotiations with them – meetings with priests always take a long time. This hour belongs to you and me. Welcome, Goldmund.'

She leaned towards him, her desirous lips approaching his. Silently they exchanged greetings in a first kiss. He slowly placed his hand on the back of her neck, and she led him through the door into her bedchamber, which was high-ceilinged and brightly lit with candles. A meal had been spread on a table, and they sat down. She placed bread and butter in front of him, and some meat, and poured white wine into a handsome goblet of bluish glass. They ate, they both drank from the same goblet, and their hands toyed tentatively with each other's.

'Where have you flown from, my lovely bird?' she asked him. 'Are you a soldier or a minstrel, or are you just a poor wayfarer?'

'I am whatever you wish,' he laughed softly. 'I am utterly yours. I am a minstrel, if you wish, and you are my sweet lute, and when I place my fingers round your neck and play on you, we shall hear the angels sing. Come, dear heart. I am not here to eat your good cake and drink your white wine – I have come only for you.'

Gently he drew down the white fur from her neck and coaxed the garments from her body. Might the courtiers and priests outside carry on their consultations, might the servants creep about and the thin sickle moon float all the way down beyond the trees: the lovers were oblivious to it all. For them, Paradise blossomed; drawn to each other and entwined with each other, they lost themselves in its fragrant night, saw its mysterious white flowers dawn, and plucked with tender, grateful hands its longed-for fruits. Never had the minstrel played on such a lute; never had the lute responded to such strong, expert fingers.

'Goldmund!' she whispered ardently. 'Oh, what a magician you are! I would like to have a child by you, my sweet goldfish! And even more, I would like to die of you. Drink up all of me, beloved, melt me, kill me!'

Deep in his throat there was a hum of happiness as he watched the austerity in her cool eyes melt and grow weak. Like the faint tremor of dying, a quiver passed through the depths of her eyes, subsiding like the silvery ripple on the skin of a dying fish, dull gold like the glinting of that magical shimmer deep down in the river. All the happiness ever to be known by a human being seemed to him to be concentrated in this moment.

While she lay there trembling, her eyes closed, he quietly got up and slipped into his clothes. With a sigh he whispered in her ear: 'My beautiful treasure, I am leaving. I don't want to die, I don't want to be killed by that count of yours. I want once more to make us both as blissful as we have been tonight. Once more – many times more!'

She lay there without speaking until he had finished dressing. Then he gently pulled the coverlet over her and kissed her eyes.

'Goldmund!' she said. 'I wish you didn't have to leave! Come back tomorrow! If there is any danger I shall see that you are warned. Come back, come back tomorrow!'

She pulled on a bell-rope. The maid appeared in the door to the wardrobe room and conducted him out of the palace. He wished he could give her a gold coin, and for a moment he was ashamed of his poverty.

Shortly before midnight he stood at the fish-market and looked up at the house. It was late, there would be nobody awake at this hour, and he would probably have to spend the night outdoors. To his surprise he found the front door unbolted, so he slipped quietly inside and closed the door behind him. The way to his room led through the kitchen, where a light burned, and he found Marie sitting at the kitchen table beside a tiny oil lamp. She had dozed off after waiting two or three hours. Startled, she jumped up when he entered.

'Oh!' he said. 'Marie, are you still up?'

'Yes, I am,' she replied, 'otherwise you would have found the house locked up.'

'I'm sorry you waited for me, Marie. It's very late. Don't be cross with me!'

'I'm never cross with you, Goldmund. I'm just a little sad.'

'You mustn't be sad. Why sad?'

'Oh, Goldmund, how I wish I were healthy and beautiful and strong! Then you wouldn't have to go out at night to other houses and love other women. Then you might stay with me one night and love me a little.'

There was no hope in her gentle voice, and no bitterness, only sorrow. Embarrassed, he stood beside her; he felt so sorry for her and was at a loss for words. Carefully he reached out and stroked her hair, and she stood without moving, trembling at the touch of his hand on her hair. She shed a few tears, straightened up again and said shyly: 'Go to bed now, Goldmund. I have been talking foolishness – I was so sleepy. Good-night.'

Chapter Sixteen

Goldmund spent a day of happy impatience in the hills. If he had had a horse he would have ridden to the monastery, to his master's beautiful Madonna. He longed to see it again; also it seemed to him that he had dreamed that night of Master Niklaus. Oh well, some other day. Even if this blissful love affair with Agnes should be short-lived, maybe end in disaster, today it was in full flower and he must not miss any part of it. Today he did not want to see people or be distracted. He wanted to spend the mild autumn day out of doors, under the trees and clouds. He told Marie he intended to go for a long walk across country and probably would not return until late. He asked her for a chunk of bread to take along and would she please not wait up for him. She made no comment, filled his satchel with bread and apples, brushed down his old jacket that she had already mended the very first day, and sent him on his way.

After crossing the river he walked up steep steps through the bare vineyards, disappeared into the forest and continued to climb until he had reached the top. There the sun shone mildly through the branches of the bare trees, and blackbirds fled from his footsteps into the bushes, where they squatted timidly as they looked out through the thicket with their bright black eyes. Far below, the river flowed in a blue curve and the town lay tiny and toylike. The only sound coming from below was that of church bells summoning to prayer. Up here were grassy mounds and knolls dating from ancient pagan times: fortifications perhaps, or graves. He sat down on one of the mounds in the dry, rustling autumn grass and looked out over the whole wide valley and beyond the river to the hills and mountains, range upon range, to the point where mountains and sky met in a blue haze and could no longer be distinguished.

All this wide country, and much farther than the eye could see, had been travelled by his feet; all those regions that were now distant and part of memory had once been close and part of the present. In those forests he had slept a hundred times, eaten berries, felt hunger and cold; he had tramped over those ridges and moors, been happy and sad, fresh and weary. Somewhere in the distance, farther than he could see, lay the charred bones of dear Lena. Somewhere over there his companion Robert might still be roaming the countryside, provided the plague had not got him. Somewhere out there lay dead Viktor, and somewhere, distant and enchanted, stood the monastery of his youth and the castle of the knight with the beautiful daughters, and somewhere, too, poor persecuted Rebekka was running away, or she had perished. All those many, widely scattered places, those moors and forests, those towns and villages, castles and monasteries, all those people, whether alive or dead, he could feel present within himself and linked together in his memory, his love, his remorse, his nostalgia. And if Death should come for him too, tomorrow, all that would fall apart and be wiped out, that entire picture-book, so full of women and love, of summer mornings and winter nights. It was time to do something before it was too late, to create something that would remain behind and survive him!

So far there was not much left to show for that life, for all that journeying, for all those years since he had first gone out into the world. All that remained were the few sculptures he had once made in the workshop, especially his St John, and then this picture-book, this unreal world in his head, this beautiful, painful world of images in his memory. Would he manage to salvage something from this inner world to display in the outer world? Or would it merely continue for ever as before: ever new towns, new landscapes, new women, new experiences, new images, one heaped upon the other, of which he carried away nothing but this restless surfeit of the heart, as tormenting as it was beautiful?

How humiliating to be so fooled by life – it was enough to make a person laugh and cry! Either you lived, giving free play to your senses and drinking your fill at the breast of the old Eve-mother – and although that did provide some intense pleasure it was no protection against impermanence: you were like a mushroom in the forest, in the full vigour of fine colours today, and decayed by tomorrow; or you tried to resist, locked yourself up in a workshop and attempted to build a memorial to fleeting life – but then you had to renounce life, become a mere tool; then, although dedicated to preserving the imperishable, you dried up and lost your freedom, the fullness and joy of life. That was what had happened to Master Niklaus.

But surely the whole of this life had meaning only if both could be achieved, if life were not split by this barren Either/Or! To create without paying the price of life! To live without renouncing the nobility of creativeness! Wasn't that possible?

Perhaps there were people for whom it was possible? Perhaps there were husbands and family men whose faithfulness did not cost them their sensuality? Perhaps there were settled folk whose hearts did not dry up from the absence of freedom and danger? Perhaps. He had never seen any.

All existence seemed to be based on duality, on contrasts. One was either a woman or a man, either a wayfarer or a complacent burgher, motivated by either reason or emotion – nowhere could a person breathe in and breathe out, be both man and woman, nowhere did freedom and order, instinct and intellect exist simultaneously. One element had always to be paid for with the loss of the other, yet each was always as important and desirable as the other! Perhaps women were better off in this respect. Nature had so created them that desire automatically bore its own fruit, and the harvest of love was a child. In the man's case, instead of this simple fertility there was eternal desire. Was the God who had created all this evil or hostile? Did He laugh spitefully at His own creation? No, He could not be evil if He had created deer and stags, fishes and birds, the forest, the flowers, the seasons. But the cleft went right through His creation, whether that creation was a failure or incomplete, whether God had something special in mind with this dichotomy in human existence, or whether this was the seed of the enemy, original sin. But why should this longing and inadequacy be sin? Were they not the origin of everything beautiful and sacred that man had created and given back to God in gratitude?

Depressed by his thoughts, he turned his gaze on the town, made out market-place and fish-market, the bridges, the churches, the town hall. And there, too, was the stately bishop's palace where Count Heinrich now governed. Under those turrets and long roofs lived Agnes, his beautiful, regal mistress who looked so haughty yet in love could forget herself and surrender so completely. Joyously he thought of her, joyously and gratefully he recalled the previous night. To know the happiness of that night, to be able to make that wonderful woman so happy; this had required his entire life, all that women had taught him, all his journeyings and sufferings, all that tramping through snowy nights and all the friendship and familiarity with animals, flowers, trees, waters, fish, butterflies. It required senses sharpened in sensuality and danger; it required homelessness, and all those mental images accumulated through the years. As long as his life was a garden where magical flowers like Agnes bloomed, he must not complain.

He spent the whole day on the autumnal heights, strolling, resting, eating some bread, thinking of Agnes and the evening. By nightfall he was back in the town, approaching the palace. The air had grown cool, and the houses looked out of quiet, glowing window-eyes. He came upon a small procession of singing boys who were carrying hollowed turnips mounted on poles. Inside the turnips, in which faces had been carved, were lighted candles. The little spectacle brought a breath of winter with it, and Goldmund smiled as he watched it pass. He spent some time loitering outside the palace. The clerical delegation was still there; occasionally an ecclesiastical gentleman was to be seen standing at one of the windows. At last he succeeded in slipping inside the building and finding the maid Berta. Once again he was hidden in the wardrobe room until Agnes appeared and led him tenderly into her bedchamber. Tenderly her lovely face welcomed him – tenderly but far from happily. She was sad, she was worried, she was frightened. He did his best to cheer her up, and under his kisses and endearments she gained some confidence.

'You can be so very sweet,' she said gratefully. 'You make such deep sounds in your throat, my bird, when you coo and talk to me so lovingly. I love you, Goldmund. If only we were far away from here! I don't like it here any more, but it'll soon be over anyway – the count has been recalled, the silly bishop is due to return soon. Today the count is angry – those priests have been pestering him. Oh, Goldmund, he mustn't catch sight of you! You wouldn't live another hour. I am so afraid for you!'

Half-submerged sounds surfaced in his memory – had he not heard this lament long ago? Thus had Lydia once spoken to him. She had been just as loving and anxious, just as tender and sad. Thus had she come at night to his room, loving and frightened, full of concern, full of terrible images of dread. He loved to hear it, that tender and anxious lament. What would love be without secrecy? What would love be without danger?

He drew Agnes gently to him, stroked her, held her hand, murmured soft, coaxing words into her ear, kissed her eyebrows. It touched and thrilled him to find her so anxious on his account. She received his caresses gratefully, almost humbly, and clung lovingly to him, but her mood was not a happy one.

Suddenly she gave a violent start: a nearby door was slammed, and rapid footsteps approached the bedchamber.

'For God's sake, it's him!' she cried in desperation. 'It's the count! Quick, you can escape through the other room. Hurry! Don't betray me!'

Even as she spoke she was pushing him into the wardrobe room. Alone and groping in the dark, he could hear the count speaking loudly to Agnes in the next room. Through the gowns he felt his way to the door to the corridor, soundlessly placing one foot in front of the other. Now he was at the door and tried to open it quietly. And only then, the moment he found the door locked from the outside, did he too feel alarmed, and his heart began to beat wildly and painfully. It might be an unlucky coincidence that someone had locked this door since he had come in, but he did not think so. He had fallen into a trap; it was all over for him. Someone must have seen him slipping in here. It would cost him his neck. He stood trembling in the dark and recalled Agnes's parting words: 'Don't betray me!' No, he would not betray her. His heart was pounding, but his decision gave him strength, and defiantly he gritted his teeth.

This had all happened in a few moments. Now the other door opened, and the count came in from Agnes's bedchamber, a lighted candelabrum in his left hand and a drawn sword in his right. That same instant Goldmund snatched up a few of the gowns and cloaks hanging round the walls and slung them over his arm in the hope of being taken for a thief – perhaps that would be a way out.

The count had seen him at once. He slowly approached.

'Who are you? What are you doing here? Answer me, or I'll run you through!'

'Forgive me,' Goldmund whispered, 'I am a poor man, and you are so rich! I'm giving back everything I've taken, sir – look!' And he laid the garments down on the floor.

'Ah, so you've been stealing, have you? It was not very clever of you to risk your life for an old cloak. Are you a townsman?'

'No, sir, I am homeless. I am a poor man, I crave your indulgence . . .'

'Be quiet! I wouldn't mind knowing whether you had the impertinence to think of molesting the lady. But since you will be hanged anyway, that need not be investigated. The theft is enough!'

He knocked loudly on the locked door and shouted: 'Are you there? Open up!'

The door was opened from the outside, and three servants stood with drawn swords at the ready.

'Tie him up securely,' cried the count in a voice rasping with scorn and arrogance. 'This is a tramp who has been stealing here. Lock him up, and first thing tomorrow hang the rogue from the gallows!'

Goldmund offered no resistance as his hands were tied together. He was led through the long corridor, then down the stairs and across the courtyard, a lackey walking ahead with a lantern. They stopped at an arched, iron-clad cellar door. Discussion and argument followed: no one had the key to the door. One of the servants took the lantern, and the lackey went back for the key. Thus they stood, the three armed men and the prisoner, waiting at the door. The one with the lantern held it up so he could peer into the prisoner's face. At that moment, two of the many priests who were guests at the palace passed on their way from the palace chapel. They stopped in front of the group and looked with interest at the nocturnal scene: at the three servants and the prisoner, standing there waiting.

Goldmund did not notice the priests, nor did he look at his guards. All he could see was the small, flickering light that was being held close up to his face and dazzling his eyes. And beyond the light, in a twilight of dread, he saw something else, something formless, vast, ghostly: the abyss, the end, his death. He stood there with a fixed stare, seeing and hearing nothing. One of the priests was whispering intently with the servants. On hearing that the man was a thief and was to be put to death, the priest asked if he had seen a confessor. No, he was told, the man had been caught red-handed and arrested on the spot.

'In that case,' said the priest, 'I shall bring the blessed sacraments to him tomorrow before early mass and hear his confession. I hold you responsible for seeing that he is not taken away before then. I shall talk to the count tonight. The man may be a thief, but he has the right of every Christian to a confessor and the sacraments.'

The servants did not dare protest. They knew the priest; he was a member of the delegation and they had several times seen him dining with the count. And anyway, why should one begrudge the poor vagrant his confession?

The priests left. Goldmund stood staring fixedly until at last the lackey came with the key and opened the door. The prisoner was led into a vaulted cellar and stumbled down the few steps. It was an ante-room to the wine-cellar and contained a few three-legged stools and a table. Moving one of the stools up to the table they ordered him to sit down.

'A priest is coming early tomorrow morning, so you'll have time to confess,' one of the servants told him. As they left they carefully locked the heavy door.

'Leave the light for me, my friend,' Goldmund asked.

'No, brother, you might get up to some mischief with it. You'll manage without. Be sensible and accept your fate. Besides, how long does a lamp like this burn? It would go out anyway in an hour. Good-night.'

Now he was alone in the dark, sitting on the stool. He laid his head on the table. It was an uncomfortable position, and the cords round his wrists hurt, but he was not conscious of these sensations until later. For the time being he just sat with his head placed on the table as if on an executioner's block. He felt the need to have his body and senses do what was being demanded of his heart: accept the inevitable, become resigned to having to die.

For an eternity he remained in that position, miserably bent over and trying to accept what was demanded of him, to breathe it in, take it in and be suffused by it. It was now evening, the night was beginning, and the end of this night would also mean his own end. He must try to grasp that. Tomorrow he would no longer be alive. He would hang, he would be an object for birds to settle on and peck at; he would be what Master Niklaus was, what Lena was in the charred hut, what all those were whom he had seen lying in the pest-ridden houses and piled high on the death-carts. It was not easy to take this in and be suffused by it. In fact it was downright impossible. There was far too much he had not yet parted from, not yet taken leave of. The hours of this night were his to do that.

He must take leave of the beautiful Agnes; never again would he see her tall figure, her fair, sunny hair, her cool blue eyes, never again watch the weakening and trembling of the arrogance in those eyes, never again see the lovely gold down on her sweet-smelling skin. Farewell blue eyes, farewell moist, quivering lips! He had hoped to kiss them many more times. Oh, this very day on the hills, in the autumn sunshine – how he had thought of her, given himself to her, yearned for her! But he had to bid farewell also to the hills, the sun, the blue sky and its white clouds, to the trees and forests, to wayfaring, to the hours of the day and the seasons of the year. At this moment Marie might still be up, poor Marie with the kind, loving eyes and the bad hip, sitting and waiting, falling asleep in her kitchen and waking again, and no Goldmund to come home any more.

Oh, and the paper and pen, and his hopes for all the statues he had still wanted to carve! Gone, gone! And the hope of a reunion with Narcissus, with John the Beloved Disciple – that, too, he must abandon.

And he must take leave of his own hands, his own eyes, of hunger and thirst, food and drink, of love, of lute-playing, of sleeping and waking, of everything. Tomorrow a bird would fly through the air and Goldmund would not be there to see it; a girl would sing at a window and Goldmund would not be there to hear her sing. The river would flow and the dark fish would silently swim; a wind would blow and sweep the yellow leaves along the ground; a sun would shine and a starry sky; young people would go off to dance on the village green; a first snow would cover the distant hilltops – and it would all go on, the trees would all cast their shadows beside them, the people would all have happy faces or sad, the dogs would bark, the cows would low in village barns – and all that without him, all that was no longer his. He would have been wrenched away from everything.

He could smell the morning air of the heath, taste the sweet young wine and the firm young walnuts: a memory, a blazing reflection of the whole colourful world, raced through his troubled heart; as the entire beautiful medley of his life was sinking away, it flashed in farewell once again through all his senses, and he broke down in an outpouring of anguish as the tears welled up in his eyes. Sobbing, he abandoned himself to his grief, his tears flowing unchecked as he gave way to his boundless agony. O you valleys and wooded hills, you streams among the green alders, O girls and moonlit evenings on the bridges, O beautiful sparkling world of images, how can I leave you! An inconsolable child, he lay weeping across the table. From his stricken heart rose a wail of entreaty: 'Mother, Mother!'

And as he spoke the magic name, he was answered by an image from the depths of his memory, the mother-image: not the mother-figure of his thoughts and artist's dreams but that of his own mother, beautiful and alive, as he had never seen it since his monastery years. To her he addressed his lament, tearfully bemoaning the unbearable pain of imminent death; to her he surrendered and gave back the forest, the sun, his eyes, his hands; to her he gave back his whole being and life, into those maternal hands.

In the midst of his tears he fell asleep; exhaustion and sleep folded him in their motherly arms. He slept for an hour, maybe two, out of reach of his misery.

On awaking he was conscious of severe pain. His bound wrists were hurting badly, and spasms of pain were shooting through his back and neck. With an effort he straightened up, now fully awake, and became once more aware of his situation. Complete and utter darkness enveloped him: he had no idea how long he had slept, no idea how many hours he had left to live. Perhaps they would come the very next moment and take him away, to die. Then he remembered that he had been promised a priest. He didn't think those sacraments would do him much good. He didn't know if even complete absolution and forgiveness of sins would be enough to send him to Heaven. He didn't know if there was a heaven and a heavenly Father, and a Judgement and an eternity. He had long lost all certainty in such things.

But whether there was an eternity or not, he did not hanker after it: all he wanted was this uncertain, ephemeral life, this breathing, this sense of being at home in his skin; all he wanted was to live. Frantic, he stood up, groped his way unsteadily in the dark as far as the wall, stood leaning against it and began to reflect. Surely there must be a way to save himself! Perhaps the priest would be his salvation, perhaps the priest could be convinced of his innocence, would put in a good word for him or obtain a postponement or help him escape? He concentrated on these thoughts, turning them over and over in his mind. And if that didn't work, he still refused to give up: the game couldn't be lost yet. So first he would try to get the priest on his side; he would do his utmost to captivate him, to win his heart, convince him, flatter him. The priest was the only good card in his hand; all other possibilities were illusions. Still, coincidences and strokes of fate did happen: the hangman might be stricken with colic, the gallows might break, an unforeseeable chance to escape might arise. In any case, Goldmund refused to die. He had done his best to absorb and accept this fate. He had not succeeded. He would resist and fight to the utmost, he would trip his guard, he would knock down the hangman, he would defend his life to the bitter end with every last drop of his blood. If only he could persuade the priest to untie his hands! That would give him an enormous advantage.

Meanwhile, ignoring the pain, he tried to work at the cords with his teeth. After an agonizingly long time his frenzied efforts did seem to loosen them slightly. With painfully swollen arms and hands he stood panting in the darkness of his prison. When he had recovered his breath he groped his way along the wall, on and on, exploring the damp cellar wall step by step in the hope of finding a projecting edge. Then he remembered the steps down which he had stumbled on entering this dungeon. He searched for them and found them. Kneeling down, he tried to rub the cord against the edge of one of the stone steps. It was difficult: mostly it was his wrist bones instead of the cord that met the stone. The pain was like fire, and he could feel the blood flowing. Yet he did not give up. At last, when a thin little strip of early-morning light began to show between door and threshold, he had achieved his object. The cord had been rubbed through, he could undo it – his hands were free! But then he could scarcely move a finger; his hands were swollen and numb, and his arms had stiffened up to his shoulders. Knowing he must exercise them, he forced them to move so that the blood would circulate through them again. For now he had what seemed like a good plan.

If he should completely fail to persuade the priest to help him, and provided he was left alone with the man for even the briefest time – well, he would have to kill him. He would do it with one of the stools. Strangling was not feasible, since he lacked the necessary strength in his hands and arms. So – beat him to death, quickly put on the priest's robe and escape! By the time the others found the body he would have to be out of the palace, and then run, run! Marie would take him in and hide him. He had to try it. It might work.

Never in his life had Goldmund watched the dawn – waited for it, longed for it and yet feared it – as he did in that hour. Trembling with tension and determination, he watched with a hunter's eyes as the pitiful slit of light under the door slowly, slowly grew brighter. He returned to the table and practised sitting bent over on the stool with his hands between his knees to conceal the absence of his bonds. Now that his hands were free he no longer believed in his death. He was determined to survive, even if it meant smashing up the whole world. He was determined to live, whatever the cost. His nostrils quivered with his craving for freedom and life. And who knows, maybe help would arrive from the outside? Agnes was a woman, and her power did not extend very far, nor perhaps her courage; it was possible that she would sacrifice him. But she loved him; perhaps there was something she could do. Perhaps the maid Berta was lurking around outside – and wasn't there also a groom Agnes had said she could trust? And if no one turned up, and he was given no sign – well, he would carry out his plan. If it failed, he would kill the guards with a stool, two or three or however many happened to turn up. He was sure of one advantage: his eyes had become accustomed to the dark room. Now in the dimness he could barely make out all the shapes and dimensions, whereas the others would at first be totally blind in here.

He sat down at the table, feverishly considering what he would have to say to the priest to win his help, that being the first step. At the same time his eyes were riveted on the modest growth of the light in the crack. The moment which only a few hours before he had so greatly dreaded, he now passionately longed for: he could hardly wait for it. The terrible tension was almost past enduring. Moreover, his strength, his alertness, his willpower and his watchfulness must inevitably subside. The guard with the priest must come soon, as long as this tense preparedness, this absolute determination to escape, was still at its peak.

At last the world outside was waking up; at last the enemy was approaching. Footsteps echoed on the cobbles of the courtyard; the key was inserted in the lock and turned. After the long, deathly silence, each of these sounds seemed as loud as thunder.

And now the heavy door opened slightly, creaking in its hinges. In came a priest, unaccompanied, with no guard. He came in alone, carrying a candelabrum with two candles. Now everything was different from the way the prisoner had imagined it.

And how strange and moving: the priest behind whom invisible hands were closing the door was wearing the habit of the

Mariabronn monastery, the well-remembered, familiar habit such as Abbot Daniel, Father Anselm and Father Martin used to wear!

The sight gave his heart a jolt; he had to turn his eyes away. The appearance of this monastic habit might be promising, a good sign. But perhaps there really was no other solution than to kill the man. He gritted his teeth. He would find it very hard to kill this member of the Order.

Chapter Seventeen

'Praise be to Jesus Christ,' said the priest as he placed the candelabrum on the table. Goldmund murmured his response while staring at the ground.

The priest fell silent. He stood waiting, not speaking, until Goldmund became uneasy and raised his eyes inquiringly to the man in front of him.

This man, he now noted in bewilderment, was wearing not only the habit of the monks of Mariabronn but the insignia of the abbot's office.

And now he looked into the abbot's face. It was a lean face, firm and clean-cut, with very thin lips. It was a face he knew. Spellbound, Goldmund looked at this face that seemed to be formed entirely of spirit and will. With a shaking hand he reached for the candelabrum, raised it, and brought it close to the stranger's face in order to see the eyes. He saw them, and the candelabrum trembled in his hand as he replaced it.

'Narcissus!' he whispered almost inaudibly. The room began to spin round him.

'Yes, Goldmund, I was once Narcissus, but I discarded that name a long time ago – you have probably forgotten. Since my investiture my name has been John.'

Goldmund was shaken to the core. Suddenly the whole world had changed, and the abrupt collapse of his superhuman exertions threatened to suffocate him. He trembled, and dizziness made his head feel like an empty bladder; his stomach contracted. His eyes smarted with welling tears. To sob, to burst into tears, to faint – that was what his whole being craved at this moment.

But from the depths of the memories stirred up by the sight of Narcissus rose a warning: once, as a boy, he had broken down and wept in front of that handsome, austere countenance, those dark, all-knowing eyes. He must not do so again. Now, at the most extraordinary moment of his life, this Narcissus had reappeared like a ghost, probably to save his life – and was he once again to break down and faint in front of him? No, no, no. He took a grip of himself. He restrained his heart, curbed his stomach, drove the dizziness out of his head. He must not display any weakness now.

In a forcibly controlled voice he managed to say: 'You must allow me to go on calling you Narcissus.'

'Call me that, my friend. And won't you shake hands with me?'

Again Goldmund took hold of himself. In the boyishly defiant, lightly mocking tone he had sometimes used as a pupil, he gave his answer. 'Excuse me, Narcissus,' he said, his tone distant and a little blasé. 'I see you are now an abbot, but I am still a vagrant. Moreover, our conversation, much as I desire it, may not last much longer, I am sorry to say. You see, Narcissus, I have been condemned to the gallows, and in an hour or less I shall no doubt be hanged. I am saying this merely to clarify the situation for you.'

Narcissus's expression did not change. He was both amused and touched by his friend's somewhat puerile attempts to show off. But the underlying pride that prevented Goldmund from collapsing in tears into his arms – that he understood and deeply respected. In truth, he too had pictured their reunion differently, but this little comedy met with his fondest approbation. Nothing could have gained Goldmund swifter access to his heart.

'Very well,' he said, likewise feigning indifference. 'Incidentally, I can set your mind at rest as to the gallows. You have been pardoned. I have been directed to inform you of this and to take you with me when I leave, for you are not permitted to remain in this town. So we shall have time enough to talk. But now, will you shake hands with me?'

They shook hands with a firm and lingering clasp, feeling greatly moved. In their words, however, asperity and pretence continued for some time.

'Right, Narcissus, so we shall leave this less than honourable shelter, and I shall join your retinue. Are you returning to Mariabronn? Yes? Very good. By what means? On horseback? Excellent. So it will be a matter of obtaining a horse for me too.'

'We shall, *amice*, and we shall be gone in two hours. Oh, but look at your hands! Dear God – all scratched and swollen and bleeding! Oh, Goldmund, what have they been doing to you!'

'It's all right, Narcissus, I did this myself. I was tied up, you see, and had to free my hands. I can assure you it wasn't easy! By the way, it was rather courageous of you to come in here like that, unaccompanied.'

'Why courageous? There was no danger.'

'Oh, merely the one small danger of being killed by me. That's how I had planned it, you see. I had been told that a priest would be coming. I would have killed him and then escaped in his clothes. A good plan.'

'So you did not want to die? You were prepared to put up a fight?'

'Of course I was. That you happened to be the priest was something I naturally couldn't foresee.'

'Nevertheless,' Narcissus said slowly, 'it was really a rather brutal plan. Do you think you could actually have killed a priest who came to you as a father confessor?'

'Not you, Narcissus, of course not, and maybe not one of your fathers either, if he was wearing the Mariabronn habit. But any other priest, regardless – oh yes, you can be sure of it.' Suddenly his voice became sad and sombre. 'It would not have been the first person I have killed.'

They fell silent. Both men felt awkward.

'Well, we shall have time enough to talk about such things,' Narcissus said in a neutral voice. 'I shall take your confession sometime, if you like. Or you can just tell me about your life. And I have a few things to tell you too. I look forward to that. Shall we go?'

'One moment, Narcissus. It has just occurred to me that I did once call you John.'

'I don't understand.'

'No, of course not. You know nothing about it yet. It was quite a few years ago that I gave you the name of John, and it will always be attached to you. At one time I was a sculptor and wood-carver, you see, and I hope to be one again. And the best figure I made in those days, a youth carved from wood, life-size, is a portrait of you, but it's not called Narcissus, it's called John. It is a St John the Disciple at the foot of the Cross.'

He stood up and walked towards the door.

'So you did still think of me?' Narcissus asked softly.

Goldmund answered just as softly: 'Oh yes, Narcissus, I did think of you. Always, always.'

He thrust open the heavy door, and the pale morning light looked in. They said no more. Narcissus took him to his guest chamber where a young monk, his attendant, was busy packing the abbot's belongings. Goldmund was given something to eat, and his hands were washed and lightly bandaged. Before long the horses were brought to the door.

As they mounted, Goldmund said: 'I have a request. May we go by way of the fish-market? There's something I still have to take care of there.'

As they rode off, Goldmund looked up at all the palace windows in case Agnes might be at one of them. He did not see her again. They went by the fish-market. Marie had been very worried about him. He took leave of her and her parents, thanked them profusely, promised to return one day, and rode off. Marie stood in the doorway until the horsemen had disappeared, then slowly limped back into the house.

There were four of them: Narcissus, Goldmund, the young monk and an armed groom.

'Do you remember my pony Blaze?' Goldmund asked. 'He used to be kept in your monastery stable.'

'Certainly I do. You won't find him there any more, but then you would hardly expect to. It must be seven or eight years since we had to put him down.'

'Fancy your remembering that!'

'Oh, indeed I remember it.'

Goldmund was not saddened by his pony's death. He was happy that Narcissus was so well informed about Blaze – he who had never concerned himself with animals and probably had never known another monastery horse by name. This made him very happy.

'You will laugh at me,' he resumed, 'for asking after my poor little pony before inquiring about anyone else at the monastery. That wasn't very nice of me. Actually I had meant to ask about quite different things, above all about our Abbot Daniel. But I assume he has died, since you're his successor. And for the time being I wanted to avoid talking about deaths. At present I'm not inclined to think too kindly of death, partly because of last night but also because of the plague, of which I saw more than I cared for. But now that we're on the subject, and it was bound to come up, tell me – when and how did Abbot Daniel die? I revered him greatly. And about Father Anselm and Father Martin – are they still alive? I'm prepared for the worst. But since the plague spared you at least, I am content, although it never occurred to me you might have died – I always had faith in our meeting again. But faith can deceive, as I have found to my sorrow. I couldn't imagine that my Master Niklaus, the sculptor, might have died either. I was counting firmly on finding him and working with him again. And yet he was dead by the time I came back.'

'It is quickly told,' said Narcissus. 'Abbot Daniel died eight years ago, without illness or pain. I am not his successor – I have been abbot for only a year. He was succeeded by Father Martin, at one time our school principal. He died last year, not quite seventy. And Father Anselm is no longer there either. He was very fond of you and often spoke of you. Towards the end he could no longer walk, and lying down was acutely painful. He died of dropsy. Yes, and the plague came to us too, and many died. Let's not talk about it! Have you any more questions?'

'Yes indeed, a great many. Above all, what brought you here to the cathedral town and to the governor?'

'It's a long story, and it would bore you – it has to do with politics. The count is a favourite of the Emperor's and in some matters acts as his deputy, and at the present time there are a number of questions to be settled between the Emperor and our Order. The Order appointed me to the delegation that was to negotiate with the count. We had very little success.'

He fell silent, Goldmund asked no more and there was, after all, no need for him to find out that the previous night, when Narcissus was pleading for Goldmund's life, that life had had to be paid for with several concessions to the tough-minded count.

They rode on. Goldmund soon felt tired and had trouble staying in the saddle.

After a long interval Narcissus asked: 'Is it true, then, that you were arrested for theft? The count claimed that you had sneaked into the palace, into the inner chambers, and had been stealing there.'

Goldmund laughed. 'Well, it really did look as if I were a thief! But I had a rendezvous with the count's mistress. Doubtless he knew that too. I am very surprised that in the circumstances he let me go.'

'Well, he was reasonable about it.'

That day they could not travel as far as they had planned because Goldmund was too exhausted and he could no longer hold the reins. They took up quarters in a village. Goldmund was put to bed with a slight fever and stayed there throughout the following day. He was then fit to continue, and soon, when his hands had healed, he began thoroughly to enjoy the journey on horseback. What a long time it had been since he had ridden a horse! His spirits rose; he became young and lively, raced short stretches with the groom, and when he was in the mood assailed his friend Narcissus with a hundred impatient questions. Calmly yet joyfully Narcissus responded with good humour; he was enchanted again by Goldmund and loved his impetuous, childlike questions, which were so filled with boundless trust in his friend's intellect and shrewdness.

'One question, Narcissus: Did the monastery ever burn Jews?'

'Burn Jews? How could we? There are no Jews where we are.'

'Right. But tell me, would you be capable of burning Jews? Can you conceive of such a possibility?'

'No, why should I do such a thing? Do you take me for a fanatic?'

'Don't misunderstand me, Narcissus! What I mean is, can you imagine a case in which you would give the order to kill Jews, or at least your consent? After all, so many dukes, mayors, bishops and other authorities have given such orders.'

'I would not give an order of that kind. On the other hand, I can imagine being in a position of having to witness and tolerate such cruelty.'

'So you would tolerate it?'

'Yes, I would, if I did not have the power to prevent it. I suppose you have at some time watched Jews being burned, Goldmund?'

'Ah, yes.'

'Well, then – did you prevent it? No? There you are.'

Goldmund recounted in detail the story of Rebekka, waxing heated and passionate as he did so. 'And now,' he concluded angrily, 'what kind of a world is it that we have to live in? Is it not a hell? Is it not outrageous and revolting?'

'You are right. That's how the world is.'

'You see?' Goldmund exclaimed hotly. 'And how often in the past did you assure me that the world was divine, that it was a great harmony of circles with the Creator enthroned in their midst, and that what existed was good, and so on? You said I could find it in Aristotle or in Thomas Aquinas. I am eager to hear your explanation of that inconsistency.'

Narcissus laughed. 'Your memory is amazing, but it has deceived you slightly. I have always revered the Creator as perfect, but never the creation. I have never denied the evil in the world. No genuine thinker has ever maintained that life on earth is harmonious and just and that man is good. In fact, Holy Writ expressly states that all aspirations of the human heart are evil, and we see that confirmed every day.'

'Good. At last I see how you scholars mean this. So man is wicked, and life on earth is vile and brutish – you admit that. But somewhere behind it all, in your thoughts and textbooks, there is justice and perfection. They exist, they can be proved – it's just that they are not put to use.'

'You have built up much resentment against us theologians, dear friend! But you still have not become a thinker – you mix everything up. You still have some things to learn. Why do you say that the idea of justice is not put to use? We do this every day and every hour. I, for instance, am an abbot and have a monastery to run, and what goes on in this monastery is no more perfect and sinless than what goes on in the world outside. Nevertheless we constantly and repeatedly oppose original sin with the idea of justice, trying to measure our imperfect lives against that idea, trying to correct evil and place our lives in constant relationship to God.'

'Oh, Narcissus, I don't mean you or that you're not a good abbot! But I'm thinking of Rebekka, of the Jews who were burned, of the mass graves, of the countless deaths, of the alleys and rooms with their stinking corpses, of the whole appalling devastation, of the homeless, abandoned children, of the watchdogs dead of starvation at the end of their chains – and when I think of all that and see those images in my mind, my heart bleeds, and I feel as if our mothers had brought us into a hopelessly cruel and devilish world, and it would have been better if they had not and if God had not created this terrible world and the Saviour had not for its sake let Himself be crucified to no purpose!'

With a smile Narcissus nodded to his friend. 'You are quite right,' he said warmly. 'Speak freely, tell me everything. But in one thing you are very much mistaken – you think that what you are expressing is thoughts. But it is emotions! The emotions of someone who is troubled by the horror of existence. But do not forget that those sad and despairing emotions are balanced by quite different ones! When you enjoy riding your horse through beautiful country, or when you recklessly sneak into the palace at night to court the count's mistress, the world looks quite different to you, and all the plague houses and all the burned Jews have no power to prevent you from seeking pleasure. Isn't that so?'

'You are right, it is. Because the world is so full of death and horror I constantly seek to console my heart and pick the lovely flowers that bloom in the midst of this hell. I find pleasure, and for an hour I can forget the horror. But it is none the less there.'

'You have expressed that very well. So you find yourself in the world surrounded by death and horror, and you escape from that into pleasure. But the pleasure does not last, it sends you back into the devastation.'

'Yes, that's how it is.'

'Most people feel that, but not many experience it with such force and intensity or sense the need to become aware of those feelings. But tell me, apart from this desperate back and forth between pleasure and horror, apart from this to and fro between love of life and a sense of death, have you not also tried some other way?'

'Oh yes, of course. I have tried art. As I have already told you, among other things I became an artist. One day – I had been out in the world for about three years and almost the whole time moving from place to place – I came upon a wooden statue of the Virgin Mary in a monastery church. She was so beautiful, and the sight of her moved me so greatly that I asked after the master who had made her. I searched for him and found him. He was a famous master. I became his pupil and spent a few years working with him.'

'Tell me more about that later. But what was it that art gave you and meant to you?'

'It was the overcoming of impermanence. I saw that, from the farce and death-dance of human life, something remained and survived – works of art. Even they perish at some point – they decay or are burned or are smashed to pieces. But still they outlast many a human lifetime and, beyond the immediate moment, form a quiet domain of images and sacred objects. To contribute to this with my work seems to me both good and comforting, since it comes close to immortalizing the ephemeral.'

'I like that very much, Goldmund. I hope you will carve many more beautiful works. I have great confidence in your powers, and I hope you will long remain my guest at Mariabronn and allow me to establish a workshop for you. For many years our monastery has been without an artist. But I believe you have not quite exhausted the wonders of art with your definition. I believe that art consists of more than wresting from death, through the medium of stone, wood or paint, something extant but mortal and endowing it with greater permanence. I have seen many a work of art, many a saint or Madonna, which I believe to be more than mere faithful depictions of some individual who once lived and whose form and colouring the artist has preserved.'

'You are right!' Goldmund cried eagerly. 'I wouldn't have believed that you know so much about art! The original that underlies a good work of art is not a real, living person, though that person may have been the impulse. It is not flesh and blood. It is spiritual. It is an image that dwells in the artist's soul. Such images are alive in me, too, Narcissus – images that I hope one day to portray and show to you.'

'Wonderful! And with that, my friend, you have unwittingly entered the realm of philosophy and uttered one of its secrets.'

'You're making fun of me!'

'Oh no! You spoke of "originals", of images that exist solely in the creative spirit but that can be realized and made visible in physical matter. Long before an artistic form acquires visible reality it has already existed as an image in the soul of the artist! And this image, this "original", is precisely what the old philosophers called an "idea".'

'Yes, that makes good sense.'

'So, by acknowledging the existence of ideas and "originals", you enter the world of the mind, our world of philosophy and theology, and you admit that, in the midst of the confused and painful battlefield of life, in the midst of this unending, senseless Dance of Death of bodily existence, there is such a thing as the creative spirit. You see, it is to this spirit in you that I have always appealed, ever since you came to me as a boy. In your case, this spirit is not that of a thinker but that of an artist. But it is spirit, and it is that which will show you the way out of the murky welter of the sensual world, out of the eternal back and forth between pleasure and despair. Ah, my friend, I am happy to have heard you acknowledge this. I have been waiting for it – ever since the day you deserted your teacher Narcissus and found the courage to be your own self. Now we can be friends all over again.'

In this hour Goldmund felt as if his life had acquired a meaning, as if he were looking at it from above and clearly seeing its three main stages: the dependence on Narcissus and its severance; the years of freedom and roaming; and the return, the soul-searching, and the beginning of ripeness and harvest.

The vision dissolved. But he had found the relationship to Narcissus to which he was now entitled: no longer a relationship of dependence but one of freedom and reciprocity. Now he could without humiliation be the guest of Narcissus's superior spirit, since the latter had perceived in him the equal, the creator. To prove himself, to show Narcissus his inner world by way of his sculptures, was something he looked forward to more and more as the journey proceeded. But sometimes he also had misgivings.

'Narcissus,' he warned, 'I'm afraid you don't really know whom you are taking into your monastery. I am not a monk and have no wish to become one. Of course I am familiar with the three great vows, and I would willingly agree to poverty, but I am no friend of either chastity or obedience. Moreover, I don't find those virtues particularly manly. And as for piety, there's not a shred left in me. It is years since I either confessed or prayed or received Holy Communion.'

Narcissus took this in good part. 'You have evidently become a heathen! But we are not afraid of that. And you need not be especially proud of your many sins. You have led a normal worldly life. Like the Prodigal Son you have tended swine, and you have forgotten the meaning of law and order. I am sure you would make a very bad monk. But I am not inviting you to join our Order. I am merely inviting you to be our guest and to set up a workshop in our monastery. And one more thing. Don't forget that, in our youth, it was I who awakened you and did not discourage you from going out into the life of the world. Whether you turned out well or ill, next to yourself I bear the responsibility. I want to see what you have become. You will show me, in words, in life, in your works. If, after you have shown me this I should find that our house is not the place for you, I shall be the first to ask you to leave.'

Goldmund invariably admired his friend when he spoke like that, when he behaved as an abbot, with that quiet assurance and a hint of mockery for the worldly life and its people, for it was then that he saw what Narcissus had become: a man. A man of the spirit and of the Church, yes, with delicate hands and a scholar's face, but a man full of confidence and courage, a leader, a man who bore responsibility. This man Narcissus was no longer the youth of the past, no longer the gentle disciple John, and it was this new, this manly and authoritative Narcissus whom he wanted to portray with his hands. Many figures were waiting for him: Narcissus, Abbot Daniel, Father Anselm, Master Niklaus, lovely Rebekka, beautiful Agnes, and many another – friends and foes, living and dead. No, he had no wish to become a member of the Order, neither a pious nor a scholarly one. He wanted to create artistic works, and he rejoiced at the thought that the one-time home of his youth was to be the home of these creations.

They rode through the crisp autumn air, and one day, when the bare trees had been thick with frost in the morning, they crossed rolling open country dotted with lonely marshy areas, and the long outlines of the hills seemed strangely familiar. They came to a forest of tall ash trees and a stream and an old barn, at sight of which Goldmund's heart began to beat a little faster. With joy yet trepidation he recognized the hills he had once ridden among with Lydia, the knight's daughter, and the heath where, cast out and despondent, he had once tramped off through lightly falling snow. The clumps of alders came into view, and the mill, and the castle. With a twinge of nostalgia he recognized the window of the study where once, in that legendary time of his youth, he had listened to the knight telling of his pilgrimage and had had to correct his employer's Latin.

They rode into the courtyard, one of the scheduled stations on their journey. Goldmund asked the abbot not to reveal his name and to allow him to have his meals with the groom among the servants. This was done. The old knight was no longer there, nor was Lydia, but there were still some of the huntsmen and servants, and the castle was ruled by a very beautiful, proud and imperious noblewoman, Julie, at the side of her husband. She was still a great beauty – very beautiful and somewhat bad-tempered. Neither she nor any of the servants recognized Goldmund.

At dusk, after supper, he slipped across to the garden and looked over the fence at the already wintry flowerbeds, then crept along to the stable door and peered in at the horses. That night he slept beside the groom on the straw, the burden of memories weighing on his chest and awakening him many times. Oh, how fragmented and barren his life lay behind him – rich in glorious images but shattered into so many pieces, with so little of value, so little of love! Next morning as they rode off he looked anxiously up at the windows, hoping to catch a last glimpse of Julie, just as not long ago he had looked up from the courtyard of the bishop's residence hoping to catch sight of Agnes at a window. Agnes had not come, nor did Julie. Such had been his entire life, it seemed to him: bidding farewell, taking flight, being forgotten, left standing with empty hands and a shivering heart. This haunted him all day long, and he spoke not a word as he slouched gloomily in the saddle. Narcissus let him alone.

By this time they were approaching their destination, and after a few days they reached it. Shortly before the monastery tower and roofs came into view they rode across those stony,

271

barren fields where, so long ago, he used to look for St John's wort for Father Anselm and where Lisa the gypsy had made a man of him. And now they rode through the Mariabronn gateway and dismounted under the Spanish chestnut tree. Goldmund touched its trunk affectionately and stooped to pick up one of the brown, prickly husks that were lying, cracked and dry, on the ground.

Chapter Eighteen

For the first few days Goldmund stayed in the monastery itself, in one of the guest cells. Then, at his request, he was given quarters across from the smithy, in one of the domestic buildings that surrounded the big courtyard as if it were a market square.

To find himself once more among all these familiar sights was inexplicably moving. Apart from the abbot, no one here knew him, no one knew who he was. Those who lived here, brothers as well as laity, did so according to strict rules; they were busy and left him alone. But the trees in the courtyard knew him, and the doorways and windows, the mill and the water-wheel, the flagstones in the passages, the withered rose-bushes in the cloister, the storks' nests on the granary and the refectory – they knew him. From every corner the fragrance of his past, of his early youth, drifted towards him, sweet and touching. Love impelled him to gaze upon everything, to listen again to all the sounds: the vespers bell and the Sunday chimes, the plashing of the dark mill stream between its narrow, mossy walls, the patter of sandals on the flagstones, the evening sound of Brother Doorkeeper's clinking keys as he made his rounds to lock up. Beside the stone gutters that caught the rain-water from the roof of the lay refectory, the same weeds – crane's-bill and plantains – grew rankly, and the spreading branches of the old apple tree in the smithy garden were still twisted the same way. But what moved him more than anything else was the sound of the little school bell and the sight of the monastery schoolboys clattering down the stairs and into the courtyard at recess. How young and foolish and charming those boyish faces were. Had he really also once been so young, so clumsy, so charming and childish?

But in addition to this familiar monastery he also discovered an almost unknown one that struck him forcibly in the very first days and grew in importance to him as it blended, though slowly, with the familiar one. For although nothing new had been added and everything was just as it had been in his schooldays and for more than a hundred years before that, he no longer saw it with the eyes of that schoolboy. Now he saw and felt the dimensions of these buildings, the vaulted ceilings of the church, the old paintings, the figures of stone and wood on the altars, in the arched doorways. And although he saw nothing that had not been in its place in the old days, only now did he perceive the beauty of these things and the spirit that had created them. He saw the old stone Madonna in the upper chapel. Even as a boy he had loved it and copied it in his drawings, but now for the first time he saw it with wide-open eyes, recognizing it for a wondrous creation that he would never be able to surpass even with his best and most successful work. And there were many such wonderful objects, none of them standing alone or by chance: each of them had its origin in the same spirit, its place among the old walls, columns and arches as its natural home. All that had been built, chiselled, painted, lived, thought and taught in the course of several centuries was of a single origin, a single spirit, and formed a harmonious whole like the branches of a tree.

Surrounded by this world, this strong, silent unity, Goldmund felt very small, and he never felt smaller than when he saw Abbot John, his friend Narcissus, at work as the ruler of this powerful yet quietly gracious community. However much the scholarly, thin-lipped Abbot John and the simple, kindly, unpretentious Abbot Daniel differed in personality, each of them served the same entity, the same idea, the same system, deriving his dignity from them, sacrificing his individuality to them. That rendered them as similar to each other as did their monastic garb.

At the heart of this monastery of his, Narcissus acquired enormous stature in Goldmund's eyes, although his behaviour towards Goldmund never varied from that of friendly companion and host. Soon Goldmund hardly dared address him as 'Narcissus' any more.

'Listen, Abbot John,' he said one day, 'I suppose I shall gradually have to get used to your new name. I must tell you that I feel very much at home here among all of you. I'm almost tempted to make a general confession to you and, after due penance, ask to be accepted as a lay brother. But that, you see, would put an end to our friendship – you would be the abbot and I the lay brother. But this living beside you, day after day, seeing you at work, and neither being nor accomplishing anything myself – I can't go on like this. I, too, should like to work, I'd like to show you what I am and what I can do, so that you can see whether it was worth pleading for my release from the gallows.'

'I am glad to hear this,' said Narcissus, speaking more precisely than usual. 'You can begin whenever you wish to set up your workshop. I shall immediately instruct the blacksmith and the carpenter to be at your disposal. As for whatever working materials are available here, just take your pick. And draw up a list of what needs to be brought in by cart from outside. And now let me tell you what I think about you and your intentions. You must allow me a little time to express myself. I am a scholar, and I should like to try to formulate the situation in terms of my world of thought. I have no other language than that. So follow me once again, just as you often used to do so patiently all those years ago.'

'I shall try to follow you. Speak freely.'

'Think back to our young days and how I sometimes used to tell you that I believed you to be an artist. At the time it seemed to me you might become a poet. In reading and writing you had a certain aversion to the conceptual and the abstract, and in language you had a special love for words and sounds that harboured sensuous-poetic qualities – that is to say, words that evoke images.'

Goldmund interrupted. 'Excuse me, but don't concepts and abstractions, which you prefer, also evoke mental images? Or, in order to think, do you really need and prefer words that don't evoke images? Is it possible to think without visualizing something?'

'A good question! But of course one can think without visualizing! Thinking has nothing whatever to do with mental images – the mind works not with images but with concepts and formulas. At the very point where images cease, philosophy begins. This, you will recall, is what we so often argued about in our youth – for you the world consisted of images, for me of concepts. I kept telling you that you lacked the makings of a thinker, but I also told you that this was not a deficiency, since instead you were a master in the sphere of images. Let me explain. If, instead of taking off into the world, you had become a thinker, you might have caused great harm, for you would have become a mystic. Mystics, to put it briefly and somewhat bluntly, are those thinkers who cannot break free of images, in other words who are not thinkers at all. At heart they are artists – poets without verses, painters without brushes, musicians without tones. There are some highly gifted and noble spirits among them, but they are all, without exception, unhappy people. You might have become one of those. Instead, thanks be to

God, you became an artist and took possession of the world of images in which you can be a creator and a master instead of being mired in your inadequacy as a thinker.'

'I am afraid,' Goldmund said, 'I shall never succeed in grasping your world of thought, a world in which the mind needs no images.'

'Oh but you will, you will succeed at once! Listen. The thinker tries to perceive and formulate the nature of the world by logic. He knows that our intellect and its tool, logic, are imperfect instruments, just as an intelligent artist is fully aware that his brush or chisel will never be able perfectly to express the luminous nature of an angel or a saint. Yet they both, the thinker as well as the artist, attempt to do just that in their own way. They cannot and must not do otherwise, for by trying to realize himself through the talents given him by nature, a person performs the supreme and only meaningful act possible to him. That is why I used so often to tell you, do not try to imitate the thinker and the ascetic, but be your own self. Seek to realize yourself!'

'I understand you more or less. But what does that really mean, to realize oneself?'

'It is a philosophical concept – it is the only way I can express it. For us disciples of Aristotle and St Thomas Aquinas, the highest of all concepts is the perfection of being. The perfection of being is God. All else in existence is only half, partial, becoming. It is mixed, consists of possibilities. But God is not mixed. He is one, He has no possibilities but is total reality. We, on the other hand, are ephemeral, we are becoming, we are possibilities. For us there is no perfection, no complete being. But from the point where we move from the potential to the deed, from possibility to realization, we participate in true being, come one step closer to perfection and the divine. That is what realizing oneself means. I am sure you are familiar with this process from personal experience, for you are an artist and have carved many statues. When you have been truly successful with such a figure, when you have liberated the representation of a human being from random elements and reduced it to pure form – then, as an artist, you have realized this human image.'

'I understand.'

'You see me, friend Goldmund, in a place and an office where it is made fairly easy for my nature to realize itself. You see me living within a community and a tradition that correspond to my nature and support me. A monastery is not a heaven, it is full of imperfections. Nevertheless, to people like myself, a reasonably well-ordered monastic life is of infinitely greater benefit than life in the world. I shall not speak of morality, but, in practical terms alone, pure thinking – which it is my task to practise and to teach – demands a certain protection from the world. Therefore here in our house it has been much easier for me to realize myself than for you to realize yourself. The fact that in spite of this you have found a way and have become an artist is something I greatly admire, knowing as I do that it has been so much more difficult for you.'

Goldmund blushed with embarrassment at the praise, also with pleasure. To change the subject he interrupted his friend: 'I have been able to understand most of what you set out to tell me. But there is still one thing I can't get into my head – that which you call "pure thinking", thinking without visualizing, and functioning with words that evoke no mental images.'

'Well, take an example that will help you to understand. Think of mathematics. What images are conveyed by numbers? Or by the plus and minus signs? What images are conveyed by an equation? None whatsoever! In solving an arithmetical or algebraical problem, there is no mental picture to help you. You solve an abstract problem within the limits of acquired thought-forms.'

'You are right, Narcissus. If you write down a row of numbers and symbols for me, I can work my way through them without visualizing anything, I can let myself be guided by the plus and minus signs, the square, the brackets and so on, and I can solve the problem. That's to say at one time I could, though today it would be beyond me. But I can't imagine that solving such abstract problems could have any value except as an intellectual exercise for students. Learning arithmetic is quite a good thing, but I would consider it senseless and childish for a man to spend his whole life sitting over such mathematical problems and endlessly covering sheets of paper with rows of numbers.'

'You are mistaken, Goldmund. You are simply assuming that this industrious mathematician would keep on solving new problems set him by a schoolmaster. But he can set these questions for himself. They can arise in him as a compulsive force. One must have mathematically calculated and measured many an actual space and many a fictitious one before daring to approach the problem of space as a thinker.'

'Well, yes. But in fact even the problem of space, as a purely intellectual problem, is not to my mind an object on which a man should waste his labours and his years. For me, the word "space" is nothing, not worth a thought, unless I can envisage an actual space, such as the firmament. To observe and measure *that* does seem to me no unworthy task.'

Narcissus broke in with a smile: 'What you really mean is that you reject thinking but do accept the application of thinking to the practical and visible world. My answer is, we certainly lack neither opportunities to apply our thinking nor the will to do so. The thinker Narcissus, for example, has applied the results of his thinking to his friend Goldmund as well as to each of his monks a hundred times and does so every hour of the day. But how should he "apply" something if he has not first learned and practised it? The artist also constantly practises his eyes and his imagination, and we acknowledge this even if the effect is evident in only a few actual works. You cannot condemn thinking as such but approve its "application"! The contradiction is clear. So let me do my thinking, and judge it by its effects, just as I will judge your artistry by your works. At present you are restless and irritable because there are still obstacles between you and your work. Remove them, look for a workshop or build one yourself and get to work! Many questions will then solve themselves.'

Goldmund could wish for nothing better.

He found a room beside the outer gateway that happened to be empty and was suitable for a workshop. From the carpenter he ordered a drawing-table, as well as various implements for which he made precise sketches; then he drew up a list of the objects that were to be brought to him in due course from nearby towns by the monastery carters, a long list. At the carpenter's and in the forest he inspected all the supplies of cut timber, chose many logs for himself and had them brought, one by one, on to the grass behind his workshop, where he stacked them up to dry and with his own hands built a roof to protect them. He also found much to occupy him at the blacksmith's, where he quite bewitched the man's son, a dreamy young fellow, and won him over. With him he spent long hours at the furnace, the anvil, the cooling trough and the whetstone, where they produced all the curved and straight drawknives, chisels, drills and files that he needed for his wood-carving. Erich, the blacksmith's son, a youth of about twenty, became Goldmund's friend, always willing to help and full of keen interest and curiosity. Goldmund promised to teach him to play the lute, something he passionately desired, and also let him try his hand at carving. Whenever Goldmund felt useless and depressed at the monastery or with Narcissus, he could recover his spirits with Erich, who loved him shyly and revered him beyond measure. Erich often asked Goldmund to tell him about Master

Niklaus and the cathedral town. Sometimes Goldmund was glad to do so, and would then suddenly be surprised to find himself reminiscing like an old man about travels and exploits, whereas his life was supposed to be only just beginning now.

No one noticed that he had changed considerably over time and had aged far beyond his years, since no one had known him before. The hardships of his wandering, irregular life may have taken their toll earlier, but the subsequent time of the plague with all its horrors, and finally his imprisonment by the count and that fearful night in the castle cellar, had shaken him to his very depths, leaving some traces behind: grey hairs in his blond beard, fine lines in his face, bouts of sleeplessness, and sometimes in his inmost heart a certain weariness, a slackening of pleasure and curiosity, a grey, lukewarm feeling of surfeit and satiety. In preparing his work, while talking to Erich, when busy at the blacksmith's or the carpenter's, he would thaw, become lively and young. Everyone admired and liked him. But often he would sit for half an hour or more, listless, smiling and bemused, given over to apathy and indifference.

Of great importance to him was the question of where to start with his work. The first piece he wanted to create here and with which he intended to repay the monastery for its hospitality was not to be a casual creation that would be installed at some random place to be gaped at; rather, like the old works in the house, it was to form an integral part of the building and life of the monastery. His choice would have been to construct an altar or a pulpit, but there was neither need nor space for either. Instead he found something else. In the refectory of the fathers was a raised niche where, during mealtimes, a young brother always read aloud from the lives of the saints. This niche was without decoration. Goldmund decided to provide the steps leading up to the lectern, and the lectern itself, with carved wooden panels similar to those of a pulpit, with figures in low relief and some almost free-standing. He described his plan to the abbot, who approved and welcomed it.

When the work could at long last begin – snow lay on the ground, and Christmas had already passed – Goldmund's life took on a new aspect. As far as the monastery was concerned, it was as if he had vanished: he was never seen; he no longer waited for the bevy of boys at the end of lessons, no longer roamed the forest or strolled up and down in the cloister. He now took his meals at the miller's – not the same one as he used to visit so often as a boy – and he allowed no one to enter his workshop except his assistant Erich, although there were days when even Erich heard not so much as a single word from him.

For his first work, the reading dais, he had after much reflection drawn up the following plan. Of the two parts of which this work consisted, one was to represent the world, the other the divine Word. The lower part, the steps, growing out of a sturdy oak treetrunk and winding round it, was to represent Creation, with motifs from nature and the simple life of the Patriarchs. The upper part, the balustrade, would support statues of the four Evangelists, one of whom was to depict the deceased Abbot Daniel, another the deceased Father Martin, his successor, while the figure of Luke would immortalize his Master Niklaus.

He encountered great difficulties, greater than he had expected. They caused him concern, but it was a sweet concern; in delight and despair he wooed the work as if it were a reluctant woman, battling with it tenaciously and tenderly as an angler battles with a big pike, becoming more knowledgeable and more sensitive with each resistance. He forgot everything else, forgot the monastery, almost forgot Narcissus who, when he did sometimes turn up, was shown nothing but drawings.

Nevertheless, Goldmund surprised him one day by asking him to take his confession. 'I couldn't bring myself to do this before,'

he admitted. 'I felt too inferior, and that I had already been sufficiently humbled in your eyes. I am more at ease now – I have my
work and no longer count for nothing. And since I happen to be
living in a monastery, I should like to abide by the rules.'

He now felt he could rise to the occasion and did not want
to put it off any longer. Moreover, in the tranquil life of the first
weeks and in his preoccupation with all the old familiar sights
and memories of his youth, also in the stories for which Erich
asked him, the review of his life had assumed a certain order
and clarity.

Narcissus received him without ceremony for his confession,
which lasted close to two hours. With an impassive expression
the abbot listened to the adventures, sufferings and sins of his
friend. He asked some questions, never interrupted, and listened
calmly even to that part of the confession in which Goldmund
acknowledged the waning of his faith in God's justice and goodness. He was moved by much of what his friend admitted; he
saw how much he had been shaken and shocked, and how close
he had sometimes been to death. Then again he had to smile
at his friend's still-innocent childishness, touched to find him
concerned and remorseful about impious thoughts which, in
comparison with his own doubts and intellectual abysses, were
harmless enough.

To Goldmund's surprise, even disappointment, his father
confessor did not take his real sins too seriously, but chided and
punished him unsparingly for his neglect of prayer, confession
and partaking of Holy Communion. He imposed on him the
penance of living in moderation and chastity for four weeks
before receiving the sacraments, of attending early mass every
morning and of saying three Paternosters and one Hail Mary
every evening.

At the end he told him: 'I exhort and beg of you not to take
this penance lightly. I do not know whether you still remember

the text of the mass precisely. You are to follow it word by word and concentrate on its meaning. Before the day is out I shall recite the Lord's Prayer and some Hail Marys with you and instruct you as to the words and meanings to which you are to direct your particular attention. You must not say and listen to the sacred words the way one says and listens to the words of men. As often as you catch yourself merely reeling off the words – and that will occur more often than you think – you must recall this hour and my admonition, and you must start again from the beginning, saying the words and taking them into your heart in the manner that I shall show you.'

Whether by happy coincidence, or because the abbot's psychological insights were so effective, this confession and penance brought Goldmund a time of fulfilment and peace that made him deeply happy. In the midst of his work, fraught as it was with tension, anxiety and satisfaction, he found himself released from the agitations of the day by the mild but conscientiously performed spiritual exercises, his whole being in renewed relationship with a higher order that removed him from the dangerous solitude of the creator and admitted him as a child to the Kingdom of God. Although he could not but wage the battle for his work in solitude and devote to it all the passion of his senses and his soul, the hour of prayer unfailingly led him back to innocence. Often fuming with rage and impatience as he worked, or in a voluptuous ecstasy, he would immerse himself in the devotional exercises as if in deep, cool water that washed him clean of the arrogance of rapture as well as the arrogance of despair.

It did not always work. Some evenings, after hours of working at fever pitch, he failed to find calm and composure. Now and again he would forget the exercises; and several times, as he strove to immerse himself, he was hindered and tormented by the thought that saying one's prayers might be no more than a childish striving after a god who didn't exist or who couldn't help him anyway. He told his friend of his misgivings.

'Just carry on,' said Narcissus. 'You have promised, and you must keep your word. It is not up to you to think about whether God hears your prayers, or whether the God you may imagine even exists. Nor is it up to you to think about whether your efforts are childish. In comparison with the One to whom our prayers are addressed, all our actions are childish. You must strictly forbid yourself these infantile thoughts during your prayers. You must say your Paternoster and your Hail Mary and concentrate on their words, become suffused with them, just as when you are singing or playing the lute, for instance, you do not chase after some clever notions or speculations but perform one sound or one fingering after another as purely and perfectly as possible. While one is singing one does not think about whether or not the singing is useful. One simply sings. You must pray like that too.'

And again it worked. Again his wrought-up and insatiable ego was blotted out in the overarching order; again the venerable words passed over and through him like stars.

With great satisfaction the abbot noted that Goldmund, after completing his time of penance and receiving Holy Communion, carried on with his daily exercises for many weeks and months.

Meanwhile his work progressed. From the sturdy newel of the steps there gradually emerged a little world of forms, of plants, animals and humans; in their midst, old Noah among vine leaves and grapes, a picture-book of Creation and a paean to its beauty, freely disporting but guided by a hidden order and discipline. During all those months the work was seen by no one but Erich, who was allowed to make himself useful and had no thought in his head other than having a chance to become an artist. Some days even he was not allowed to set foot in the

285

workshop. Other days Goldmund devoted time to teaching him and letting him try his hand, glad to have a believer and a pupil. Once the work was successfully completed, he would ask the boy's father to release him to be trained as his permanent assistant.

He worked at the figures of the Evangelists on his best days, when everything was in harmony and no doubts cast their shadows over him. His most successful figure, it seemed to him, was the one he endowed with the features of Abbot Daniel. He felt a great love for it – the face radiated innocence and goodness. He was less satisfied with the figure of Master Niklaus, although Erich admired that one the most. This figure displayed inner conflict and grief; it seemed filled with lofty creative plans yet also with despairing knowledge of the vanity of all human endeavour, grieving for a lost wholeness and innocence.

When his Abbot Daniel was finished, Goldmund told Erich to clean up the workshop. He draped cloths over the rest of the work and placed only this one figure in the light. Then he went to Narcissus and, finding him occupied, waited patiently until noon the following day, when he brought his friend to the workshop to show him the figure.

Narcissus stood and gazed. Taking his time, he studied the figure with the meticulous care of a scholar. Goldmund stood silently behind him, trying to subdue the turmoil in his heart. If one of us fails the test now, he thought, the worst will happen. If my work isn't good enough, or if he can't understand it, all my labours here will have been valueless. I should have waited after all!

The minutes dragged on like hours. He remembered the time when Master Niklaus had held his first drawing in his hands, and in his tension he pressed his hot, damp hands together.

Narcissus turned to him, and immediately Goldmund knew he had nothing to fear. In his friend's lean face he saw something blossom that he had not experienced since his boyhood: a smile, an almost shy smile in that strong, spiritual face, a smile of love and devotion, a gleam as if the loneliness and pride in that face had for a moment been pierced, as if all that shone from it now was a heart overflowing with love.

'Goldmund,' said Narcissus very softly, even now weighing his words, 'you are not expecting me suddenly to turn into an art connoisseur. I am not one, you know that. There is nothing I can say about your art that you would not find ridiculous. But let me just say this. The moment I saw your Evangelist I recognized our Abbot Daniel, and not only him but also everything he used to mean to us – the dignity, the goodness, the simplicity. Just as Father Daniel used to stand before us, the object of our youthful veneration, now again he stands before me here and, with him, all that was sacred to us and renders those times unforgettable. By letting me see this you have made me a precious gift, my friend. Not only have you given me back our Abbot Daniel, but for the first time you have completely opened yourself up to me. I know now who you are. I shall not talk about it any more – I must not. Oh Goldmund, that such an hour as this should have come to us!'

There was silence in the big room. Goldmund saw that his friend was deeply stirred. His chest tightened with embarrassment. 'Yes,' he said curtly, 'I am glad. But now it must be time for you to go to dinner.'

Chapter Nineteen

Goldmund spent two years on this work, and starting with the second year he was given Erich as a full-time pupil. In carving the steps he created a miniature Paradise; ecstatically he shaped an exquisite wilderness of trees, foliage and undergrowth, with birds in the branches and bodies and heads of animals emerging everywhere. In the midst of this peaceably flourishing primeval garden he set a few scenes from the lives of the Patriarchs. There was seldom a break in his busy life. It was a rare day when he found it impossible to continue, when restlessness or tedium turned him against his work. Then he would set his pupil a task, walk or ride out into the country, and in the forest breathe the nostalgic scent of freedom and the vagabond's life. Here and there he would seek out a farmer's daughter, or go hunting or lie for hours staring up at the canopy of treetops overhead or into the dense wilderness of ferns and gorse. He never stayed away for more than a day or two. Then he would return to work with new passion, to his rapturous carvings of rankly proliferating plants, to gently and tenderly bringing forth human heads from the wood, incisively carving a mouth, an eye, a wavy beard. Apart from Erich, only Narcissus knew the work. He would often come across to the workshop, at times his favourite room in the monastery, and look on with joy and amazement. Here was the flowering of what his friend had been carrying in his restless, defiant, childlike heart; here it grew and blossomed, a creation, a small, burgeoning world: playful perhaps, but certainly no worse than playing with logic, grammar and theology.

One day he said pensively: 'I am learning a lot from you, Goldmund. I am beginning to understand the meaning of art. I used to believe that, compared with thought and scholarship, it was not to be taken very seriously. I saw it roughly as follows. Since man happens to be a dubious mixture of spirit and matter, and since the spirit opens the way for him to perceive the eternal, whereas matter drags him down and shackles him to the ephemeral, he should strive to move away from his senses and towards the spiritual in order to enhance his life and give it meaning. Although I pretended, from habit, to have a high regard for art, actually in my arrogance I looked down on it. Only now do I see how many paths there are towards that perception, and that the spiritual path is not the only one, perhaps not even the best. It is my path, to be sure, and I shall stay on it. But I see you on the opposite path, on the path through the senses, with a profound grasp of the mystery of being and a power to express it much more vividly than most thinkers can.'

'Now you understand,' said Goldmund, 'why I can't grasp what thought without images is supposed to be.'

'I understood that some time ago. Our thinking is a constant process of abstracting, a turning away from the sensual, an attempt to build a purely spiritual world, whereas you concern yourself with what is most insubstantial and mortal and proclaim the meaning of the world in terms of the ephemeral. You do not turn away from it, you dedicate yourself to it, and through your dedication it achieves the sublime, becomes an allegory of the eternal. We thinkers attempt to approach God by stripping the world away from

Him. You approach Him by loving His creation and re-creating it. Both are the work of man and inadequate, but art is the more innocent.'

'I don't know about that, Narcissus. But when it comes to coping with life, to fending off despair, you thinkers and theologians do seem to be more successful. I have long ceased to envy you your scholarship, my friend, but I envy you your calm, your equanimity, your peace.'

'You should not envy me, Goldmund. There is no such thing as peace the way you mean it. There is peace, to be sure, but not a peace that dwells permanently within us and never leaves us. There is only a peace that has to be fought for over and over again, in never-ending battles one day after another. You do not see me fighting. You are not aware of my battles either in my studies or in my prayers. And it is good that you should not be. You see only that I am less subject to moods than you are – that is what you assume to be peace. But it is a battle – it is a battle and a sacrifice as in every honest life, as in yours too.'

'We won't argue about it. But you don't see all my battles either. And I don't know whether you can understand my feelings when I realize that very soon this work will be finished. It will be taken away and put in place, I shall receive a few words of praise, and then I shall return to a bare, empty workshop, depressed about all the shortcomings in my work that you others can't even see, and in my heart of hearts I shall be as empty and bare as the workshop.'

'That may be,' said Narcissus, 'and neither of us can fully understand the other in that respect. But what is common to all men of goodwill is this: that in the final analysis our works disappoint us, that we must always start again at the beginning, that the sacrifice must always be made afresh.'

A few weeks later, Goldmund's great work was finished and installed. The all-too-familiar experience was repeated: his work became the property of others, was examined, judged, praised, and he was acclaimed and honoured. But his heart and his workshop were empty, and he was no longer sure whether his labours had been worth the sacrifice. On the day of the unveiling he was invited by the fathers to a banquet, at which the oldest wine in the house was served. Goldmund feasted on the good fish and the wild game, and what moved him more than the aged wine was the interest and pleasure with which Narcissus welcomed his work and the honours conferred upon him.

A new work, desired and commissioned by the abbot, had already been planned, an altar for St Mary's Chapel in Neuzell, which belonged to the monastery and where a Mariabronn father officiated as priest. For this altar Goldmund wanted to carve a figure of the Madonna, intending to immortalize in it one of the unforgettable figures of his youth: the beautiful, timid Lydia, the knight's daughter. Apart from that, the commission was of no great importance to him, but it seemed a good opportunity for Erich to work on it for his qualification as a journeyman. If Erich should pass the test, Goldmund would always have a good partner in him, one who could take his place and free him for the only projects on which his heart was still set. Together with Erich he selected the wood for the altar and told him to prepare it. Goldmund often left him to himself, having resumed his ramblings and long walks through the forest. Once when he stayed away for several days, Erich reported his absence to the abbot, and even the abbot worried that he might have left for good. But he returned, spent a week working on the Lydia figure, then went back to roaming the countryside.

He was troubled. Since the completion of his great work, his life had become disorganized. He skipped early mass; he became profoundly restless and dissatisfied. He thought often of Master Niklaus, wondering whether he would soon become like him – hard-working, respectable and artistically competent, but no longer free and no longer young. A recent minor experience had given him food for thought. In his wanderings he had come across a young peasant girl by the name of Franziska who attracted him greatly, so that he did his best to charm her by applying all his former arts of courtship. The girl enjoyed listening to his chitchat and laughed merrily at his jokes, but she rejected his advances, and now it dawned on him that to a young woman he seemed old. He did not go back there, but he did not forget the incident. Franziska was right. He had changed, he could feel it himself, and it was not merely the few prematurely grey hairs, the few lines round the eyes: rather it was something in his nature, in his feelings. He felt old, felt he had acquired an uncanny resemblance to Master Niklaus. He observed himself with distaste and shrugged his shoulders at what he saw. He was no longer free, he had become settled; no longer an eagle or a hare, he had become a domestic animal. On his ramblings he sought the aroma of the past, the memory of his earlier journeys, rather than new journeys and new freedom: sought them longingly and warily, like a dog searching for a lost scent. And whenever he spent a day or two away, indulging himself, he felt irresistibly drawn back to the monastery; with a guilty conscience he felt the workshop waiting, felt responsible for the altar that had been begun, for the wood that had been prepared, for his assistant Erich. He was no longer free, no longer young. His mind was made up: when the Lydia-Madonna was finished he would go on a journey and have one more try at the life of a wayfarer. It was not good to live for so long in a monastery among nothing but men – good for monks, perhaps, but not for him. With men one could have clever, uplifting conversations, and men understood the work of an artist; but everything else – idle talk, tenderness, playfulness, love, contentment unmarred by thought – did not flourish among men; for that there had to be women and new places and constantly new impressions. Everything round him here was a little grey and solemn, a little heavy and masculine, and he had been infected by this. It had crept into his blood.

The thought of the journey consoled him. He kept steadily at his work so as to be free that much earlier; and as the figure of Lydia gradually emerged from the wood, as he carved the austere folds of her robe to make them flow down over her aristocratic knees, he was seized by a profound and painful joy. He found himself falling nostalgically in love with the image, with the beautiful, shy, girlish figure, with the memory of the past, of his first love, of his first journeyings, of his youth. He worked reverently at the delicate form, sensing it to be in harmony with the best in him, with his youth, with his fondest memories. It was bliss to shape the curving neck, the sweet-sad mouth, the fine hands, the long fingers, the exquisitely arched fingernails. Erich also contemplated the figure with admiration and awe-struck love as often as he could.

When it was almost finished Goldmund showed it to the abbot. 'This is your most beautiful work, my friend,' Narcissus said. 'We have nothing to equal it in the entire monastery. I must confess that there have been times during these last few months when I was worried about you. I saw that you were restless and unhappy, and when you disappeared for more than a day I would sometimes think anxiously, perhaps he will not come back. And now you have produced this wonderful statue! You have made me glad and proud!'

'Yes,' said Goldmund, 'the statue has turned out quite well. But listen, Narcissus! For this to happen, my entire youth was needed, my life as a wayfarer, my falling in love, my wooing of many women. That is the well from which I have drawn. Soon the well will be empty, my heart is drying up. I shall finish this Madonna, but then I mean to go away for a while, I don't know for how long, and I shall revisit my youth and all that was once so dear to me. Can you understand that? Very well. You know, I have been your guest, and I have never taken any payment for my work here . . .'

'I have frequently offered it to you,' Narcissus broke in.

'Yes, and now I'll accept it. I'll have some clothes made, and when they are ready I'll ask you for a horse and some money – then ride out into the world. Don't say anything, Narcissus, and don't be downcast. It's not that I don't like it here any more – there's nowhere I could be better off. There are other reasons. Will you grant me my wish?'

Little more was said on the subject. Goldmund ordered a simple riding outfit and some boots, and while summer was approaching he finished the Madonna as if it were his last work, with loving care, giving the hands, the face, the hair, the final perfect finish. It might have seemed that he was delaying his departure, as if glad to let himself be repeatedly held up by those finishing touches to the statue. One day succeeded another, and still he found more instructions to give. Narcissus, although saddened by the impending farewell, sometimes had to smile a little at Goldmund's infatuation with the statue and his inability to tear himself away from it.

But then Goldmund surprised him one day by suddenly turning up to take his leave. He had made up his mind overnight. In his new riding outfit and a new cap he came to Narcissus to say goodbye, having already confessed and taken

Holy Communion. Now he came to say farewell and to ask for a blessing on his journey. Both men found the parting painful, and Goldmund was brisker and cooler in his manner than he really felt.

'Shall I ever see you again?' Narcissus asked.

'Oh yes – provided your handsome horse doesn't break my neck, you'll certainly see me again! Otherwise there would be no one left to call you Narcissus and be a worry to you. Depend upon it! Don't forget to keep an eye on Erich. And make sure no one touches my statue! It is to remain in my room, as I have said, and you must never let anyone else have the key.'

'Are you looking forward to your journey?'

Goldmund winked. 'Well, I was looking forward to it, I must admit. But now that it's time to leave, it doesn't seem as much fun after all. You'll laugh at me, but I find it hard to break away, and this dependence bothers me. It is like a sickness – young, healthy people don't have that. Master Niklaus was the same. But enough of this useless talk! Give me your blessing, dear friend, it's time for me to leave.'

He rode away.

Narcissus's thoughts were much occupied with his friend; he worried about him and missed him greatly. Would he ever come back to him, that fugitive bird, that dear, happy-go-lucky fellow? Now once again this strange, beloved person was on his twisting, aimless path; once again he was roaming the world, filled with lust and curiosity, following his powerful, dark urges, impetuous and insatiable, a big child. May God be with him, he thought, may he return safely. Once again he was flitting about, a butterfly, sinning, seducing women, following his desires, having perhaps to kill again, landing in danger and prison and perishing there. What a worry he was, that fair-haired boy who complained about getting old and looked at one out of such childlike eyes! How much one had to fear for him! Yet Narcissus rejoiced over him. At heart he was very pleased that this stubborn child was so hard to control, was subject to such moods, and that he had broken out again and was sowing his wild oats.

Each day, at some hour, the abbot's thoughts would return to his friend, in love and longing, in gratitude and anxiety, sometimes also with misgivings and self-reproach. Should he not perhaps have revealed to his friend more of how much he loved him, how little he wished him to be other than he was, how enriched he had been by him and by his art? He had told him very little about this, much too little perhaps – who knows whether he might not have been able to hold on to him?

But he had not only become richer through Goldmund; he had become poorer – poorer and weaker, and it was no doubt just as well he had not shown this to his friend. The world in which he lived and had his home, his world, his monastic life, his office, his scholarship, his nicely organized thought structure, had often been violently shaken and cast into doubt by his friend. Without question: from the point of view of the monastery, of reason and morality, his own life was better, more correct, stable, more orderly and exemplary. It was a life of order and strict service, a perpetual sacrifice, a constantly renewed striving for clarity and justice – very much purer and better than the life of an artist, vagabond and rake. But seen from above, through the eyes of God, was the order and discipline of an exemplary life, the renouncing of the world's sensual pleasures, the distancing from dirt and blood, the withdrawal into philosophy and meditation, better than Goldmund's life? Had man really been created to lead a regulated life whose hours and functions were announced by prayer-bells? Had man really been created to study Aristotle and Thomas Aquinas, to master Greek, to repress his senses and flee the world? Had he not been created by God with senses and urges, with pits of blood-stained darkness, with the capacity for sin, lust, despair? It was around these questions that the abbot's thoughts revolved when they dwelled on his friend.

Yes, and perhaps it was not only more childlike and human to lead the life of a Goldmund: it might be greater too, more courageous, to abandon oneself to those cruel currents and confusions, to commit sins and accept their bitter consequences instead of washing one's hands and leading a spotless life set apart from the world, instead of planting a beautiful, harmonious intellectual garden and promenading without sin among its carefully tended beds. Perhaps it was harder, braver and nobler to roam the forests and highways with ragged shoes, exposed to sun and rain, hunger and privation, playing with the pleasures of the senses and paying for them with suffering.

However that might be, Goldmund had shown him that a person destined for higher things can plunge deeply into the blood and drunken chaos of life and cover himself with much dust and blood without becoming petty and mean, without killing the divine spark within him; that he can go astray among the dark depths without the divine light and the creative force in the sanctuary of his soul being extinguished. Narcissus had looked deeply into his friend's life, and neither his love nor his respect for him had been diminished. Oh no, and since seeing those wonderful images, motionless yet alive, transfigured by inner form and order, emerge from Goldmund's sullied hands, those soulful, shining faces, those innocent plants and flowers, those imploring or blessed hands, all those bold and gentle, proud and holy, gestures, he was fully aware that a wealth of light and divine grace dwelled within that inconstant heart of an artist and a seducer.

It had been easy for him in their conversations to appear superior to his friend, to contrast his friend's passion with his own discipline and ordered thought. But was not each small gesture of a Goldmund figure, each eye, each mouth, each tendril, each fold of a garment, more – more real, more alive and more irreplaceable – than anything an intellectual could accomplish? Had not this artist, whose heart was so fraught with conflict and anguish, erected images for count-less people, now living and still to come, of their agony and their striving – images to which the prayers and rever-ence, the deep-seated fears and longings of the unnumbered could appeal in order to find consolation, confirmation and strength?

With a wistful smile, Narcissus recalled all the scenes since his early youth in which he had guided and advised his friend. Goldmund had accepted this gratefully, constantly acknow-ledging Narcissus's superiority and leadership. And then, out of the storms and sufferings of his tumultuous life he had quietly brought forth his works: not words or lessons, not elucida-tions or admonishments, but genuine, enhanced life. How poor in comparison was he, Narcissus, with all his knowledge, his monastic discipline, his dialectics!

These were the questions around which his thoughts re-volved. Just as many years ago he had so drastically intervened in Goldmund's youth and given a new dimension to his life, so since his return his friend had unsettled him, forced doubts and self-examination upon him. Goldmund was his equal; there was nothing Narcissus had given him that he had not received many times over in return.

The friend who had ridden away allowed him time for his thoughts. Weeks passed: the chestnut tree had long since blossomed, the milky, pale-green foliage of the beech trees had turned dark, firm and hard, the storks on the gate tower had hatched their young and taught them to fly. The longer Goldmund stayed away, the more Narcissus realized what he had meant to him. He had a few learned fathers in the house, an expert on Plato, an outstanding grammarian, one or two sophisticated theologians. Among the monks he had a few loyal, honest souls who took their vocation seriously. But he had no equal, no one against whom he could seriously match himself. Only Goldmund had offered this irreplaceable quality. To be deprived of this a second time was a hardship. He yearned for his far-off friend.

He would often go across to the workshop to encourage Erich, who continued to work on the altar and was very anxious for his master's return. Sometimes the abbot would unlock Goldmund's chamber, where the Madonna stood, then carefully lift off the cloth and spend some time with the statue. He knew nothing of its background, Goldmund never having told him the story of Lydia. But he could feel it all, could see that this young woman's figure had lived for a long time in his friend's heart. Perhaps he had seduced her, deceived and deserted her, but in his soul he had taken her with him and guarded her, more faithfully than the best husband; and eventually, perhaps after many years in which he had never seen her again, he had shaped this beautiful, touching figure, endowing her face, her pose, her hands, with all the tenderness, admiration and longing of a lover. In the carvings of the refectory lectern, Narcissus could also read some of his friend's history. It was the history of a wayfarer and a man of impulses, of a homeless, faithless person, but what had remained of it here was all good and true, full of vital love. How mysterious was that life, how turbid and sweeping were its currents, and how noble and clear were the results displayed here!

Narcissus struggled. He mastered his doubts, did not break faith with his course, neglected none of his strict duties. But he suffered from his loss, and suffered also from the realization of how deeply the heart that was supposed to belong only to God and his office was attached to this friend.

Chapter Twenty

The summer passed; poppy and cornflower, campion and chick-weed withered and vanished. The frogs in the pond fell silent, and the storks flew high in preparation for their departure. Then Goldmund returned!

He arrived one afternoon, in a gentle rain, and did not enter the monastery, going instead directly from the gate to the workshop. He had arrived on foot, without a horse.

Erich was shocked when he saw him enter. Although he recognized him immediately and his heart went out to him, it seemed to be an entirely different person who had come back: a false Goldmund, many years older, his eyes lacklustre, his face dusty and grey, looking ill and gaunt yet showing no pain – rather, something like a smile, a good-natured, tolerant, old man's smile. He walked with difficulty, dragging his feet, and seemed ill and worn out.

This altered, unfamiliar Goldmund looked his assistant strangely in the eye. He made no fuss about his return, behaving as if he had only come from the next room and had been there just a moment ago. He offered his hand with no greeting, no questions, no story, saying merely, with an air of terrible fatigue: 'I have to sleep.' After sending Erich away he went into his chamber adjoining the workshop, where he removed his cap, let it drop, took off his shoes and headed towards the bed. At the back of the room he saw his Madonna, covered with cloths. He nodded at her but did not go to remove the cloths and greet her. Instead he crept to the little window, saw the perplexed Erich waiting outside, and called out: 'Erich, you needn't tell anyone I've come back. I'm very tired. It can wait till tomorrow.'

Then he lay down in his clothes on the bed. After a while, since sleep eluded him, he got up, walked stiffly towards the wall where there was a little mirror, and looked in it. He carefully examined the Goldmund looking out at him from the mirror: a weary Goldmund, a man grown weary and old and withered, his beard now quite grey. It was an old, unkempt man who was looking back at him out of the dim little mirror, a face he knew well enough but that had now become unfamiliar, a face that seemed not quite real, seemed not to concern him. It reminded him of various faces he had known – a little of Master Niklaus, a little of the old knight who had once ordered a page's outfit for him, a little also of the St James in the church, the old, bearded St James who beneath his pilgrim's hat looked so ancient and grey yet also so cheerful and benign.

With minute care he scanned the face in the mirror as if anxious for information about this unfamiliar person. He nodded at it and recognized it: yes, it was he, it corresponded to his sense of himself. A very tired and somewhat dispirited old man had returned from a journey, an insignificant old man with little to boast about, yet he had nothing against him, in fact he liked him. There was something in his expression that the former, handsome Goldmund had lacked, despite all the fatigue and decrepitude – a look of contentment or at least of equanimity. He laughed softly to himself and saw the mirror-image laugh with him: a fine fellow he had brought home from his travels! He had come home from his little horseback journey penniless and pretty much in rags, and not only his horse and his satchel and his money were gone. There were other things, too, that he had lost along the way or that had deserted him: youth, health, self-confidence, the colour in his cheeks and the vigour in his look. Nevertheless, he liked the reflection. He preferred the feeble old fellow in the mirror to the Goldmund he had been for so long. He was older, feebler, more pathetic, but he was more harmless, more content, easier to get along with. He laughed and lowered one of his wrinkled eyelids. Then he lay down again on the bed and this time fell asleep.

The next day he was sitting bent over the table in his chamber, trying to draw a little, when Narcissus came to see him. Stopping in the doorway he said: 'I was told that you were back. God be praised, my joy is great. Since you did not come to me, I have come to you. Am I disturbing you at your work?'

He came closer. Goldmund straightened up from his paper and reached out his hand. Although he had been prepared by Erich, Narcissus was shocked at the appearance of his friend, who gave him a friendly smile.

'Yes, I'm back again. Greetings, Narcissus, we haven't seen each other for a while. Forgive me for not coming to see you yet.'

Narcissus looked him in the eye. He, too, saw not only the apathy, the pathetic deterioration of that face; he also saw that other, that oddly engaging look of equanimity, of indifference even, of resignation and the serenity of old age. Experienced in the reading of human faces, he also saw that this unfamiliar, altered Goldmund was no longer entirely present, that his soul had either detached itself from reality and was moving along dream-paths, or was already standing on the threshold of the gateway to the Hereafter.

'Are you ill?' he asked gently.

'Yes, that too. I became ill right at the beginning of my journey, in the very first days. But you'll understand that I didn't want to come home right away. You would all have had a good laugh if I had turned up again so quickly and taken off my riding-boots. No, I didn't want to do that. I continued on and drifted about a bit. I was ashamed because my journey was a failure. I had bitten off more than I could chew. All right, I was ashamed. Oh, but you can understand that, you're so clever! I'm sorry – did you ask me something? It's maddening – I keep losing the thread. But all that about my mother, you did a fine job there. It hurt quite a bit, but . . .'

His murmurings trailed off in a smile.

'We shall see that you get well again, Goldmund, you will lack for nothing. But why did you not turn back right away when you began to feel ill? Surely you have no reason to be ashamed on our account? You should have turned back immediately!'

Goldmund laughed. 'Yes, I remember now. I didn't dare turn round and come home again. It would have been a disgrace, you see. But now I'm here. Now I feel well again.'

'Did you have much pain?'

'Pain? Yes, I have more than enough pain. But, you know, the pain is not such a bad thing, it's brought me back to reason. I'm not ashamed any more, not even in front of you. That time when you came to see me in the prison in order to save my life, I really had to grit my teeth, I felt so ashamed. That has all passed now.'

Narcissus laid his hand on his arm, and he immediately fell silent and smiled as he closed his eyes. He fell peacefully asleep. Greatly perturbed, the abbot hurried away to fetch Father Anton, the monastery physician, to attend to the sick man. When they returned, Goldmund was asleep at his drawing-table. They put him to bed, and the physician remained with him.

He found him to be hopelessly ill. Goldmund was taken to one of the sickrooms, and Erich was assigned to keep permanent watch over him.

The full story of his final journey never came to light. A few things he told, some could be guessed. Often he lay apathetically; sometimes he was feverish, his speech confused. Sometimes he was rational, and then Narcissus was always summoned, those final conversations with Goldmund being very important to him.

Some fragments from Goldmund's account and confessions were passed down by Narcissus, others by Erich.

'When did the pain begin? It was at the start of my journey. I was riding through the forest, and my horse and I took a tumble. I fell into a stream and lay all night in the cold water. Right here, where I broke my ribs – that's where the pain has been ever since. At the time I wasn't very far from here, but I didn't like to turn back – it was childish, but I thought it would look ridiculous. So I rode on, and when I couldn't ride any farther because of the pain I sold the horse, and after that I spent a long time in a hospital.

'I'm staying here now, Narcissus. It's all over with the riding. It's all over with my wanderings. It's all over with dancing and women. Oh, my friend – otherwise I would have stayed away a long time, for years! But then when I saw that there was no more pleasure for me out there I thought to myself, before I peg out I'd like to do a bit more drawing and a bit more carving – a man needs to have some pleasure, after all.'

'I am so glad you have come back,' Narcissus told him. 'I missed you so much. I thought of you every day, and I often feared you would never want to come back.'

Goldmund shook his head. 'Well, it would have been no great loss.'

Slowly, his heart burning with agony and love, Narcissus bent down to him and did what in the many years of their friendship he had never done: he touched Goldmund's hair and forehead with his lips. Startled at first, then moved, Goldmund realized what had happened.

'Goldmund,' his friend said softly into his ear, 'forgive me for not being able to tell you earlier. I should have told you when I came to see you in your prison, in the bishop's residence, or when I was shown your first carvings, or any other time. Let me tell you today how very much I love you, how much you have always meant to me, how rich you have made my life. It won't mean a great deal to you. You are accustomed to love. It is nothing exceptional for you – you have been loved and pampered by so many women. For me it is different. My life has had little love in it – I lacked the best part. Our Abbot Daniel once told me that he considered me guilty of pride, and probably he was right. I am not unjust towards my fellow-men. I endeavour to be just and patient with them, but I have never loved them. Of two scholars in the monastery I would rather be with the more learned one. I have never felt love for a weak scholar despite his weakness. If, nevertheless, I know what love is, it is because of you. It is you I have been able to love, you alone in all the world. You can have no idea of what that means. It means a spring in the desert, a blossoming tree in the wilderness. It is you alone I have to thank for my heart not drying up, for a spot remaining within me that can be reached by grace.'

Goldmund smiled, happy and a little embarrassed. In the low, calm voice that he had in his coherent hours, he said: 'At the time when you saved me from the gallows and we were riding home, I asked after my pony Blaze, and you told me what had happened to him. I realized then that you – someone who hardly knows one horse from another – had taken an interest in my pony Blaze. I knew that you had done it for my sake, and that made me very happy. Now I see that it really was so, and that you really feel love for me. And I have always felt love for you, Narcissus – half my life has been spent courting your affection. I knew you cared for me too, but I would never have hoped that you with all your pride would one day tell me so. Now you have told me, at the very moment when there is nothing else left for me, when travel and freedom, world and women have deserted me. I accept it, and I thank you.'

The Lydia-Madonna stood there in the room looking on.

'Are your thoughts always of dying?'

'Yes, they are, and of what has become of my life. As a youth, when I was still your pupil, I wished to become as spiritual a person as you. You showed me that that was not my vocation. So I threw myself into the other side of life, into the world of the senses, and women made it easy for me to find my pleasure there – they are so willing and so eager. But I don't mean to speak disparagingly of them, or of sensual pleasures. I have often been very happy. And I have also been fortunate enough to discover that sensuality can be inspired. This is the origin of art. But now both flames are extinguished. I no longer know the animal delights of lust, nor would I even if women were still chasing me. And I no longer have the desire to create works of art. I have carved enough statues, the quantity doesn't matter. That's why it is time for me to die. I'm ready, and I'm curious.'

'Why curious?' asked Narcissus.

'Well, I suppose it's a bit silly of me, but I'm really curious about it. Not about the Hereafter, Narcissus. I don't waste much time thinking about it and, to be frank, I no longer believe in it. There is no Hereafter. The withered tree is dead for ever, the frozen bird will never come to life again, no more than a man after he has died. He may be remembered for a while after he's gone, but even that won't last very long. No, the only reason I'm curious about dying is that it is still my belief, or my dream, that I am on the way to my mother. I hope that death will be a great happiness, a happiness as great as that of the first consummation of love. The thought persists in me that instead of Death with the scythe it will be my mother who takes me to herself again and leads me back into Non-being and innocence.'

On one of his last visits, after Goldmund had not spoken for several days, Narcissus found him awake and eager to talk.

'Father Anton says you must often be in great pain. How do you manage, Goldmund, to endure it so calmly? It would seem that you have found your peace.'

'Do you mean peace with God? No, I have not found that. I don't want peace with Him. He has made a mess of the world, we don't need to praise it, and after all He won't care very much whether I sing His praises or not. Made a mess of the world – that's what He's done. But I have made my peace with the pain in my chest – that's correct. At one time I couldn't bear pain very well, and though I sometimes thought that dying would come easily to me, I was mistaken. When death seemed imminent, that night in Count Heinrich's prison, it became obvious – I simply could not die, I was still much too strong, too wild, they would have had to kill each of my limbs twice over. But now it is different.'

Talking tired him; his voice grew weaker. Narcissus begged him to save his strength.

'No,' he said, 'I want to tell you about it. In the old days I would have been ashamed to tell you. It will make you laugh. You see, when I mounted my horse and rode away that day, it wasn't entirely without an objective. I had heard a rumour that Count Heinrich was back in the country and that Agnes, his mistress, was still with him. Well, that doesn't seem important to you, and today it doesn't to me either. But at the time the news affected me powerfully, and I could think of nothing but Agnes. She was the most beautiful woman I had ever known and loved. I wanted to see her again, I wanted one more chance to be happy with her. I rode, and after a week I found her. It was there, in that hour, that the change in me took place.

'So I found Agnes, she had lost none of her beauty. I found her and also an opportunity to appear before her and speak to her. And imagine, Narcissus, she wanted nothing more to do with me! I was too old for her, I was no longer handsome and amusing enough for her, she saw no prospect of further pleasure with me. That was really the end of my journey. But I rode on, reluctant to return to you all so disappointed and ridiculous, and as I rode along my strength and youth and good sense had already entirely deserted me, for I fell with my horse into a gully and a stream and broke my ribs and lay there in the water. That was my first experience of real pain. As I was falling I could feel something crack in my chest, and the cracking pleased me – I was glad to hear it, I found it satisfying. I lay there in the water knowing that I must die, but it was all quite different from that night in the prison. I didn't mind at all – dying no longer seemed bad to me. I was suffering that violent pain I have often had since, and at the same time I had a dream or a vision, call it what you like. I lay there with that burning pain in my chest, and I fought it and yelled, but then I heard a voice laughing – a voice I hadn't heard since my childhood. It was my mother's voice, deep, full of sensuality and love. And so I saw that it was she, that my mother was with me and had me on her knees, and that she had opened my breast and had her fingers deep inside it between my ribs so as to lift out my heart. As soon as I saw and understood that, I felt no more pain. Even now, when the pain returns, it is not pain, it is not an enemy, it is my mother's fingers that are lifting out my heart. She works hard at it. Sometimes she squeezes and groans as if in sensual ecstasy. Sometimes she laughs, then hums a little tune. Sometimes she is not with me but up in the sky. I see her face among the clouds, as big as a cloud. There she floats, smiling sadly, and her sad smile sucks my heart out of my breast.'

Over and over again he talked of her, of his mother.

'Do you remember?' he asked on one of the last days. 'At one time I had forgotten my mother, but you recalled her to me. That was very painful too, as if wild beasts were tearing at my guts. In those days we were still young – what handsome young fellows we were! But even then my mother was already calling me, and I was compelled to follow. She is everywhere. She was the gypsy Lisa, she was Master Niklaus's beautiful Madonna, she was life, love, lust. She was also fear, hunger, desire. Now she is death – she has her fingers in my breast.'

'Don't talk too much, dear friend,' urged Narcissus. 'Leave it till tomorrow.'

Goldmund looked into his eyes with that new smile he had brought back from his journey, a smile that seemed so old and fragile and at times even a trifle feeble-minded, while at others it conveyed sheer goodness and wisdom.

'Dear friend,' he whispered, 'I can't wait till tomorrow. I must say goodbye, and before we part there is still so much to tell you. Listen to me for just a few more moments. I wanted to tell you about my mother, and that she is holding her fingers around my heart. For many years it has been my fondest and most secret dream to carve a mother-figure. To me she was the most sacred of all images. I always carried it around in me, a figure of love and mystery. Only a short while ago I could not have borne the thought that I might die without having carved that figure, my life would have seemed wasted. And now, see how strangely things have turned out between us! Instead of my hands forming and shaping her, it is she who is forming and shaping me. She has her hands around my heart and is lifting it out and emptying me. She has enticed me to die, and with me my dream – the beautiful statue, the image of the great

Eve-mother – will die too. I can still see it, and if I had enough strength in my hands I could shape it. But she doesn't want that, she doesn't want me to make her mystery visible. She would rather have me die. I am glad to die, she is making it easy for me.'

Narcissus listened in dismay to his words; he had to bend low over his friend's face to understand them. Some he could barely make out; others he heard clearly enough, although their meaning remained a mystery to him.

And now the sick man opened his eyes once more and looked long into his friend's face. His eyes bade him farewell. And with a movement as if trying to shake his head, he whispered: 'But how are you going to die one day, Narcissus, since you have no mother? Without a mother one cannot love. Without a mother one cannot die.'

His few remaining mutterings were no longer intelligible. Narcissus spent the two last days at his bedside, day and night, watching the spark of life grow dim and flicker out. Goldmund's last words burned like fire in his heart.

STEPPENWOLF

Hermann Hesse

At first sight Harry Haller seems like a respectable, educated man. In reality he is the Steppenwolf: wild, strange, alienated from society and repulsed by the modern age. But as he is drawn into a series of dreamlike and sometimes savage encounters – accompanied by, among others, Mozart, Goethe and the bewitching Hermione – the misanthropic Haller discovers a higher truth, and the possibility of happiness.

This haunting portrayal of a man who feels he is half-human and half-wolf became a counterculture classic for a disaffected generation. Yet it is also a story of redemption, and an intricately structured modernist masterpiece. This is the first new translation of *Steppenwolf* for over eighty years, returning to the fresh, authentic language of Hesse's original.

'The gripping and fascinating story of disease in a man's soul' *The New York Times*

SIDDHARTHA

Hermann Hesse

Siddhartha, a handsome Brahmin's son, is clever and well loved, yet increasingly dissatisfied with the life that is expected of him. Setting out on a spiritual journey to discover a higher state of being, his quest leads him through the temptations of luxury and wealth, the pleasures of sensual love, and the sinister threat of death-dealing snakes, until, eventually, he comes to a river. There a ferryman guides him towards his destiny, and to the ultimate meaning of existence. Inspired by Hermann Hesse's profound regard for Indian transcendental philosophy and written in prose of graceful simplicity, *Siddhartha* is one of the most influential spiritual works of the twentieth century.

'Hesse sensed, decades before my generation . . . the necessity we all have to claim what is truly and rightfully ours: our own life' Paulo Coelho